# On Dulcimer Strings

# On Dulcimer Strings

To Bobby + Debbie
Something to remember
me by!
Enjoy!
Your neighbor
Angela

Angela Lebakken

| Library of Congress Control Number: | | 2008900888 |
| --- | --- | --- |
| ISBN: | Hardcover | 978-1-4363-1976-8 |
| | Softcover | 978-1-4363-1975-1 |



This is a work of fiction. Names, characters, places and incidents either are the product of the author's imagination or are used fictitiously, and any resemblance to any actual persons, living or dead, events, or locales is entirely coincidental.

This book was printed in the United States of America.

**To order additional copies of this book, contact:**
Xlibris Corporation
1-888-795-4274
www.Xlibris.com
Orders@Xlibris.com
46097

# ACKNOWLEDGMENTS

~

Without the support and encouragement of my weekly writer's critique group I fear this story would have languished in my mind or in a dark drawer. Thank you Ina Christensen, Phil Hahn, Sandy Kretzschmar, Faye Newman and Betty Wetzel for demanding the best I have to offer. And thank you, too, for the groans, laughter and camaraderie over the five year period it took to complete this project. What else could one expect from a group called Naked Wednesdays? A name ever reminding us that "writing is like running naked in the streets."

I also thank my daughter, Margie and my sister, Marlys for their enthusiastic response after reading the final draft of *On Dulcimer Strings*.

# ONE

~

*I'll be with her again, in this life or next,*
*I'll go back to the past if I must.*
*I'll be with her again in time out of mind,*
*Where who hate us ne'er were, or are dust.*
—C. G. Sterling, "Outback"

Molly Carpenter strode down the grassy hill, determined to shed her troubles along with her clothes. Burnt-orange curls tickled her face where they'd escaped yellow ribbons. She untied her denim wraparound skirt and let it fly. Unbuttoned her checkered blouse as she marched and watched it snag across a shrub. Knowing full well where she headed and why, she had squeezed into an old bikini she'd discovered while unpacking some breakable doodad. On her exploratory walk last week, she had glimpsed a secluded retreat with a fast-moving creek. The idea of a swim and a sunbath alone had drifted in a backroom of her mind ever since. As it floated, the thought grew, filled one room and then another like a hot air balloon inflating, until encompassing every nook and cranny. Until the stream and solitude meandered through her waking moments and seeped into her dreams. Yearning to be unfettered and childlike drove her stride now. Suffocated by Jake's demands and criticism, Molly needed freedom to breathe.

So many promises had been made and broken, she feared she'd never trust him again. Could she continue living with a man she didn't trust? She shook off doubts and fears, intent on enjoying this experience moment by moment. The very ground beneath her feet seemed buoyant and alive, the air a sweet taste of honey.

With a tree stump as a perch, she removed her tennis shoes and socks. Her toes wriggled as blades of cool grass slid between each one. She sighed. Standing, she brushed twigs and grit from her fanny, then stretched her arms wide, leaned her head back and smiled as summer breezes fondled her. Out of sight, a dove cooed a sad song as if in mourning. Crows responded with harsh caws, scolding the dove to suck it up and quit whining. Molly pondered both messages and dismissed them. *Not today. Not now.* She gingerly tiptoed to the gate of an unpainted, weathered fence that enclosed an abandoned cabin and separated her from the stream she sought. Her slender hands couldn't get a grip, and the rusty latch held firm. She spied a hole where the fence had rotted through, and she slipped between two of the remaining rails, glad for having trimmed extra weight from her six-foot frame. More wildflowers of varying heights, shapes, and shades here but less grass for her tender feet. Thistles abloom in purple hues poked and scratched but didn't deter her.

At water's edge, she paused, allowing the sun's rays to penetrate the white skin of her belly and thighs. At forty-nine years, she rarely exposed so much body. Freckles lay in wait and tomorrow they'd bloom. She waded into the brook and cringed as icy water swirled at her knees. Colder than she expected, it must be spring fed. Gasping, she sank deeper, ripples covering her breasts. *Might as well go all the way,* she thought, leaning forward immersing her head. The world sparkled when she came up for air and gazed through droplets clinging to her eyelashes. In the shallows, the sandy river bottom cushioned her in a soft seat as she played the water with her fingertips. Something tiny and lively squiggled by and tickled her leg. The squirm, bloom, caw and coo of nature's magic held her captive. She picked up a smooth stone and turned it over and over in her hand. It shone with wet energy and she connected with its place here, as if even inanimate objects had a story of their own. Just as this clear water rinsed dust and grime from her skin, the birds, stones, and shimmering leaves soothed her dis-ease.

Molly longed to linger but forced herself upright, allowing warm sunshine alleviate the shivers as she picked her way to shore. Her clothes, scattered pell-mell in the tall grass, looked like someone's clothesline had been hit by a whirlwind. She shrugged, stripped off her wet suit, and spread a towel in a patch of blue and white flowers. New to Appalachia, she couldn't name these blooms. Names normally mattered to her, but not today. Packing, leaving, and then the search for a new home had left her exhausted. She should be there now, settling in and getting rid of the clutter. But she had seen an opportunity to flee Jake's judgmental eye, and she'd snatched it.

Perfumed flowers lulled her, iridescent blue dragonflies landed and rose again. The creek gurgled, as if rocks and pebbles had burst into song. Faraway strains of a stringed musical instrument carried to her on the breeze. Tears came whenever her ears picked up that haunting sound, unknown but familiar.

She rose up on one elbow and gazed at the battered structure on the knoll. In her flurry and quest for freedom from a self-imposed cage, she had seen a dilapidated, shoddy shack. Now as she stared until her eyes glazed over, she noted the large oak logs chinked together with precision; the field rock chimney and shingled roof looked weathertight, secure. This building had held its ground through far more winter storms than she had. Hadn't buckled under pressure. It stood two stories tall, and her toes curled as if around the rungs of a ladder climbing to a loft she pictured within. Four poles supported the roofs of two porches. Stacks of flat rocks created a solid foundation for the floors. Three level boulders formed steps to the front landing and small doorway—the door long gone. She imagined one though, with an inside latch identical to the one on the gate. This windowless north facing gave the interior a damp, dark appearance. The south side, out of her view, would have windows, for warmth and light when days were short and air so cold it crackled. The split rail fence encircling the yard appeared stable, but sections had caved to time, weather, and vandalism.

A footpath led from the back stoop through the fence and into nearby trees. Overgrown with weeds, only a faint outline announced its presence. One day she'd explore, venture in, maybe even tromp that trail. For today the view from her flowery bed satisfied her curiosity. A stray black-and-white cat darted from beneath the building. The cat froze as if paralyzed and glared at her. A pretty-enough kitty but with an ominous look, as if warning of danger or commanding her to follow. She shuddered as it ran off.

She lay back, closed her eyes, and pictured in her mind the building as a home with smoke puffing from the chimney, the fence sturdy and strong.

. . .

A little girl with curly blonde hair in snarls and straggles plays with a pointed stick, pokes holes and pretends to dig. Her faded blue dress drags on the ground and hangs loosely from thin shoulders. It bunches at the waist where a string pulls tight and ties in back. Her chubby hands and cheeks are smudged and grimy. The yard has a few chickens, grass stubble, stones, and dirt. Trees signal autumn with red and gold leaves.

"Sophia, Sophia, careful with that stick. C'mon. The boys'n Papa are gone up the hill already." A washed-out woman in her late forties, clad in a shirtwaist of some coarse fabric, hurries into view. A scarf tied behind her ears holds back wisps of hair loose from her long braid. The woolen shawl wrapped around her shoulders is pulled tight against chill air. In one large bony hand she carries gunnysacks and a stick with a small blade bound to the end by flexible twigs.

Sophia takes her mama's free hand. She likes to go "Sanging." A safe time close to Mama as she uncovers strange roots. This year she has a stick of her own.

Sophia half skips to keep up with Mama's pace. They pass the vegetable garden, now a rubble of dead plants. First frost has blackened the squash and tomato leaves. Potatoes deep in loamy soil are surely ready for harvest. Today the sun is bright, but its fire has cooled.

"Mama, Mama, will I see a blubberfly?"

"Might, chile. Soon enough it'll be too cold, and butterflies will go to sleep. Birds will fly away."

"Blutterfly. Bl . . . bl . . . butterfly." Sophia grins.

When they enter the woods, Mama pauses, blinks in the dimness and Sophia relaxes a bit. Then they rush on. At a deep gully covered with blackberry vines they stop.

Mama drops her gunnysacks and says, "Now, look for red berries, yellow leaves and tell me. Don't go fur, y'hear?"

Sophia nods and turns. With her eyes to the ground, she moves away, skirting the brambles. The sun warms her where trees have bared their branches. Robins chirp, sparrows flutter about, a mourning dove coos. Intent on red berries and big yellow leaves, Sophia skips and chants, "Sanging, sanging, Mama and me are sanging." Gusts of wind whistle by, swirling fallen leaves. A butterfly trembles and lands on her arm. Distracted, she smiles and follows as it flutters away behind a tree, then disappears in a thicket.

When a dead branch breaks with a sharp snap, Sophia notices noises around her. Alert for danger, she stops, catches her breath. Now she simply hears dried leaves rustle as jays and squirrels poke through. The butterfly forgotten, she stands alone in a small glen overshadowed by leaves still clinging to broad arms of old oak trees. Having pivoted in circles listening for noises, she doesn't know which way her mama is. In dappled light she spots a grassy patch by a rill. She sits on its bank, her elbows on bent knees, the long skirt tucked around her legs and her chin cupped in the palms of her hands. Sophia scrunches her eyes tight and refuses to cry. A thundering crash. Eyes fly open. Fear races through her.

. . .

Opening her eyes in this bed of flowers by the creek, Molly wondered what had just taken place. Something about a little girl and "sanging." *What is "sanging?" And the name Sophia.* She must have fallen asleep and dreamed. Or had her imagination run wild?

The air grew cool against her naked body and she shivered. She thought of gathering her clothes and getting dressed. But that would break the spell. A breeze as light as fairy wings whispered and pleasured her skin. Clouds, like fields of flowers, turned kaleidoscopically pink and orange, yellow, red, and deepened to purple as the sun sank low to the horizon. Breathing deeply, she felt herself melding with breezes, flower scent, and color-filled skies. Adrift in a sensuous land of ghosts from the past, her mind floated as if in her hot air balloon hovering high in the sky. Sensing movement, she sat up and watched as two white-tailed deer, a doe and fawn, drank from the stream.

"Molly! For Pete's sake! Come home and fix my supper!" Jake's voice, even from a long distance, shattered her tranquility. Her eyes filled with tears as she did what she was told. Again. She stumbled into her skirt and tattered tennis shoes. Stuffing the damp bikini and her socks into pockets, she buttoned her shirt as she hurried up the hill toward home. Had she really walked this far? Bits of grass and flower petals snagged in her hair, as Sophia and sanging tangled her thoughts.

Molly hung her towel on the coat hook by the back door and started to ask about his binoculars dangling by their strap. He interrupted.

"It's after seven. You know I've got the church board at eight," Jake scowled.

Nodding, she sent potato peelings skidding in the sink. "This won't take long. Some fried potatoes and that ham left from Sunday."

"I ate the ham for lunch when I couldn't find you. Were you out there naked all day? What if some of the congregation had seen you? You haven't even met them yet, for God's sake."

"You were spying again, Jake. With those binoculars of yours. You promised. You . . ."

"You have to trust me, or we might as well quit now. I went looking for you . . ."

Somewhere in this tirade, she tuned him out. She knew he wouldn't be ranting if she had gotten home by four. If she had been made up and in a dress. If she'd fixed a complete meal and had a smile ready for the litany of his day. Depositing the makeshift supper of scrambled eggs and potatoes in front of him, she grabbed a carrot and slipped from the room but could have stormed out unnoticed. Engrossed now in his meal and his Bible, he'd begun preparing Sunday's sermon.

In the bedroom, she kicked off her scratchy tennis shoes and wiggled her toes into soft slippers. The rumpled rag of a bikini she pitched into the waste basket. Last time for that excursion. Although she did feel a naughty rebellion with no underwear beneath her skirt. Maybe she *would* go swimming again—next time naked. Then freckles could play where they may.

As she sat folding laundry, her thoughts wandered to when she had first met Jake. Now a kinky full beard and mustache covered his receding chin and thin lips. Then, clean shaven, he had reminded her of a young Clint Eastwood, exuding a mysterious energy. She had been turned on by what she'd seen as a cocky air of confidence when he stopped and greeted most everyone as he crossed the social hall toward her. When she held out her hand, he clasped it in both of his. She noted the stubby, thick fingers with nails bitten short. *Nervous,* she thought.

"Hi," he said as he stepped closer. "I'm Jake Carpenter." He had entered her comfort zone and her heart raced, but she didn't back away.

"I'm glad to meet you. I'm Molly. This is my first time here. Actually my first experience at a Baptist church. Have you been attending long?" She had pulled her hand from his, embarrassed by her sweaty palm.

"I'm the assistant pastor. The older ladies keep trying to match me up. I wondered why they hadn't introduced me to you."

"Well, now you know. Besides, I've just ended a ten-year marriage and not ever going to marry again." *Shut up,* she'd scolded herself.

"Okay, so we aren't getting married. How about sharing a plate of this potluck with me?"

Heads turned at her loud and nervous laugh. "Of course, let's eat."

From there she'd lost her grip on sense and had given lust a carefree ride.

. . .

Jake, heading out for his meeting, hollered good-by and slammed the door, rattling the dishes he'd stacked on the counter. The idealistic man with hopes of being a second Billy Graham was now this impatient, arrogant preacher. Oh, he could still charm the ladies and buffalo the men of the congregation. For a time anyway.

"Hi, I'm Jake Carpenter," he'd be saying soon. "Call me JC."

They'd uprooted and moved across country to Tennessee only weeks ago to avoid a scandal back in Tucson.

Molly plopped folded underwear on the dresser and headed for Jake's office, maneuvering around a jumble of cardboard cartons. Much still remained packed, but all the books lined the shelves. She switched on a light and pulled down the dictionary. S A N G—she supposed the spelling as she ran her finger down that page. Nothing. S E N G—nope. Perplexed, she gave up the search.

She moved to the opposite wall and sat at her mahogany writing desk. Pulling a spiral notebook from the top drawer, she found the next blank page and wrote June 19 on the top line. Shocked, she realized they hadn't celebrated their twentieth wedding anniversary. Her pen flew over the lines as thoughts and feelings tumbled onto the page about this sad oversight, the delightful experience at the brook, the puzzling Sophia dream, the blue flowers. She finished with a new resolve to be and do what Jake wanted. This move was a new start. He'd made promises and she would believe him. Again. Spent, she closed her journal and tucked it under a household file and old letters.

Searching for a book to take to bed, Molly pulled one and then another from the shelf, always returning them precisely. She needed an interesting distraction, or she'd be reliving the balloon-ride sensations all night. A tome, with reference to the symbolism of the flowers and plants mentioned in the Bible, caught her eye. When she flipped it open, a folded paper fluttered to the floor. Retrieving it, she recognized her daughter's precise handwriting. Before she had a chance to reread the letter Amy had written, a car pulled into the driveway. Jake home already? Molly glanced at the schoolroom clock on the wall. Goodness, she'd been fussing in here for hours. She slid the letter between pages, closed the book, stuck it on the shelf, and hurried to meet her husband with a smile and "Happy Anniversary."

# TWO

~

*Catch for us the foxes, the little foxes that ruin*
*the vineyards, our vineyards that are in bloom.*
—Song of Solomon 2:15

Molly woke late, the corners of her mouth turned up as if she'd been watching a child at play. When she reached to pat Jake and whisper good morning, her hand encountered an empty space, a rumpled sheet. Disappointed, she let her mind embrace yesterday's finale.

When she'd opened the door last night to greet Jake, a bouquet of long stem roses in shades of pink, red, and yellow peeked around the corner in front of his sheepish frown.

"I'm sorry, Molly. I didn't mean to snap at supper. Nervous, you know, about the church board. Happy Anniversary, honey." He placed the flowers in her outstretched arms and filled the sink with water. "Here," he whispered, "this will do until later." And as he took the roses from her, he traced his fingertips slowly down her arms.

She had snugged into his embrace, turned her face to his, and succumbed to feathery kisses as his fingers tangled in her hair and applied slight pressure; a hint of herbal tea flavored the kiss. His wiry whiskers tickled and scratched in pleasant familiarity as the essence of fresh air and roses settled her scattered emotions. Her left hand found and caressed the velvety hollow behind his ear lobe while her right hand slid down his back, along his spine to his buttocks, and she, too, applied pressure. The kiss became more intense, his breath quicker. Without a word, they kissed again; and with hands interlocked, they turned out lights, stepped around the cartons that littered the way, and, once in the bedroom, dropped their clothes and crawled beneath cool sheets.

In the morning light, she remembered the flowers. As if he'd read her thoughts, Jake came in, a vase filled with roses in one hand and a steaming mug of coffee in the other. The two scents commingled in a soothing, stimulating aroma.

"Here you go. How'd you sleep?" he asked.

"Heavenly, thank you very much," she said, patting the bed. Inviting him. She reached for the coffee. "This is nice too."

"Well, don't get too comfortable. You've got a meeting with the Ladies Guild at ten o'clock, you know."

She glanced at the radio alarm. She had over two hours to prepare. Still, she sulked. These "teas" were awkward when she was one of many. She dreaded being the center of attention—the need to choose her words, pretend propriety.

Jake proceeded to her closet and rifled through her clothes, pulling out one dowdy dress and then another. "Wear the brown suit. And this cream silk blouse," he said.

She seethed inside. *Did I ask you, damn it?* Didn't he even think she could choose proper clothes?

"All right. Except, please. I want a few minutes with my coffee." She liked to float into morning as if she reclined on a breeze-swept feather. He, most often, burst into the day ready for a marathon.

She wished Jake would sit a minute now. Instead, he mumbled something and walked out. Had they even made love? Or was last night just another appetite sated? *Prostitution* crossed her mind as she hauled out of bed. And yet the heady, sweet fragrance of his roses filled the air. At the window, she stared long moments into the distance and imagined waking alone in the cabin by the gurgling stream. Yesterday's retreat ignited her as a lover's tryst might. Within her a pool of gentle euphoria gradually soothed a hot spot of trepidation, as if she were a refugee, home after long exile. Soon she *would* return and explore. However, not today—it was show-up and show-off time. Good ladies of the church awaited.

Fortunately the brown suit included both pants and skirt. Jake hadn't been specific, so she chose pants. June heat already pressed in tempting her to wear T-shirt and shorts. Wouldn't that set quite a tone? But a preacher and his wife came as a package, and she must be approved too or there would be no contract. With Jake's cloudy past, job choices were getting fewer all the time.

So, dressed properly, subdued make up and jewelry applied, and with frizzy curls tamed, she sought Jake for his okay. She found him in the study, shifting away from the empty shelves by her desk.

"How do I look, sir?" she asked turning a slow pirouette.

"Why not the skirt? I'd think it would be cooler and certainly more ladylike." The scowl had crept back to its comfortable fit across his face.

She didn't bother explaining that a skirt required tight panty hose and high-heeled shoes. Sometimes she hoped his next life would be as a woman so he could suffer feminine complications.

"I don't have a clue when I'll be back," she called on her way out, deliberately not slamming the door.

As she drove to the church, she struggled toward a pious frame of mind. Geez, she'd forgotten her Bible, which should have been as natural to carry as her purse. The air conditioner in her old Chevy station wagon chugged and coughed with not a note of coolness in it. Beads of sweat formed across her forehead and at her nape. *There goes my makeup and hairdo,* she shrugged. Her slacks weren't as loose and comfortable as she remembered either. And silk that had felt cool against her skin now clung to her back. She wanted to be peeled, naked, and dunked in ice water or at least dusted with talcum powder. Almost running a four-way stop, she jammed on the brakes. Her eyes shot to the mirror and met an irate grimace informing her she'd narrowly escaped being rear-ended. "Oops," she hand signaled and continued on. She'd better pay closer attention. Now look, a broken fingernail. The final blow to her careful grooming.

A mere ten-minute drive and her guise of cool confidence had disintegrated until she felt like a bedraggled, unkempt klutz. Small talk would add witless to the list.

The church sat back from the street, a small white building with a rock foundation, tucked among old oak and maple trees. A gravel driveway wound around them in gentle curves, leading her down a hill to the parking lot by a large addition unseen from the street. Partially hidden by trees, until almost upon it, a magnificent spire reached toward the sky.

As she entered the fellowship hall, twenty matrons posed like drooling bears, ready to slobber over her. She blinked in the intense light reflected from stark white walls and bears became ladies again. Cooler air tingled her skin and refreshed her mind. She looked for faces she could relate to but saw only the self-assured demeanor of the staid and settled. The president, perfectly coiffed, rose and bore down on her, dangling bracelets swaying in rhythm with her chins.

"I'm Mrs. Fletch, call me Diatrice," she said, holding out her hand. "And you, of course, are Molly. So good to meet you, dear."

Molly suffered a soft, doughy arm and, trying for a handshake, settled for a powdery slide. One by one women came, introduced themselves and greeted her. Priscilla, Gertrude, Mildred and . . . each doused in their own brand of perfume. Each eyed the slacks she wore. They had all donned skirts and twisted into hose.

One of the Gertrudes served tea and typical sugary pastries, a welcome few minutes of distraction. With an exhausted smile, she listened to Diatrice describe her and Jake as "answered prayer." "Praise the Lords" and Biblical passages flowed from one painted mouth and then another. Molly scanned the walls in search of a clock; she didn't dare squint down at her watch. Her heart sank. She'd been on display for barely twenty minutes. She envisioned a reward. A pastime she dabbled in often these days. Perhaps a drive to the bookstore they'd passed in the next town.

"Monday mornings, then?" Diatrice asked.

Molly nodded, unsure what she'd committed to.

"And what book do you prefer to start with? Psalms are always an uplifting study."

Molly's mind went to the Song of Solomon—the rose of Sharon and lily of the valleys. To study the plants, the trees and animals, how they related to womanhood and God's eroticism enticed her and might even prove beneficial in relationships. The little foxes and all that. But one glance around and she guessed *that* study would be stifled. At least they hadn't clamored for Leviticus with its sin and punishment.

"Which translation do you prefer?" she asked, certain of the answer, still hoping for a modern version.

"Why, King James, of course." Diatrice pursed her lips as if someone had slipped a pickle in her pastry. "Now about Wednesday night choir practice, we understand you play piano?"

"No, I'm sorry." At least she would escape those few hours every week.

"Well no matter, dear. We'll simply enjoy your lovely voice. Certainly you sing?"

"That's at 7:00 PM, Wednesday?"

"Yes, and we look forward to your joining us on Friday afternoons as we quilt and crochet coverlets for the children's hospital."

"Now, dear," Mildred or Gertrude or . . . said, "do you have any ideas? We *are* always open to suggestions."

"Well, I'm thinking how about some pictures on these white walls? Jake's mother painted with oils, and we have lots more paintings than we have wall space. We have landscapes, flowers, bowls of violets. We'd be happy to . . . ," she heard herself prattle and couldn't stop.

"Molly, how generous," Diatrice interrupted. "Someday soon *our* decorating committee will come by and choose *appropriate* pieces. How gracious an offer."

The tea and commitments continued until she thought she would burst mentally *and* physically. She knew, too, she'd be expected to close the meeting with prayer.

The audition having finally concluded, Molly retreated to her sunbaked car, climbed back out, and stripped off her jacket. In the car again, she rolled down the window and, deciding to drive barefoot, she leaned over and through the steering wheel, pulled off her shoes and knee-high hose. Her toes itched, and she fumbled in her purse for her lavender water. Ah, relief as she sprayed her feet. She turned and saw most of the women lined up at the curb eyeing her as if she were an escaping prisoner. *Shit,* she thought, *I've got to get out of here, now.*

The countryside offered cooler air, and for a few miles she breathed in the fresh, earthy scent. One of her favorite childhood songs came on the "oldies" radio station; and she cranked the volume to a deafening level, stepped on the gas, and sang with gusto, "Good Golly, Miss Molly." The music's beat coursed through her and, like a cathartic, flushed out and away church responsibilities and Jake irritations, setting her spirit free. The song ended as she entered the speed zone, indicating the outskirts of town. Barely larger than Sweet Hollow, the main street did contain some interesting shops. Past the bank, the post office, a church with high steeple, she pulled to the curb. She scrambled around the steering column as she squeezed her feet into shoes once more. Linty hair pins, scrounged from the bottom of her purse, pulled damp curls away from her neck. With the sleeves of her grimy silk blouse rolled up, she was out of the car, headed for anything that would distract her.

Without thought, she popped into a resale shop, found a rack of shorts, grabbed a pair in her size and a large T-shirt and beelined for the dressing room. The clothes fit—baggy and breathable. Now the brown pumps looked ludicrous. Barefooted, her street clothes over her arm, she paid for her purchase and asked for a sack and directions to the shoe store. As she crossed Main Street, the pavement burned her feet like flames from hell licking at the soles.

"I'll take a pair of white sandals in size 9 1/2," she blurted.

"Flats or heels?" the pimply teenager whined.

"Flat," she said. "And cheap."

"Here's a pair on sale, half price. They're last year's."

Her tired feet relaxed as she slid on the sandals and buckled them loosely.

"Great, I'll take 'em. I'll wear them."

Carrying the "church tea" attire back toward her car, she noted the drugstore. A quick trip matched her up with a straw hat and giant sunglasses. If she met Diatrice now, she wouldn't be given a second look. Molly pranced down the street, her unintentional disguise an invigorating elixir. Where was that bookstore? An antique shop looked interesting, and she entered its quiet, dim atmosphere. Music played—faraway plucking of a stringed instrument whispered through her veins and quieted her mind. Once her eyes adjusted, she saw fine old furniture, lamps with baubled shades. Doilies and needlework draped the arms of couches and chairs.

A rolltop desk at the back wall attracted her. Headed there, she bumped into another desk made from rough-cut wood. She caressed the writing area worn smooth by use.

"Handcrafted. One of a kind."

Molly jumped, looked up from the desk and met soft brown eyes.

"Sorry, I didn't mean to startle you. Just surprised to see anyone wandering through the dust today. I've admired this desk myself, but don't know where I'd put it," he said, charming her with his Southern drawl. Any minute now he'd be calling her "darlin."

"Well, it certainly wouldn't take up as much space as that huge rolltop. I don't even need a desk, but something about this one . . ." When she took off her sunglasses and met his eyes again, gold flecks danced on a brown background. Tears began rising. *Why? God, why now?* She never dropped her guard with strangers, no matter how kind they seemed. Besides, this afternoon was a frolic, no snifflers allowed.

He merely nodded, smiled, and walked away. Trying not to stare, she noted his curly chocolate-brown hair streaked with gray, the slight downward curve of his shoulders, the loose-fitting dress pants. She returned her attention to the desk, pulled open a drawer, feigned interest in its construction. Glancing up, she blushed when she was caught, or he was caught, looking. They both grinned. She slapped her glasses back on.

"Hey," she called, "do you work here?"

"Oh, no," he said, retracing his steps. "My name's Royce. I like to browse and covet odd pieces . . . I mean, uh, of furniture, I mean."

"Hello, Royce. I'm Molly," she said, a smile twitching her lips. "I'm new to this area and shopping for a diversion." Now it was her turn to be flustered. Her cheeks burned. She wanted to hide, but, at the same time, couldn't take her eyes off him. Handsome devil with classic features and a beguiling smile. "I really like that music. Do you know the instrument?"

"Ah, the dulcimer. You'll hear it a lot in the shops. Soothing isn't it?"

"Oh my, yes. Say . . . uh, I thought there was a bookstore around here? New Age stuff?"

"Actually it has a little of everything. The shop's a block down, across from the bowling alley. I'm headed that way, I'll walk with you."

"Thanks, but I want to see more of this place first."

"Bye, then. Nice to meet you, Molly."

"Bye." *Hmm,* she thought and then caught a glimpse of herself in a filmy mirror. Curls, with a hairpin attached, poked out from under the huge straw hat. A giggle bubbled up when she spied the price tag still dangling from the brim. I must have reminded him of Minnie Pearl, and the chuckle became a full belly laugh. He wasn't flirting with her, he surely thought she was batty. The T-shirt she wore displayed a Harley logo and slopped on her, big enough for a biker. Another laugh burst forth as she peered down at white knees and still whiter thighs jutting from baggy shorts. She couldn't imagine who and what he thought she was. She didn't care.

"May I help you, uh, ma'am?" a proper voice asked.

Molly pulled her shoulders back, managed a serious expression and asked, "What can you tell me about this desk?"

"Well, *madam,* this piece is at least 125 years old," he said. "Of course, you know, the age is determined by the construction and type of wood. This is rough-hewn walnut plank. A rather expensive item. *Miss*? I do have other, shall we say, less pricey desks in the sale section. You might find something suitable to *your* needs there."

Suddenly she felt like a child, small, unimportant. A nuisance. Worse than that. As if he had ridiculed her while playmates watched. *How ridiculous,* she thought. I tower over this snob, and he'll not be a spoiler of my afternoon.

"Thank you. Uh, where is your ladies' room?"

Once inside, she yanked off the straw hat, ripped away the price tag, which left a small hole. She giggled. She cried. Tears rolled down her cheeks, mucking up the remains of this morning's makeup. She splashed cold water on her face and arms, brushed and pinned up her hair, ran a once over of lipstick, and thought, *Good enough.*

Scurrying away from the dim confines and snooty salesman she headed back to the resale shop, smiled politely at the clerk's raised eyebrows, but refused to explain her return. She chose a white cotton blouse with pink rosebuds and glass buttons with a snug ribbing at the bottom and a floppy straw bag to replace her dressy purse. There, now she'd go to the bookstore, certain that Royce Whoever would be long gone.

Vending machines, sticking out like McDonald's arches on this quiet street of turn-of-the-century buildings, reminded her she was hungry. Before this move, she'd always carried a health bar and bottled water in her car. Today she had neither and selected some junk food. As she moseyed along, balancing the soda and savoring forbidden chips, she spied a phone booth tucked between the drugstore and a lawyer's office. Setting her snacks on the ground between her feet, she rummaged with greasy fingers for her new phone number. When the answer machine picked up instead of Jake, she said her own "praise the Lord." "The meeting went well. I'm shopping. Will be home to fix supper." Molly quickly hung up and then dipped a finger into the coin return, just in case.

The bookstore was larger than she expected, narrow but deep, with shelves to the ceiling. She paused and inhaled the comfortable bouquet of old books and dust. After a browse through a good selection of both new and used books she found one on native plants, including color plates. This might identify the blue and white flowers she'd bedded in. She took it to the desk for purchase and found herself bewitched by those same gold-flecked brown eyes.

"Wait a minute. You work *here*?"

"Well, actually I'm the owner. And you have chosen a comprehensive volume on the flora of this area," he said as he rang it up and slipped a bookmark under the cover.

He lingered a moment longer than necessary with a quizzical expression as if he expected something. Had he noticed her tidier appearance? She squelched the urge to ask, "Don't I look better?" Tongue-tied, she shook her head, left the store, and strolled toward her car.

Two teenagers scuffled ahead of her, and, as a dog lifted its leg at a hydrant, she stumbled, caught herself and cried, "Good Golly." The boys turned and laughed, the dog ran away—job half finished, she presumed. Pushing her hat down over her forehead, she winked and grinned at the kids.

Into the resale store one more time, steeling herself for raised eyebrows but greeted instead by a different clerk, she headed for her dressing room. She wrinkled her nose and bit her lip as she switched back to Molly Carpenter, preacher's wife. Avoiding eye contact, she slipped out of the shop. In her car, a trapped fly buzzed incessantly until she rolled down the window and waved the pest to freedom. *For some, freedom is only a wave away,* she mused.

Molly stopped at the grocery store and picked up a rotisserie chicken and a deli pasta salad. Dinner made. As she neared home, the temperature dropped rapidly. Dark clouds, from nowhere, accumulated. A summer storm brewed. She called out as she entered the house and then relaxed. Jake wasn't home, giving her time to change into jeans and tuck her "costume" to the back of the closet.

At her desk she titled the journal page "Day of Disguise" and jotted the highs and lows of it. Was she an "odd piece?" She, who would never have been seen in public so askew. Until Tennessee, that is. Here she acted on strange impulses, as if another version of herself had taken residence in her body. As she journaled, enthusiasm and angst drifted in layers onto the page.

A flash of lightning, clap of thunder, and there stood Jake looking grim. Was she about to catch hell? Again? No, this was different.

"What, what's the matter?" She dropped the pen and rose to take his arm.

"Have you seen today's mail? No? Well, here."

# THREE

~

*The gloaming, when a man cannot make out if the nebulous figure he glimpses in the shadows is angel or demon, when the face of evening is stained.*
—Homero Aridjis, [2]1492: The Life and Times of JuanCabezon of Castile (translated by Betty Ferber)

The letter Jake handed her was short and blunt, typical of his sister. "Dear Jake, I am dying, and I must talk with you right away. This is urgent and private. Please come alone. Joanne."

"What is she thinking? I can't go running off to Denver. I haven't even given one sermon."

"Call her. You haven't seen her in years. Maybe she's overreacting. Find out how urgent this really is."

Molly only heard the "uhs" and "yeses" of Jake's monosyllabic responses.

"I'm amazed. Joanne. Crying? I don't think she's ever cried before in her life," Jake said after he'd hung up. "I guess that's why she wrote in the first place. Knew she'd lose it over the phone."

"Did she tell you what's so important?"

"No. And she won't, except face-to-face. I guess I'd better go."

"When?"

"I don't know. Now . . . okay, here's what I'll do. Preach Sunday and lead evening prayer and praise. Leave on Monday as soon as I can get a flight."

On Sunday Jake delivered Molly's favorite sermon. Every church that hired him received this message first. In a gentle, soft voice as if wooing a lover, he read 1Cor.13: "Love is patient, love is kind. It does not envy, it does not boast, it is not proud . . ." and Eph. 5:7, "Husbands, love your wives just as Christ loved the church . . ." Laying the Bible down, he leaned forward at the pulpit, an expression of compassion and sincerity in his eyes. With hands open, palms offering, he spoke of love.

Always she had warmed to his smile, his singsong delivery, his inviting manner. She wanted to believe he loved this way but suspected he was conning them, sucking them in, painting a false picture of his heart. She didn't want to know if deceit lay behind his words of love, and so she daydreamed. About a kiss good-bye at the airport Monday evening, coming home to a quiet, empty house. Clean, too, since she'd finished unpacking. The plan was a quick trip, with him gone until Thursday. Guilt niggled at her for selfishly coveting a peaceful time alone. A family crisis shouldn't trigger gladness in her.

Startled, she realized the congregation was on their feet singing the closing hymn, "Shall We Gather at the River." Yes, a gathering of one at the little river by the cabin would be grand.

The heat wave had broken, and humidity didn't press her down as she and Jake stood at the open church door. They smiled, repeated names, and shook hands with the flock as they filed out. From church they followed Diatrice and her husband Richard to their home for brunch. The "chosen" members caravanned, creating a procession through narrow streets and quiet neighborhoods.

Richard proved charming and unpretentious. With a sparkle in his deep blue eyes, he regaled them with stories about the Scots-Irish settlers. The hillbillies. How they farmed from "kin see to cain't see." When someone asked about the "Indian savages," Richard spoke in a hushed tone of the Trail of Tears, when thousands of Native Americans—Cherokee—were marched forcefully from this land for resettlement seven hundred miles away in Oklahoma. How they departed in autumn to avoid the heat that had killed so many of the first contingent. And then they encountered snowstorms and freezing temperatures with little protective clothing.

"Scores of them died from pneumonia brought on by ill-treatment and exposure," he said. "However, a remnant escaped the roundups and hid in the forest. Today many of their descendants live on the Cherokee Indian Reservation."

Molly listened, in awe of his demeanor. Never had she heard the Trail of Tears told with this tenderness. He hadn't given a history lesson; he had spoken, with reverence, of a people and their pain. She hardly knew him, but Richard had earned her respect, and a seedling of trust had been planted.

When the group clustered on the lawn to say good-by, Richard amused them with his stumbling demonstration of native clogging. His middle-age paunch jiggled as he stomped his feet and skipped a little hopscotch. Out of breath within moments, he seemed as delighted with himself as Molly was with him. She shook his hand, pressed her cheek to his, and whispered, "Thank you." His blue-eyed twinkle softened to velvet as he looked into her eyes and squeezed her hand. She felt comforted as though she'd met a kindred spirit. Driving away, she wondered how and why such a sensitive man had mated with Diatrice. Who could figure?

Monday, while Jake packed and made his arrangements, she led the Bible study. Curiosity about the new preacher's wife brought in a much larger group than expected, even requiring more chairs. Filled with chatter and commotion, the fellowship hall took on a relaxed and friendly atmosphere. Most of the women, dressed casually, carried Bibles filled with notes and scribbles, dog-eared badges of achievement. Except for a shy young woman named Beth, her Bible crackling new. Her green eyes, set off by waves of long black hair, glanced one way then the other. So skittish. Molly ached for her and kept a watchful eye while Beth seemed to shrink smaller than her already-petite stature.

"Diatrice suggested Psalms for this study. I have another book in mind," Molly began. "Why don't we study James?" She waited until the groans died down and said, "Let's give it a try. James isn't *all* about keeping watch over our tongues. While we study James, we'll get acquainted with each other and learn how to become 'better, not bitter' through our trials and temptations." Molly noticed Beth fumble through the pages of her unsullied Bible and added, "You'll find James near the back between Hebrews and 1Peter."

Diatrice puffed up, opened her mouth to speak, sat back deflated. Protest daggers flashed in her eyes. Molly, confident in her knowledge of the subject matter, refused the invitation to intimidation. She continued the lesson, certain the book of James, with its plain truths, could be an equalizer in this group.

After class, she invited Beth for coffee. With one eye on the time so she'd be sure to get Jake to the airport his customary three hours before flight, she and Beth chatted.

"How long have you lived here?" Molly asked.

"Oh, all my life," Beth answered. "My mama was born in the hills and came here to town when she married Papa. Papa, he died ten years ago from too much moonshine, and Mama passed this April . . . I don't know why I'm troublin' you with all this."

"No, I'm glad. It's nice talking with you. Say, do you hike or take long walks?"

"Oh, sure. Walking is one of my favorite pastimes. Especially in summer. Why?"

"Well, I'm curious about the wildflowers. I was thinking maybe we could explore together. I bought a book with good pictures."

"Shucks, with me along, don't need a book. I've been naming flowers long as I can remember."

"That sounds great. By the way, were you at church yesterday? I don't remember seeing you."

"I was there, I slipped out the side door after. I really loved your husband's talk. He sure is a gentle, kind man."

Molly forced a placid expression. The "Love" sermon had pleased. *But,* she thought, *there is another side.* Will you be enamored when he leans on the pulpit, points his index finger one moment, and raises his fist the next? Or when he glares and, with a condescending smirk planted across his face, shouts, "Gawd will punish the sinner . . ." Kind and gentle is not how you'll see him then, I'm afraid. But maybe this time he *has* changed and won't pound and shout, she told herself.

"I'm glad you liked the sermon. Will you be at Bible study next week?"

"Oh, I don't fit in. They all know so much."

"Or think they do. You are fresh air in a stale room."

"I don't even have the right kind of Bible."

Molly noticed the New International Version that lay beside Beth's cup. "Ah, but you have my favorite translation, and it will work fine. Please come. Oh, and here's my phone number in case you want to talk or something. And I've got yours from the sign-in list. If you get a chance I suggest reading the Song of Solomon, about in the middle. Well, here let me show you."

"Thank you," Beth whispered

"This has been nice, let's go for that walk soon," Molly invited as they rose to leave.

When Beth smiled, Molly was reminded of a lipstick commercial and wondered if Beth knew how beautiful she was.

. . .

She was eager, now, to hike and contemplate her surroundings, but first breakfast. A bowl of steaming oatmeal was what she craved. Savoring it brought back childhood memories of howling wind and blowing snow on winter mornings where she'd grown up. Those were the times when she'd had her fill of hot cereal, fortifying her for her trek to school. She thought of North Dakota and her little hometown in the Red River Valley. A flat and fertile country of rich black loam where crops of wheat, soy beans, sugar beets, and fields of sun flowers thrived during long summer days under a blistering sun. But winter snows whirled into blizzards as winds whipped and met no heap or hill to slow them. Temperatures plummeted to thirty or forty degrees below zero without considering windchill. The river froze along with the land.

She had been young, and it was summertime when she left the valley. Her wedding day. Eighteen, a high school graduate—fearless and naive, unaware of the commitment she made. She had left her home, her mom and dad, without looking back. No hugs, no tears, no regret. Like a leaf blown in the wind, she had fluttered away. Her teenage vows to love, honor, and cherish lasted ten years, and then her marriage grew ugly and shattered. Goodness. What brought all that back? Like wind across that prairie, memories had swept over her. Now, here she sat eating oatmeal for the first time in years and struggling not to fail again.

She determined not to brood today. Jake was gone, and she had a day of exploring ahead. Last night, alone and quiet, she'd paged through her new plant book and would tote it along this morning. And a notebook. And some lunch.

Whistling, she tucked in her camera, shouldered the pack, and walked out the door, a whole day at her disposal. The sky, heavy with dark clouds, softened her mood. Striding down the hill, she imaged earth energy drawing up through her boots' thick soles, through arch supports and two pairs of socks. Life-enhancing energy traveled up her legs and torso; wholesome well-being spread from her spine to every line and wrinkle of her body. She stopped often, hunched down in wet grass, brushed away mosquitoes and examined flowers. She found daisy fleabane in her book and named the tiny white blossoms. Blue miniature iris, with petals moist and soft as a lady's tongue tasting honey, and with leaves as slim as grass flourished on the slopes. Wild onion she recognized by pinching off a blade and sucking pungent juice. A mockingbird filled the air with a medley of other bird's song. A soft mew turned her thoughts to the cat. Kittens, maybe. No, it was a bird. What bird? She needed a bird book too, or maybe Beth would know.

Wedging through a thicket, Molly stopped short at the spectacle of a woman in a rocking chair on the cabin porch. A stringed instrument lay on her lap and dulcimer music floated in the air. She wondered if she should call out her presence. Crouching behind a rhododendron scraggly with dead blossoms, she snapped a couple of pictures. As she searched out the rotted section of fence and cautiously advanced, her lips puckered, but a whistle wouldn't sound, so she coughed and hummed loudly, wishing a bell hung around her neck. Instead of turning toward Molly's commotion, the woman faded, the music stopped. Molly breathed deeply, calming her racing heart and wobbly knees. There was nothing here except her imagination. As she mounted the three boulders and stood on the deserted landing, tree branches moaned in the breeze. Shadows fell and rose again.

She gulped and stepped into the cabin. Did a body memory tighten her toes at the sight of a ladder leading to a loft? A memory of what and when? I'll climb up since my feet are itching to, she decided, with a backward glance toward the entrance. No apparition followed her, just a gust of cold air. Four steps up and she looked into the loft. Unease leached from the sloped ceiling and echoed from low walls as she crawled about scanning her surroundings. Emptiness, save for a hunk of corncob and bits of cloth covered with cobwebs. A nest for some rodent and his family, she assumed, repulsed and longing to gather the scraps to her bosom at the same time. Musty air smelled of varmints, droppings, vacancy. She strained for a glimpse out a small window, but the glass was cloudy and covered with bird droppings. A rag became the first item on her "bring along" list. The loft appeared large enough to sleep two or three children. And parents would, no doubt, make their bed in the nook directly below.

Within minutes, her claustrophobic discomfort sent her scurrying down the ladder.

Surveying the ground floor she noted windows on the south side. Perhaps there had been glass in them at onetime. Now, they were gaping holes, letting in air as well as anything else that wanted a home. Boards hung loosely on either side of each window, makeshift shutters that had fought the winter cold. Peering through one of these windows she could see a garden patch and a stone walk, gone weedy, leading to an outhouse. Her eyes closed. Could she conjure up Sophia? Silly. That was only a dream.

Molly hoisted her bag, stepped outside, and breathed deep. Sitting on the edge of the porch, dangling her legs, she pulled out her notebook and pen and scribbled a few lines about her "lofty" feelings. Not having recaptured Sophia magic, she felt disheartened, empty. Her pen quit its effort, and she dropped the supplies into her pack. She leaned against a support pole, tucked her knees under her chin, and contemplated resting here after a day of toil. The porch had held up well through time, though the floor boards appeared worn where she had imagined the rocking chair.

Maybe a swim would clear her mind of cobwebs and fancied ghosts. Today was ideal for that nude dip she'd promised herself. She stretched and sauntered to the creek. Soon boots, jeans, and the rest of her clothes lay in a pile. Naked, she stretched again. No sun today to freckle her and the water cool, not biting. Pan-sized fish darted off when she waded downstream. In a deep pool she lay back and floated for long, silken moments. The clouds danced together and away, as if they stepped to a Virginia reel for no other reason than the joy of it. Two hawks circled high on motionless wings, and she marveled at their seemingly effortless pairing. A flight simpatico.

When she emerged dripping, a shiver ran through her from the breeze against her wet skin. But also, an eerie sensation, as if someone watched her. She shook the feeling off along with as much water as she could and then allowed some air drying before struggling into jeans, a sticky effort. Socks tugged and twisted on her wet feet. Towel would go on her list. She ambled back, swinging her arms and shaking her dripping mop of hair. Tucking bra and panties into her pack, she spied her lunch and sat to eat a tuna sandwich and more forbidden chips.

"Meow." Molly looked up at a black and white cat, a few feet from her. Smelled tuna, no doubt. She offered a piece. The cat came, sniffed, looked at her, sniffed, meowed, and backed away.

"Come here, kitty, I won't hurt you. Here kitty, kitty." She put the bit of tuna on the floor, an arm's length away. And waited.

"Meeoow." The cat stared, demanding, insistent. She pretended to dismiss its presence, continued eating her lunch, and soon felt the tentative touch of a paw on her leg. Then another and the cat nestled on her lap. "Oh, sweet kitty. What's your name, huh?"

"Meow."

"I don't think so. I'll call you Cat until I know better." Cat purred as she petted, and the sun peeked through clouds and hid again. When a drop of water from her wet curls landed on Cat's nose, he jumped down and ran, looked back, meowed.

"Okay, Cat, I'll follow you for a little while. I have all day."

Cat scurried ahead, tracked back as if making sure she still followed. The stone walkway was fairly clear until they passed the privy. Then an overgrowth of shrubbery blurred more than the edges. Maidenhair fern, with its delicate black spine, thrived. Dips in the trail were puddled and muddy. Her boots squished and slipped, and she reached for branches to steady herself and keep from plopping in the mire. She breathed in clean, earthy evidence of decaying vegetation. Straggly trees leaned over in places, forming moss-covered arches. The moss reminded her of fur, and when she ran her hand across it, she was pleasantly rewarded. Soft light, deep shadows of gray and green captured her mind and led her thoughts away to a fairy tale of far-reaching forests and gnome-shaped growths on the trees. Awakened awareness propelled her in wide-eyed wonder as if she were a child on her first excursion outdoors. Would there be a troll beneath a bridge soon? Cat's impatient meowing kept her from pausing long. The trail climbed steeply, and she grew tired but trudged on.

"How far, kitty?" she asked as she bent and picked Cat up, surprised that the kitty allowed her to. Around one more bend and she recognized the twists and turns as the path in her Sophia dream. Molly leaned against an old chestnut tree and gulped from her water bottle, tried to get her bearings but felt bewildered, as if she'd walked through a wall into undefined space and time. The sun's rays, when they penetrated the clouds, angled at a different slant. A faint autumn smell and chill surrounded her. Cat scrambled from her arms and meowed frantically. No, not a meow. She heard the sobs of a little girl.

"Mama, Mama."

Creeping slowly, Molly approached. Cat stayed back, and when she looked again, Cat had disappeared. Goose bumps prickled her neck and arms as the unknown cloaked her like a fog. Her nerves nettled, red and burning cold like the leaves of the sumac that surrounded her. Moments ago—a century ago—those sumac had been adorned in wooly, hairy leaves of green. Now they sported autumn scarlet.

Curiosity laced with fear goaded her on. She remembered this place. Sophia had wandered off here. Coming to a glen, her fog lifted; and she saw the child on the ground, dirty, curled in a ball with grubby little hands clasped over her head. Molly heard someone call, "Sophia, where are you?" And as the careworn woman came through the bushes, Molly caught a movement on the far side of the clearing. In the gloaming, a golden light. Another little girl, the same size as Sophia, took hazy shape. Dressed in white with eyelet ruffles and delicate pink ribbons along the hem and the pink and white pinafore. Her feet were clad in black patent leather and white anklets with pink lace trim. Blonde hair flowed in curls shiny as a halo. With a caring look at Sophia, and a glance toward the frowning woman, the golden light was gone. The woman rushed toward Molly, and Molly stammered to explain her presence there, stopping when it became apparent she wasn't seen.

Transfixed, slack-jawed, she watched.

"Mama," sobbed Sophia as her big tear-filled eyes looked through Molly.

"Hush, chile, Mama's here now."

"But, Mama, where'd Susie go?"

"Hush, hush, don' you cry."

"But," Sophia hiccupped, "she was here. They hurt me and scairt me til she came and taked me away. Susie kept me safe, and she is purty. She be my friend." Sophia shook with sobs, and her mama held her tight against her breast. The little girl hunkered down and murmured about a bridge to cross.

"Hush, baby, hush."

Molly supposed this woman had once been pretty. Her high cheek bones and full lips spoke of a bygone beauty. Now her cheeks were sunken with deep lines, the bones jutting and red raw. Good bone structure gone awry. Her face had been chiseled by hard work, suffering, and disappointment. Pain seemed to pull the woman's shoulders down as she slowly raised Sophia's tattered dress, exposing scraped knees, bruises, a trickle of blood on her thigh.

Molly gasped, sobbed. Wept uncontrollably. Her knees burned, her belly ached. She, too, rolled up in a ball, covered her head, and cried out for her mama.

. . .

Fingers of icy air dragged Molly from a mindless stupor. Her arms ached as she pulled them from over her head, opened her eyes, and peered into darkness. Save for the full moon high in the sky and fox fire glinting beneath shrubs, she was alone in the glen. Or so she thought until she heard a snap and a crunch made by something large. A faint shadow crept across the clearing. Panic rocketed through her, her lungs refused air, her heart pounded as she fought the urge to bolt and chase after reality, hoping she'd catch it somewhere in time. But what was time anymore? Where did it start, and where did it end? Silently she begged, *God help me. God, please help me.*

Inch by inch she unfolded, gasped for breath, rose to her feet, and, with only pale moonlight as guide, she retreated from the glen. She tripped on roots, scratched her cheek across a branch, and snagged her pack on rocks as she dragged it until she came to the chestnut where she had stopped so long ago. She rested. Thirsty for air and water, she drank of both and continued on. The moon and fox fire gave way to twilight. The way was visible now, warm breezes raised her curls, squirrels chattered. Trees held full heads of green leaves, and flowers bloomed. Gone was the autumn chill and dark night. Still she hurried, blindly running at times, headed for home and sanity behind locked doors. To safety from the harsh static of an ominous presence.

Molly bolted the door and latched the windows as twilight lost its grip and slipped into dark.

A whippoorwill began his nightlong serenade.

# FOUR

~

SOPHIA

*All that we see or seem is but*
*a dream within a dream.*

—Edgar Allan Poe

Someone big, like a monster man, had clamped his hand across her mouth and knocked her to the ground. Held her facedown. His hand was rough, dirty, and manure smelly. His knees were hard and pushy between her legs. A rustle in the bushes scared him. When he ran off, he yelled, "bitch" and she'd better watch out. His voice told her it was Jimmy, her big brother, being mean and bad to her again.

Now, Sophia is home, safe in Mama's arms, swaying gently back and forth. Her knees are dirty, and blood oozes through the grime. Her head hurts, her mouth tastes of manure smells. Sobbing, she reaches for a fold of Mama's dress and sucks on a corner. And Mama sings

O, they tell me of a home far beyond the skies,
O, they tell me of a home far away;
O, they tell me of a home where no storm clouds rise,
O, they tell me of an unclouded day.

Too soon, Mama stands and helps her climb the ladder to the attic loft, lays her down, and tucks the feather quilt under her chin. Sharp points of straw from her bed poke through, scratching her back as Mama's warm tears puddle on her forehead. Beside her is Mandy Lee, her corncob doll. Still sniffling, Sophia closes her eyes and surrenders to sleep. Soon the pretty girl just her age, Susie, enters. She smiles and wipes away Sophia's tears and smudges, kisses her cheek, and sits beside her.

When Sophia opens her eyes, the room has grown dim. She moves to the window and looks at her world through dirty, torn curtains. Almost everything is hard around her. The packed dirt of a front yard, the stones on the way to the privy, the chair she sits on for supper, the hands that scrub her face at night. Her dress is torn, dirty, stained. Her other dress, made of brown flour sacking, is coarse and scratchy, but pink and blue flowers that skipped around the skirt make it her favorite.

Food smells drift up—fried potatoes, she thinks. Her tummy growls. Papa's roar startles her as he tells Mama to just shut up.

"She's lyin', Marta. She don't mind and makes up stories. Let her jest stay up thar and miss her supper. See if'n she likes that."

"George, you weren't there. You didn't hear and see. He's been at her, I tell ya."

"What kin I do anyhow!" his big voice shouts. Mama murmurs. And then his same angry bellow, "We ain't got no money for no such stuff. We ain't got nothin' more t'sell."

The desk and chairs, she thinks Mama says. Her eyes slide shut, and she waits. Tired and sick, frightened, she thinks, *If only I weren't so hungry.* She curls up in the quilt with Mandy Lee in her arms and cries until sleep slips over her tears. Susie appears in front of her—beautiful and light. Her eyes twinkle as she beckons Sophia to come.

"But I not s'pose t' leave the house."

"Sh, sh, follow me."

Sophia rubs sleep from her eyes, climbs down, and walks out the back door. Down rickety steps, across the yard. Chicken droppings squish between her toes. First stars flicker in a sky still blue. Birds have quit singing except the nightingale. She follows Susie to a cottage where daisies bloom. In the doorway, a plump, grey-haired lady opens her arms. Fragrant, warm air greets her.

Sophia pats down her crumpled dress and, with eyes so wide her forehead hurts, steps into a room of soft colors and flowers. Candle lights glow in the window.

"Hello, my name is Lily. I'm Susie's mother," the round lady says.

"You look like assers," Sophia stammers.

Lily frowns, and Sophia is afraid she said something bad. In a flash, the lady smiles big. "You mean my lavender dress. The same color as the asters blooming on the sunny slopes. In full flower right now."

Sophia nods and whispers, "Purty assers."

Lily rubs Sophia's face and hands with a soft, wet cloth, sits her on a stool and brushes her hair. She gently works her fingers through the snarls and keeps brushing for a long time. Susie brings a looking glass, and Sophia giggles. Her hair shines bright and smooth, and she even looks like Susie. Except her cheeks aren't as round and pink. Susie's rosy and I'm gray, like when Mama washes my dress too many times, she thinks. 'Cept for my hair. Now it glows like a new penny.

Lily takes her hand, and they all sit at the table, where bowls of soup send steam rising. The soup is spicy and thick, with bread, too, for sopping it up.

"Eat all you want. There's a good girl," Lily coos.

And Sophia eats every bit in her bowl. She wants to pick it up and lick the very bottom, but Susie doesn't, so neither does she. She folds her hands on her lap, her legs swing free from the tall chair, and she hums while Lily plays the dulcimer.

"My mama had a dul-see-mir onct."

Lily hands her the stringed instrument. And Sophia strums, making music.

"Do you like cookies?" Lily asked.

Before she can nod her head, a glass of creamy milk and a ginger cookie are set before her. The cookie, spicy and sugar crusted, snaps when she bites and then melts in her mouth. Rich, cool milk slides the cookie sweetness down. Clean, warm, and filled, Sophia licks her lips of the last drops of milk and sugar. Susie's mama pats her head and kisses her cheek. She smells like ginger cookies and is soft and smooth like the milk. Lily's apron is white as white can be and has ruffles around the edges. *Even her apron is purty,* Sophia thinks. Susie is lucky living here.

"It's time for you to go home now. You don't want your mommy worrying," Lily says as they walk toward the door.

Susie leads the way, through the woods and toward her house. Looking back, Sophia sees the grey-haired lady wave good-bye. An owl asks, "Who, who?" Then Lily and the cottage and flowers fade away. Sophia awakens to darkness, cold and more hurt in her stomach. She hears noises and she jumps.

Mama, by moonlight, creeps up the ladder with a plate of cold supper for her.

In the morning, Mama throws a rope with buckets tied to each end across their old mule's back and hauls water from the well. She heats the water on a fire pit and fills a round metal tub. In summer, Sophia takes a bath outside, but this morning is cold, so Mama has carried the tub into the kitchen near the fire. With a soap sliver and a rag, Mama dabs at Sophia's scraped knees and all the tender places. After toweling Sophia dry, Mama helps her into her brown dress with the blue and pink flowers.

Sometimes Papa and Mama go to town, taking dried sang roots to sell. When they come back, they have a store box full: a sack of flour, some sugar, raisins. Usually a dress and shoes for her—too big—to grow into.

She doesn't know where Mama and both her brothers are going today or why. There is no more sang done; it still needs to be hung and dried. But today Jimmy and Joe hitch the old mule to the wagon and load the broken desk and four rickety chairs. They take food from the root cellar and bread, dried apples. Sophia, all clean and dressed up, is ready. Mama shakes her head and strokes Sophia's cheek with her calloused hand.

"Be good girl," Mama says with tears in her eyes. "Papa will watch out fer you." Mama says it will be the next day 'fore they be home.

Papa tromps into the woods as soon as the wagon rounds the bend.

All day Sophia waits, hoping they'll come back for her. No one comes and she climbs to bed with an aching rumble inside. Sometime after dark, Papa comes home and staggers up to the loft. Sophia's eyes are wide as his fist shakes a warning in her face. He smells strong like moonshine when his mouth gets close to hers. "*If only* I weren't here," she whimpers silently. Just then Susie skips across the attic floor and takes Sophia's hand. Off they go to play.

Sunshine in a narrow shaft passes over Sophia's eyes, startling her awake. It must be very late. She can't recollect sunshine in her bed before. Why is Papa still snoring and so loud?

Stretching, she looks for golden-haired Susie, who had been here a moment ago. Susie has disappeared again. Sophia crawls from her warm bed and climbs down the ladder stairs, tiptoes past Papa, out the broken door to the privy. Coming out, she squints in the bright sun and remembers that Mama is gone.

In the kitchen she searches for food. Way back in the crate that is the cupboard is an old rusty tin that rattles when she shakes it. She tugs at the lid. Her little hands keep slipping, so she squats on the floor, places the tin between her knees, twists and pulls at the cover. It holds tight. There is a knife somewhere. A sharp knife she has been warned not to touch. What else can she do? Climbing on top of the wobbly cupboard, she reaches high where the knife is hanging from the ceiling. On tiptoes with her arm and fingers stretched, she can touch the blade as the knife dangles from a hook. The cupboard teeters and sends her sprawling with a clamor. On the floor, with her hand tight across her mouth, Sophia holds her breath, afraid the noise has woke up Papa. He'll be mad and do bad things. Sophia cries without a sound.

Maybe she better climb back in bed or go outside and be quiet. But her tummy hurts as if an angry hand is squeezing it tight. A flat, dull piece of metal is under the fire pit grill. It works. Pop—the lid is off. Peering into the can, she sees a small box tied tight with a string. She sniffles, replaces the lid, and slides the tin back.

With nothing in the house to eat, she thinks of Mama's garden and goes outside again. The ground is wet from last night's rain, so a carrot pulls up easy. It is muddy, but the rain barrel is full. She dips the hollowed-out gourd, drinks, and cold water aches into empty spaces of her stomach. Sophia clutches her middle a moment and then pours water over the carrot, wipes it back and forth on the rag that always hangs near the dipper. Sitting on a big rock she bites, chews, swallows. The carrot is sweet, and juices slide down her throat, filling her tummy. What else is in the garden? There are potatoes, she knows. Will she get in trouble for digging one? She looks around for the shovel. She needs to put on her shoes too, if she's going to dig.

A wagon creaks and clanks up the rutted road, and she runs to meet her mama. It ain't Mama or nobody she knows. The horse stops, and a man in all black clothes jumps down. He tips his tall black hat and, with a bow, says, "Howdy, there, little miss. How are you?"

Sophia stares. He is long and skinny and scary looking. His thin lips stretch into a smile, but his eyes stay cold.

"My name's Reverend Hebbins. I'm the new travelin' preacher man. Is your mammy or pappy here?"

Sophia shakes her head no. Papa will be mad if he gets woke up before he's ready.

"Well, then, little miss, come on over here. I got something for you. Gimme a hug first."

She backs away, but he swoops down and swings her up in his arms. High. She catches her scream back quick before it makes any noise. He slides her down his body until her toes touch the ground again. Her dress is all scrunched up, and she twists around to make it straight and cover her knees. He reaches in his wagon and hands her a loaf of bread.

"My missus baked this for y'all. You see you give it to your mammy, hear? And this here Bible too."

"Thank you," Sophia mumbles, gripping the book in one hand and the bread under her other arm. She wishes he would go away so she could get a hunk of the bread. He stands with hat in hand, waiting. For what? *If only Mama were here.* His mouth smile sends shivers down her arms and the Bible falls in the dirt. Picking it up, he says, "I'll put this on the stoop here. Don't forget it, ya hear?"

Sophia nods and backs toward the house, trips over a tree root and plops down hard on her fanny. Seeing Susie skipping across the yard toward her keeps her from crying. Preacher man laughs but his eyes don't.

"Bye now, little miss. Tell your mammy I come this way once a month," he calls as he climbs into his wagon, swats his horse with the reins, and continues down the road.

Susie spins around and hopscotches out of sight.

Sophia dashes into the house, pulls off big chunks of the brown loaf, and gobbles it down. Will Mama be mad that she ate so much? Should she hide the rest? No. Mama won't be mad, but Papa might. Maybe if she does a good thing, he won't think about her eating so much. *I could go sanging,* she thinks. That's a good thing. The sanging stick is leaning against the wall.

Barefoot, Sophia runs past the privy, past the shrubs and into the forest until her throat itches, and coughing makes her stop for rest. This doesn't look like where Mama and me were sanging. Another track leads through some ferns and flowers, and she follows it a long, long way. The path ends in a sunny clearing. This isn't it either, and she sinks to the ground, lost.

A huge black-and-orange bee touches down on her arm. Sophia doesn't move a muscle, doesn't even blink. It's a bubble bee, she knows. The bee crawls to her sleeve and lifts off slowly as if half asleep or too big to fly. She trails after the bee, in a trance, as if there is no choice.

Sophia stumbles and falls, hitting her cheek on a sharp rock. "Ouch," she cries, and tears form a film over her eyes. She picks up the hem of her dress and bends to wipe her eyes and runny nose. Blood stains the cloth. Her cheek is bleeding, and now she can't stop crying.

Something scratches her leg, tugs at her dress. Thorns on blackberry vines. She has found the berry patch, so there must be sang too. Careful of the brambles, she stretches to pick berries first. They almost fall into her hand—ripe. Sweetness fills her mouth but then, gagging, she spits it all out. Juice stains her fingers, runs down the corner of her mouth, drips on her dress, mixing with drying tears and blood. The berries are moldy from the rains and cold. Suddenly tired, she sees where fallen leaves have been blown together forming a pile. She takes the few steps, licking her sticky fingers as she goes. When she lies down on the leaf bed, her ears fill with crackles as dry leaves break and settle. Dust puffs make her sneeze. The sun is warm, and breezes keep bugs away. Murmuring, singsong noises reach her from a creek she can't see. *If only I wern't alone,* she thinks. The breeze, the creek, the dusty leaves lull her. She dreams.

"Who are you?" Sophia asks Susie, who has curled up beside her. "Why are you here?"

"I've been looking for you. Please come be with me."

"Oh I cain't," Sophia says.

"You came last night."

"But weren't that a dream?"

Susie nods and slips away.

Sophia is awakened by a nudge to her shoulder. A monster man stands over her and she screams.

"Hush, Soph, hush. It's me. Joe. Ma sent me fer you. She's scairt about you. Git on home, right quick. I gotta git Pa. He here?"

"Na ah. I'm lost." She crawls to her knees and then, standing, looks at Joe, her big brother. She brushes at leaves stuck to her clothes and legs. Her dress has tears from berry brambles. Oh no. Her purtiest dress is ruint. Papa's gonna be so mad. Mama won't be mad. Mama will be sad and try to make everything all better. But Papa will be so mad. She wants her mama. Joe takes her by the hand and walks to the path. "Now jest go straight. Don' turn. Y'hear? Y'gotta go a long ways."

"I cain't."

"Sophia, I cain't git you home . . . Oh, all right but hurry. Cuz I gotta fin' Pa too. And Ma, she's worried. C'mon."

Sophia scurries after Joe. His steps are big, and he jumps easily over a fallen log. She must stop and climb over, scraping her arms and legs as she goes.

"I forgot my sanging sack and stick. Wait fer me."

"No, you cain't go back. We're late, and Ma is worried, I tell ya." Joe bends forward and motions for her to climb on his back and they go fast until he is out of breath and sets her back on the ground.

"You can make it from here, Soph," Joe says and gives her a little shove.

Sophia walks on, alone, making sure not to turn any which way. *I kin, I kin get home,* she thinks over and over. "I kin," she says aloud as she comes to a clearing. The privy appears, then the garden patch and then the lean-to. Home.

"Mama," she cries and runs to the back door. Mama is in the kitchen.

"My sweet Sophia, where y'been, chile? And look at you."

"I been sanging. I forgot my stick."

"Yer papa with you?"

Sophia shakes her head. "I was scairt while you was gone and a preacher man came with this bread. And I were hungry fer sumpin'. I didn't eat it all."

"Well, I'm home now and got the fire goin' fer supper. First, I got somethin' fer you. Come."

She follows Mama up to the loft. On the straw bed is a big box. Mama places a soft tiny ball of fur in Sophia's outstretched arms. A black-and-white kitten looks in her face from wide green eyes.

Sophia sits close to Mama, lets her hands slide over the kitten and giggles when it purrs.

"Where y'been? Why'd y'go?" Sophia asks

"Jimmy needed to go fur away fer a while so me and Joe took him."

"He ain't here no more?"

"No," Mama says and shakes her head.

Jimmy gone. He won't chase her no more or yell mean things at her when Joe ain't there. Sophia wants to lay her head in Mama's lap, hold the soft, soft kitten and rest. Gently Mama sits her up, places the kitten in the deep box, and beckons Sophia to follow her downstairs. There on the kitchen table is the wooden "town" box. A new pair of shoes for Sophia, with bits of rags stuffed in the toes so they'll fit.

Mama hums while she tends the fire and starts biscuits and greens for supper. Sophia's belly rumbles with the aroma, and she wriggles in her chair. It is just Mama and her. And the kitten in the box who needs a name. *I'll call it Biscuit,* she thinks. Turning her head she is spooked when a shadow passes by the little window. Oh, its Mama coming from the rain barrel with more water to heat. Mama pours hot water in the wash basin, carves a sliver of soap, and sets Sophia to washing herself—ridding her of crusts of blood and blackberry juice and salty tear stains. The warm water stings and sinks into her. She closes her eyes and lays the wet rag on her face, over and over again. Until Mama says enough and she sees two plates of biscuits and greens on the table. Suppertime.

While they eat, the afterglow of a setting sun fades. Darkness settles down, like a blanket, over the house. An owl hoots from a distant tree.

Stars blink as Sophia approaches the privy one more time before bed. Mama is close behind, lighting the walk with a kerosene lantern. Shadows, cast by the swinging lamp, dance in and out of the bushes. In the outhouse she goes as fast as she can and comes out still pulling up her panties. The lantern light glows, but she doesn't see Mama. And then a loud noise and a big movement in the bushes makes her cry out and shake . . . It is Mama, having gone potty behind the outhouse.

"Jumpy little chile tonight. You must be tired. How about a story now and some sleep?"

"Uh-huh." Sophia nods.

Hand in hand they walk the stony walk to the back stoop. Mama puts out the lamp so they can watch the night sky. In a moment they catch the flash of a falling star. "Oh," they say together.

"Make a wish," Mama says.

Sophia squinches her eyes tight and wishes she never has to be alone again.

# FIVE

~

*Soft is the music that would charm forever*
—William Wordsworth

Hot water coursed down Molly's body as she stood in the shower with eyes closed one minute and wide-open the next. Seeing first Sophia, tattered and hurt, then Susie, polished and smiling. She had scribbled in her journal all she had seen. Every detail flung on to the page. Perhaps writing helped. Herbal tea helped too. Before bed she'd brewed a mix of chamomile, kava kava, licorice root, and catnip. She did sleep eventually, but dreams dropped her into a dark abyss and then spiraled her up to the ethers. When phantoms at last evaporated and she rested in her bed, in familiar surroundings, the sun shone high in the sky.

Instead of coffee this morning she'd prepared another cup of calming tea. At the last moment she'd added a bit of ginseng and chicory root for a pick-me-up. As soon as her mind said ginseng, she made the connection—sang. That's what Sophia and her mama were digging. Of course, red berries and yellow leaves in autumn. One mystery solved, although, for her, autumn was months away.

She sipped the sweet, warm liquid while standing at her bedroom window, watching puffy, innocent clouds move slowly across the sky like colorless helium balloons afloat. Funny how billows in the heavens could balance her—her head in the clouds and feet on solid ground. As she drank and gazed at the flowerbed rampant with daisies gone wild, a cat jumped off the garden gate and into the yard. It turned its black-and-white face and looked directly at her.

"Oh no, not today, Cat." And she yanked the curtain closed. *So much for being grounded,* she thought, holding her breath. Cat was the constant in both her waking and sleeping dreams, enticing her down dim forest paths and to shocking scenes.

She must get composure before driving to the airport tonight. The morning newspaper had told her today was Thursday, the only piece of news she could concentrate on. She'd have coffee, eat lunch, and then go to the bookstore, look for history of this place. Maybe that would answer some questions. The water ran cold, and she turned off the tap in time to hear the phone ring, so she grabbed a towel and, dripping wet, rushed to answer.

"Where have you been?" Jake's angry voice responded to her out-of-breath hello.

"Why? What do you mean? I was taking a shower." Molly glanced down and saw six messages on her machine. Geez.

"I've called three times. The last time I told you to call me immediately. Where the hell have you been and with whom?"

She stammered, said nothing. Jake's voice softened.

"What's the matter? Are you sick?"

"Yes, well, sort of sick, yes. But I can pick you up." She heard his exasperated exhale over the line. Her mind pictured his thin lips taut like a wire, barbed by his whiskers.

"Molly," he sighed again, "that's why I called. I'm staying 'til Saturday. When I couldn't get you, I called the board president and explained—well, gave him an excuse anyway." Jake told her what time he would arrive and insisted she write it down and repeat it all back to him.

Off the phone, Molly stared at the blinking answer machine, at the slip of paper with Jake's arrival information, at the little puddle from her dripping body, at the soggy towel that was coming untucked and slipping. She had two more days to get herself centered. Normally a long hike would calm her, but the thought of a walk alone, now, made her dizzy and nauseated. Molly knew she must make human contact to bring reality underfoot.

After dressing and drying her hair, she listened to her messages. Yes, three from Jake, the last one angry and scowling.

Intermingled was Diatrice's voice. "We missed you, dear, at choir practice. Can only assume you are ill. Do call if you need anything." Geez, she had forgotten.

Next, a connection so garbled she couldn't identify the caller or the words. Nothing but static and a high-pitched whine. She fast-forwarded.

"Hi, Molly, it's me, Beth. Jest wanted to thank you for your friendly invitation. Oh, and I'm reading Song of Solomon. Thanks. Bye."

Molly smiled for the first time since her haunting experience. Beth's soft voice soothed her and reminded her of Amy. She missed her daughter and ached to talk all this through with her. At one time Amy would have listened and perhaps laughed and teased but not scorned. The last few phone calls, she had been vague and cut their conversations short, with what seemed like lame excuses. Molly had written and gotten no response. Either Amy was miffed or busy with no crisis in her life that required Mom. Now she remembered the letter Amy had sent that Molly wasn't even sure she had seen come into the house.

In the study, she reached for the book she'd stuck it in. The door bell rang and she jumped. She hesitated. She'd never see who was there except by opening the door. Did she want to do that? Don't be silly, she scolded, probably just a neighbor from down the road.

She marched into the living room and threw open the door. She gasped. An ancient man stood grinning toothlessly at her. Skinny and unkempt in baggy bib overalls with, of all things in summer, a long-sleeved underwear shirt beneath. His yellowish gray hair hung to his shoulders. A sparse beard and mustache drooped down his face and onto his chest. From deep beneath bushy eyebrows, his weary eyes gazed, as if this were his last chore and then they could close forever. He held a three-stringed musical instrument, beautifully carved and polished.

"Yes?"

"This here's fer you," he said as he twisted his head and spit over the rail.

"I don't understand."

"Take it, its you'rn. Be hunderd dollars cash money." He thrust the object at her.

"But I don't have a hundred dollars. And I can't play this anyway."

"Made this here dulcimer, m'self, fer you."

"No, thank you. It's beautiful. But no, I'm sorry, I can't buy it."

He shook his head, turned and gimped down the steps, to the street and into a battered pickup that looked as old as he did. Before driving away, he treated her to another toothless grin.

Molly gawked. What on earth was going on? Who were all these strange people? She grabbed her purse, locked the doors, and hurried to her car. As fast as she dared drive she headed to the next town, the bookstore. *I'll dig up some history of this place, maybe it's haunted,* she thought. *Could I have stepped through a veil and unleashed strange spirits?* Shaking and frightened she screeched into a parking space. As she got out of her car, she saw Royce, through the store window, peering over his reading glasses. Probably heard her tires squeal. Another good impression. *Maybe he won't remember me,* she hoped.

"Well, if it isn't Molly."

"You remember my name?"

"You aren't an easy lady to forget," he said with a wink.

Was he making a pass at her? She glanced quickly at his left hand. No wedding band. But she wore hers.

As if reading her mind, he said, "Don't worry. The last thing I need is an irate husband on my heels."

"Oh," she said and fondled her ring. "My husband is gone." What had gotten into her, why did she say that? Well, it's true, he *was* gone for today. But the implication. Now he's got me pegged as a merry widow. *I don't care,* she argued with herself, *I need someone to talk to. Someone who won't whisper, "the new pastor's wife is crazy."*

"Well, what can I do for you—first, how'd you like the book on plants?" he asked.

"It's good. Helped me a lot."

"And today?"

"I'm not sure. I think I'm looking for some history of this area. Around the civil war era?"

"I may have just the book for you. But I sold my last copy yesterday. It'll be a couple weeks before my order arrives. What's your number? I can call when it gets here."

"Ah, ah . . . well all right. My name is Molly Bell." Why had she given her maiden name? Anonymity, that's why, damn it.

He laughed.

"I know. I've heard it plenty. Ma Bell," she said.

"Actually, no. I laughed because it made me think of the Bell Witch."

"Huh?" Prickles covered Molly's skin as if she'd rolled in a cactus bed.

"Well, there was this witch tormenting the Bell family in the early 1800s. Except that was over the mountains in West Tennessee. The frontier of that time."

"Have there been witches and ghost sightings around here?" she asked as her breath came back.

"Oh, sure. I've got a few books on the subject." He led her down one long shadowy aisle to a far corner. She followed as if on a treasure hunt and about to uncover the chest of gold.

"There's this one," he said, handing her *Ghosts and Haunts from the Appalachian Foothills*. A phrase on the back cover gave her pause "Hear the cries and meet the spirits that inhabit the region."

"Here's the one I was thinking of," he said, pulling a small book from the shelf.

*Haints, Witches, and Boogers: Tales from Upper East Tennessee*, by Charles Edwin Price.

Her hands shook slightly as she took the book from him. She studied the colorful cover. The title in dandelion yellow on a purple night sky, a red mansion in a forest of green, and a midnight blue lake. One of the chapter titles intrigued her. "Part of the Dark Is Moving: The Haunted Bridge at Stony Creek." And then another. "The Hainted River."

"I'll take this," she said with an effort at nonchalance as they walked to the front of the store.

"I'm interested in your opinion. After you read it, give me a call, would you?"

At her puzzled look, he continued, "I put a bookmark in every book I sell. It has the store's number. And here, here's my home phone."

"Okay." Molly moved toward the door, hesitant to leave but at a loss what to say.

"Wait a minute. I'm, ah, it's almost closing time. I could lock up early, and we could stop at Sam's café . . . have some supper."

"Oh, I don't know, thanks but . . ."

"Come on, you've got to eat—and tonight's special is catfish. Or, uh, unless you've got other plans?"

The question came with a raised eyebrow, an eager half smile. An encouraging nod of his handsome head. This would give her a chance to talk about ghosts and seeing things and feeling a presence.

"Sure, why not? Catfish it is." Molly attempted a dazzling smile and then bowed her head, suddenly shy. She waited outside as he closed up and locked the door.

"Let's walk. It's only three blocks down and around the corner. Nice afternoon anyway. Look, no clouds. No storm tonight."

As Molly strolled alongside him, she was aware their stride matched effortlessly. She fished out her big sunglasses and put them on, in case one of the Sweet Hollow Baptist congregation should be in town.

They passed a beer joint as an old codger came out, bringing with him dank tavern odors and the twang of jukebox honky-tonk.

"Whew," they both said, turned to each other, and crinkled their noses.

When they paused at a junk store window, Royce leaned close and pointed out a wooden butter churn; his scent, untainted by cologne or artificial flavorings, seeped into her skin like warm almond oil. His face was close as she turned toward him. He didn't back away, and neither did she.

They both chuckled. She nervously. She suspected he'd felt the tug of her scent also.

He asked, "What is the fragrance you're wearing?"

"Oh, you must be smelling remnants of my aromatherapy concoction I used this morning."

"Therapy? Have you been ill?"

"I've had some anxious moments, and my tranquility blend helps calm my nerves."

"I think I smell lavender, right? And sandalwood?"

He leaned toward her hair and inhaled. As he exhaled, his warm breath caressed her cheek.

"You're right. And chamomile, frankincense, and patchouli," she murmured. She could like being with him. *Goodness, he must be ten years younger, and please don't forget you are no longer Molly Bell.* Her first marriage was the mistake of teenagers. This one with Jake, she'd entered as an adult, and if it failed, she'd be a failure too. But for today she didn't want Jake's shadow walking with them down this quiet street.

"Interesting," Royce said. A woman in a yellow convertible beeped her horn and hollered, "Hi." Royce smiled and waved. "My sister-in-law."

"Oh, your family lives close, that's nice."

"Well, just my brother and his wife and their teenage daughter."

"Do you have children?" she asked, thinking of Amy and making plans to call her tonight. They hadn't talked for too long.

"No kids. My niece is like a daughter to me, though. I'll probably never have any kids of my own."

"Why? You're still young."

"Fifty isn't that young."

Molly stumbled and burst out laughing. "Go on. You're not fifty. Are you? You sure don't look . . ."

"No kids." He laughed, and she almost reached for his hand to swing as they sauntered along.

"Actually, I'll be fifty next month. Well, here we are at Sam's. Nothing fancy, but he can fry a catfish."

They took a rear booth, and she deliberately sat with her back to the room and the door. A gum-snapping waitress in a gray uniform appeared with water and menus. Tall and slender with bleached blonde hair rolled in a bun and hairnet, she tilted so one hip jutted out.

"Hi, Royce. Early tonight, huh?" She blew a little gum bubble and popped it back behind full, smiling red lips.

Royce introduced her as Sam's wife, Ellen.

"Good to meetcha, hon," she chewed, giving the appearance of a friendly horse.

"Hi, Ellen." Molly smiled.

After they ordered the special, she broached the subject of ghosts. She started with the least traumatic. "Remember the music at the antique store? You said it was dulcimer, and I'd hear it in lots of establishments? Well, I'm hearing that music in the woods too when *no one* is around."

"Hmm. Maybe the forest is haunted, and you'll find your answer on those pages." He pointed to *Haints, Witches, and Boogers* . . . lying on the table.

"I'd like to, believe me."

"Where abouts are you hiking?"

"Well, we, uh, I live on the other side of Sweet Hollow, on the outskirts. I walk until I come to an old two-story log cabin by a fairly large stream. The woodland is just past there."

"I think I know where. That cabin has an interesting history."

Before she could pursue what he meant, Ellen, still chewing gum, served platters of fried fish.

"Enjoy." And off she snapped.

"So tell me. What is it you do besides frequent the wilderness and mix potions?"

"I'm a writer," she said without hesitation. How had lying become so easy? Well, she did write in her journal all the time, she rationalized.

"What sort of writer? If you don't mind my asking. Fiction, true life, haunting?"

Laughing, she said, "A little of all three, right now."

"Published? I could feature your work?"

"Nothing published yet." *Yeah, right, yet.*

"Well, when you do, keep me in mind. How's your fish?"

"Delicious, thank you. A nice surprise to this day. Here's to dinner with a new friend." And she held up her glass of water for a toast.

The golden flecks danced in his brown eyes when they met hers. He clinked with his glass and said, "For me too. I thought I'd be staring at a crossword puzzle over my plate. This view is far nicer."

His smile created a dimple in his right cheek. Molly went soft inside and changed the subject.

"Getting back to dulcimer music. An old man came to my door this afternoon with a handcrafted instrument for sale. Are there such craftsmen in this area?"

"Oh, sure. Though they don't usually go door-to-door selling their wares. Did he give his name?"

"No. Just that he made it for me. Gave me the jitters."

"Hmm. What'd he look like?"

She described him, and Royce shook his head.

"That sounds like a lot of guys around here. Did you buy the instrument?"

"No. Now I wish I had. I didn't have a hundred dollars, and besides, he made me edgy. I wanted him gone."

She considered relating her encounter and dreams about Sophia, Marta, and Biscuit. She held her tongue, saving that whole scenario for another time, if there was one. And she found herself hoping there would be.

"Guess I'd better head home," she said and they got up.

"See ya in church," Ellen said with a pop and crackle of her gum.

They glanced sidelong at each other and Molly mouthed what. Her mind raced. Had Ellen recognized her from services Sunday? Royce just turned and waved at her as they stepped through the door.

"She says that to me all the time. Doesn't mean anything. You had a strange panic look in your eyes, as if you had been caught with your hand in the cookie jar or something."

"Surprised, more like it. Neither of you seem churchy to me. Whatever that means."

Walking back to her car, he put his arm loosely around her as they stepped off the curb. Just gentlemanly behavior but pleasant shivers shot up her spine, and she tingled like a teenager on her first date.

"I'll call when the civil war book comes in," he said as he opened her door.

Molly pulled a pad of paper from the glove compartment and jotted down her phone number. "Here," she said. "I never did give you this."

"That's right, we got caught up in haunts and witches. Thanks for a nice dinner hour. Bye."

As she started for home, Molly tried not to think about Royce. But his smile, the dimple in his cheek, and his velvety brown eyes kept creeping forward in her mind. Finally she succumbed and relived the interlude. Innocent enough but enticing all the same. The last glory of twilight waned as she pulled up to the house. In the deepening shadows she could see something leaning against the front door.

She set her purse down and picked up the package swaddled in brown paper and tied with string. A penciled note scribbled on the wrapping read, "Made fer you. Leave money under the rocking chair." She looked to the road and down the country lane. No sign of anyone. Carrying the parcel and her new book, she scurried inside, locked the door, switched on lights throughout the house, and sat to untie the string and let the paper fall. Her jaw dropped as she gazed at the highly polished dark wood of the dulcimer that lay on her knees. She caressed the satiny surface, admiring its intricate design. The wood felt familiar to her hand, and her fingers began to strum.

# SIX

~

*Do not go where the path may lead,*
*go instead where there is no path and leave a trail.*
—Ralph Waldo Emerson

The music Molly made with her inexperienced strumming sounded like banjo, with a delicate jingle overtone reminding her of tiny bells on lilies of the valley in springtime, raindrops at the beginning of a summer storm. Autumn leaves floating to earth on a gentle breeze would sing like this if they could. And yes, the dulcimer music she brought forth could make the first snowflakes of winter dance.

Her shoulders rounded gently, her jaw slacked, and she felt the curve of a contented smile glide into place upon her face. Her eyelids became heavy, and she let them fall. Her body no longer weighed her down; she was light as if she were a fluff ball floating on an air current. She continued to strum with a sense of familiarity unexplainable. As her shoulders drooped, her neck lost its will to hold her head up, and so it rolled to one side, seeking a resting place. She let gravity have its way and now understood what a puppet felt like when the strings had gone limp. Eventually her hands released their tension and ceased playing. Still, music filled the room. Filled her world.

A far-off ringing woke her muscles and brought them to attention. She opened her eyes, straightened her spine, and listened to her own voice, "Please leave a message."

Beth chimed, "Hi. My boss is closing shop tomorrow, and I have the day off. Wondering if you're up fer a hike. Call me."

Molly couldn't muster the tautness to move through the room and pick up the phone. Instead she rested the dulcimer on the coffee table, tipped herself sideways on the couch until her head lay on a throw pillow. She tucked her hands under her cheek and slept.

When she roused from a deep, dreamless sleep her concerns had retreated to a dusty corner of her mind, and she had no intention of stirring them up. It was only nine thirty in the evening, and she considered calling Beth, then remembered her manners. *Phone calls from nine in the morning to nine at night—unless an emergency.* Her mother's voice echoed in her brain. Her plan to call Amy passed through her reverie. Tomorrow, maybe. She stumbled through the house, flicking off lights, shed her clothes, and crawled into bed.

Waking before dawn, refreshed and relaxed, she thought of the dulcimer. Magic, she decided. White magic. She sauntered to the kitchen and brewed a pot of coffee. In the living room, she brushed the instrument with her fingertips and breathed, "Thank you." Gathering up the brown paper and string, as if it were holy, she read again the shaky handwriting. "Leave money under rocking chair." She'd scrape together one hundred dollars somewhere. Her front entry contained two lawn chairs and a small table. Could he mean the rocking chair she *thought* she'd seen at the cabin? After pouring a cup of coffee, she went in search of her camera. Finding it in her backpack, she noted the pictures she'd taken that day were the first on the roll. Maybe she could finish it today on a hike with Beth.

She dug out her Bible Study papers and found the sign-in sheet. Spying Diatrice's spidery script reminded her of the sewing circle that afternoon. Molly rang her first, hoping a machine would pick up.

"Hello," the pursed lips twanged.

"Hi, Diatrice, this is Molly."

"Goodness, dear one, how are you?"

"I'm okay. I'm sorry I missed choir practice." Another lie. She was getting too good at this. "And I'm afraid so much has come up with Jake out of town that I'll not be available to quilt this afternoon," she said, sounding snooty to her own ears.

"Well, dear, we certainly hope you and Reverend Jake will fulfill your commitments. Now, I really must rush. As I said, if you need anything, please call."

She considered the veiled warning, but nothing could drag her to church on this clear, cool day. She shook her head and directed her eyes farther down the list. Beth answered halfway through the first ring.

"My goodness. You were right next to the phone. Oh, this is Molly."

"I was jest ready to try you again. Hoping I'd catch you home."

"I'm sorry I didn't return your call last night. I dozed and then it got too late. I do want to hike—you still game?"

"Sure. Let's pack lunch and make it all day, okay?

"How about in an hour? Can you come to my house?"

"I'll need directions, I reckon."

Molly gave them and they said good-bye. She hit the play button to hear her other messages. A garbled one again, then Beth's, and then more static and shrill whining, eerie, like a distant air-raid siren. She erased them all and then wanted to undelete. That's three peculiar recordings in two days. Her phone line must need work, and yet her other calls were clear. Could someone be trying to reach her from outer space? She smiled. But then the thought came, *Or from beyond the grave*? Her smile faded. Still she hummed as she moseyed in to get dressed.

. . .

"Right here should be the chestnut. Where *are* all the chestnut trees? I guess I'm not where I thought I was," Molly said as she pivoted with her arms spread and gazed in all directions.

"Taint chestnuts in these woods anymore."

"Why? I thought I saw them everywhere."

"They used to grow all over these parts 'til 'round 1900 or sich. Then a fungus got 'em. Took several years but when people saw 'em dyin' off, they logged as much as they could. No matter if the tree was healthy or not. Woodpeckers, wind, rain spread the disease; and man didn't give the strong trees a fightin' chance. They used chestnut wood for most everything. Those split rails around that cabin, the shingles too—probably chestnut—it decays so slow. But now . . . well, the American chestnut is long gone."

"But . . ." She decided to keep her argument to herself, after all Beth knew what she was talking about. Had she really experienced stepping back in time? Somewhere before 1900. She knew she'd seen majestic chestnuts flourishing among oak, hickory, maple and birch. The deep, spiraling fissures in the bark of the trunk she had leaned against that day with Cat could be nothing other than a chestnut. And the ground had been thick with large nuts.

Trying to wrap her mind around this, her eyes met Beth's quizzical expression.

"Thar's a dwarf chestnut that seems immune. I don't see those here either."

"No, no. It's okay. I must have been mistaken."

Their hike led them deeper into the thick stand of trees than she had ventured before. Climbing a steep stretch, they fell silent, reserving their breath for oxygen intake.

"Ah, here's ginseng nestled alongst maidenhair fern," Beth squatted and swished the fronds to one side.

"I'd have missed that. It's almost cowering now. In late fall it takes center stage. Could it be Virginia creeper instead? Here I am, questioning you."

"No, you could've been right. The leaf clusters are akin. I reckon I know sang when I see it."

Molly smiled. Ginseng—sang. A little thing, but significant enough to instill a feeling of place. "So do you harvest sang yourself?"

"Shucks, not much anymore. My mama and I useta years back."

"I gather it was considered valuable long ago."

"Oh yeah. Fer Cherokee, ginseng was the plant of life, fer all its power. And we used it fer digestion, fer energy. An all 'round tonic. Mama gave sang to us girls fer cramps too."

"The roots, right?"

Beth nodded.

As they traipsed, Molly heard the soft nasal mewing she'd mistaken for a kitten on one of her walks. "Listen," she said.

"Look," Beth pointed to a birch tree. "About midway. See 'em?"

She spied two birds and twisted her pack around to pull out one of the small nature books she'd brought along as Beth continued, "That one's a yellow-bellied sapsucker. It's a male—see his red throat? He's probing fer insects. He'll be back feeding at those same holes again."

"Guess I didn't need these books, huh?"

Beth shrugged, grinned. *There's that lipstick commercial again,* Molly thought as she took pictures of the birds. They stood silent with necks cricked and watched until they flew.

When they rounded a bend, a raccoon stared at them. They stared back, inching toward him. Molly and Beth beamed at each other as if they shared a delicious secret. The raccoon allowed them near enough to see his eyes peek through his mask. His size and stillness told them he was adult. They hesitated, and Molly tried to communicate with her eyes as she eased her camera up and snapped two pictures. He turned and ambled off as if saying, "I've posed long enough, get the message?"

They walked in silence for several minutes. In a hushed voice, Beth said, "You know, in lore raccoons stand fer disguise. It's said if a raccoon happens on your path you should pay close attention. Maybe someone you know is wearing a mask, not lettin' you see who they really are. Or, you may even be hidin' from your own self."

"You mean living a lie or being lied to?"

"Well, yeah, but not like a deliberate thing. More of a not knowin'."

"Or maybe like going to a masquerade ball. Hiding behind a mask. Pretending you are royalty or living out a fantasy," Molly said.

"Dressin' up and pretendin' is like knockin' on the door of another world."

"Or dimension?"

"It's worth studyin'. It's an important sign fer both of us. Most likely different fer you than me."

*Another trip to the bookstore,* Molly thought.

"Beth, where's the closest library? Maybe they'd have books about animal signs."

"Oh, I reckon you'd need to go to a bigger place. The libraries here are small. Though they might could order books. I know someone who . . . ah, here we are. The headwaters of Sugar Creek are just beyond this waterfall."

"Should we rest here and have lunch?"

"Let's climb over these boulders. Thar's a clearing at the spring. If I remember right, some nice fallen logs to sit on. Sunshine and shade to choose from."

They scrambled on, and when they reached the glen, Molly plopped down on a log and untied her bootlaces. "I'm getting my feet in that stream. Now. Cool 'em off."

Beth laughed. "That's what I always do. Sometimes I strip and swim. 'Specially when it's really hot weather. Today's not too bad."

"Sounds tempting. Let's eat first. Do you ever worry about being caught naked? I had a sensation of someone watching me when I took a quick dip one day."

"Naw. Jest a few locals come up here, and they'd pay no mind."

Tiptoeing out of the creek, they sat side by side, barefoot with jeans rolled up. Like a couple of kids gone fishing. Unwrapping her tuna sandwich, Molly got a whiff and half expected Cat to appear even though they were nowhere near the cabin.

"What kind of shop do you work at that can close at a moment's notice?"

"Well, I only work there two mornings a week. I jest got a divorce, and I'm needin' more money," Beth said. "I'm savin' up to take some classes so I can get better work than cleanin' houses."

"Does it bother you then, losing a day's work?"

"Oh, no. My boss is so kindly. I'm sure I'll get paid fer today since he's the one who canceled."

"Nice."

Molly realized Beth hadn't told her where she worked, but didn't pursue it. They ate in comfortable silence, each to her own thoughts. During the pause, their surroundings came alive with more noise than squirrels and birds. A larger animal prowled. Beth held a finger to her mouth as they listened. Molly wondered if there were bears around here but kept still, alert, and looking for a good climbing tree. They both grinned when they heard a low human whistle. Just another explorer. Sure enough, the bushes parted and into the clearing strode a man.

"Beth," he said, "and Molly."

"Royce," Beth and Molly said with one voice. Molly straightened her shirt, ran her fingers through her fly-away curls. *Preening, for God's sake. Stop that.*

"Molly, you know Beth? Well, clearly."

Beth eyed them both. Then two pairs of eyes rested on Molly as if she needed to explain. She had been enjoying the show until she remembered that Royce and Beth knew two different Mollys. A long pause as they looked from one to the other. Then all three spoke at once and stopped. Laughed.

"You go first," Royce said to Beth."

"I jest met Molly at church where she . . ."

"I'm taking a Bible study with Beth," she interrupted.

"Molly's the . . ." Beth caught Molly's abrupt shake of her head. "The new member," she added quickly.

"How do you know Royce?" Molly asked.

"It's his shop I work at," she said, laughing.

"The bookstore." The old saw about tangled webs we weave ran through her mind. Now she knew why she avoided lying. It just complicated life. What must Beth be thinking? And how was she going to explain herself without looking exactly like the liar she'd become?

Meanwhile, Royce made himself comfortable and was eating the lunch he'd brought along.

"Hey, hope you ladies don't mind if I join you," he winked.

"Not at all," they both said.

"Looks like you two have been wading. Surprised you haven't gone swimming."

Molly laughed, remembering their planned dip in the stream. Beth caught back a chuckle, her mind must have gone there too.

"Well, we considered a dip . . . briefly," Molly said through her giggle. "It's pretty shallow and a footbath was enough."

"So what brought you out here?" Beth asked as she packed away the remains of her lunch.

"Molly's been telling me about strange noises coming from a cabin up this way. Curiosity got me. I walked all around the cabin and in it, even climbed to the loft. No music played for me."

Molly watched their interaction, looking for signs of romance or flirtation. She perceived a platonic friendship even though they would make a striking couple. Both had beguiling smiles capable of entrancing anyone. A twinge tugged at her heart. *Jealousy? Oh, come on, get a grip.*

"Say," she said, regaining her composure, "you said there was an interesting story about that old house. How about telling us?"

Royce moved to a large tree. Sank to its base and stretched his legs out in front of him. He took off his cap, ran his fingers through wavy hair. Seemed he was preparing to regale them with a long tale. After a swig from his water bottle, he said, "Well, folks here 'bouts tell . . ." And when he grinned the dimple deepened, his eyes sparkled.

"Actually, though, there is a story, passed down and around. Beth, you probably know it better. You've lived here longer. So jump in and correct me or add any details I may overlook."

Molly and Beth slumped off their perch and sat on flower-covered ground, using the fallen log for a backrest. Molly wriggled her toes and relaxed her mind. She'd worry later how to repair her little web of lies. Now, the sun warmed her, and a breeze whispered through the trees. Both reminding her of Royce's breath across her cheek. Jake and the church, with their choke hold, seemed far away. She breathed deeply as Royce began.

"Well, the place was built 1800 or so by a trio of brothers. They'd left their home and land and almost all their belongings in Scotland. Paid passage to America took what was left of their wealth. They had nothing except for a few coins, a rag filled with dried twigs and blossoms, and their willingness to work. After living up north with cousins for a few years, they eventually settled in Sweet Hollow. They came to these parts with a reputation for craftsmanship. The one called Doc, because of the herbs and healing potions he concocted, was the only one to marry . . ."

At the mention of herbal healing, Molly dropped the stick she'd been absentmindedly using to doodle in the dirt and gave her full attention.

"It was the abundance of herbs in these parts, I reckon, that attracted them and kept 'em here. The ginseng prob'bly most important, but others too. Blue cohosh, goldenseal, mayapple, all the berries, 'specially the blackberry and wild cherry," Beth commented.

Royce nodded. "Anyway, Doc, he married one of the distant cousins and brought her here. She was a beauty, the story goes. Slim and tall with long thick copper-colored hair. She and Doc, with his two brothers' help, cut the trees and built the cabin. Eventually, after babies started coming, the brothers moved on. Doc would go off riding a mule, making rounds to the neighbors, who lived miles apart and miles from anyone. He'd be gone weeks at a time. Helping people, doling out magic potions of . . ."

"Don' forget the still," Beth interrupted.

"That's right. Far up here somewhere, Doc built a still to make alcohol he needed for medicinal purposes." Royce smiled. "Mostly for medicines, I'm sure. Honey, vinegar, and moonshine for arthritis. Red pepper tea and 'shine for a bad cold."

"A lotta home remedies and sich come down from ol' Doc. And not all call fer 'shine," Beth added.

"Right. Even today people will try different concoctions before seeking medical help. And quite often they work. I've got a couple reference books that give details on mixing roots and berries. But you know more about that, Molly, than I do. Back to the story. Doc and his lady had a sweet romance. Same values, work ethics and all. Life turned especially hard for her when he was gone, as you can imagine. The isolation and danger and all. Her name, um . . ." he looked at Beth.

"I've heard 'twas Marlene," she said.

"Marlene and Doc had three children. Two sons who, as soon as they could, took off to the nearest town. Any size community was better than a wilderness farm. The girl, though, she grew to be the real beauty in the family. Tall and strong and comely is how locals say. Didn't even resemble old Doc. Looked exactly like her mama. Doc loved her all the same and protected her. Kept her away from any travelin' vagabonds.

"On one of his trips, however, a sweet-talking young man come along and the daughter run off with him. Well, when Doc came home and heard, he was furious and hied out after them. Nobody ever saw Doc again. Supposedly, Cherokee took him. They always got blamed for any mishap that couldn't be explained . . . but the daughter—do you know the names?"

Beth nodded. "Marta 'n' George."

Sophia's parents! Molly's eyes shot open, and her mind slammed shut. She heard Royce's voice but no longer deciphered his words. His tone became a murmur beneath strains of dulcimer music coming closer and louder. His voice faded completely.

Molly stares as she sees Joe, Sophia's brother, run through the clearing. She crumbles like a rag doll with its stuffing pulled out. She is small, childlike, and frightened. Joe chases and hollers right past or through Royce. But no, this is a different glen, and the air is chill, the light diffused by clouds of dust stirred up in fallen leaves. In minutes, Joe reappears helping his pa, who staggers, drunkenly scowling at her.

Molly trembled as if riding out an earthquake. Was this the big quake of 1811? And how would she know about that? When was this? Where had she gone? From a far distance she heard a deep voice crooning, "Molly." Another voice, higher pitched but soft, joined in. "Are you okay?" Her body expanded to adulthood, the stuffing in place again. The air was summer sweet and humid.

"Wow. What happened? You all right?" Royce's concern soothed her, his strong hands on her shoulders settled her safely.

"I think I'm okay . . . but honestly, I'm getting scared. All the strange goings-on since I came to Sweet Hollow."

"Maybe you should talk with a professional," Royce said.

Beth opened her mouth and closed it again. *Thank you,* Molly thought. Thanks both of you, my friends.

# SEVEN

~

*You cannot change the music of your soul.*
—Katharine Hepburn

Thunder rumbled, like a bear growling before lumbering off. An afternoon storm was still distant clouds, but boomers increased in volume. Not wanting to get drenched, Molly and Beth laced their boots, then followed Royce through the bushes and along a trail rather than over the boulders. They trekked together until they neared the log cabin, then Royce veered off. He'd parked on an old wagon road and had cut in on another trail.

Lightning crackled to thunderous applause, and the skies opened up. Beth and Molly took shelter in the cabin.

"Well, I hope he makes it without getting soaked," Molly said.

"I reckon. I've come that way a time or two, it's not fur."

"About Royce. You must be wondering what's going on."

"Shucks. No need to 'count fer me."

"No, I put you in an awkward position, forced you to lie. I'm sorry. Please don't say anything to Royce about me until I've had a chance to set the record straight."

"Sure," Beth said. "It's not my business. But I'm right curious."

"It's that he doesn't know I'm Jake's wife. I want him to hear it from me. That sounds mysterious, and I don't mean it to be. Maybe someday I'll be able to explain."

They watched in silence as rain beat down and lightning flashed. Molly exhaled the breath she hadn't realized she'd been holding. Something brushed her leg. Cat rubbed by her and meowed. Beth squatted, held out her hand, and the kitty stuck his head beneath her palm, eking out a petting. Molly sat on the floor and a purring Cat crept into her lap.

"That's queer," Beth said. "A peek at him is all I've gotten afore he darts away. Likes you, plain t'see."

"I've named him Cat. Do you know, does he have another name?"

"He's Smart Alec t'me. He's gotta be, survivin' here with wild animals, owls 'n' sich."

Molly had a sense he'd conquered more than that. Right now he behaved like an ordinary family pet. But when he wanted to lead her or convey a message, he glared, his body stiffened. No purring voice or floppy tail then. She considered describing all this to Beth but still felt disconcerted from having been buffeted about in a time warp.

The rain calmed her, as it usually did. All those negative ions from falling water, she supposed. She inhaled deeply, feasting on the nourishing air. When the storm ended, afternoon had slipped away, and soft gray light settled around them. They said good-bye to Smart Alec Cat and hurried back to Molly's house. Beth climbed into her car, and Molly mentioned Bible study on Monday.

"Be there," she said and waved as she drove away.

Molly lingered at the road, weighing the day's events. The evening hour and earlier rain had stirred up mosquitoes and no-see-ums. Swatting biting insects and waving her arms at gnats, she surrendered the sliver of moon and first star to darkening skies. Tired and hungry, she made toast and a cup of tea, took them to her bedroom window, and stared into the garden. She really must prune the daisies, pull some weeds. Journal pages in mind, she closed the blinds as Cat jumped over the fence into the yard.

She placed the dulcimer on her desk, retrieved her notebook and recorded the day. Chestnut trees that were no more, a raccoon's message about masks, Royce showing up and her reaction to him.

How she'd remembered his warm breath across her cheek. How he stretched out beneath the tree and slipped into local dialect as he told the cabin story. When she wrote of being transported by mention of Marta and George, her script became childlike, mostly illegible. Automatically her free hand touched the dulcimer, her fingers picked at its strings. Finally, having emptied her mind and heart on several pages, Molly placed her journal in a drawer beneath a clutter of computer software. She gently picked up the dulcimer and slid it under her bed.

She woke early Saturday morning, jumped up and scurried around the house—vacuuming, doing laundry, washing dishes, dusting. Chores she should have been doing all week. In the flurry of flying weeds and daisies, the phone rang. She almost let the machine answer, instead rushed in.

"Hi," Royce's voice greeted her.

She closed her eyes and reminded herself to breathe. "Hi."

"I'm just checking. You seemed flustered when I left you yesterday. Just wondering how you are. Did you get caught in the cloud burst?"

"We took cover in the cabin. We wondered about you."

They had a pleasant few moments, and she asked to meet him Wednesday, late afternoon. She would identify herself, apologize for lying, and then put in an appearance at choir practice. She'd tell Jake she was going to the bookstore before church. Not a lie at least.

On the drive to the airport she switched radio stations until she had spanned the dial and back again. With a huff of disdain, she settled for silence. She was torn about Jake's return. Dreading it but needing some routine to give her a sense of stability. She wished she could talk to him about Sophia. And the dulcimer. How could she explain a dulcimer under their bed? He'd never find it, she was certain. Still she yearned to share it, to strum the stings, make sweet, mesmerizing music.

Poor Jake. Spending all that time with his sick sister. And she had hardly given either of them a thought. Even now she wished he'd stay longer. So she wouldn't have to cook or clean, true. More, though, she treasured solitude. Sleeping alone, thinking a thought through without his demands intruding. She feared she'd live to regret her longing for more space. Who was she beyond the minister's wife anyway? A crazy woman with delusions of a past life? A woman who heard music where there was none? Saw people who lived 150 years ago? No, without her marriage she'd shatter into a million pieces. Irreparable. Tears flowed, tracing past her open lips. She tasted salt and wiped her nose as she pressed down on the gas pedal.

She put on a happy face.

. . .

Preparing for church, Molly had determined to stay alert and hear Jake's sermon. Maybe she'd get an inkling of what transpired with his sister, though she doubted it. Oh, he implied certain idiosyncrasies from the pulpit, giving the impression of actually revealing himself. But he mostly separated church from his personal life.

Now, as she settled in the front row, she thought about his behavior at the airport. He'd strutted toward her with a cocky attitude and called back to a fellow passenger, "Jake Carpenter. That's J.C. for short."

The closer he'd gotten, the farther away he'd seemed, as if a concrete block wall surrounded him. With averted eyes, he'd given her a cursory peck on the lips, but his hands roamed her back as if he were checking the ripeness of a melon he'd just purchased. Molly shivered and swallowed. Forcing a pleasant expression, she'd said, "I'm glad you're home."

As they walked to the car, she'd asked, "How is your sister?"

"Oh, um, fine."

"Fine! She said she was dying!"

"Well, she is. I mean she wasn't sick in bed."

When she asked what had been so urgent, he had grunted that he was tired and didn't want to talk. He drove faster than the road warranted, his face calm while his hands clutched the steering wheel, knuckles white. Silence prevailed. Coming upon the scene of an accident, he'd been forced to brake and slow to a crawl as traffic funneled into one lane.

"What did you and Joanne do all week?" she asked to break the tension.

"What does that mean? I could ask you the same damn thing."

His words bit, and she wanted to slap at them like the pesky mosquitoes of the night before. Instead she murmured, "I wish you wouldn't snap at me. The question wasn't snap worthy. I'm interested, is all."

"You're right. I'm sorry." He'd turned to her as lights at the accident scene lit up the interior of their car. Her heart sank when their eyes met. His were black marbles, dull and lifeless. She had jerked away and looked out her window into darkness as they'd sped on.

. . .

She rose now for the opening hymn, reminding herself not to drift again . . . What was going on with Jake? She'd seen him this remote and sullen once before. When his oldest daughter almost died in an accident. Molly couldn't reach him then either. That had been one of the darkest times in their marriage. He wouldn't talk to her, he wouldn't visit his daughter in the hospital. And then he'd behaved so outrageously he'd been arrested, pleaded guilty, and ordered into therapy.

"God," she prayed, "help us all."

Dulcimer music from far, far away pulls her thoughts from terrible imaginings. She moves toward the strings, wanting to be swallowed in them. As she shrinks into a child's skin, something warm and soft and small is being yanked from her arms. The air is shattered by a cry as if a banshee screamed.

Another screeching noise plows her back into adulthood and the church. The soloist had missed a high note at full volume. Molly panicked, glanced from side to side, looked up at Jake. No one seemed to notice that she'd succumbed to the call of another time.

The congregation stood for the final hymn. Shocked, she realized she had missed the whole service and had no idea what Jake had preached.

"Thanks a lot for your rapt attention," he said through gritted teeth as they neared the door to shake hands and say polite good-byes to parishioners.

. . .

Arriving at the church for Bible study, Molly was greeted by Diatrice standing guard at the door.

"You're looking well, my dear. We are all so glad you could be here," Diatrice remarked, peering down her nose.

Molly just nodded, turned, and greeted other women. She was pleased when Beth joined in the discussion of the first verses of James about having faith, not doubting. "He who doubts is like a wave of the sea, blown and tossed by the wind." Exactly how she felt these days. What was she to have faith in? She left with more questions than answers.

One-word sentences were the norm the next few days. Even when she surprised Jake with a dinner of collard greens and corn pone fried in bacon grease. He'd raised his eyebrows but asked for seconds. "Good," he mumbled.

Late Wednesday morning Jake turned talkative. With the sheepish smile that had always melted her heart, he said, "Maybe tonight we could light some candles, put on that Rod McKuen poetry you like and exchange massages."

"What? You snap and snarl. You breathe down my neck without a word about your whole trip. Now I'm asking myself why we are even still married, and you think sex is the answer?"

"Molly . . . I love you. You must know that."

"I don't know anything, anymore. Saying 'I love you' is just words, Jake . . ."

"I fell in love with your laughter, your spunk. You brought a new dimension to my life. You were always so open and honest, but now . . . now you've been so preoccupied. Jumpy. Lying naked by a river one day. Daydreaming in church, another. Diatrice tells me you missed every meeting while I was gone. I'm afraid for us, and I don't know how to fix it." Looking at his watch, he said, "I can't be late for these meetings. Tonight, Molly? Please. Let's at least light some candles and talk. I'll get home as soon as I can."

The day was muggy. Heavy, like her spirits. Jake's pleading and tender good-bye kiss mingled in her mind when she thought of Royce and the friendship that was ending before having a chance, like a trillium blossom plucked in the wild, the flower gone forever and the bulb not producing another for years. Still, she applied makeup and coaxed her hair into a tidy mop behind her ears in preparation for meeting Royce.

*Why bother?* she thought. *Once he knows all my lies the relationship will surely be over*. Just as well. Too much sexual energy danced between her and Royce for a simple friendship, and she sure didn't need an affair complicating her life.

Driving to the bookstore, she listened to her oldies radio station. Sure enough, Stevie Wonder's voice boomed, "Good golly, Miss Molly." Oh, if she could go back to her first encounter with Royce, when she'd been riding high on that song. Now a sigh sank back down her throat, and she whispered, "Right, some folly, *Miss* Molly." With windows open, hot, humid air fanned her curls and pulled hairs loose into a frizz around her face. She stuck out her lower lip and blew upward, cooling her forehead and chasing tears back to their source.

Royce was locking the door when she pulled up. She poked her head out the window and hollered, "Hi."

He turned, and she caught her breath. Clean shaven, eyes sparkling, his hair slightly tousled, he charmed her completely. The faded blue chambray shirt he wore complemented his coloring and hinted at muscles beneath.

"Howdy," he said.

She motioned for him to hop in. "Is there a park nearby where we could walk and talk?"

"There is. Along the river. But it may be pretty buggy . . . no, wait. The county sprayed two nights ago. It should be fine."

"Good. Which way?" She kept her voice nonchalant.

He gave her quick directions and then said, "That shade of green becomes you."

"Thank you. It's called sea green and is supposed to have a calming effect."

"I imagine you are still in a stir about whatever happened up at the spring."

"That and the conversation we are about to have."

"Oh really? Hmm." His tone sounded intrigued rather than concerned.

Molly pulled into a parking spot near the playground, deserted at this dinner hour. They got out and started down the dirt lane that followed the river. When she stumbled over a large stone, he took her elbow and electric shock pulsed through her. She jerked away.

"Sorry," he said. "Just didn't want you to take a tumble here."

"No, I, I. Um." She paused and then said so quietly he leaned close, "It's just that I'm afraid I have already taken a tumble . . . over you."

"Is that a bad thing?" Royce put his arm around her, his hand resting on her shoulder. He stopped, turned her to him, and placed his lips lightly on hers. When she opened her eyes he was opening his. Molly whimpered, put her hands on his face, and answered his kiss, passionately. Pent-up emotion spun her as if she were caught in a whirlpool—heavenly sinking.

She sobbed and pulled away. "This is a mistake. You are going to hate me."

They walked on, holding hands, saying nothing. They hardly knew one another. And so much was based on lies. He thought she was single, that her last name was Bell. This must be a mammoth-size case of lust. The same lust that had led her to marry Jake those long years ago. *At my age, I should know better,* she thought. They came to a picnic table and sat side by side facing the river. Tall rhododendron and elderberry shrubs secreted them from passersby. She turned to Royce and blurted, "Here's the thing. I've created a picture—no. I've *lied* to you. I am not who you think. I am Molly Carpenter. Very much married, and my husband, Jake, is pastor at the Baptist church in Sweet Hollow. I wish you wouldn't think of me as a liar, except that is what I've become, I guess. If Beth hadn't shown up as a mutual acquaintance, I probably would have kept on lying. I'm so sorry." She choked and bowed her head.

It seemed an eternity before his hand caressed her cheek. He cupped her chin in his palm and gentled her face toward him. She kept her eyes closed until he said, "Molly, look at me, please."

A lock of hair had fallen across his forehead. Two vertical lines formed between his eyebrows. His mouth was grim. "Now, you are going to hate me . . . I've known who you are all along." He put his arm around her but turned his eyes to the river. They watched the water flow by. A pair of ducks swam lazily with the current, a tree branch drifted past.

"How did you know? And why did you let me go on like that?" she whispered. Long moments passed, and she thought he hadn't heard. Still, she waited. She took his hand and rubbed the knuckles smooth. Her thumb paused in its caress when she eyed the ring on his finger. Not a wedding band, more like a class ring—the size anyway. The design had a prominent filigree cross with a large emerald in the center. Five tiny gemstones, like points of a star, defined the outer edge, giving it a sinister look. Was he a member of some secret society?

The occult? He did seem inordinately informed and interested in witches. The Bell Witch and all that. *Oh my God,* she thought, *I must have seemed that way to him*. Did he think she was one of *them*? She knew he was too good to be real. *Snap out of it, Molly. Where has this dark imagination come from?* Still, a mixture of dread and déjà vu cloaked her, making breathing difficult, clear thinking a strain.

"This much I know for certain, Molly. You do not lie often, you are too inept a liar." He paused. "First of all, these are small communities. A new pastor is news. Before you and Jake arrived, there was an article about the two of you in the local paper and a picture. So when you said your name was Molly . . . well, how many Mollys have just moved to these parts? I didn't recognize you with your outrageous floppy hat and biker shirt. However, you were on my mind a lot, and when you came in the second time, the resemblance was clear."

Royce finally faced her; and when he did, he took his arm off her shoulder, leaned his elbow on the weathered gray picnic table, and rested his chin in his hand. He shrugged his shoulders.

"When you implied your husband was dead and gave me a false last name, I knew you were lying, but your body language told me you weren't a liar. The discomfort was obvious. You looked down or around me, you blushed and stammered. Quite charming, actually. I wondered why you were lying . . . I'd be happier if you were single, but darlin', I want us to be friends. You've captivated me."

Not knowing what to say, she rose and they strolled on. His ring flashed in her mind. She wanted to ask but was afraid to know. A breeze blew cool across the water. Royce crammed his hands in his pockets and she crossed her arms. He stooped, picked a handful of sky blue flowers, presented the bouquet with a gallant bow. *Forget-me-nots, the symbol of love lost.* Certainly he didn't know that. Such a simple, kind gesture of friendship. A smile spread across her face for the first time that evening as she curtsied and said, "Thank you, sir."

"That glow is what I was hoping for," Royce said and smiled in return. "Now, how about some supper?"

At mention of food, her stomach rumbled. "Do we dare go back to Sam's? Or will we be noticed?"

"I know a better place. The food might not be as good, but there's plenty. And it's much more private."

Once in her car, he guided her down a quiet residential street. The pavement ended, the street narrowed and curved through a copse of maple and oak. No more houses nor manicured lawns. With every inch they traveled, she grew more nervous.

"Where are you leading me?" Her laugh sounded hysterical to her ears.

"We're almost there. Around the next curve."

Sure enough, a tidy bungalow nestled in the trees. Her mind raced with doubts.

"Is this a good idea?"

"Food and conversation is all. I promise I'll behave, if you will."

When she didn't move or say anything, he continued, "You look petrified. I'm not an axe murderer or a Don Juan. Besides, I'd like to hear more of your incident the other day if you want to talk."

"It may shock you, if I can even explain—it's so weird." She really did need an interested ear for her Sophia experiences. And his ring could mean nothing. Maybe he just liked the shape and stones. Still, when he stepped from the car, she slipped her cell phone into her purse. Just in case.

Royce unlocked the front door, and they entered a tiny room, one wall lined with books, floor to ceiling. Her trepidation slunk to a corner of her mind when she spied a small delicate harp. She had seen similar harps at a museum and couldn't resist crossing the room, touching its dark polished wood. There were no foot pedals. Instead, attached to the harp's neck were levers, which enabled a player to shorten the strings and change key, she knew.

"Oh, do you play?"

"Afraid not. But here . . ." he flipped on the stereo and bell-like ethereal music filled the room. "It's Celtic harp."

A doorway led to the kitchen, a warm little space with painted white cabinets and deep maroon flooring. She perched on the lone bar stool and watched Royce scramble eggs, chop bell pepper and mushroom. He prepared two plates, adding a dollop of deli pasta salad, poured tumblers of iced tea. They sat at the breakfast nook and ate.

"So, darlin', any more strange happenings lately?"

"Keep calling me darlin' like that and I can't promise propriety." She thought this would bring a laugh; instead, he looked seriously at her, and she blushed. He reached for her hand, and she told him about having seen Marta and George, Sophia and her brothers. The whole story unfolded, including the dulcimer at her door, the sense of living as a child in another time. How she feared she would crumble into a heap or meld with the other side and remain there. He listened without interruption, nodding, encouraging her. Someone else now shared her burden. Wrung out, she gulped her tea.

"Thank you," he said when in silence she met his eyes. "Come." And they moved to the living room sofa. From their seats at the window they watched the sun's final raspberry pink light sink behind a small lake.

"I know someone who I think could help you sort all this out. He knows more about local folklore than I do. He's a trained counselor too. Comes into the bookstore often. He and my brother work together on community projects. His name is Richard Fletch."

"This really is small town, isn't it? He and his wife go to our church—well, more than that. They're on the board that hired us. Or Jake, I mean. Feels like they hired both of us. I've dealt with Diatrice a lot and was surprised when I met Richard. A charming, kindly man married to such a stuffy old biddy," she said.

"They make an odd pair, true."

"I've thought of talking with him, but I'm concerned about Diatrice finding out and then heaven only knows where the story would go."

"Poor Richard. He's been paying for a teenage mistake all his life. Got her pregnant in high school and a shotgun wedding ensued. She's old money and expects devotion. But I'm certain your story is safe with him. His office is the one place she doesn't call the shots. He tells her *nothing* of his counseling, I'd swear. Think about it."

"I will. I know he'd be easy to talk with. Now I'd better go. What time is it?"

"Almost nine."

She shook her head. Another choir practice missed. They'd probably given up on her.

At the curb, Royce wrapped her in his arms. Their lips brushed, she kissed his cheek, and he whispered, "Good night, darlin'." Halfway home she realized his car was still at the bookstore. He'd have a long walk in the morning. When memory of the strange ring sidled forward, she shook her head and refused to entertain the thought.

Jake's car wasn't there when she pulled into their driveway. So much for his promise not to be late. But she sighed in relief. She wouldn't be confronted with questions or a romantic setting. A scribbled note on the front door read, "Dulcimer money." She stuffed the paper into her purse and unlocked the door. Jake stood waiting for her with feet apart, hands on hips, eyes beady and glaring. Instead of asking where she'd been, he pointed at long scratches on his forearm.

"All I did was park in back and walk through my own yard. Next thing I know there's a goddamn cat hissing at me, jumped me—look at this. Well, I kicked that damn cat so hard he bounced, let out a yowl and leaped over the fence."

She slumped against the door with her hand over her mouth, dropping it to ask, "Black-and-white?"

"What? Yeah, the cat was black-and-white. What's the difference? Just some vicious alley cat." Then he pivoted, stomped out of the room, his voice trailing, "Goodnight. I'm going to bed."

Molly ran to the bathroom, afraid she would throw up. She composed herself and retreated to the office. Opening the drawer containing her notebook, she gasped and felt bile rise to her throat. Her skin prickled as if something evil had been lurking in the drawer and now, set free, invaded her aura. The software, once in a jumble, now arranged in neat stacks, making her journal visible beneath them. Had Jake been snooping again? No, she must have tidied them after she put her writings away. But what of that pent-up, dirty energy when she opened the drawer? There had been no odor but rotten eggs came to mind. Instead of writing, she laid her head on her folded arms and wept. For herself and Jake, but mostly for Cat. Had Jake injured him? Had she lost him? There seemed to be no integrity here—none.

"God help us all," she prayed like a mantra until she slept.

# EIGHT

~

MOLLY and SOPHIA

*The virtues we acquire, which develop slowly within us, are the invisible links that bind each one of our existences to the others —existences which the spirit alone remembers*

—Honore Balzac

Howling black cats jump over the fence in Molly's mind. White ones follow and stare menacingly at her. As she watches, all of them merge into Cat, mewling in pain. Molly floats into a dark, moonless night, and Cat crawls to her. She gently scoops him into her arms. "Poor kitty. I am sorry." Stroking him, her hand traces the cold, hard cross and stones on a collar that disintegrates beneath her fingers, leaving only his soft, warm fur.

"Mew, meow." Cat inches his mouth to hers and sniffs. His nose is cool and wet as it bumps her face. He trembles with a faint purr.

With her head high and shoulders back, she glides across the lawn, her feet skimming the ground. She passes through a gate and onto a trail, all the while petting and soothing Cat. Scurrying critters stir up spooky noises, but she continues on with calm assurance, escorted by an indomitable force.

Every footfall lands on a slate-gray cobblestone of memory. Each stone wet and sleek with pain from the past. Her steps remain steady and sure, spurred on by the pungent odor of rotting autumn leaves, and the bite of winter's wind filled with a promise of snow. When she blinks and sets Cat down, he becomes a kitten and she a little girl. The sun is starting to lighten the sky, and a rooster crows his good morning.

Sophia is jumping-up-and-down excited as she waits in the frosty yard while Joe hitches the mule to the wagon. She wishes she could take her kitten, Biscuit, with them. Mama says no, there will be too many people and too much commotion. But there will be kids her age to play with. The McCalls live far away so they must get an early start and may sleep in the rig tonight before coming home tomorrow.

In the wagon, Sophia and Mama settle on a bed of straw and snug crockery jars to keep them from breaking when they travel over rutted roads. Joe and Papa climb up top to drive the mule. The crocks will be filled with molasses as pay for helping with Pearl and Dave's stir off.

For the first few miles they bounce and jostle on nothing more than two packed furrows gouged out over the years. The air is brisk and the sky cloudless. Blackbirds flit by and land in the ditches they've passed over. Sophia holds her breath and squeezes her eyes tight when they come to the lopsided bridge scarcely wide enough for the wheels. If they go off, it is a deadly drop to the river below. The mule almost stops, finding his footing step by step. When he trots again, Sophia relaxes and leans back.

"The way's more toler'ble from here, chile," Mama soothes.

First to arrive, Joe maneuvers the rig far into the trees, leaving room for guests to park. Sophia watches Papa and Dave feed cane between rollers that crush it dry. Juice comes out into a trough that runs down to a container. Joe hauls buckets of the green liquid to Mama and Pearl who take turns pouring it over layers of cloth, straining it into the boiler. A big wood pile stands close by, and they stoke the fire to boil down the juice. There is no work for Sophia, and she wanders to the road. When the first visitors pull in, three little girls pile out. Someone has brought a ball to kick, which they chase every which way. More families come, filling the yard with talking, laughing people.

An old man plays a fiddle while women and children sing songs and dance little jigs. Mama has quit working and rests under a chestnut tree, next to a heap of nuts, raked and ready to store for winter. At lunchtime, Mama fetches the hamper she has packed; and when Sophia is done eating, she curls up in the wagon for a nap. A hand musses her hair, and when she opens her eyes, she is looking into the mean black eyes of the preacher man. She gasps and shuts them tight again.

"Molly, look at me."

"Sophia," she mumbles.

"Molly, Molly, come now." He shakes her shoulders.

"Me Sophia," she yells and then sobs.

"Fine!" he snarls and stomps away.

Sophia lies real still except for her hiccups. She smells molasses cooking, and when she is sure Preacher Man is gone, she sits up and looks around. Mama waves to her from her spot by the tree. The men have finished their job and join the festivities. Sophia is surprised when her papa jokes and laughs. Afternoon and evening fly by with laughter, songs, and sampling of yellow foam from the boiling juices.

"I cain't 'member sich fun. Ouch," she says, grinning as her mama spits on the hem of her dress and scrubs sticky sweetness off Sophia's face. Mama smells like fresh air and new-mown hay when she hugs her.

Early the next morning they say good-bye to Dave and Pearl. Sophia and Mama each sit with a molasses crock between their legs. Mama moans when the buggy jolts over rocks and holes. At the bridge the mule balks. Papa and Joe holler and cuss and whip at him; he won't budge. Mama climbs out, lifts the crockery to the ground. Sophia follows. Joe pulls the mule, one step at a time, while Papa beats it with a board. On the other side of the span, Joe runs back for the molasses. In the wagon again, Mama shades her face with her arm and curls up with her head on Sophia's lap.

Back home, as Mama puts the molasses away, she says, "I gotta rest. Y' be good, chile, an' let me be."

Sophia runs out and calls for Biscuit. Her kitty comes and jumps as she giggles and kneels with her arms wide. Biscuit is getting bigger every day, and the black spot on his upper lip stands out like a smudge on his white face. Sophia twirls around, and around and kitty does too. Chasing his tail.

"Mama, Mama, see what Biscuit does," Sophia chants as she and kitty run into the house.

Mama leans against the door frame, her face pale and thin. Gaunt eyes smile weakly at Sophia, and she pats her head.

"C'mon, Soph. Git Biscuit outta here. Pa tol' y' he don' want no cat in here," Joe says.

Sophia picks up her kitten and skips outside. Mama, dashing past her, crumples to the ground and heaves into the bushes. Sophia sits beside her and slides under Mama's arm, hunkers close with her face against the scratch of Mama's sweater. They sway gently. A cold wind gathers strength, pulls dark clouds across the sky, stirs up fallen leaves in little whirlwinds.

"I'm cold," Sophia says.

"Snow tonight. I kin smell it."

"What do snow smells like? I cain't 'member smellin' snows afore."

Mama shakes her head and says, "Let's go on in. Time to fix supper fer yer pa."

"I kin hep. I'm big now."

Biscuit sneaks in after them and crawls behind the rickety cupboard. Sang hangs in long ropes from the rafters everywhere. The house is warm with fragrant air. Mama has started the stove and is frying parsnips with bits of salt pork. Just as Papa stomps in, Mama gasps, "George," and falls to the floor.

"She's done passed out!" Papa yells.

"Is Mama daid?" Sophia chokes.

"No, Soph, she's jest feelin' poorly," Joe says and hugs her.

Papa glares. "Come mornin' y' go fetch yer granny. Yer ma's sick and needs hep around here."

"But Granny done said . . ."

"Don' argue wit me, boy. Reckon Granny'll come if'n she knows her darlin' girl is bad sick." George lifts his wife and carries her to their bed. He lightly slaps her face, and her eyes flutter open. Papa says, "Joe will fetch yer ma. Where's the box, Marta?" He shakes her shoulders.

"Fer Sophia," Marta murmurs.

"The ring," Molly cries out, bolting upright. "The ring, the ring, the ring." Her head falls back onto her folded arms.

Biscuit darts from his hiding place, stops and hisses at Papa. "What I tell y' 'bout that cat? Tol' y' if'n I caught it once more time in th' house you'd never fergit."

Papa snatches the kitten and grabs Sophia with his other hand. Half drags her out to the yard.

"No, Papa, please, no, Papa, please, no."

He shoves her into the shed, throws Biscuit in, and slams the door. Sophia hears the latch slap into place. There are no windows. It is so dark she cannot even see her kitty who is clinging to her. She coughs from dust and smells rodent droppings.

Suddenly Sophia is all grown up and a man is patting her, calling her Molly, whispering that everything is okay. He guides her to a pretty room and a soft bed. Now little again she mutters, "Biscuit, *if only* you'd stayed a hidin'." A small dim light appears far back in a corner. Her friend Susie's hand is smooth and velvety as flower petals as she caresses Sophia's cheek and croons her to sleep. Biscuit wakes her with a yowl. Scratching sounds make her think of rats and snakes. She cries, "No no no no."

"No, what?" The man is back and she is big. "Molly, wake up, you're having nightmares."

Someone is shaking her, but she is too little to wake up here. She clings to Biscuit, and Susie holds her hand. Now there is a grating noise on the door. When it opens, she feels a gust of cold air and sees the ground covered in snow.

"Here, Soph, I done brung y' some supper. Sh, now, sh. Brung some fer Biscuit too. Kin only stay a bit, don' want Pa to fin' me out cheer." Joe helps her eat and feeds some to kitty. The parsnips are cold and greasy but sweet. "Mama wrapped these fer y'." Two biscuits with molasses in between make her remember all the fun at the stir off. She slurps cold water from the dipper. Joe covers her with a blanket, gives her a hug, and leaves, quietly slipping the latch in place. She sleeps.

The door is flung open and white sunshine hits her eyes so she can't see in or out. "Ma wants y'," Papa says.

Sophia cowers as Susie whispers, "Stay with me. No one can hurt you if you stay with me."

"Kin Mama come too?"

Susie shakes her head no.

"C'mon now!" Papa growls. "No more cat in th' house. An' no lying to yer ma. No makin' up tales 'bout bein' in thar all night. That's a lie, and y'll git soap in yer nasty mouth agin, hear?"

Sophia sobs as he shoos her toward the house. Biscuit jumps from her arms and runs away, leaving little paw prints in new snow.

Mama stands over the fire, cooking grits while Joe packs food and water for the trip to get Granny.

"Kin I go? I wanna."

"No, Soph, y' cain't."

"Please, Joe, don' leave me 'lone. I scairt. *If only* I kin go."

"I'm droppin' Pa at McCall's t' werk fer some days. Y'll be all right cheer wit' Ma. Y'll hep her whilst we're gone. You kin feed them chickens, cain't cha?"

"Susie! Susie's here!"

Susie holds a finger to her mouth and shakes her head. "Sh, sh," she whispers.

"What y' say?" Papa asks.

"Nothin'." Sophia wipes her nose, looks at Susie in the corner and smiles.

"Quit that snifflin' and eat yer grits," Papa says in a strange quiet voice.

. . .

"I fixed you some oatmeal, Molly," Jake whispered from the doorway. "I'll be right back with it."

She shook her head and examined her surroundings. The bed was a tousled mess as if there'd been a hoedown in it. *What a funny comparison,* she thought. Then the night's dreams swirled her in a maelstrom of emotions. The dark, locked shack and high narrow bridge filled her with terror. Two intense phobias she'd held all her life. Then delectable molasses flavor lingering on her tongue reminded her of childhood happiness.

When Jake walked in with the breakfast tray, Molly's mouth fell open.

"You shaved off your beard? Why?"

"It was too scraggly. Time to see my chin again."

"But why?"

"You're still half asleep. We'll talk after you have your coffee and eat. You had an awful night, crying out, nightmares. I half carried you in to bed. I finally moved to the couch out of your way," Jake said as he backed out the door, leaving her in utter confusion.

She sipped coffee but had no appetite for food. Dreams ricocheted off the walls of her mind. Molasses stir off. *How could I dream something I've never heard of?* She needed to record this information. Setting the tray aside, she crawled out of bed to fetch her journal. As she walked past the window, she saw Jake, in the back yard, spraying his car with the hose until mud slid down the side. Where did all that muck come from? And why wash it now, at sunrise?

At first she was shocked that her notebook lay in plain view, then remembered the black energy from the night before. Molly felt battered and bruised, wishing for escape, wanting to cry. Back in bed, propped up on pillows, she was scribbling frantically when Jake came in.

"Honey? Can we talk about all this now?"

She let her pen fall, folded her hands on her lap, heaved a sigh, and said, "All right."

"A menacing tone, Molly."

"I'm tired. I'm confused. I'm trying to sort things out. There is too much going on here."

"I thought I could help if you would talk to me about your dreams."

"Why don't you wait and read all about it in my journal? You were into it yesterday, weren't you?" And then she did cry. Deep, wrenching sobs of hurt and betrayal.

"I didn't read it. I swear to God." He clasped her hand in his, lifted it to his lips, and murmured, "I love you too much to invade your privacy again."

He walked to the window. Stared into the sunshine, said nothing until, "There's that cat again. Not in the yard at least. He's sitting on the fence."

"How could you kick an innocent cat? What is the matter with you?" Her tears dried up as anger took their place.

"Listen, you are overreacting to damn near everything. It's not as if I threw the cat to its death off a cliff. And by the way, I stepped on an ant yesterday too."

He walked across the room, sat on the bed, put his arm around her and whispered, "I'm sorry, again. That was sarcastic. Listen, I'm thinking maybe your hormones are messed up. You are forty-nine years old. Why don't you go to a doctor and have them checked?"

With that, she leaped out of bed, grabbed some clothes and slammed into the bathroom. Immediately she stormed back and retrieved her journal. In the shower she beat her fist into her palm and held her face under pulsing hot water.

The sweet taste of molasses gone, replaced by bitter coffee and frustration.

# NINE

~

*How shall we tell an angel from another guest? How, from the common worldly herd, One of the blest?*

—Gertrude Hall

Molly worried her grandmother's hanky until violet flowers on mellowing linen and lavender lace became a wadded mess in her hands. Palms damp, foot tapping, she sat in a small private waiting room, alone with her thoughts and potted plants. She'd made this therapy appointment two weeks ago when she'd been desperate. Now, consumed with doubt, she forced herself not to bolt. A small needlework, "Thou Shalt Not Smoke," hanging on the wall merely awakened an old desire. She hadn't smoked a cigarette in years, but the habit lay dormant in the basement of her mind. If she had one, she *would smoke it now*. Three slow, deep breaths relieved the craving, and her mind wandered back to last Sunday's service.

She'd yearned to stay home and avoid the same old teachings that she now doubted. None of the church's interpretations of life and death fit with what she was experiencing. Then the opening hymn:

> O Lord my God! When I in awesome wonder
> Consider all the worlds Thy hands have made,
> I see the stars, I hear the rolling thunder,

> Thy power throughout the universe displayed:
> Then sings my soul, my Savior God, to Thee:
> How great Thou art. How great Thou art!

And she'd wept. Dabbing her eyes, she glanced up to see Jake smile like a Cheshire cat. And when, instead of an altar call, they closed with "In the Garden":

> I come to the garden alone,
> While the dew is still on the roses; . . .

She knew he'd chosen those songs for her. Her face still wet with tears, she had smiled a thank you and squeezed his hand as they walked up the aisle to the door. She felt flustered by the singing of the beloved hymns and her husband's effort to please her, as if she'd imagined dissension between them and her doubts about him and the church. They'd gone for a long afternoon drive, enjoying hilly, verdant countryside at a leisurely speed. Instead of turning toward home, Jake had pulled off the main highway and traveled some distance on a winding, narrow road. She'd been delighted when an idyllic country inn came into view.

"I hear their Sunday dinner is delicious," he said, lightly running his fingertips across her forearm.

Over a quiet dinner, with Jake seeming open and loving, she dared, "I've lived here before."

"You mean as a little girl?"

She shook her head so hard she could see her curls flying. "No, no. I mean another lifetime."

He placed his fork on the plate, patted his mouth with a napkin, and said, "Molly, Molly, Molly, you can't be serious." His eyes hardened as he assumed his preacher persona. "That idea goes against everything we believe. Everything I teach. Think about Heb. 9:27, 'Just as a man is destined to die once and after that to face judgment.' Now, really, where are you getting such a foolish idea?"

Maybe he hadn't read her journal or he wouldn't have to ask. "There's this little girl named Sophia . . ."

"Oh, please. That is all fantasy in your head. I mean, *where* in the Bible can you find any reference to past lives?"

"I don't know, and right now I don't care. The books that ended up in the Bible are fine, but what about those that weren't politically acceptable? What about old Pope, what's his name—Vigilius? And the Council of Chalcedon? When they squelched anything that gave a person a chance to think. So the church could control? You know the history. What about that?" Her voice had risen, people at the next table glanced over. She fumed, more at his superior tone and pontificating air than at his actual words. But, most of all, her anger turned inward for even offering her ideas. Dinner sat like a burning coal in her belly. She gulped water.

"Calm down. You're making another scene," he hissed. "Tomorrow make an appointment with a doctor and get tranquilizers or something. Now, let's pray." He bowed his head.

She slapped her napkin to the table. She stood tall, with her head held high. And, as if to a slow cadence, marched from the restaurant.

. . .

Resigned to obligations, she had dragged herself to Bible study the following day. Not seeing Beth or any other welcoming face, she'd walked toward the group of matrons in a corner, just in time to catch the end of a sentence.

"So *pedestrian,*" Diatrice smirked. When she turned and saw Molly, her agitation left no doubt who had been the subject of conversation. Diatrice's flabby jowls colored crimson, she gasped, recovered, and gave Molly a perfunctory cheek-to-cheek greeting. Without a word, Molly wheeled, took her position at the podium, and began the meeting. *Pedestrian, tranquilizers, hormones.* The words had throbbed behind her eyes until, claiming a sick headache, she'd fled the class.

Maybe Jake was right about menopause. Books she'd read referred to feeling irritated and anxious. None of them predicted hallucinations or past life regressions. Since her blowup over the cat and her journal, she'd begun taking a capsule called Change of Life, containing black cohosh, sarsaparilla, ginseng, licorice, and other minor herbs. When she'd read the label, she'd flashed to Sophia and all the ginseng root hanging from the rafters. Herbs were slow acting, she knew, so she wasn't surprised that she had seen no change in her emotions. But really, did what was going on have anything to do with hormones anyway?

. . .

The door opened and Richard met her with a fullface smile. He took both her hands in his and said, "Good morning, Molly. Come on in."

Determined to be casual and speak solely of the cabin, to ask for legend details, she followed him into a softly sunlit room. He sat at his cluttered desk and she across from it.

"So what brings you to my office?"

"Oh, I'm curious about . . . I mean, a friend told me that you . . ." Her throat closed, her eyes filled. She shrugged and scrambled in her purse for a tissue. He offered a box of them and sat beside her on the couch.

"I'm sorry," she muttered.

"Go ahead and cry. This is a safe place."

She sniffled and picked up the tattered brown teddy bear cozied next to her and hugged it in her lap. Leaving the tissue box, he returned to his desk and waited. When she met his gaze, she was rewarded with an expression as gentle and soft as the teddy bear in her arms.

"I don't know where to start."

"What's your most pressing concern? Let's start there."

"Well, first, I'm afraid Diatrice and then the whole church is going to find out I've come here and that Reverend Carpenter's wife is crazy." She challenged him with an unblinking, square-in-the-eye look.

He nodded and said, "Good for you. Honest and straightforward. Half our work is done. Nothing leaves this room, I promise."

Molly leaned back, crossed her legs, loosened her death grip on Teddy. The room was quiet except for the aquarium's pump bubbling air into the water. She watched brightly colored tropical fish swim back and forth in a hypnotizing slowness. Closing her eyes, she brooded. Where *should* she begin?

"Do you believe in reincarnation?" she blurted.

For a fleeting second, his blue eyes danced, reminding her of his clogging demonstration. The twinkle faded and he paused.

"It really doesn't matter what I believe. Why the question?"

"All I know is, ever since coming to Sweet Hollow, I've been drawn back in time to perhaps . . . uh, maybe the mid 1800s. I hear dulcimer music and at first I'd see this family living in an old log house. Now, though, it is more than seeing them. When visions come, I *am* Sophia, a little girl." She stopped, caught her breath, and waited for a response.

"How do you feel as Sophia? Are you happy?"

"Sometimes. With Biscuit or Mandy Lee. I don't know. Sometimes the whole world seems sad and hopeless, as if Sophia is crying out and no one is listening. As if somehow I could change the outcome . . . prevent disasters in my, uh, her life." Molly prattled, realizing the gushing of words, unable to stop. "A voice in Sophia's head whispers, 'die and get it over with,' while Susie tugs and urges me, uh, her into a magical land. I want to help, but I'm afraid I'll go over to that dimension or time and not come back. Now my life has gotten so convoluted, I'm hoping for magic somewhere, anywhere."

Without taking notes, Richard listened. One minute with raised eyebrows, the next a grimace and then a questioning tilt of his head. Compassion watered his eyes. When she came to a halt after describing the taste of molasses, delight flashed across his face and, like a shooting star, vanished. Replaced by concern.

"Biscuit and Mandy Lee?"

"Oh, Biscuit is a kitten and Mandy Lee a corncob doll. My . . . or Sophia's only playthings."

"And you've discussed this with Jake? Does he have an opinion?"

"I can't talk to him about reincarnation, past lives. I tried. He doesn't even know I'm here. He thinks I should take hormones and I'll be fine."

Richard's teddy-bear cheeks twitched, and she gathered he was restraining a smile.

She exhaled deeply and stopped torturing the stuffed animal's ear.

"I'm locked in to so many church commitments too. Bible study, choir practice that I haven't been to yet, something on Friday, and it's all closing in on me. I want to back off from all responsibility.

"I thought I came here to learn more about the cabin's history. Royce told me some and believes you know more. But now I want permission to quit."

The aquarium gurgled. A cobalt blue fish swam lazily while a gray one with orange lines and splotches darted in and out of underwater figurines. One hyperactive and one almost sluggish. Two sides of her personality? She set the teddy bear in its corner of the couch, pulled up another tissue, blew her nose. The clock on the wall ticked. Molly heard birds singing, and wind forced a tree branch back and forth across the outer wall.

Finally, Richard spoke, "You don't need my approval for anything. But, I do think a sabbatical from church duties would be wise. At least a short one.

"You've given me a lot of information to consider. Since you can't talk to Jake about this, I'm wondering if you've made friends you could confide in. You mentioned Royce. I imagine you met him at his bookstore?"

"Yes." She cast her eyes down, her cheeks grew hot, and she knew she looked guilty. "He and I seemed to be . . . uh," she stammered.

"Go ahead. It's okay."

With a nervous laugh, she picked up the teddy bear again. She wished she'd never mentioned Royce's name. Why did she? She had to share her feelings with someone, that's why.

"Do we have time for this today?"

"Let's start anyway," he said.

"All right." Molly straightened, pulled her shoulders back and down, squeezed the teddy bear. She bit her lip and began, "Actually, we met over a rickety old walnut desk in an antique shop. We both felt drawn to it. And then to each other, I think. I lied to him about who I was. So out of character, but I couldn't stop. There is an energy between us that I don't need right now. And yet a camaraderie too. Like he's a long lost—brother or something." Molly paused. She'd never thought of him that way. *Geez, what does that mean? Sexual urges and brotherly love?* No. "Not a brother. More like a love from long ago. Do you see how crazy this sounds? He knows almost as much about Sophia as I do. Well, no. I've been avoiding talking with him since my nightmare."

"Why?"

"I'm too attracted to him. But I'm leery of him too. I don't know what the fear is about."

"Writing might help you clarify some of these intense emotions. Have you considered keeping a journal during all this?"

"That's another issue. I've kept journals for years. And now I think Jake's been reading them all along. I suspect, though I can't prove, he read it two weeks ago. And, of all things, I'd written about Royce."

"Did you ask if he'd read it?"

"He denies it. Says he respects me too much. I vacillate between feeling betrayed and blaming paranoia or hormone deficiency." She hiccupped and almost laughed. But, either way, it wasn't funny. "Maybe my marriage is what we should have been talking about."

"Let's address that next time, okay? Don't stop writing in your journal and keep it with you. Then you'll know he hasn't read it. How about next week, same time?"

Richard gave her a comforting hug and whispered, "Remember, you already have the magic you seek."

. . .

Jake was now gone more than he was home, claiming church business. Frequently he took her old car, leaving her with air conditioning and leather seats. Still, she mostly stayed home. She called in sick for Bible study and begged out of ever attending choir practice. Royce had phoned a couple of times, sounding worried. Molly had thanked him for his concern but skirted the issue of meeting again by saying she needed rest and quiet. Often she didn't answer the telephone, just let the machine take it. The majority of calls were hang ups and static messages.

Sitting in the kitchen, cup of coffee in hand, she listened to the phone ring and heard, "Hi. This is Royce . . . uh, from the bookstore, remember? I'm calling to let you know the Civil War book is in." He was clearly covering with the "remember" remark, in case Jake played the tape. She'd been tempted to pick up. To say, "I'll be right over." She didn't.

Instead, she pulled on old jeans, T-shirt, and her hiking boots. She scribbled a note for Jake, promising to be back by five. Grabbing her notebook, she poked a pen into the curls behind her ear, retrieved the dulcimer from under the bed, and headed out. Stopped, turned back. She keyed in Royce's home number, and when his recording answered, she said, "Please call me after five tonight. Uh, I'm going to the cabin and . . . and I'm not sure, but need someone to know, in case, uh, something happens. Thanks." She wished she could erase that and start over, be more casual, certainly less intense. She started to call again, hung up, and sallied forth.

The sun beat hot, and she rued having left her cap hanging on its hook. *Well, tough,* she thought. She walked with purpose, not slowing to examine flowers or spy on birds singing in the trees. When she arrived at the fence, she stopped. Listened. No far-off music. Relieved and disappointed, she surveyed her surroundings. The empty porch. No rocking chair. Still, she approached slowly, lest she frighten any unseen occupants. Stepping up the three boulders, she felt, once again, a chill breeze. *Some sort of air pocket here,* she rationalized.

Today Molly had no intention of even entering the house. She sat near the door exactly where she thought she'd seen the rocker. With the dulcimer resting on her outstretched legs, she leaned back. Goose bumps covered her arms, and she donned the sweater she'd tied around her waist. Warmer and fairly comfortable, she settled down and closed her eyes. Waiting for the past to appear. Nothing but the murmur of the stream tumbling over rocks. Nothing but the sweet fragrance of clover in bloom. Nothing but the strange combination of warm sunshine sliced by drafts of chilly air. She felt calmer here, now, than she'd been in a long time. Reminiscent of her first visit when she'd been filled with euphoria and tickled by dragonflies. Quiescent, she dozed.

. . .

A shadow passes over her, and she opens her eyes one millimeter at a time. So at peace and self-assured, nothing save a ghost could disturb her. Up the walkway an old man gimps. As he draws closer, Molly sees the long gray whiskers of the man who'd come to her door one evening. Same bib overalls and yellowing long-john shirt. He stops, yanks a faded blue-and-white bandana from his back pocket and mops his brow. Twisting his head, he spits tobacco juice before ascending to stand in front of her. Strangely, her heart doesn't jump nor her pulse race. Her breath flows easy, and her body remains loose. She has a sense of being in the presence of an angel. An odd old-codger angel.

"Hello. I know you . . . You brought me this dulcimer. Why?" Molly asks.

"It's fer you. Do you have the money?"

"No. Here. Here, you take this back. It is a beautiful instrument, and I love it. But, no, I don't have the money."

"Keep it then. It's fer you, Molly. To help you."

"Help how? Help with what? Why are you here?"

He squints his watery blue eyes as if either pondering the question or the questioner. "I've been here all the time. You asked fer help. All anyone has to do is ask."

She glances down and examines the dulcimer. When she lifts her head, he is standing close. He squats to her level and peers deeply into her eyes, as if reading her thoughts or planting ideas.

"Listen to the dulcimer. Trust where the music leads. Ask and watch fer the answer. You are not alone. Molly, my own. Even now there are friends who walk close and need you to help them find their way."

Unkinking his old knees, he stands with a grunt. When he pats her shoulder, heat radiates across her back, travels up her neck and out the top of her head. Falling warm air surrounds her, floats between her and the hard wood surface. She smiles and sleeps again.

. . .

When she awakened, she was alone. Save for the black-and-white kitty purring beside her. A mourning dove cooed. Distant thunder rumbled, and as she strolled home, she heard herself intoning, "Then sings my soul, my Savior God to Thee, how great Thou art, how great Thou art."

# TEN

~

*Not dancing is also a dance*
—Author Unknown

Molly stood at the kitchen sink rinsing salad greens when Jake walked in and the phone jangled.

"Hi, honey. Look what I brought home."

"Just a second . . . the phone."

"Hello, Molly." Royce sounded husky with concern.

"Hi."

"I got your message. Are you okay? Did anything happen in the woods?"

"Yes. It did."

"I've missed you. Will you meet me for lunch tomorrow? Say, Sam's at 11:30?"

"Great. Yes. I'll do that. Thanks again."

Had she arranged for a tryst? Is that why her heart raced and her whole body tingled? *It's wrong!* she told herself. She'd simply have a cup of coffee, buy the book, and come home. "Oh, I think not, Molly," another inner voice chimed. The old man appeared in her mind. Disapproving? No. Nodding his head.

What did Jake think of that conversation? She turned as he unboxed a cheesecake, looking pleased with himself.

"Looks delicious. And a surprise. What's the occasion?"

"Just a whim. I was passing a bakery and decided we deserved a treat. Now, what's for supper?"

They shared a rare pleasant meal and took their dessert outdoors. Molly lit a citronella candle to keep bugs away, and they laughed as he related silly mistakes he'd found in the church bulletin just before sending it to the printer. Even as she wished they could always enjoy each other's company this way, she questioned his motives. Was he being loving and kind? Or afraid she would quit excusing his surly outbursts? Or had he slipped again, fallen into his addictive behavior? She didn't ask, refused to dwell on her fears, and took the evening as a gift.

Dinner over and the kitchen cleaned, she retreated to her desk and wrote. Delighted with her courage to enter the past, delighted with the unusual angel in bib overalls. Bothered, anticipating tomorrow's encounter with Royce. She scribbled it all.

That night, after a luxurious bubble bath, she slept like an innocent. Teddy bears and bright yellow flowers danced in her dreams. Finches, larks, and robins sang her awake. Stretching, she smiled. The smile froze when Royce and the day ahead came to mind. An adrenaline rush tightened her jaws, tensed her shoulders, knotted her stomach, and even twitched her toes. *Calm down,* she thought. *Royce is a friend. Sam's is a public place.*

"You awake? It's 7:30," Jake called from the kitchen. "Coffee's on. I'm going for a walk. I'll be back by nine." The door slammed.

As she enjoyed her coffee, Molly wondered how to spend this unexpected solitude. She considered photographing the flower garden and finishing the roll of film she'd started at the cabin. Had there been a young woman and a rocking chair, or was it an illusion? This film may tell her. *Well, I could simply take the film in partially exposed.* That decided, she retrieved the dulcimer from beneath her bed and sat at the kitchen table admiring the craftsmanship. Maybe she should learn to play. Was the old man right? Would music really lead her? Sipping her second cup, she strummed, expecting the pleasant bliss of the last time she'd fiddled with it. Then a vision of Beth looking startled. Poof—the picture disappeared. Molly stopped, shook her head, and negated the image as a trick of memory or light. She played for several minutes when, again, a glare like an old-fashioned flashbulb. Jake's face and then gone. *I don't like this much,* she thought. Beth. Jake. Both alarmed.

Molly took a few deep breaths, calming her mind and body. She positioned the dulcimer in her lap and again toyed with the strings, this time plucking. But her fingertips were soft and sensitive. The strings hurt. While placing the instrument on an overhead shelf in her closet, she felt something on the bottom. A quill was taped to the underside. With renewed interest, she carried the dulcimer to her easy chair by the living room window. The quill, new to her hand, felt awkward and clumsy. Still, it produced a delicate series of notes. More melodic than her fingers had.

Music she and the dulcimer create eases concerns and complications. Forty-nine years of learning and conditioning fade to simple thoughts of fluttering butterflies and warm, gentle breezes. She surrenders life to the moment and the music. The world diminishes and becomes natural and quiet. Molly knows this as a child's carefree mind and she willingly succumbs. Her eyelids fall, and she watches fairies dance on gossamer strands while clouds play peekaboo in a rainbow sky. She giggles as a soft little kitten tickles her cheek.

Petting the black-and-white kitty, she glides to a cottage nestled in the trees. Smaller and smaller her world becomes until she cuddles in her mama's arms. Sophia, snug in her mama's bed.

"Are y' bad sick, Mama?"

"No, chile. I jest need a restin'," Mama whispers. "Sophia, in the cupboard, to the back, is a tin. Run, fetch it t'me."

Sophia remembers the can that had been so hard to open. Scooting out from under warm covers, she squeals as her feet meet the cold floor. There is food in that cupboard now. A sack of flour, a sack of sugar. Coffee. Moving it all to one side, she squirms in and gropes for the old container. Neatly, she replaces everything exactly and scampers back to bed.

"Ouch." Mama yelps with a chuckle as Sophia's icy feet snuggle against her leg.

Mama struggles at opening the tin, leans back, closes her eyes for a moment. Then makes another attempt. Sophia's nose is right in the mix, almost getting swatted when the lid pops off. Mama removes a little gray box tied tight with twine.

"This here's fer you. Fer when you git big. It was yer grandpa's, and I know he'd want you to have it. S'posed to be magic."

"Kin I see? Please, kin I?"

Mama pulls open the knotted string. Lays her head on the pillow, rests. As she opens the box, they both jump, startled by a clattering from the kitchen. "Must be Biscuit," Mama sighs and gives Sophia a squeeze.

"Molly, Molly." Jake's harsh, high-pitched tone jolted her to the present. "You scared me. Here it is after nine o'clock, and you're not dressed. Your coffee almost tipping off the chair. And I can't get your attention until I yell. As if you were in a trance."

"Oh my goodness. I must have dozed." There was no point explaining where she'd been. Arguments took too much energy. Besides they'd had a quiet evening, and she liked the comfortable atmosphere.

"What's with this?" Jake lifted the dulcimer and plopped his hand across the strings.

"It's a long story. Belongs to a woman at Bible study." Not a lie, that. "I may learn to play." She took it from him. He looked askance, opened his mouth, closed it again, and shook his head.

At the closet, she pondered what to wear. White. She'd wear white for protection, purity, and truth. As she pulled a ruffled sundress from its hanger, the doorbell sounded.

"Well, hello, Diatrice. Ladies. Come on in," Jake bellowed. "This is a surprise. Molly didn't tell me she was having company."

"Oh, dear, no. We're on our way to a meeting. We are the decorating committee, and Molly invited us by any time to choose from your mother's oil paintings. For the fellowship hall. You know, on those blank walls that seem to *bother* poor Molly."

Molly heard it all as she scrambled into her dress and sandals. How long was this going to take? And why today? And what was the "poor Molly" business? Condescending . . . She ran a brush through her tangles, planted a smile, and went to greet them.

Diatrice and Gertrude, in pink flowered dresses, settled on the couch, like overstuffed pillows with flounce. Two slender women, she couldn't remember having met, perched on easy chairs. Molly performed polite greetings and immediately made an excuse to cut the visit short.

"Gosh, I wish you would have called. I'd like to serve coffee and visit. However, I need to leave at eleven."

"Molly, dear. We'll barely stay a minute. We won't disrupt your busy schedule."

"Well, then. The paintings are in the spare bedroom. Let's go have a look."

Jake displayed the art and regaled them with how each piece had come about. Where the three-story red house in this one had actually been, the bouquet of pansies in that one. The African violet, in the blue-and-white bowl, that had been his grandmother's. The good ladies oohed and aahed, and Molly watched the clock. Jake thrived as the center of attention, and Diatrice, in particular, was practically fawning over him. *This could take forever*, she thought, when, as if on cue, each woman picked up a large painting. Out to the car they all trooped. One by one she grazed them in halfhearted hugs as Jake arranged the artwork in the trunk.

He held her close at his side as they waved good-bye.

"How about lunch out today?" he asked.

*What next?* "I've got a, uh, an appointment. In fact, I only have time to brush my teeth and smooth on a dab of make up."

Jake's lips curved down, his head bowed slightly, shoulders slumped. Little boy manipulation. She wasn't falling for that today. In fact, no more, she hoped.

"Lunch with a friend and then the bookstore," she proclaimed, hurrying out the door. In the car she remembered her journal. When she reentered the house, Jake moved from her desk to the window.

"I get one day off. And want to spend some time . . . . At least give me a kiss." He ran his hand possessively over her. A reminder she *belonged* to him?

"I've got to go. I just came back for my notebook. A list I need."

"Tell me you love me."

"You know how I hate being late. I love you," she babbled, pecked his cheek and headed out.

"I love you too. Drive safe."

A morning of distractions had kept her from agitating about this rendezvous. Now, thinking of Royce in his faded blue shirt that made him look virile, strong, innocent, and charming, she almost missed her corner and swerved on squealing tires. An irate or indignant driver leaned on his horn. She took a deep breath and slowed down, noticed her surroundings. Queen Ann's Lace, with its fernlike leaves and flat-topped creamy flowers, flourished on lush green hillsides. Hawks glided overhead. Summer in full glory, and she'd almost missed it in her flurry. She slowed further.

Nearing Sam's, she saw Royce, standing in the sunshine, the buttons open on his white polo shirt. He smiled and came to her door.

"Hi," he said. "Don't you look pretty in white."

"Hi yourself. And so do you—look pretty in white."

They laughed. Awkward tension dissolved.

"Listen," he said, "it's such a nice day. I wonder if you'd like to picnic?"

"Uh, yes, I guess." She thought of the table by the river.

"I ordered lunches to go, hoping you'd say yes." He opened his car door for her.

"Let me get my camera. I want to use up this roll of film. Maybe the ducks will be there. How long do you have for lunch?" she asked.

"I've taken the afternoon off. Beth is minding the store."

"I haven't seen her for a while. How is she?

"Fine, I think. I asked how you were, and she froze. Stammered something and got busy in a hurry. Strange, don't you think?"

"Oops. She must still think you don't know who I am. I'd better give her a ring later."

It soon became apparent, by turns he took, they weren't going to the river. Royce drove down a side road, onto a dirt track that ended in a small clearing.

"I don't know about this," she muttered. Still, Richard seemed to think Royce would make a good friend.

"I promise. I will protect your honor with my life," he declared with his hand over his heart.

They climbed out, collected their things. He, the picnic lunch and a blanket. She, her camera and notebook.

"Where I have in mind is a ways but the trail is level and cleared. Least it was awhile back."

The path led to a lake with a sandy beach. She paused, but he continued on, so she traipsed along. Pebbles and sand caught in her sandals as she followed the lake's contour. Royce glanced back, saw her stepping lightly.

"I'll carry you, if you like," he teased.

"I think not." She laughed.

"Well, we're almost there. We'll have to wade in to get around these brambles."

They bent, slipped off their shoes, and then sloshed to midcalf around the shrubs.

"Here we are," he said as they entered a secluded cove. He spread the blanket, plopped the picnic supplies, and grinned.

"All alone in the world, aren't we?"

"My honor, remember?"

"Yes, darlin'. But this is so much nicer than Sam's. Agreed?"

"Hmm." She rested on the blanket and gazed at the lake. Ducks swam, but she let her camera lie. "Do many people come here?"

"I don't think so. Especially on weekdays. Teenagers sometimes at night, I've heard. Maybe that's why the name—Lake Romance."

He unpacked their lunch. Turkey on hearty dark bread. Coleslaw, lightly dressed. Corn chips and salsa. Bottled water. Green chili and jack cheese on the sandwich surprised her.

"Ellen caters to my Southwest appetite. I took a chance you'd like it. I have one plain, just in case."

"Delicious," she mumbled, her mouth full. *You would think I hadn't eaten all day*, she thought. And realized she hadn't. Molly stopped midbite and admired the handsome man sprawled beside her. Leaning on one elbow, he seemed to be relishing his lunch too.

"What is it about us?"

He raised his head, searched her eyes. "I don't know," his voice choked. "I do know I've missed you. I'm fascinated by what's happening with you at the cabin. I feel connected to those events in some way. I also find myself planning to tell you whenever something interesting occurs in my life . . . I really do *not* want to be involved with a married woman . . . I hope we can be friends and maintain our integrity."

"I tried to stay away," she said, her voice quivering. "I had a session with Richard. You and I—our relationship—came up. He seems to regard you highly." And then she talked. About her therapy, bad dreams, the angel, even her stresses with Jake. Royce listened, not touching her; though she yearned for his hand on hers, his breath against her cheek. When she finished, a comfortable silence lay, like eiderdown, between them. Ripples lapping the shore, and the distant laughing yodel of a loon created background music. As they watched the lake, puffy gray clouds drifted in front of the sun. Lord and Lady Duck glided by. He, with a regal head of brilliant green, slightly forward of Lady, more sedately adorned in taupe with ecru flecks. Even in the world of waterfowl the male took the lead, the female acquiesced. *Did Lady Mallard ever protest?* Molly wondered.

"Oh look," she cried. "A swan. Beautiful."

"Yes. Beautiful," he said, but she, not the swan, was the target of his brown eyes.

Molly gasped, reached for her camera, stood, and walked to the waterline. She snapped a picture as the pure white swan spread its powerful wings. On a whim, she twirled and clicked two of Royce, silent and strong as he lounged with eyes half closed. He laughed. She fought the urge to pounce on him. To accost him. To throw their honor to the wind. The stones in his ring caught the light and glittered. A faint foreboding passed through her, as if she'd seen an apparition. Taking a deep breath, she dared ask, "Is there a story behind your ring?"

Molly settled again on the blanket, this time a little closer. She focused her gaze on his long tapered fingers. An artist's hand. She took a picture of his ring.

"I've had this since my father died when I was seven years old. It's been in our family for generations, coming from Scotland originally. This is a Celtic cross and an emerald. These smaller gems represent birth months of some far-removed ancestors. After Dad's funeral, Mom told me the legend of the ring's magic powers. Then she put it in a box for safekeeping until I graduated high school. Apparently, due to its age, the ring has considerable monetary value. I, of course, treasure it as a family heirloom. And since I have no children, it will go to my niece. That's my plan, anyway."

Had she been apprehensive for no reason? What caused this qualm?

"Hmm . . . The design looks familiar in an odd way. I wonder why. Where did you grow up? Where were you born?"

"I was born in Los Angeles and grew up in Albuquerque, hence the green chili craving. I think my great-great-grandfather was from around here, though. And when I arrived fifteen years ago, I did feel at home. I came because of the Appalachians. Well, to get out of the desert, true, but I felt called here. I'm still not clear why."

Seeing an inch-long jagged scar above his elbow, she reached, caressed his arm.

"What's this? Looks like a pretty wicked injury from a long time ago."

"No. A birthmark. It's faded a lot since I was a kid."

She continued stroking the mark with her fingertips as he spoke. He paused with a questioning look and then drew her to him, wrapped his warm, strong arms around her. Kissed her eyelids, the tip of her nose. She felt soft and velvety, like the petals of a rose in full bloom. His masculine scent more intoxicating than any rose. She begged silently for his mouth. He finally gave his lips, and she melted into him. Her heart pounded, or was it theirs? His hand pressed her head with gentle insistence. Tears came to her eyes, ran down her face and, when the salt mingled in their passion, he drew away. Inches from her face, he said one word in a throaty exhale, "Molly?"

She knelt, brushed a lock of hair from his forehead, and shook her head. Slowly she stood, walked to the water's edge and prayed, "What now, God?" Without a backward glance, she moved into the lake. Soon her dress billowed atop the water, and the cold quieted her fervor. She dove under and swam until her lungs screamed, and she came up for air. Looking back, she saw him stand, remove his shirt, advance toward the water, and then swim until she was in his arms once more.

"I think so, yes," she said, swallowing her words.

"Our honor?" he asked.

"Thank you, sir," she moaned and floated away.

When Molly came ashore, her white sundress clung to every curve. Water dripped at the hem. Water dripped from the end of her nose. She felt young, alive, and aware.

Royce walked toward her, shaking his head and smiling. "The beautiful nymph of Romance Lake," he said.

"Shall I be Daphne to your Apollo?"

As he bowed in courtly fashion, thunder cracked, and an afternoon rain storm set out to drench them. "Thor has spoken," he said.

Soaking wet already, they laughed. Until they spied the camera, blanket, and shoes. While raindrops sizzled on the water, they dashed. As they climbed into the car, she chuckled, "Saved from becoming a laurel tree."

"For now." He winked and handed her a folded sweatshirt. "Why don't you put this on, you're shivering. We'll stop at my place and dry your clothes, okay?"

# ELEVEN

~

*Knowing is not enough; we must apply.*
*Willing is not enough; we must do.*

—Goethe

Wrapped in Royce's white terry bathrobe, Molly curled up on the sofa. She'd called and left a message for Jake, and now she blew on piping hot cocoa while her clothes tumbled in the dryer. Serene and secluded, this place offered solace like nature, but with creature comfort added. Floor-to-ceiling bookshelves, casually filled, bestowed a relaxed ambiance. Even the potted ivy seemed to meander with strength and nonchalance. Molly's mind quieted as she sipped her chocolate and breathed in gentle energy. Royce, stretched out in an easy chair across from her, looked as content.

"What should we do? How do we keep seeing each other and prevent sparks from flying?" he asked.

"Mmm . . . let's make a pact. First, what gets us in trouble?"

"Well . . . I think I was okay until you walked your fingertips across my arm. My mind shouted no while your eyes and hand whispered yes. So maybe number 1, for friendship's sake, no physical contact."

"You're right. And I'd better get a grip on my emotions. I can't lose you now."

They paused, listening to Celtic harp music frolic around the room. The antique Franklin clock on the mantel reminded her to enjoy these few minutes and then hurry home. She felt certain they could achieve a wholesome understanding. After all, they were not hormone-crazed teenagers. Adults knew what was imperative, and it wasn't sex. *Still, look at him lounging there scrutinizing me.*

"Number 2, you've got to stop looking at me that way! I'm not a hot fudge sundae."

He raised one eyebrow as if challenging her accusation. Then he threw his head back and laughed. "Darlin' Daphne, you saw right through me. You, a portrait in white, brought to mind—what's it called? Food for the gods. *Ambrosia.* That's the word. Well, if ambrosia ever appears on a menu, this vision of you in my bathrobe will flash before me."

"Here's the thing, Apollo . . . no, you aren't leading me down that lane, please. Maybe we can't just be friends." Tears came at the possibility of this loss. "I'm fighting the desire to charm you into my arms right now."

Saying nothing, he concentrated on his hot chocolate as if he sought answers in nonexistent tea leaves. Was he considering what she'd said? Molly had noticed how he seldom replied immediately when she stopped talking. A characteristic she found charming and complimentary. Now he studied her, and the dimple deepened in his cheek. He started to rise. She held her breath.

"Molly," he murmured.

The dryer buzzer sounded. She exhaled. His smile shifted to a rueful expression. They trooped to the laundry room, and he handed her the warm bundle. She shook her dress and thanked God for timing and permanent press.

Clad again in summer dress and sandals, she realized how warm she'd gotten. From the cocoa? Or from her passion, tightly leashed? Or simply from a rain storm too early and so short it served only to create saunalike conditions?

As he drove back to Sam's and her car, she voiced her plan, "Tonight I am going to discuss you with Jake . . . No. Wait. It's okay. I'll tell him you are a friend of Richard's and that I will be seeing you to help me get over my past life trauma. He'll be glad of that, and it is true. I need your counsel, and there could be a revelation waiting for you too. The old dulcimer man said some people in my life would benefit from staying with me through this. I think it's you. And maybe Beth. But she's another subject. Well, wait. If we met with Beth along, then we'd maintain our focus, I think."

"Do we really need a chaperone? I'd rather be alone with you . . . I'll settle for seeing you with Beth if I have to. Oh, by the way," he said, "Beth's done some sort of makeover in the last few weeks."

"How do you mean?'

"Well, a short haircut. And not so modest and shy. She's more outgoing."

"That sounds like a good thing. She's a beautiful woman, don't you think?"

"I guess."

As they neared the bookstore, Molly asked, "Do you mind stopping? I, we, could talk to Beth now. See if she'll conspire with us."

"Good idea," he said and pulled to the curb.

When they walked in, Beth blushed. Jake stood eyeing them.

"Jake. This is a surprise. I didn't expect you here," Molly said, running a hand through her curls, flattening an imagined wrinkle in her skirt.

"Well, you said bookstore, and I came looking for you. Who's your friend? For some reason I expected you were lunching with a woman."

"Shucks, Reverend Jake, this is jest Royce. He's my boss, owns this place," Beth said.

Royce held out his hand. Jake shook hands, but frowned at Molly.

"Let's talk at home, all right?" she said and directed her attention toward Beth.

"My goodness! I'm not sure I would have recognize you without your long wavy tresses. The pixie cut is becoming. And nice for this hot weather, I bet."

"I reckon. I, uh, needed a change. I'm jest havin' some fun." Her voice was still small and shy. And she seemed nervous, as if she'd rather be somewhere else. But then, no doubt, every one of them wished they were anywhere but in this muddle. Jake sullen, Beth stuttering and blushing, she perspiring. Molly glanced at Royce. He stood back, observing with interest.

"Listen, Beth. Royce and I have an idea. How about you and I getting together for coffee soon."

"Uh . . . I'm right busy now . . . two jobs and sich. Well, okay, uh, I'll call you . . . soon."

Royce looked at Jake, who was looking at Beth. Molly stared at them all and said, "Well, I'm going home. I can walk to my car."

"I've got a few stops and then I'll be home," Jake said.

"I'll take you, Molly," Royce offered.

Jake scowled, then shrugged and nodded. They said good-bye and left.

"What on earth was that about, do you suppose?" she asked.

"Beth was obviously uncomfortable. What about Jake?"

"Jake was on the defensive. I recognize that tone. I'm not sure why. At least he'll know who I mean when I talk about you and me getting together."

"That's his Ford across the street?"

"Yes, why?"

"It looks familiar. I can't remember from where."

"A maroon sedan. Common enough, isn't it?"

"No, it has those fancy wheels. Sporty for such a sedate automobile. Hmm."

At her battered old station wagon, they stood and talked with the doors open, cooling the interior.

Royce put his hand on hers. She tensed but met his gaze.

"Why do I have the feeling nothing is ever going to be the same again?" he asked, squeezed her hand and released his grip.

"Because nothing will be. Shall I call you?" she asked.

He nodded and backed away as she slid behind the wheel. When she drove off, she glanced in her rearview mirror. He stood, leaning on his car, hands in his pockets.

. . .

Standing barefoot on a stool, Molly yanked a heavy tome from the shelf, flipped the pages, shook it with both hands, and tossed it. Books lay open on the desk, jumbled on the floor. They continued flying as if a tempest had chosen this one room for a destructive dance. Tears streamed down her cheeks; her nose ran. Another tissue mixed in the fray. Breathing hard, cursing under that breath, she had dismantled half the precisely aligned library by the time Jake arrived.

"I'm home," he sang as he came in the front door.

"Where's the letter?" she screamed.

"What the hell are you doing?" he shouted, staring at the chaos.

"Where's the letter from Amy?" she yelled.

"I do not know what you are talking about. What were *you* up to all afternoon with Royce?" He sneered the name as if he had a nasty taste in his mouth.

"Don't start with me. Listen to this," she snarled.

Molly hit the answer machine play button. First came her message to Jake. Then another static one. Then Amy's voice. "Mother!" A pause and what sounded like tears. "Here's my new phone number . . . I'm in therapy, and childhood crap is coming up. I wrote you a letter and waited, waited to hear. I didn't call. I couldn't stomach hearing *his* voice or having to talk to him. Please, please call as soon as you get this."

"I do not know what she means. I swear to God, Molly."

"Damn it, Jake. Stop lying! I *saw* a letter from her in one of these books. Now where the hell is it?" She shook with anger. Bile rose in her throat as she glared at him.

He came toward her, his arms spread as if to hug her. Her mouth fell open.

"What are you doing? Do . . . not . . . touch . . . me!"

"You're hysterical. Calm down. She's probably having one of her little crises. Looking for someone to blame. Calm down." He took another step toward her, and she raised her arm, almost slapped him. Instead, gasping for air, she covered her mouth and gaped at him. She'd never hit anyone in her life.

Jake began methodically stacking books even as she ripped through more of them; she slammed some and hurled others.

"I'll search every damn one of these books. So just tell me where the letter is. If I don't find it in a book, I swear I'll dump out your desk drawers next."

He threw up his arms and shrugged his shoulders. "You have lost your mind. There is no letter, damn it." Panting now, he paused, glowered at her, walked to the window, and stood with feet apart and clenched fists on hips. Pivoting, he scowled. She met his stare and did not back down. A long moment later, as light faded from his eyes, he looked away.

"I'm getting a beer and then I'll watch the news. We'll talk when you've come to your senses," he said, as if placating a child throwing a tantrum.

After he left, she flung the door shut and played back the messages. She heard pain and urgency in her daughter's voice. Her hand trembled as she wrote down the number. A new area code; she didn't even know where Amy was. She wished she had the letter, so she'd have some idea what was going on. How could she be so out of touch with her precious daughter?

Inhaling deeply, exhaling slowly, she placed the call. The phone rang and rang. Expecting voice mail or something, she instructed herself to breathe in and breathe out, seeking the composure to leave a coherent message. Nothing but the never-ending ring, ring, ring. She hung up and headed for the bathroom. From the hall she heard the TV blaring. How could he sit there? His wife had called him a liar, had almost hit him, was in dire trauma, and he watched *Wheel of Fortune*. Who was this man she'd lived with for twenty years, this man she'd given her heart to? *A liar. A con man. A selfish, self-centered son of a bitch.*

Molly washed her face with a cool cloth. She rummaged in the cabinet until she found the valerian root and kava kava blend. Blurry eyed, she attempted to line up the bottle's arrows and, with shaky hands, pushed at the cap. She wiped her nose, squinted, realigned arrows, and succeeded in opening the bottle. Swallowing three capsules with a glass of water, she thought of Sophia trying to get that damn can open. *Not now. Oh, Sophia, not now.* Molly slumped to the floor.

. . .

Sophia cowers in a corner, hugging Mandy Lee. As soon as they'd heard the horse and buggy, Biscuit had run into the woods. She'd wanted to run too, but Mama called to her. Now her eyes follow the tall, skinny preacher dressed all in black as he walks across the room and pats Mama's head.

"George told me you were feeling poorly and asked me to stop in. Rest now. I'll watch out for the little girl there."

"But I'm needin' t'cook or find somethin' to eat."

"It's a mite cold in here, missus. I'll start a fire and set a pot of soup to cookin'. McCalls sent fixin's. Girl, put that dolly down and run fetch some kindlin', quick."

When Sophia comes back, arms loaded with sticks and twigs, Mama is asleep. Preacher Man, his lips thin and tight, smiles at her. His eyes are black and give Sophia a sickness in her throat. She thinks of Susie and looks for her.

"Here, Mister." She hands him the bundle and starts to climb in bed with her mama.

"Oh, no you don't," he hisses. "Your mammy's a-restin'. You're a big girl now. You git out to my wagon and bring in that box of food."

Sophia backs away to the door, turns and runs. The box is big and heavy. She tries but can't budge it. On top is bread. She picks that up and a sack of cookies and a jar of molasses. Carries them into the house. Mama coughs hard, moans.

Fire snaps and crackles, and Preacher Man is adding a big chunk of wood. She'll be warm soon, and the man is humming. Sophia relaxes. Maybe she is safe.

"Fetch the rest now, little girlie."

Next she brings a chicken and a sack with onions and turnips. Now she can handle the box. As she lugs it toward the house, it slides. She stops and, with her knee bent, pushes the crate back up, gets a better grip. Sharp corners dig into her arms; she bites her lip and climbs the rock steps. She slips on a patch of ice and snow, almost dropping the box, but Preacher Man catches her in time.

"Not as big a girlie as I thought. How old are you, little miss?"

"I be six." Sophia doesn't feel good again. Preacher Man is too close and he smells funny. Sweet, but too sweet.

"Come in here. It's warmer now. Y'can help with the cookin'."

The big iron pot hangs over the fire, water already steaming. Preacher withdraws a pouch from his pocket and pinches some dried leaves into a tin cup. He ladles hot water in and covers the cup with a piece of crockery. Then he puts the whole chicken in the pot and chops onions and vegetables. Picking up the tin cup, he walks to the bed and nudges her mama awake.

"Now, let's drink this before it gets cold. Now, now, missus, jest a nip of belladonna. Not enough to do you harm. It'll help you rest." Preacher Man spoons tea medicine into Mama's mouth and chants,

The Lord is my shepherd; I shall not want.

He maketh me to lie down in green pastures: he leadeth me beside the still waters.

He restoreth my soul: he leadeth me in the paths of righteousness for his name's sake.

Yea, though . . .

As he drones on, Sophia stands against the wall, Mandy Lee in her arms again. She is confused. Mama sleeps, breathing soft, not coughing. Mama's restin' and soon there will be soup, but she is scared.

Preacher Man pulls up the rocking chair, sits, and reaches for her. She quickly backs away, shaking her head, clutching her doll.

"What's your name, pretty little girlie?" he asks as he motions her nearer the fire.

"Sophia," she whimpers, creeping forward, stopping.

"Come here, now," his voice rasps hard and mean like her papa's sometimes. He pats his leg. "I'll tell you a story while the soup stews and your mammy sleeps."

Sophia tries to hurry past him to get to her mama's bed. Preacher Man grabs her and sets her down hard on his lap. Instead of telling a story, his hands hold her tight and one hand covers her mouth.

"Your mammy's not waking up for a long spell. You make a fuss, Miss Sophia," he spits, "and I'll tell your pappy you were sassy t'me."

Sophia can't stop crying and wants Susie. *If only I wern't alone.* Biscuit meows at the door. Then Susie is taking her hand, walking with her and kitty to the pretty cottage and the lady dressed like asters. Snow is gone and flowers bloom.

Susie's mommy, Lily, stands at the door, her arms open wide.

. . .

When Sophia wakes up, the cabin's sole light is the fire's faint glow. Mama is coughing next to her in bed. The last she remembers was morning and making chicken soup. Now its aroma fills the house, and her tummy growls. But her arms and legs ache, and her face burns.

"Mama, Mama, you 'wake?" she whispers.

"Yes, chile. I'm hungry, ain't you?" Mama sits on the edge of the bed and then shuffles to the fire. She adds a log from the high stack. "That preacher brought in a whole heap a' wood. I reckon he's a nice man. More belladonna right cheer, an' water fer heatin'. An' smell this soup, Sophia."

"I kin hep," Sophia says, jumping out of bed. She climbs on a chair, takes bowls from the shelf and peers out the little window. "Look, Mama. Snow. Where's the flowers?"

"Goodness, ain't been no flowers fer months, chile."

"Oh, but . . ." Sophia's lip quivers.

"Musta been a dream you were havin'. Now run t' the stoop an' see if'n thar's milk an' butter."

As Sophia opens the door, a blast of cold air hits her. A wooden box lined with straw snugs against the outside wall. Tucked inside is a jug of milk and a package that must be butter. She hasn't had milk in a long time and hollers, "Mama. He done brought milk."

Sophia and Mama slurp hot soup, dunk buttered bread. "I'm feelin' better," Mama says and finishes her special tea. After supper, they close the shutters, and Mama puts another log on the fire and carries the pot of soup out to the straw-lined box. Instead of venturing to the outhouse in the dark and snow, Sophia uses a bucket behind a curtain. They crawl into bed.

"Tell me a story, please, Mama."

And Mama says, "Once a long time ago, in a faraway land across the ocean, lived a right strong an' handsome man. Yer grampa. He were smart an' kindly an' loved making music.

"Where's the ocean? What's it look like?"

"Sophia, so many questions. The ocean is big waves of water higher than th' house, an' you can look forever an' not see th' other side, so I'm tol'.

"Now yer grampa was needin' to leave where he lived afore they throwed him in jail fer somethin' he didn' do. So he got hisself to the waterfront. He had all his clothes on—two pairs of everythin' 'cept shoes. When the big ship left the land, yer grampa were on it. After his food run out, he worked fer his dinner. He could empty slop buckets an' mop up messes an' that thar's what he done. He never got poorly like some. He didn' know nobody when they started, but soon most knew him cuz he took care when they got to thowin' it all up. Doc, they called him. I wished I'd learnt 'bout his herbs an' sich. When he come to this new world, he married a right purty lady—yer granny. Maybe t'morrow she'll be here with Joe an' Pa. Be sure Granny tells y' all 'bout Doc an' his bag o' magic potions an' th' trinket in that tin . . . Lord, I hope they come soon, sweet chile. I'm worn an' weary."

Sophia, sedated by warm soup and the happy story, sleeps.

# TWELVE

~

*Oh the drums are so mournful*
*My dear and my love*
*My thoughts they are turning your way.*
—Donovan

A lilting soprano awakens her with a lullaby, the words delicate and sweet. "O, they tell me of a home far beyond the skies, O, they tell me of a home far away."

Someone whispers, "Molly, Molly."

The voice grows louder, clearer. "We hear your song. You're safe, come home." A gentle hand pats her arm. She opens her eyes to see a teddy-bear man kneeling in front of her. A teddy bear named . . . what?

"O, they tell me of a home where no storm clouds rise, o, they tell me of an unclouded day." This voice is her own.

"Molly, come home, I'm waiting. You are safe."

The aroma of coffee brewing mixed with cinnamon wafts to her place on the porch. Shades of pink appear in the eastern sky. But something is wrong. She feels pushed, then pulled, loved, then despised.

"Who are you?" Her tone sounds strange, and her mouth is dry.

"I'm your friend, Richard."

"Who?" The word, like a swallowed bone, catches in her throat.

"Molly! You scared me! Wake up! LOOK AT ME!" A demand from a different voice. From a different man.

"Preacher Man, get away," she wails, clenches her fists, and cowers in the rocking chair, whimpering, "I want Susie." This preacher man isn't wearing black, but his lips are thin and his eyes cold.

Voices hiss behind her. A door slams. Her tormentor gone, she is alone with the soft-eyed man in vaguely familiar surroundings.

"Who are you right now?" he asked.

"I don't know . . . Sophia. No—Susie." She glances at her hands spread atop a notebook. "But, no, see. I'm old."

"Listen carefully. You have been away—on a dream trip—into a vision. Now you've come home. You are Molly and I am Richard. No one will harm you."

Hearing the distant roar of a jet plane, she opened her eyes wide and looked at her bathrobe thrown on over a wrinkled white sundress. She stared at Richard. *Yes. Molly. That's me. And I know him. Yes. And this is my home. I live here.* But this rocking chair belonged in the living room. *Oh, I dragged it out here last night.* And then the whole night came into sharp focus . . .

She had twisted her neck one way and then the other, had rolled her head around and forward and back. Her backside had throbbed with a dull ache, her temple with a sharp one. The windowless bathroom was as dark as a cave, the tile floor unrelenting. What time was it, anyway? Feeling caged, as if a prison door had been slammed, she had turned slowly onto her knees and crawled her hands up the wall until she stood. A lotion bottle clattered to the floor as she fumbled for the light switch. Groping to the door, she peered down the hall into darkness. The house lay quiet, Jake either in bed or gone. She flipped on the light and squinted in its brilliance. Her bottle of herbal tranquilizers, cap off, sat on the counter, and she gulped three with a full glass of water. The day's fear, anger, betrayal, and sweet passion came back to her like a blast from a furnace.

Molly searched for her journal. Frantic, she even rummaged through the clutter in her car. Her camera wasn't there either. *Were they at Royce's?* Yes. The image of them in the backseat with the picnic paraphernalia came to mind. Her face grew hot as she imagined him reading her private thoughts. He wouldn't, would he?

Back in the office she stepped over piles and stacks of books, pulled another notebook from a drawer, grabbed a pen, and moved outside to sit in the moonlight and write. First she would compile a list for morning. Number 1. Call Richard. Beg for a time slot. Again her cheeks flushed when she scribbled, call Royce about journal and camera. She scratched that out, and in big bold letters drew a number 2. Call Amy. Jake must have destroyed Amy's letter. If he hadn't before, he surely did last evening after her tirade.

Her mind wandered. *What did that preacher do to Sophia? Okay, odd codger angel, you said ask. I'm asking. Help me.* She lay her head back and waited. A faraway train whistle mourned and beckoned . . .

Now, in morning's light, with hands balled and bare feet cold, she looked at her list. Maybe Jake had tried rousing her and panicked when he couldn't. He must have read her note and phoned Richard. That's why he knelt before her now with furrows deep between his kind eyes.

Seeing the second item, Molly shot her hand into her pocket. Yes, the crumpled scrap. She grabbed Richard's arm, begging him, "Call Amy. Please, tell my daughter I phoned last night. No one answered."

Richard held her hands and said, "Breathe slowly, Molly. Take a deep breath, hold it, that's good. Exhale slowly. Again . . . again."

"I can't explain and Jake is lying and won't help. Will you listen to what I heard? Then you'll know what to say."

They rose slowly and made their way through the house. They passed Jake standing in the kitchen, Bible open in his hands. He peered at them, his pious facade in place. Molly cringed. Richard motioned him not to follow. In the office she groaned, noting that all the books held their perfect place. If not for exhaustion, she would sweep them from the shelves again. She played back the tape.

"I don't even know where Amy lives anymore, how can that be? I've thought about her every day. I should have . . . been better."

"Once you talk to her, she'll understand. Let's check the area code. Where's your directory?"

She pulled one from a drawer and handed it to him. "Would you look it up, please? I'll be right back." And she fled the room.

In the bathroom, she quietly closed the door. Where were the pills? They'd been lying right here at the sink. She needed something to numb her heartache. *What I really need is a knock-out dose of belladonna to put me under. Maybe forever. Would anyone care?* Horror-struck by the enormity of that idea, she leaned against the sink, heaving great sobs until a knock came and Richard said, "Are you all right?"

"Yes, I'll be there in a second." She splashed cold water on her face and ran a brush through snarls that tangled every which way.

Back in the office, Richard and Jake were sitting almost knee to knee, speaking in hushed tones.

"Get out, Jake."

"Molly, I . . ."

"I said get out of this room!" She looked to Richard and pleaded with her eyes.

Richard nodded at Jake, and he walked out, head bowed like a naughty little boy being sent to the corner.

"He seems genuinely concerned. He thought maybe you've taken too many of these for a long time. That they've made you hallucinate about past lives." Richard held out the bottle of herbs. "I don't see a problem with them as long as you follow the dosage."

"Thank you," she said and pocketed the pills. "He hid her letter. I thought it was an old one I'd read before. I meant to reread it. I didn't and now it's gone. Will you help me make this phone call, please?"

"Okay. Area code 701 is North Dakota. It's an hour earlier there. Shall we wait?"

"No, no. Amy would want me to wake her up."

He keyed in the number, and she paced the small room for long moments. Finally, he hung up and said, "I'm sorry. No one answered."

The phone rang immediately, and Molly gasped, motioned, and Richard picked up.

"No, you've got the right number. She's right here. Uh, she's shaking her head no. Hold on a second."

"It's Royce."

Molly forced a calm greeting. "Everything is okay. I mean, nobody died or anything."

"I won't keep you. Just so you'll know, I have your camera and a spiral notebook."'

She blushed. "Please don't read what I've written."

"Of course not."

"Just a minute." Putting her hand over the receiver, she whispered, "I think Jake's on the other phone." Richard left the room.

"I'm back. I'll explain all of this one day soon. I can't talk now."

"When you're ready, you'll call me? I'm here for you, darlin'. You know that."

"Thank you . . . Bye."

She found Richard speaking with Jake and said, "Could I talk with you a minute outside?"

Jake pouted, and Molly choked back every nasty name in her vocabulary. She and Richard walked to his car.

"I will call Amy's number again. I feel strong enough and maybe at least I'll get an answer machine. Or, hopefully, she has caller ID and will know I've been trying."

"Listen, I have a nine o'clock opening today. Would you come in?" Richard asked.

"Oh, thank you. Yes, I'll be there."

Back in the house, Jake was hanging up the phone. "Please. Talk to me."

"All right . . . where . . . is . . . the letter?" she demanded.

"I'm telling you, there is no letter that I know of. Maybe it got lost in the mail. Maybe your daughter didn't even send one."

Molly questioned her own memory. Had she even seen a letter? Yes. The paper had fluttered to the floor. But had it been from Amy? She closed her eyes and imagined it in her hands. Yes. The handwriting was hers. Damn it. Jake had her discounting her own knowing. Again. This time, though, there was no doubt.

"Let me hug you. I need a hug," Jake whined.

"This is not going away." And she marched from the room. She'd call Amy, clean up, have some coffee.

. . .

Richard greeted her at his office door, and Molly went immediately to the couch and the teddy bear waiting there.

"I've made so many bad choices. This is my second marriage, and I've screwed this one up too. I don't know if I can live with him anymore. I'm so confused and muddled. I feel like I'm going insane. Twenty years of marriage, but I can't tolerate his lies, the smothering, the disrespect. I'm so afraid, though, of making another mistake. Help me make the right decision."

"You don't have to make any decision about your marriage right now. And you'll know, when the time comes, what you must do."

"This morning I wondered if anyone would care if I died." And she told him about the preacher and Sophia's mother and the belladonna. "I know that stuff is poison if you take too much, and I wished I had some. Considered suicide." Ashamed, she bowed her head.

"You love your daughter. You wouldn't put her through that. Remember, there is peace beneath the chaos. I'll help you. Call on me or Royce. Don't do this alone. Now, can you tell me how old you were when the notion of suicide came?"

"Huh?"

"Next time you have a feeling or impulse uncharacteristic of you or what's going on, ask yourself, 'How old am I with this feeling?' Be still and listen. The answer will come. Then, if you can, take a minute to validate her feelings. Yes, I think Sophia needs to be heard."

"I've got to get away. For today anyway. I cannot stop thinking about the sturdy little log cabin that refuses to fall. It has weathered blizzards outside and emotional storms within. It's quiet. I could go there now. Listen to the creek and the bluebirds sing. But I'm afraid. Can I spend this day in solitude and take what comes my way?

"Sometimes I actually yearn to become Sophia. An innocent child, you know? Innocent but . . ." And she cried. How long would tears flow before they ran dry? "I'm learning I've never, ever, been innocent."

Richard searched her face, as if silently assessing her stability. He scratched his chin and gazed at a point far away. Molly picked up the battered teddy bear, held on, tight, studied the bright tropical fish, and listened as the pump gurgled. Her jaw slackened, teeth unclenched, and she exhaled. Holding her breath was new behavior, and it always felt so good when she breathed again. Finally, he spoke, "I'd advise that you rest and wait until you're stronger before going into the wilderness by yourself. Is there anywhere else you can go for solitude?"

"Yes, there is a lake with a secluded cove. Maybe I'll go there tomorrow. Today I'll keep trying to reach Amy."

"One more assignment for the coming week. Define your boundaries with Jake."

"I thought I did."

"Be specific. The journal, your mail, your very privacy and need to be alone."

"He'll leave me, I bet."

Richard shook his head. "Jake isn't going anywhere."

As they walked to her car, he said, "Take care of yourself. Do what you need to do for your health and peace. Please call me anytime."

"What about Diatrice? I don't want her finding out."

"Here's my card. Call my pager, and I'll get right back to you."

Molly drove into the countryside, pulled off the road at a wide spot, and contemplated her situation. *Am I going insane? Or sane, like Richard said?* She wanted to close her eyes to all trauma, sadness, wickedness revealing itself. To fall face-first into denial and blessed escape.

The radio played a fluid melody by Donovan.

> Where are the eyes I beheld with my own on that long
> ago lazy day?
> Green are the leaves on the old apple tree,
> the sweet perfumed blossoms of spring entwined in your hair
> the smile in your eyes, a soft blade of grass for a ring.
> Warm are the loaves that cool on the sill to the song of the clear
> trickling stream.

The song made her think of Dulcimer Man and a voice deep within or high above, whispered, "Breathe. Relax and breathe." Several breaths later and Molly heard faraway music, closed her eyes, smiled her first smile of this day. A narrow bridge formed, and she walked down the center, dropping Jake's smirk over one side, her own guilt and shame over the other. Dropping every worry until her mind was white, clean, ready.

. . .

She comes to a porch and wraps herself in a faded quilt, sits next to her mama in bright winter sunshine.

"I reckon they're comin'. Hear the wagon, Sophia chile?"

A moment later, Joe is giving her a big hug. "Soph, my big girl. We're home. This here's Granny. Say howdy."

A tall white-haired lady climbs out of the loaded wagon and unties a cow. "Howdy, Granny. This here's Biscuit. Is that a cow? Kin I touch it?"

With large, gnarled hands, Granny pats Sophia's face. "Honey chile. Why you're the spittin' image of yer mammy when she were six. I reckon you kin pat this cow. Then take this here rope and lead Bessy out a the way. Why, t'night you's goin' t'have milk with yer grits."

"Hello, Ma," Marta whispers.

Granny's wrinkled smile fades as she looks at her daughter, then says to Sophia, "Honey chile, reckon y' kin help Joe with them goods I brought? Yer mammy and me want to say howdy."

One at a time, Sophia carries blankets and quilts while Joe hauls their old walnut desk and chairs. There's a rocking chair, a wooden butter churn, gunnysacks of food and clothes. Excited, Sophia totes what she can. Papa even smiles at her.

. . .

A car whizzed by with horn blasting and slammed Molly back to the present. Tears streamed down her face. Why? And how could the sun shine, daisies bloom, and birds sing when her world had turned dull gray? Richard's assignment came to mind and she asked, "How old am I with these tears? Silence. Another car cruised past, radio throbbing hard rock. *I want to go back to the wagon full of fun.* Now she feels like a sad nine-year-old, weeping but not knowing why.

For long moments, she sat, wondering what next. Then, carried like a leaf in a stream, she started the engine and headed back to Sugar Creek.

Her purpose still unknown, she parked and walked into the antique shop. The same man who'd been such a snot came toward her with an obsequious smile.

"Ms. Carpenter? Reverend Carpenter's missus? From Sweet Hollow?" He handed her his card. The proprietor. Hmm.

"Yes. The same Ms. Carpenter. I've been here before."

"I'm sorry, I don't remember. Perhaps I wasn't here that day? Would you like to browse or is there something in particular?"

"There was a walnut desk. Of rough hewn planks."

"Yes, yes, of course."

They threaded their way through cluttered aisles and soon stood admiring the small old piece of furniture. She ran her hand over its smooth writing surface. Sophia's desk?

"How much are you asking?"

"Well, since it is battered and since it's for you, Ms. Carpenter. Why . . . three hundred, I believe. Yes, three hundred."

"I'll take it. I think it will fit in my station wagon. You accept credit cards?" What was going on? There had been no consideration or thought behind this purchase. And Jake would have a fit about the price and the frivolity. One more mistake?

Molly stopped at a pay phone, dialed Amy's number. Again, no answer. Just barely a day since Amy's call; everything must be all right. *Soon we will connect and talk, and I'll go there if she wants me.*

Hungry, she drove the few blocks to Sam's.

"Would y' look what the cat drug in. Hon, let me get you seated and bring you some java," Ellen chimed, chewing gum, and smiling her horsey smile. After Molly ordered, Ellen slid into the seat across from her.

"Molly, right? You came in with Royce one night. I was hopin' I'd see more of the two of you. He's been alone, nursin' a broken heart, for too long. I asked, and he said you were Jake Carpenter's wife. Well, you win some, you lose some."

Interested, Molly frowned at the gum chomping that kept time to the beat of her sad heart and dull headache. The bell rang, and Ellen sauntered off for her order.

She set a bowl of chowder on the table and plopped down again. Molly stared.

"Oh, hope y' don't mind. I know you ordered a BLT, but this here's watcha need. Just what the doctor ordered." She winked. "Looks like Sweet Hollow got a winner this time. Everybody's ravin' about your hubby. Old Diatrice must a done her homework finally, instead of going for looks and charm. 'Bout time. Not that your hubby isn't charmin', though I've never met him, y'know. But that church sure had a string of piss-poor preachers—pardon my French."

"What do you mean?" Now Molly was perversely fascinated. Ellen seemed to have leaped a chasm from Royce to the church and Jake.

"Well, the last minister gambled and drank and sich. Became the butt of ridicule and bad jokes. Off he went on a toot, and we ain't seen hide nor hair of him since. Then there was the guy who weren't here long 'afore talk of him and Royce's wife spread like wild fire. She was a real looker, but beauty is what beauty does, I always say. Royce said it was just gossip. But where there's smoke there's fire, y'know? Soon enough they ran off together. Royce took her leaving hard. For a long time he claimed she was seduced. I said good riddance to bad rubbish, and it takes two to tango. Why I was glad to see you with him. But I'd bet the farm he'd never even think to do t' Reverend Jake what that other preacher did to him. The shoe's been on the other foot, y'know? Oh, Royce comes in once in a while with Beth. There's nothin' there. Not his type and she's looking for bigger fish to fry. But here I am prattling on. Eat up. Put some meat on those bones." Ellen smiled, winked again, and swished her tush to the kitchen.

What a treat, that woman. Molly liked her in spite of the gum and clichés. Ellen had given her a great bowl of soup and much to think about. Royce had been betrayed! No wonder he protected their honor.

Leaving the café, Molly heard, "Y'all come back now, y'hear?"

She considered walking to the bookstore for her journal and camera, then couldn't wait to show Royce her purchase, so she drove.

Entering the shop, Molly inhaled the familiar bouquet of old books and dust, finding serenity in that homely scent and the quiet, sleepy air. Royce came around a corner and stopped short.

"Darlin'," he said and crossed the room. He enfolded her in his arms and said nothing more. Finally she broke away and reached for a tissue.

"I'm a mess, Royce."

"A beautiful mess, though."

A chuckle deep in her throat brought a curve to her lips. "A compliment from the handsome bookseller, what better reason to come here? I just had lunch at Sam's and a conversation with Ellen. Well, a monologue from Ellen."

He smiled. "And now you know the saga of the preachers, I bet."

"Only the last two. And she's got a lot to learn about Jake."

"Ellen will hear the gossip first, if there is any dirt to dig. Now, I'm doing it—the clichés."

"I know, I know. I was thinking in them after her little spiel while I had soup I didn't order." She hesitated, then said, "You're laughing now, but it must have been a hard time for you."

"Imagine how much chowder I consumed that year. Got so I didn't even order. Just went in, sat down, and ate my soup."

"Some day could we talk about that time? I'm interested."

"Yes," he said so low she hardly heard him.

Silence surrounded them. He took her hand, guided her to a dim recess. He kissed her then. In his store, in the middle of the day, as if the rest of the world slept or was blind. Molly responded for a slow, sweet moment. Coming to her senses, she quickly stepped back.

"Wrong. I know," he said. "I couldn't resist."

"Not here," she whispered.

The bell above the door jingled as a customer walked in. "Yoo-hoo, Royce," he said as he came around the corner.

Royce smiled and nodded at him. Molly caught her breath. He could as easily have come in a minute earlier and caught them.

"Well, I did have a mission when I arrived. My stuff?" she said, forcing a light tone.

"Sure. It's in my trunk."

At her car, she said, "Look, I bought that desk. I don't have any idea why or where I'm going to put it, but I had to have it." They stood, with car door open, admiring the rickety antique.

"I'm glad it's going home with you." He paused for so long she nudged him.

"Uh, there's something I think you should know," he said, looking directly into her eyes until she felt faint. "Jake called me this morning."

"He did? Here? Why?"

"No, at home. He told me to stay away. That I was upsetting you."

She laughed. A rueful one, but at least a laugh. "Upsetting. Good word. He's got that one right." Then she got mad. Indignant. "How dare he? This is ridiculous!"

"Maybe I shouldn't have said anything. Still . . ."

"Oh no, I'm glad you did. Don't ever keep anything from me, please," she said as she got behind the wheel and started the engine. "Bye. I'm heading home. He and I are going to have a talk." She waved, and her tires squealed as she sped away.

# THIRTEEN

~

*Facing it, always facing it,*
*that's the way to get through. Face it.*
—Joseph Conrad

"Leave that in my car, Jake."

"Hey, I want to see what you bought."

"Fine. But don't move it."

"What are you thinking, Molly? How much did you pay for this piece of junk? And why?"

She didn't respond, but continued into the house. Tired and wanting a nap, she'd been met in the driveway by Jake, pacing. He'd looked at his watch as if to say, "Where the hell have you been?" Instead, he smiled and opened the driver's door. No doubt he would have helped her out if she had allowed. Now he stormed in after her, demanding to know what the desk cost and where they'd put the thing. Molly stood at the kitchen sink, gulping a glass of water. Her hands trembled, her bones ached. A fly crawled lazily up the window and there wasn't a swat left in her.

"Sit down. We need to talk," he ordered.

"Not now, I'm tired." Her urgent need to confront him about calling Royce had subsided and she wanted to be left alone.

"Now."

So she sat across from him at the polished kitchen table with a bouquet of garden flowers between them. Jake's efforts at appeasement. As if flowers and a clean house made everything all right.

"I've got a lot to say. First, how much did you pay for that desk?"

"Three hundred dollars."

"For God's sake. We don't have that kind of money to throw away on junk. I thought we agreed to discuss big purchases."

"We've agreed on a lot of things, Jake. And none of them are being held to. I wanted it. I bought it. Watch me. I'll buy what I want, when I want to."

"We can't afford this. Just because you're mad."

"Take it out of the money your mother left. The money you promised me for taking care of her those last years. Merely one of many, many promises you've reneged on. Take the three hundred out of that. But leave me be. I'm tired."

After a long silence, she started to get up when he reached for her. She cringed and sat.

"That money's gone," he said.

"What do you mean, gone? Twenty-five thousand dollars! Gone where?"

"You know the trouble we had in Tucson. I was headed for jail."

"I thought the judge dismissed the case."

"Well, yes. He did. But that cost money."

"Twenty-five thousand dollars! And you didn't tell me?"

"I knew if I told you . . . Well, look how agitated you are now . . . Listen, I bought him off for both of us. For a new start," Jake said in a calm, quiet voice as if attempting to hypnotize her.

She opened her mouth, closed it again. She was holding her breath and couldn't exhale. Who was this man? What next?

"I give up. I give up." Her only words, her only feelings.

She rummaged through her purse, gripped her valerian root, and went to the sink for water. Swallowing three, she realized the bottle was empty. *I've got to stop taking so many of these. The directions are for two at bedtime. Are they addictive? I quit. I'll take no more.* "Enough, Jake. I'm tired."

"No, wait. I need to tell you. Sit down." He posed stiff in his chair, shoulders back and a defiant glint in his otherwise dull eyes.

She fell into her chair. There was no use trying to get away, short of leaving the house, so she listened.

"Yes. I read Amy's letter and didn't tell you. Don't look at me that way. It came when we were settling in here, and you were jumpy and high-strung, running out to that deserted shack. I was waiting for the right time. So we could handle her delusions together. I thought maybe that would bring us closer."

The phone jangled, and Molly jumped. Jake rose to answer, muttering as he did. She got there first, and after her breathless hello, a woman's voice said, "Are you Molly Carpenter? Amy's mother?"

"Yes, yes. Is she all right?" Molly closed her eyes and prayed. When she opened them, Jake motioned and left the room. As if she gave a damn at this point.

"I'm a friend of Amy's. She's right here."

"Amy!"

"Mom." Her little girl's sweet voice. Well, twenty-eight now, but she'd always be her little girl.

"Are you all right? I've phoned and phoned."

"I'm sorry, Mom. After I left the message for you, I had a fight with my boyfriend and turned off my machine. So I wouldn't have to hear his voice. I didn't mean to scare you."

Molly relieved but suddenly alert, impulsively rushed through the house. The office door was open a crack, and she charged in. Jake had picked up the receiver. She glared, and he huffed past her and out of the room.

"Are you okay? I never saw your last letter. You sounded so upset when you called. My imagination has been all over the place. You're in therapy?"

"Yes. I'm so angry. Jake . . ." Her voice quivered and went up an octave.

"What? What happened? Did he . . . ?"

"No, Mom, not exactly. It was more subtle than that. Innuendoes and invading my privacy. He read my diary, letters. He went through my drawers and left disgusting photos in my room. A lot of bossing us kids around. Threats and stuff."

"Where was I during all this? Why didn't I see?"

"Mostly the worst happened while you were out. I almost told you, but you seemed so happy. There's a lot more that I won't talk about over the phone."

"Should I come? I will. If you want me to."

"It's okay, Mom. I'm fine, really. I'm making friends and have a good job. I just have so much anger, and it spills into my relationships with men. I blow up, yell, and scream. Like yesterday. That's why I'm in therapy. Listen, I have a new address. Have you got paper and pen?"

Molly's hands shook, and the pen slipped from her sweaty fingers. She had forgotten to breathe again and gasped for air as she wrote.

"I'm so sorry, Amy."

"Mom, no. It's not your fault. I love you."

Molly knew better. Whatever happened had to be her fault. What had she been thinking? She'd seen what appealed to her and married him. There had been no thought of possible consequences when she'd brought a stranger into her home. What had she known about him? Assistant pastor and his age. With blinders on, she had trusted him with her children. Her innocent eight-year-old daughter. Yes, this was her fault. No one else's. How could Amy ever forgive her? Molly doubted she'd forgive herself.

"Oh, Amy, I love you so. I'll do whatever you ask. Remember that . . . I didn't even know you'd moved to North Dakota. How long have you been there?"

"Since June. The letter you didn't get. Mostly I wrote about my move and why. I'd like to write again, but . . ."

"You know what? Monday I'm getting a post office box. I'll call with the address. Leave your machine on." She heard her daughter chuckle and she smiled, relieved.

"Well, on a lighter note, how's everything else going, Mom?"

"A lot is happening here. And not so light either. I'll write you a long letter with details. I've started therapy too. I think about you all the time, honey. I'm sorry."

"Mom, don't cry or I'll start. I'm okay."

Molly listened eagerly to Amy's news about her job and the church she attended. Not like any church Molly had ever been to. Long quiet times of meditation and songs about peace. Interesting.

"How are your brothers?" Amy had always been close to Nat, a year older, and Gust, three years younger and had kept Molly informed. "Have you seen them? Talked to them?" Molly asked, anxious for any word. Knowing they were well and safe would be enough.

"No. They don't even know I've moved. I'll call them today and let you know. I better go now, Mom. Smile."

"I am smiling, Amy. I don't want to hang up. I'll call you Monday. I love you."

"I love you too. Bye."

Molly took her scrap of paper, folded it small, and crammed it deep into her jeans pocket, put her head on her folded arms, and wept sobs of regret and relief. Tears for Amy and an aching, burning sensation that at some level she, as a mother, must have known. How could she not? Now that her eyes began to see, they saw and saw and saw. How could she have been such a fool?

Under a thin veneer of calm and control, she went looking for Jake. Her stomach churned—a cauldron of rage. She shouted his name while pacing around the house, inside and out, then checked for his car. Gone. *He'd left. Probably figured I'd calm down and swallow more betrayal. Not this time.*

She made up the bed in the guest room and tossed her possessions into that closet. She took his mother's oil paintings and heaped them in the living room. Who cared any more?

There was no solid ground beneath her feet. Even cobblestones of past-life pain would be better than this quivering, spongy earth on which she sought footing. Her thoughts turned to gentle, compassionate Richard. Knowing she could call his pager anytime was enough. Weary, she retrieved her notebook from the car and foraged in the kitchen for ice cream, chocolate, or any other comfort food; what she really craved was a cigarette. Smoking wouldn't help. Instead, she lay down on the bed and began a letter to Amy, closed her eyes and slept.

When she awoke, Jake was standing over her, and she leaped up, terrified. "What are you doing?" she screamed.

"Watching you sleep. I love you. I'll do anything. Give me another chance. Everyone deserves a second chance."

"How many second chances are there?" She spit the words. "Only days ago, I was horrified that I almost hit you. Now I'm telling you. If I were you, I'd watch my back. Because right now, I could kill you. I'm that mad. How dare you mistreat my daughter. You sorry son of a bitch."

He bowed his head and shuffled to the window. She continued to sit on the bed, staring at his back. Daring him to make excuses. After twenty years she should have known better. When he turned to face her again, he wasn't groveling. He was JC, the Reverend Jake Carpenter. The self-righteous, indignant, condescending preacher.

"Molly, Molly, Molly. You've got yourself all worked up. Remember, you made a vow to God to love, honor, and obey. Your first loyalty is to that vow. Everything I've done has been to protect you and . . ."

"What about Amy? And you called Royce, for God's sake. You are listening to my phone conversations, destroying my mail, reading my journals! I don't know who you think you are. But you are not *my* God."

"I just told Royce you were upset and needed time alone. And whatever Amy's saying about me isn't true. I swear to God. And when the phone rings I'm curious. That's normal. Now let's get back to the main issue here. I see you've moved out of our bedroom. Ephesians 5:22 says, Wives, submit yourselves unto your own husband."

"You bombastic hypocrite, get the hell out of here."

He shook his head and, muttering Bible verses, he left. She fumed. *What should I do? Where can I go. No wonder I'm not breathing. Okay . . . I know Amy is safe and getting help. I know I can speak with her and hear her voice. I must leave here. So I won't kill him.* She opened her journal and began making plans.

Dinnertime came, and she made a peanut butter sandwich. She took it and a soda and, on second thought, the cordless phone back to her room. The sandwich lay there like a plastic replica, uninviting, inedible.

Jake hollered, "What's for dinner?" Molly moved slowly into the living room and pronounced, "I have eaten," then turned on her heels and marched to the office. Retrieving some books, she hurried back to her room, closed the door, and settled in for the evening. Tomorrow was Sunday, and while Jake tended to his flock, she would leave. She couldn't read, couldn't think. She cried. Curled in a ball, she finally lost consciousness.

The room was dark and the hour late when something raised goose bumps. From a deep sleep, she opened her eyes as the door inched closed; the knob turned with a soft click. Jumping out of bed, she shot into the hall. Nothing stirred. Panting, she crept on tiptoes to the master bedroom. Jake lay there, sound asleep or so it seemed. Had a bad dream awakened her, made her skin crawl? She didn't know but wouldn't put anything past him anymore.

Back in her room she closed the door and hooked a chair under the knob. *This is no way to live. I can not do this anymore.* She lay for unending hours, eyes wide in the dark, her thoughts ricocheting from Jake's insane behavior to Amy's pain, her own guilt. Somewhere in the long night, she slept. Until the sun lit the room and birds sang.

With a clarity of purpose, Molly donned jeans, T-shirt, and sneakers. When she entered the kitchen for coffee, Jake raised his eyebrows and started to speak. She shot him a scowl, "No. I am not going to church with you today. I may never go again. No. I am not going to Bible study tomorrow," and stomped from the room.

Again she closed her door and blocked it with the chair. Until he left, she would stay in her room.

Jake knocked and muttered, "I have to go. Please come out and talk."

"There is nothing more to talk about. Just go."

"I'll see you in a few hours then. Maybe we can take a drive, have a nice dinner, and I can make you understand."

After a few minutes she came out, checked the driveway, and saw that his car was gone. She dialed the phone and exhaled in relief when Royce answered.

# FOURTEEN

~

*And the day came when the risk it took to*
*remain tight inside the bud was more painful*
*than the risk it took to blossom.*

—Anaïs Nin

"Hi, Royce. I'm so glad you're home."

"Me too," he said with an early-morning sleepy voice. "I didn't expect a Sunday-morning call from you. A pleasant surprise. What's up?"

"I've decided the little walnut desk belongs in the cabin. And I remembered that old wagon road you came in on one day. How do I find that?"

"I'm not sure where you live exactly but you take . . ."

"It sounds complicated," she said while jotting down his directions.

"Once you turn on the gravel road you won't have a problem. Are you and Jake going there today?"

"Oh, no. Things are impossible here. Jake's at church, and I'm leaving before he comes home. I plan on spending the day. In fact, I think I'll be using the cabin as a daytime retreat. At least for a while. I'll come home at night until I decide what to do."

"Sounds serious. Do you want to talk?"

"Yes," she whispered. "I do. Not now. I've got to go."

"Remember, darlin', you're welcome at my place, anytime."

"I know. Thank you. But . . ." Molly closed her eyes, bit her lip, and murmured good-bye.

Then she flew around the house, packing. She filled a cooler with ice and food. One eye on the clock, she spent an inordinate amount of precious time searching for an oil lamp tucked away somewhere. Finding it and a bottle of lamp oil behind the linens, she wrapped them in towels and nestled them in the desk. A box filled with books, matches, a few toiletries, and a bucket of cleaning supplies and rags. After hauling those and a comforter and pillows to the car, she grabbed her purse and took off. A half mile down the road she squealed a U-turn, sped back, ran in, and snapped up the dulcimer. She spied her camera and snatched it up.

On the kitchen table, with the vase anchoring a corner, lay her note:

> Jake,
>
> I need time to sort out my feelings and cannot think in this house with you. I'll be back late tonight.

Driving into town, she stopped at the drugstore with the film she'd taken since coming to Sweet Hollow. What, if anything, would develop of the mysterious lady on the front porch?

Sliding the envelope across the counter, she asked, "Do you have twenty-four-hour service?"

The clerk raised an eyebrow and scratched his head. "Oh. Uh, no. Let's see . . . today's Sunday. You can pick this up Thursday afternoon."

Molly shrugged. She'd waited this long. But still. She picked up another roll of film, a case of bottled water, and, on a whim, several scented candles. The ATM doled out one hundred dollars.

She drove out of town and fumbled in her purse for Royce's directions, glad for sunshine in a cloudless sky. Taking each described turn, she soon bumped along the rutted road. Walking would have been faster but now nothing felt urgent anymore, and she exhaled.

Blackberry branches and underbrush scraped the old gray Chevy as the tracks dwindled to mere grooves. She maneuvered to a wide spot, turned her car around, and backed in as far as she could, stopped, killed the engine, and surveyed her surroundings.

The path to the cabin must be here somewhere, but she had no idea how long the hike would be. Even opening the car door proved difficult until she leaned against it and shoved. *Can I do this? Well, how will I know unless I try? Angels, if you're there, help me.* With a comforter over one arm and a bucket in the other hand, she trampled brambles and made her way. Ten minutes later, dirty, and with sweat tracing rivulets down her face, she dumped her cargo at the front doorway. Could she haul the desk all that way? Through thorns and knee-high weeds? And over rocks and ruts? Tears of frustration burned her eyes. *Damn it! Jake wouldn't think twice. He'd just do it.* Would she always need a man to get things done? Maybe she wasn't capable of living alone. Maybe she'd better not even consider leaving him. Shoulders back and head high, she turned, determined to bring the desk back with her.

At the car, she spread an old rug she'd brought, lifted the desk on to it, and removed the drawers. *There. I may not be as strong as a bull, but I do have a brain. I will do this.* She tugged on the rug and moved her load a few feet, straightened, brushed hair from her eyes and sweat from her brow. Bent again and pulled. And again. When she stepped in a rut, turned her ankle and fell backward, she remained on the ground and rethought the situation. Her back ached and perspiration blurred her vision. She shook her head. She'd work at it more when the sun went behind the trees. Instead of her treasured desk, she carted pillows and some supplies.

Tiring of the trek, she tackled her cleaning project. The loft drew her first and when she swept up bits of corncob, she spoke out loud, "Could this possibly be what's left of the doll, Mandy Lee? No. That was far too long ago." The thought comforted her, though, and she smiled as she worked. And so the morning went, alternately cleaning and toting.

After several hours, she declared her tasks complete for the day. Her journal lay in a corner; reluctantly, she reached for the tattered notebook. She had to face her real-life situation, and the best way she knew was through writing. The rocking chair squeaking near the front door was but an illusion, so she sat on the floor and wrote with paper propped on her knees. She looked at her wrist and frowned. No watch. Her face smoothed to a half smile when she realized what gift forgetfulness had given her. A timeless afternoon lay ahead. Perfect. She began her journal entry by reporting this fact. Then describing her surroundings brought her into the moment. A woodpecker hammering at a tree far away—a yellow-bellied sapsucker? The mourning dove's coo, soft and soothing on this mild August day. Gentle breezes carrying fragrances from wildflowers unseen.

A squirrel skittered across the porch's far side, and Molly thought of Cat, wondering if he were all right and where he'd gone off to. Finally, she addressed her blowup with Jake, recording every detail, viewing the whole scenario, especially the duplicity she'd closed her eyes to for years.

Yes, Jake had been a strict disciplinarian and she'd often felt like a referee between him and her children. What Amy had said about threats and strange pictures put his behavior in another light. No wonder Molly's sons stayed away. Maybe the problem wasn't that she'd divorced their father. In the past, she'd written them letters apologizing for her mistakes. Then she'd waited anxiously for a reply; when none came, she vowed to leave them be. Now she wondered. If she left Jake, could she rebuild a relationship with her kids?

The idea of a second divorce, a second failure, brought a sad ache and apprehension. Would the scandal in Tucson come to light here? What would Royce think of her for having covered for Jake? What about her kids? Would they think she knew how Jake had treated Amy because Molly had known his history? And really, where could she go? What could she do? She'd be penniless with no skills that she could think of. Did she have a choice?

*Breathe*, she thought. Breathing helped. She didn't believe anything about Jake now and would never trust him again. Lies, lies—twenty years of lies. When he said his sister needed him, where had he actually gone? Had he really spent the thousands his mother had left them? She cringed. Turning a page, she scribbled a gratitude list, thankful for her health, friends, this quiet afternoon.

When her fingers cramped and her back ached, she closed the book and stood. Stretching, she gazed upward. Wisps of white clouds reassured her that no thunderstorm brewed. The little desk would stay dry standing in the middle of the trail. She grabbed a towel and headed for the stream. In cool, clear shallows, she lay facedown, turning her head one way and then the other. Hard work and writing had purified her emotions, and this interlude in the creek cleansed her body. Pebbles pressing into her breasts, belly, and thighs awakened a sensual sense of aliveness. From the first day she'd come here, this place had soothed her soul, as if answering a yearning for home. *Why hadn't the past made an appearance yet? Have I been so preoccupied and annoyed I've missed a window that might not come again?*

From a distance came a faint whistle. A hiker? Grabbing her towel, she slapped it against her wet skin and squirmed into her jeans and shirt. She stuffed her bra in her pocket and sat on a rock to dry her feet and get into socks and shoes. Feeling less vulnerable, she strolled toward the sound.

As she drew closer to her hideaway, the whistler became apparent, and Molly hurried her pace. Wet curls flying, tears streaming, and, with a broad smile across her face, she ran into Royce's arms.

"I, you . . . I, your whistle," she blubbered.

"Hush, darlin', hush."

"You make me cry. No. I mean it," she sighed as they strolled hand in hand. "The first time I met you, tears came to my eyes, and I had not a clue why. I don't know why I'm weeping now. Except that you are the only person in this world, besides my daughter, I'd want here this afternoon."

On the porch she reached down and examined Cat as he dozed in the sunshine. "Oh, kitty. Where have you been?" she cooed.

"This cat was at our house late one night and clawed Jake. He kicked him, hard. I was mad enough to kick back. I'm so relieved he's here . . . He seems all right."

"Your house must be fairly close," Royce said as he squatted and petted Cat.

"It's a good walk. Quite a bit farther by the wagon road."

"Has Jake ever come here with you?"

"No. Well, almost. You see that hill? Not the one closest. That one with the big trees. He yelled at me from there once. And over the hill, our house is still at least another hundred yards away. Why?"

"I got the impression you wanted time away from him. Won't he come here looking for you?"

*Would he?* "I don't think so. I took my car, and I doubt he knows about the old road . . . No. He won't." But she was guessing and hoping. As she spoke, Molly formed a makeshift lounger by spreading the comforter and two pillows near Royce's backpack and small cooler, resting in a shady corner.

"I have a frosty iced tea and an Ellen Special for a hardworking woman." He opened his cooler and handed her a cold drink and a sandwich. "I took a tour inside. You haven't been dawdling today."

They stretched out, leaning against the wall. She closed her eyes and thanked the universe for its loving kindness in providing a friend, a cat and nourishment. In her mind, the old codger limped down the walk, turned, and nodded. Ask, he'd said. And ask she had.

"You must be an angel," she said, sipping tea.

He didn't speak for so long she prodded, "Royce?"

"Oh. You surprised me with that. I've been called many names over the years, some going in the other direction, but angel? Maybe when I was four years old, scrubbed and ready for bed. But . . ."

"Well, here you are, like a guardian angel, keeping me from despair. Hey, maybe you can help me move that desk. I tried to but . . ." Enthusiasm in her voice rang like a crystal bell, making her realize how much she'd yearned to have that little piece of furniture nested here.

He smiled and nodded. "My logical reason for coming. I thought about the trail in from the road and knew one person couldn't haul anything that size. But I didn't know how I'd be received." His eyes questioned and golden flecks danced at her unspoken response. "I'm not even sure the two of us can cut through the brush. After we eat, let's try."

"I'm really glad you said that. Here I thought a man would just hoist it on his head and charge."

He threw his head back and laughed. "Some things take more than brute force, darlin'."

She grinned at him, feeling strong and capable again.

"This sandwich is delicious. Did you tell Ellen who else would be sharing your meal?"

"No. Why?"

"I guess I didn't think I'd graduated from chowder yet."

"She'd be mighty pleased if she knew we were here together, though."

"She's quite a gal. I like her," Molly said. "And her sandwiches."

"Ellen and Sam are good people." He turned to her and, with a soft voice, said, "So. Things getting worse between you and Jake?"

"Oh, Royce . . . I" She bowed her head and fought her tears. When she spoke, anger, fear, and frustration tumbled out in her words and flailing arms. At last spent, she leaned back and closed her eyes.

"Betrayal," he murmured. "I understand betrayal of trust. Is Amy your only child?"

"No. I have two sons. But, well, I don't hear from them much."

She pictured them. Nat, with his curly blond hair and sparkling blue eyes, was so sensitive as a child. He even cried when someone complimented him. And Gust, dark-complexioned and strong-willed, very much like his father. Both such sweet little boys. Both so defiant as their turn came to leave home. How had Jake treated *them*? Her mind slammed shut. "Enough of all this for one day."

They finished their meal, focusing on ordinary things, cats asleep in the sunshine and wildflowers in bloom, the unexpected respite from summer heat.

"If we're going for that desk, I guess we'd better go soon," Royce said.

Molly placed her palm on his cheek, ran her fingers through his wavy hair as she slid her hand to the back of his head and pulled him close. *Kiss me first,* she thought.

And he did. Picnic wrappings tumbled between them, crackling as she softened against him.

"Hmm," she said as she looked into his eyes, seeing desire but determination overriding passion.

"We can't do this. I won't do this," he said.

"I know. It's just . . . I can so easily get lost in you."

"I don't want to be an escape. Look at me," he said as he tilted her chin. "You mean more to me than . . ." He shook his head. "Not now. Not while you're in this turmoil."

"Thank you again, sir," she said, forcing a smile.

"C'mon, darlin'. The desk, remember?" He pulled her to her feet.

They stuffed the supper clutter in a sack, gathered up crusts and bits for Cat, and started back to the car, his arm snug around her waist, her hand in his hip pocket.

A half hour, a lot of laughs and some bramble scratches later, the desk stood indoors. A ludicrous effort, she supposed, since someone must own this property, and she'd need to haul the charming addition back out soon. One piece of furniture brought life to the room. Especially after she placed the oil lamp on one corner.

As they stood hand in hand admiring their efforts, the air took on a different quality . . .

A fire crackles in the fireplace. Her senses fill with the pleasant aroma and sound of soup bubbling in a pot. Lamplight casts shadows here and chases them away there. The shadows take form, begin moving about.

Sophia stands quietly in the corner, uncomfortable in her clothes, in her skin. Her brown hopsack dress flows well below her knees, but the bodice is snug around her changing shape. Susie still wears her pretty pinafores, and they aren't too tight so Sophia had asked her mama, "Why do I look this way?"

Mama had sighed and whispered, "Ask yer granny."

She hadn't dared trouble her granny; she looked glum and crotchety. Still Granny had taken time to pretty her dress with blue ribbons and even tied one in Sophia's long copper hair. She wished she had light, bouncy curls like Susie's instead of heavy waves that weighed her down. She could go with Susie and be a little girl again anytime. Susie had promised. But Sophia wouldn't leave her mama, and so she only went for visits.

A murmur of voices, a woman and a man. The man stomps out the back door and cold mixed with snow rushes in before he slams the door shut. Winter wind howls around corners and sneaks in beneath the door.

A weeping old woman says, "Honey chile . . . Joe. Yer mammy's done gone t' meet her maker. Ya'll come here an' hep send her on th' way."

Sophia holds her breath until she gasps for air. Her fingers tremble as she fiddles with the ribbons, tying and untying the bows.

"Yer a big girl now, honey chile. Yer mammy were poorly fer a long time. Reckon she done stayed 'til you growed up some.

Now you two come 'long. Yer pa's gone so thar's nothin' to be scairt of."

Joe puts his arm around her, and she cries on his shoulder. "Hush, Soph. I'll take care."

Lamplight dimmed and shadows disappeared. The fireplace cooled, and late-afternoon sunshine once again lit the room. Molly found herself sobbing uncontrollably. As Royce held her tight, his voice husky, he repeated over and over, "Hush, hush. Molly, you're safe."

Conscious of the present moment, she stepped back and, wide-eyed, gazed at him. "Were you standing next to me all this time? Did you go there?"

Tears glistened in his eyes, his voice cracked, "I don't know. Sadness filled me, as if someone I loved had deserted me. And then you said something. Except your voice wasn't yours. You spoke with a much younger tone. Lilting. Even in incredible sadness it was lilting when you said, "Granny. My mama. Is she daid?"

"Daid? I said that? Out loud? Did you hear anything else?"

"I thought I heard voices. I don't know. Everything was the same and different."

After a long pause, she said, "I feel as if I've always known you. That . . . that we . . ."

He put a finger to her lips. "Ssh," he said and enfolded her in his arms.

# FIFTEEN

~

*Millions of spiritual creatures walk the earth Unseen, both when we wake and when we sleep.*

—John Milton, *Paradise Lost*

Shocked into silence by visions of Sophia and her granny, Molly and Royce settled on the porch with a blanket. Cat curled on her lap. The air had cooled, and as the sun set, clouds shifted in pastel shades of gold, yellow, pink. Molly's tension eased, her shoulders released their cares. In her search for solid ground beneath her, she reminisced about their first encounter, that hot afternoon in the antique shop.

"You were looking at odd pieces," she said. "And it sounded like you meant me!"

"Well, you implied I was your diversion."

"You remember that?"

"I remember. And your floppy hat with the price tag hanging from the brim. Come to think of it, you were an odd piece," he teased. They chuckled.

"Look," she said, "the moon."

In the twilight, the crescent moon and Venus shone with promise. An owl's muffled *hoo, hoooo, hoo* spoke to her of wisdom and respect. Breezes stilled. Silence descended. His head rested on hers with a pleasing pressure. The world and her troubles were far away. She heard him breathe, felt his heart beat, his hand warm at her waist.

He straightened and considered the dulcimer that lay beside him. "This is finely crafted. A treasure."

"I brought the hundred dollars the old man asked for, and I want to leave it. He said under the rocking chair, but there is no rocking chair."

Royce untaped the quill and plucked the strings. "Oh, they tell me of a home far away," he crooned.

"You play the dulcimer and know that lullaby?"

"Well, no. I play *at* the dulcimer, and I've always known the song. Why?"

"I'd never heard those words until Sophia's mama sang them."

"It's a common enough song. I think."

They lingered until daylight's last trace disappeared and the night sky filled with stars. Then, by the beam of Royce's flashlight, they made their way back to their cars. He followed her home and drove on.

The house was dark and silent as she entered but immediately a bright light flashed on. She squinted into its glare and, for a moment, stood blinded and vulnerable.

"Where were you? One more hour and I would have called the police."

"I left you a note," she said. Her eyes adjusted to the light, she saw Jake standing with feet apart, hands on hips and eyes darting. Was he going to hit her? He never had, but he looked wild, disheveled.

Breathe, she told herself. And in a deliberate voice, she said, "I'm going to bed. Good night." He followed her down the hall but turned and slammed the master bedroom door. There would be no fight tonight.

The guest room—her room—seemed in order, but she knew different. Everything was too precise. All drawers were closed snugly when she had deliberately left some ajar. Jake had rummaged. The fact disgusted her. She closed her door and wedged the chair beneath the knob again. One more night locked in. *How many more would there be? Am I locking him out or me in? What am I searching for with Royce that I've locked away in my home?* Writing these questions in her journal, she pondered the wrongness here—in this marriage. Where was her "happily ever after?" Nothing but a veneer, and she had always refused to face anything that would tarnish her dream. Had she expected Jake to fulfill childhood fairytales of prince charming? Imagining growing old alone brought beads of sweat to her brow. Her heart ached as if being pierced by thorns. She kicked off the blanket, sobbed, blew her nose, and forced herself to continue writing. Like a dried-up sponge, she felt herself shrivel, contract. Needing, needing, needing. Was she being reasonable now? No. No, she wasn't. Sure he had faults. Doesn't everyone? She had married him for "better or worse." She could have peace, but could she pay the price? Jake, her husband, lay alone in another room. *I won't go back to the woods. I'll stay here and live up to my vows. He loves me, isn't that what counts?* With that, she crawled out of bed and padded down the hall, stifling the small voice that cried out, "What about Amy?"

Fingertips tapping on the door, she whispered, "Jake, may I come in? I want to talk."

. . .

Confused and angry, Molly approached the shed with trepidation. It had seemed ominous last night while she stood back and Royce placed her cooler inside. Now, in the bright noon sun, she studied the structure. This building was larger and sturdier than the inky black shack she—Sophia—had been locked in. Anticipating a dark, moldy space, she creaked open the door. Dim light, coming through a small window on the far side, surprised her. She hauled her cooler out of the way so she could venture in.

The floor was dirt, but a covering of straw remained. Spider webs sent shivers of disgust as they cloaked her face. She spit and sputtered, flailed her arms, then brushed the webs off and peered at a heap against the back wall. Cautiously she drew aside an old quilt, uncovering a straight-backed chair atop a jumble of junk. Could sorting out this discarded clutter help her put her own life in order? She shrugged and carried her find to the sunlight for inspection. Made of maple wood with a seat of woven cane, the chair held her weight with only a slight wobble when she sat. Perfect for the little desk.

A long straight branch that resembled a walking stick interested her, and she pulled it out. Laced to one end was a gunnysack. She marveled—a mop? A wooden butter churn, with all its slats still holding firm. Lugging a rusty cast-iron cauldron with three nubby legs, a handle and a lid—heavy, awkward, and dirty—she heard a cough or growl. She gasped, dropped the pot, slapped a dirty hand across her mouth, and waited.

She relaxed as Beth walked toward her, then tensed again. When they'd met in the bookstore, Beth had seemed nervous, even blushed when she introduced Royce to Jake. And Jake's expression as he eyed Beth? Molly was fairly certain he wasn't interested in an affair. He wasn't the type. But, then again, what the hell type was he? And Beth, involved with a married man? Molly no longer knew what to expect from anyone, even herself.

She wiped her hands on her jeans, breathed in and out, and dredged up a smile.

"Hi, Beth."

"Hi. Are you okay?" Beth seemed apprehensive.

"Sure. What about you? You look upset?"

"I need to talk to you. But . . ." Beth's voice trailed off.

"I want to talk to you too. Let me get washed up first. I'm filthy."

They walked down a slope where tufts of grass fought for survival among spent thistles and dandelions in full bloom. Close to the ground a delicate vine covered with tiny white flowers tangled around the stems of larger weeds. Molly squatted and slid her hand under a section.

"This is pretty," she said, looking at Beth for information.

Beth bent, picked a stem, and tasted. "Yes, chickweed. If we had a salad, we could add some of this."

"Hmm. No salad, but I have sandwich makings. Can you stay and have lunch with me?"

"Thanks, Molly," Beth said, looking a little bewildered.

"I've really missed talking with you. I don't know what happened. I thought we'd become fast friends, and then something came between us."

"That's why I came lookin' for you today," Beth said.

They were close enough to the stream now to hear water splashing over rocks.

"I reckon there's a well or spring here somewhere. Prob'ly filled in after all these years."

"Oh yeah. I remember that."

"Huh?"

"Oh, nothing." She bit her lip.

"Look here. There's been a building of some sort." Molly held up a rotted piece of lumber.

"The springhouse, I reckon."

They inched their way over and through rubble of field rocks that created a mound in the landscape.

"Somethin' right strange. It's as cold as a haunt here. I cain't figure it."

"I've felt that eerie cool air on other hot days," Molly said. "But only in certain places. Like sometimes by the front door."

At the stream, she knelt and splashed her face and arms. Not having a towel, she dried off on her T-shirt. As an afterthought, she pulled the shirt over her head and rinsed it out, wringing as hard as she could.

"Okay. Now I need a dry shirt. Then we'll eat and talk."

Later, sitting in the shade on the porch, sandwiches in hand, Beth spoke, "I don't wanna be meddlin' in yer business. But Reverend Jake . . ."

Molly waited. When Beth sat silent, with head bowed, she finally asked, "Has he talked to you about me?"

"Yeah. You know that day you and Royce came into the bookstore together? Well, Reverend Jake—"

"Please," Molly interrupted. "Just call him Jake."

"Well, he had been in the shop awhile. He told me you were poorly, and he was concerned and sich. He asked me to spend time with you as much as I could. Then tell him what y'all were doin'. I was tryin' to explain I didn't take to the idea when you two showed up." Beth paused, looked down at her sandwich, took a bite, and stared at the floor as if she could see into the crawl space beneath the boards. She faltered as if choosing each word. "Him bein' the reverend and all, I didn't feel right saying no. After you left, he got right mad. Wanted me to spy on you. See how y' carried on. When I wouldn't, he left in a huff."

Had Jake trailed them that afternoon? Was he now following Beth?

"Did anyone see you come here?" Molly asked, wanting to shake Beth for an answer.

"I reckon not. I came the old wagon road. But he called last night asking questions."

"What? What questions?"

"Seems he thinks you went to Royce's yesterday. But Royce jest has a post office box listing and Rev . . . uh, I mean, Jake wanted his address."

"Did you tell him?"

"No. I lied. Said I didn't know."

"Thank you." Molly relaxed even though she hadn't been at Royce's at all yesterday. "Did he ask for anything else?"

"No. Jest fer me to tell you, if I saw you, that you'd better git home. I like you, Molly. And Jake bein' the preacher an' all. But I don't wanna be in the middle of this . . ."

"Oh. I know. I know. But can you just talk with me a little more? I need . . . well, I, uh, I went to the post office this morning, and who should be strutting out but Diatrice. And, well, you know her."

Molly mimicked Diatrice and her puffed-up stance, "'I'm surprised to see you. *Dear*. After what Reverend Jake said yesterday, dear. He read Prov. 2:12-22. You know the passage, of course. About a wayward wife with her seductive words, who leaves her partner and ignores the covenant *she* made with *God*. Well, since you weren't there, what *were* we to think? But he explained how unwell you were. Why, with your nerves . . . dear me. How *are* you? I imagined you lying in bed distraught. And here you *are*. At the Sugar Creek post office? Well.'" Molly aped Diatrice's smirk. "'So glad, *dear*, that you recovered.' Then she waddled out the door. No doubt on her way to a phone."

Beth shook her head, unfolded her arms, stretched her legs. Molly took a slow breath and, in her natural voice and manner, said, "I know that wasn't very kind of me, but you can imagine. My mind raced. What was Jake implying? How dare he say something about me from the pulpit?"

"I reckon he did. He asked fer prayer. Said you were feeling anxious and upset. Sick with a headache and sich. And then at the end, he announced the final hymn. "How Great Thou Art." Said it was your favorite, and I declare he could hardly finish talkin'! Cryin', I reckon. I called you in the afternoon, but no one answered. Then I rang up Royce. Left him a message."

"Here's the thing . . ." Without relating any details about Amy, Molly described the situation between her and Jake. She cried as she explained how she'd intended to stay home and make the best of her marriage. Until her encounter with Diatrice, that is. Now here she was again, spending another day alone and struggling with decisions. "I don't know many people here, especially women I can talk to like this. So you see, I really want us—you and me—to be friends."

Beth stood, and with her yellow sundress swirling in a gentle breeze, she opened her arms. They hugged with a wry chuckle at the difference in their height as Molly bent to put her cheek on Beth's.

They walked in silence over the now-beaten track to Beth's car. Warm sunshine, a quiet breeze with robins and sparrows flitting about, making soft background music. To an onlooker the scene would seem idyllic.

"I'll be up here most days. Please come back and see me. I hope Jake leaves you alone."

Beth nodded, started her engine, and maneuvered over the ruts. Molly watched until the car disappeared behind trees and brush. Her friend was gone. Even as worries prodded and poked at the edges of her mind, blackberries caught her eye. She stooped, plucked a plump one, and tasted. Sweet and ready. If she came back tomorrow, she'd gather blackberries. For now the stuff in the shed would occupy her for a while.

. . .

After depositing the chair and other finds, Molly grabbed her notebook and walked to the springhouse ruins. Climbing over debris, she slipped, and her journal went flying. She fell to her knees, dislodging rotting remains. Her hand landed on something slimy and foul smelling. She grimaced, wiped her hands on her jeans, and poked around, uncovering fungi of some sort. Flies swarming. *Yuk,* she thought. *Still, interesting the strange shapes and sizes mushrooms could take.* Would this be the cause of fox fire's eerie glow after dark? She'd never smelled such stink, though.

Recovering, she scooted from rock to rock. Once again cold air contrasted with the warmth of the late-summer sun. Dulcimer music played, and she glanced around, expecting the old codger or some other sign of human inhabitants. Nothing. But a cool wind and a softer light. When, at last, she sat on damp earth next to the spring itself, her mouth dropped open and she said aloud, "Would you look at this. It's been freshened." Water, seeping from under collapsed fieldstone and boards, formed a pool. Watercress, green and healthy, thrived. Large pebbles formed a low enclosure, preventing dirt and debris from clogging the flow. A bucket stood clean and ready as if the spring had never been abandoned. Expecting more slimy fungi, she dipped the bucket, cupped her hands. When the water ran clear, she drank. Cool and refreshing as it must have been a hundred years ago.

A tall tree stood nearby, one she hadn't noticed before. The trunk with deep, spiraling fissures in the bark reminded her of the chestnut tree. Beth had said they were no more, but certainly this was one. She sank to the ground and recorded the miracle of the sweet well water in her journal. Cat crawled onto her lap, and as she petted, she hummed in tune with tinkling music that floated in the air. Swaying branches seemed to whisper, "Molly, Molly. Help her." A shadow passed over her face, and she looked about. Cat jumped down and ran off. The wind intensified, the air chilled her, and she heard a low, throaty sound, "Belladonna. They dose her with belladonna." She cried out, and her body slumped over, her head hitting a rock . . .

. . .

In the cabin, she sits on the floor by an old lady in a rocking chair. A fire blazes in the stove. Granny holds a little box. Sophia knows it is the one her mama had shown her long ago.

"Sophia chile, yer mammy's gone an' I'll be followin' her. Listen t'me, chile." The old woman lays the box in her lap, takes Sophia's face in her hands, and turns her chin up to look in her eyes. "C'mon back here, chile. Thar now." And they smile at each other. "Afore I pass on I want y'to have this an' know what it means. Keep it close and keep it hidden—hear? I'm gonna be leavin' ya soon."

"No. No. Granny." Sophia panics.

"Now, now. Joe's right cheer t'watch o'er you." She turns and Joe nods, his mouth grim.

Granny opens the box, and Sophia sees shining gold and sparkling stones. Granny gently lifts the jewel-embellished breastpin and holds the treasure in her palm.

I'm gonna give this t'you, chile. But first I'll tell you where it come from. 'Twas yer grandpa's. He brought it t'America. In Scotland, in a village fur away from everythin', yer great-grandpa lived. He had the smithy craft this fer his beautiful wife, Blythe, yer great-granny. She had jest birthed their fifth chile that September day. A wee lass. This sapphire's her stone. The papa named the chile Maggie, fer he hoped this lass would bring light back t'his wife's eyes. The other four chillen were rough and tumble lads. This here is a ruby fer the chile born in July; he was a big strapping' lad of fifteen when Maggie was born. An' this is a garnet fer the second son, born in January. A sly, happy little guy, he offen hid from his mama or hid her needlework an' scissors. Then this turquoise is fer the third chile. At twelve, a scholar. His nose in books, he already knew more 'n' his mama an' jest gawked at her when she asked him t'do somethin'. That boy was a dreamer and spent hours walkin' in the wooded land near their home. A pickin' flowers and dryin' em. That be yer grandpa."

"What happened to Grandpa?"

"We called 'im Doc. Well, Doc, he disappeared afore y'were born. See . . ." Granny pursed her lips and fumbled in her apron for a kerchief, wiped her nose, and sat silent for a long time. "Yer grandpa Doc was right angered 'bout yer mama and papa runnin' off like they did. I tried . . . Anyhow, he took out after 'em. Ne'er came back. I ain't seen 'im since. Cain't see 'im, but I hear 'im play his dulcimer . . .

"Here . . . here now is the diamond. The most precious o' stones. Danny, born in April, woulda been 'round ten on that September day. But Danny was sickly, weak, and frail. When he was three, he was left in the cold and rain fer a time. When the nanny found him, he were a shiverin', quiverin' wet l'il lad. He ne'er spoke no more, jest got worse til he died in his mama's arms. The mama ne'er left her chillen again. The papa cried and sweet-talked her. Begged her fer 'nother chile. But she was scairt an' grievin' an' with three lads t'raise.

"The tale goes that durin' a cuss fight, the papa done forced hisself on her and Maggie came along. What li'l git up the mama had was gone. This here purty was t'cheer her and bring her luck. See—this big emeral' in the middle, 'tis all 'bout love. An' the cross is fer Jesus. No doubt Preacher Man tol' y' 'bout that . . . Sophia chile . . . look, look here."

*Preacher's not here, Susie. I'm safe with Granny.* Sophia shook her head as if coming out of a trance. "I'ma hearin', Granny."

"Sure 'nuff. Where was I? Oh . . . The mama jest sat, holdin' her baby an' rockin'. One day, in dead o' winter, the mama and her baby didn' open their eyes no more.

"On her desk was this breastpin and note:

> Baubles for naught.
> Love 'tisn't bought.
> No rogue finds rest. Kindness be blest.
> On to the last. The spell is cast.

The papa put the jewel and paper in this li'l box and ne'er looked at it again. Fer years he took t'drink. Runnin', he were, from the haunts. After squanderin' his riches, he died a broken man. What li'l money was left went t'his new wife. She right quick chased the three half-growed lads from their home. The dreamer and book learner, yer grandpa, knew 'bout this box and smuggled it out with him.

"Doc tol' 'twas a curse his mama put on th' pin. Cursin' his papa fer his betrayal and sinnin' against her. But he knew it a blessin' fer those who were good an' kind. He made me promise t'keep this safe iffen he couldn't stop yer mammy from wedden yer pa. I think Doc knew he weren't comin' back . . ."

Granny slips the jewelry into a small cloth sachet. "'Tis yers now, chile. I'll tie the ribbon round yer neck. Tuck it under yer frock next t'yer heart. Feel yer mammy an' yer grandpa thar with you. And keep it always. Someday 'twill bring good luck."

. . .

Molly's head pounded, and her moans blended with dulcimer music. A blanket had been tucked around her, but she shook with cold or fear or both. Where was she? Who was she? So dark and the ground hard. Someone leaned over her, gentled her head, and kissed her cheek. Her eyelids lay heavy, and she struggled to open them.

"You've come back. I've been waiting," Royce said as he held a cup of warm, sweet tea to her lips.

# SIXTEEN

~

*There is no chance, no destiny, no fate, that can circumvent or hinder or control the firm resolve of a determined soul.*

—Ella Wheeler Wilcox

"My head," Molly murmured, closed her eyes, and shifted into Royce's arms.

"You've got quite a bump there." He brushed her curls aside and ran his fingertips across the lump on her head. "You're still shivering too." He held her tighter.

The overcast, darkening sky brought foreboding disquiet; the distant hammering of a woodpecker kept time with the pounding pulse point in her forehead.

"Smoke? Fire in the stove? I smell smoke."

"There is no smoke or fire. You're dreaming."

She opened her eyes, lifted her head; and as if she looked through a velvet mist, the tree she'd sat by lost its leaves, its branches, changed shape and hardened into a boulder.

"The chestnut tree?" she asked.

"There's no tree here. You must have fallen against this rock."

He relaxed his hold, and she sat up. Looking around at the rubble, she remembered the spring. Her mouth felt dry, and she yearned for a drink of the fresh, cool water. Now only debris cluttered the ground around her. No limpid pool or trickling rill.

"Someone called me. I heard my name."

"I did. A few minutes ago when I came looking. I went to the cabin with . . . well, never mind. But I saw your gear. I knew you must be around somewhere."

"I heard music . . . my name . . . wanted to write. Can't go home." Tears welled up as she spoke. "Something wrong there. Something wrong . . ." Molly lay back, her head resting on Royce's rolled-up jacket. He must have placed it there while she slept or was unconscious, or in a trance. Time had passed, now late afternoon, and she shivered. What if he hadn't come? What if she'd woke after dark? Not knowing where she was? With no flashlight?

She sat up again, scanned the area, twisting to see behind her. A shadowy movement in the shrubs, or her imagination? The music stopped.

"Royce, I'm afraid."

"C'mon. I brought soup and bread. Can you walk? Or should I carry you?" That image made her smile. When was the last time she'd been carried anywhere? Standing, she cried out. Her whole body ached, and her head throbbed. Holding his hand, she trudged up the slope, her legs heavy. Startled, she jumped as something disturbed the bushes close to her.

"What's that?"

"What? The rustling noise? Just a squirrel or some other critter, I imagine."

Stopping to rest, they listened to a dove coo, as if in sympathy with her pain. "I heard a dove the first time. And music . . ."

"That's wind, not music. Or birds. Or even the creek."

"I know what I heard," she snapped.

"Sorry."

"So am I. It's just that . . . I know what I heard." *Do I have to defend myself with you too?*

He hugged her then, with an urgency that seemed too intense. She stepped back and tried to read his expression. He looked angry. With her?

Nearing the cabin, she saw a redheaded young woman sitting in a rocking chair. The same woman she'd snapped a picture of weeks ago. She couldn't mistake all those tousled red and gold curls. Grabbing Royce's arm, she stopped and said, "Look. Look at that woman and the chair. And see, there *is* smoke coming from the chimney. Smell it? I do."

"Calm down, Molly. The smoke you think you see is clouds blowing across the sky. There is no woman. But the chair is real. My surprise."

Molly ran the last few yards, stumbled, recovered her balance. At the porch she paused and watched the woman disappear. The empty chair rocked gently. But, damn it, she knew she smelled smoke. Rushing in to the wood stove, she grazed the surface with one finger and quickly pulled away, fearing a burn if she lingered. Nothing. She placed her whole hand on the surface. The stove was cold. When she turned around, Royce stood, shaking his head.

"Maybe you'd better stop coming here."

"I'm a little confused, is all," she said as she looked from him to the stove and back again. *Breathe. Take a deep breath. Okay. Breathe. Why did I quit bringing valerian root with me? The smoke, and the woman were just my imagination playing tricks. Something solid. I need something solid.* With her head held high, she said, "Come, I want to see that rocking chair."

Molly stared at Royce's gift. Aware of his eyes on her, she examined roughly crafted rungs, bold, and strong with peeling green paint.

"Like it?" he asked.

She ran her hands over the wide, flat arms, the cane back and seat. Her hands encountered static, warm and somehow alive, as if a ghost resided there. Sophia's ghost? A coolness replaced the warmth. The phantom had dissipated. A pleasant sensation of calm, of serenity, hung in the air, as if two worlds were melding and flowing together and apart. Molly wanted to curl up in this chair as if she were a baby in a mother's arms. "Where did you find it?" she whispered.

"Oh, this rocker's been with me for years. I guess we picked it up at a yard sale somewhere."

"This is exactly where I saw the other one. How did you know?" She gazed at him and, for a moment, his eyes twinkled, then the light dimmed.

He looked away. "Sit, I'll pour us some soup."

She eased herself onto the seat, rested her head, and closed her eyes. A cloud enshrouded her, evaporated, formed again.

"My god, Molly. For a moment you had a glow around you. There it is again. Like a halo covering your whole body." Then his face relaxed. "It's gone. A ray of sunlight must have cut through the clouds. Now *I'm* getting spooked. I'll get us something to eat."

Soon a mug of hot chicken soup rested in her hands; garlic and onion steam filled her nostrils. She admired the bright-colored chunks of carrots and peppers. "Nice job, sir."

"I can't take the credit." He smiled. "Ellen." His smile vanished, replaced by a frown.

"What's wrong?" she asked.

"Well . . . now's not a good time to bring this up."

"Is Ellen okay?"

"She's fine."

They ate in silence until Royce looked up and said, "Molly, I'm worried about you. This place is sucking you in. I wish you'd bring someone with you. Just in case."

"I wasn't planning to come back. But . . . well, this morning I went to the Sugar Creek Post Office. Opened a PO box and sent Amy the number. Then I encountered Diatrice who said Jake's calling me a wanton woman."

"Oh, c'mon. Would he say that? When?"

"In his Sunday sermon. He implied as much. Why do I feel like I've got to justify what I say to you today?"

"Sorry. Again."

"Anyway," she said with a heavy sigh, "I wasn't about to go home after hearing all that. So I came running here. Beth showed up a couple hours later. We had lunch."

"Does Beth know you're here a lot?"

"Yeah, she does, and I told her about Jake and me. But I haven't said much about the music and visions. I did ask her to come back. I think she will."

"She's going to be busy for a while." He set his cup down, inched nearer the rocking chair. Sitting at her feet, he reached for her hand. She heard a rasp as he exhaled deeply. "I've asked her to mind the bookstore for me." After a long pause, he added, "I'm flying to California tomorrow morning."

"Oh," she said, trying to hide her disappointment.

"I wouldn't go if it weren't important. I don't like leaving you now. Damn it."

"I'll be all right." She tried to keep her voice from quivering. "I do believe in a loving universe, angels, and all that. It's just that I can't go home. I lose my integrity there." *What am I going to do? I can't be in the same house with Jake. If I drop my guard in the least, I sink into his energy until I lose myself. I spiral down and have to struggle to the surface. This place, like a handhold, pulls me out of a quagmire. Then I come and hear music and cries for help. Strangers tell me strange tales about jewels.*

She closed her eyes, conjured up the brooch Granny had given Sophia. Small gemstones with a cross and emerald in the center reminded her of . . . She stared at the hand holding hers. His fingers were bare. She bent to see his other hand. The whole scene paraded past her. Birthstones, a little boy dying and a spell. *The spell.* Royce was no rogue, though. Even if his ring came from that piece of jewelry, he's kind. It would be a blessing for him.

"Molly. Molly."

She looked into Royce's startled, frightened eyes as he shook her.

"What?" she said.

"What happened just now?"

"I . . . uh, I was daydreaming, I guess." *Why don't I tell him? Why don't I ask about his ring? He's already worried enough.* "You said California? Why? Or shouldn't I ask?"

The sun set behind dark clouds and gloom descended. Rain fell and chilled the air. Molly pulled a jacket from her pack as Royce walked to the railing for his. Cat jumped up, meowed, and crawled to her lap.

With his back to her, Royce said, "It's . . . my ex-wife. She called last night. About an hour after I left you."

*He was talking with his ex at the same time I was lying in Jake's arms sharing . . .* She cringed, blushed at how open she'd been. Telling Jake about seeing Richard for counseling, about considering leaving their marriage. Forever this time. *Stop it, Molly. This isn't all about you.*

"Why you? Why California?" she asked.

Royce swung around and, even in the gloaming and from a distance, she could sense his ambivalence. "She's in trouble. Why me, you ask?" He turned again, clutched the railing, and faced the rain. "Cecilia and I were married a long time, Molly. I've got to help if I can."

Her stomach jerked as a niggling twist of mistrust and fear poked at her. What brought that on? It didn't sound like he was planning to reconcile. Besides, they had no commitment to one another. And just last night she . . . Her throat closed on bile that rose as she remembered how Jake had massaged her back, her legs, her . . . *Oh no.* She clutched her belly with one hand. The other, in a fist, flew to her mouth. Anger, like a demon, flared up screaming, *You little fool. Stop thinking about it,* she scolded herself as she walked to him and tried to reassure him.

"Of course, you should go."

The rain came harder with no sign of letup. He unclenched from the rail and, with hands cool on her face, kissed her forehead, her eyelids, the tip of her nose. And then with a groan, he wrapped his arms around her, kissed her mouth. She clung to him. He offered such comfort and strength. The thought of losing him . . .

"I have to do this. I have to go."

"Don't worry about me. I'll figure something out."

"Listen," he whispered, "I know an out-of-the-way motel. Clean and safe, and this time of year, rates are reasonable. Mostly used when leafers arrive in droves. Why don't you go there tonight?"

"But that's just one night. There's tomorrow and . . ."

"I leave in the morning. I'll give you a key. You can live at my house 'til I get back."

"Thank you. Maybe I'll take you up on that. I know I can't stay here. I won't. But something calls me. I don't know. I wonder if you're . . ." *That's for him to figure out. Don't distract him now.*

Wordlessly they gathered up what they'd take with them. Cat nested in the old quilt on the rocking chair.

"I wonder how he survives out here. Why an owl or something doesn't get him?" she said as she petted him. "Wild instinct, I guess. But then, with us, he's so tame—almost like a house cat. As if there were two of him." Cat's warm softness made her wish she could take him with her. What good company he'd be.

"Oh, the money." She pulled out an envelope with five twenty-dollar bills and slipped it under a rocker. *The old man said under the rocking chair. How had he known?*

"Do you really intend to do that? If it rains any harder, it'll get wet," Royce said.

*Aha. I wasn't a Girl Scout for nothing*. Digging in her tote, she pulled out a bag containing fresh socks. She'd had wet feet once too often. The envelope would stay dry in plastic until she came back and pocketed the money. Even if there were such things as ghosts, what would they want with money? Silly. She went inside and retrieved the dulcimer, tucked it among her belongings. "Now I've bought it, maybe I'll learn to play. While you're gone."

Royce stared at her as if he were miles and years away. They slugged through the rain, silently keeping counsel with their own thoughts. Her heart heavy, her body wet. The rutted old road was barely passable, and she prayed she wouldn't get stuck as she watched Royce's truck slide sideways.

. . .

"Where are you?" Jake hissed into the phone. Then, as if realizing how mean he sounded, he added, "Honey."

"Don't honey me, Jake. I called to tell you I won't be home tonight."

"What? Why? I thought after . . ."

"Well, you thought wrong."

"For God's sake, Molly. What now?"

"Just hearing your voice disgusts me. I know what you said from the pulpit. Your little act."

"I said you were sick. We even sang your favorite hymn. And that was before last night. Before our talk, our love—"

"Stop. I'll be home tomorrow to pack some clothes. Good night."

She looked around the motel room. Clean and quiet and nothing fancy. Standard room, right down to the faint musty smell. Good enough for one night. At least she could think here, and Jake didn't know where she was. Sometimes she wondered if he was basically evil. Was that possible? Or just her paranoia?

Molly took off her shoes, frowned at her dirty wet clothes and draped them over a chair. She crawled into bed, unkempt, feeling homeless and poor. A poor, sad Raggedy Ann.

Raggedy Ann—she scribbled. Is that where her journey led? No home, no bank account. Nothing. Nonsense, she wrote.

Having no sleeping potion, she knew only one way she'd get any rest—meditation. She closed her eyes and floated on a placid pool, welcoming warmth from an autumn sun, the water smooth like a blue liquid balm. Drifting slowly toward the lake's center, she relaxed and smiled at puffy white clouds that occasionally shadowed the golden sun. As she neared the center, she fell asleep and no longer drifted but was being pulled faster and faster. Water slapped at her, rolling over her head, leaving her gasping. Dark, angry clouds clashed and dispersed. United again. Thunder rumbled like booming timpani, and lightning crackled across the sky. A whirlpool sucked at her. She cried out, but no one came. Kicking and flailing, she tried to swim away. The current flipped her over, and a vortex pulled her straight down, head first into a cavern beneath raging waters. A pocket of dank air surrounded her, and she gulped. A mammoth-sized troll, smelling of decay and covered in rubies, sapphires, and diamonds appeared.

He held a huge gold filigreed cross and, over the water's roar, he growled, "Sell your soul."

She screamed no, and was flung to the surface. A calm lake. Geese honked overhead. All she could see for miles were geese, in formations ever changing. Honking, flapping their wings, they landed around her. First a few, then more and more until, with a threatening ruckus, they surrounded her. The honking stopped. A blonde witch, with piercing green eyes, cackled, "You silly goose." The giant gray birds took flight with the cackling witch among them. Molly was alone. A boat approached. Two little girls with orange moplike curls giggled and held up their dolls. Raggedy Anns, dressed in red-and-white gingham. She hauled herself into their boat and rowed toward shore. Following the dolls as they skipped up a hill, she slipped and sprawled on thorns and stones. Turned her ankle, scraped her knee, tore her cheek. Still, she struggled on, clawing at prickly shrubs while the girls floated above the ground. "Wait for me," she cried. They laughed and waved their pudgy hands for her to hurry. When she staggered onto a footbridge, the children disappeared, but a baby bawled as it crawled toward her from the other side. The trestle, no wider than a catwalk, was rotting and rickety, the canyon it traversed, deep. She scrambled on all fours and reached, yelling, "No, no." Inches from her grasp, the baby fell over the side just as a board gave way beneath her. With outstretched hands, she caught the child in midair, and they plunged through space. Falling, falling.

Molly bolted upright. Panting, sweating, trembling. A nightmare. Her mind reeled, her heart pounded. Eyes wide and darting she took in her surroundings. The light was on, her notebook crumpled in the sheets. With a shaky hand she recorded key words. The bridge. So familiar, had she dreamt of it before? What about the baby? Why couldn't she save the baby? She sobbed. Vowing not to fall asleep, she switched off the light and lay back on her pillow. "God," she prayed aloud. "Please help me."

When she woke, dust particles hovered on sunlight streaming in. She looked around, bewildered. Yesterday flooded her memory. Alone in a cheap motel, with a headache and a lump, yearning for coffee, her stomach growling. No room service here; she was lucky to have a telephone. Padding into the bathroom, a one-cup coffee maker and a packet to brew met her eye. Ah, God is good. When the cup filled she took it and crossed to the one window, peeled heavy orange curtains back a crack and peered out. Robins drank from puddles dotting an asphalt parking lot. A couple of cars were parked beside hers. A gas station and café and past that were woodlands. Through the trees she could make out a few ducks swimming on a pond, reminding her of that lovely romantic day she'd spent with Royce at a lake called Romance. Now he had gone to rescue his ex-wife, Cecilia. Such a pretty name. Would Molly ever meet her? Surely she wouldn't be coming back with Royce.

What time was it? Looking for her watch, she rummaged through her possessions, caressed the dulcimer, and closed her eyes for a moment. Pulling out a clean shirt, underwear, socks, she shook her head. She should have looked last night. Pleased to have fresh clothes, she traipsed back to the bathroom and stood under a hot shower until the water ran cool.

Clean, dressed, and invigorated, she piled her stuff into her muddy car and walked to the café. A bell tinkled as she entered; the scent of pine cleaner and freshly brewed coffee greeted her. Toward the rear of the small diner she slipped into a booth, so she faced the door. She wished she had driven to Sam's. Ellen could have distracted her with her prattle and platitudes. As she imagined clam chowder for breakfast, the waitress set a bowl of oatmeal in front of her, refilled her cup, and went back to reading a newspaper at the counter. Eating hot cereal sent her mind to childhood winters and from there to Amy and then Sophia. Little girls, all of us. How can this be? Looking up, she thought she saw the dulcimer man as he limped through the door.

"Hey," she called.

The waitress rushed over. "What's the matter?"

"Who was that man who just left?"

"You're the only customer here."

"Oh," Molly said, blinking back tears. Her hands shook. Was she losing her mind? She paid for her half-eaten breakfast and hurried out to her car.

Not wanting to get where she was going, she drove slowly with the window down. Air, fresh and cool after last night's rain, calmed her jitters. She glanced at her watch. Nine o'clock already. Good. Maybe Jake wouldn't be there.

No such luck. Not only was he there, he was outside. Waiting for her? No. A hose in his hand, he was about to wash his car. Again.

# SEVENTEEN

~

*What lies behind us and what lies before us*
*are tiny matters*
*compared to what lies within us.*
—Oliver Wendell Holmes

"I'm going stark raving mad. Nightmares about geese and cackling witches and falling off bridges and seeing ghosts. Hearing voices. I don't want to go to that cabin ever again, and yet I can't stay away. Thank God, Royce came and found me, but now he's gone too. My marriage has completely fallen apart. I'm scared. What do I do now?"

"Tell me, Molly," Richard said.

"I can't." No longer able to sit still, she jumped to her feet and paced the tiny office. Three steps from the couch to the fish tank. Three steps back. Faster. Huffing, she pushed up her sweatshirt sleeves and yanked at the collar of her blouse. She'd been so cold. Cold since her confrontation with Jake yesterday. Now she felt like she was strangling in her heavy clothes. Was this a hot flash? Maybe Jake was right. She should take some pills, hormones, or tranquilizers and everything would be just fine. Her blend of essential oils sure hadn't done much to calm her, and she'd run out of valerian root.

Richard rose from his desk, opened the small window behind her, and then laid his hands on her shoulders. She stopped, looked up at him, and bit her lip.

"Cry. It's okay. You aren't going crazy. Trust me."

Molly sank back on to the couch, pulled the teddy bear into her arms, and cried, hot tears seeping from under closed eyelids. No sobs arose, her tension didn't mount. Instead, she felt her shoulders loosen and her heartbeat subside.

Richard's voice, soft and soothing, encouraged her to take a deep, slow breath, hold it as he counted to four, then release the air through her mouth, again to the count of four. "Again," he said. "And again . . . Open your eyes. Look at me."

She obeyed like a well-behaved child. He sat on the corner of his desk, near enough to take her hand, though he didn't.

"Tell me how old you feel right now."

At first she shrugged and then said, "Teenager. Fifteen or so. Sometimes I feel as old as the world itself. When I'm there—on that porch or . . . or even just hearing the music. I'm compelled to be Sophia with all her pain. I feel it, as if doors in my heart that were closed tight are being torn open. No . . . as if the doors are made of glass, and each memory is a rock that shatters them. And Susie . . . Susie makes the hurt go away. Susie seems to sweep away the shards and fill my heart with mellow energy." As she spoke of Susie and felt that cocoon of love, she heard her voice become smooth, no longer cracking and quivering as it had when she'd first arrived. "But it's not real . . . is it?"

"You're real, Molly. You are," Richard said. "Tell me about Susie. Is this a playmate of Sophia's? Or an imaginary friend of hers?"

"I don't know. Both? Could she be both?"

Richard waited.

"No," Molly frowned. "Susie is more of a place. A quiet, safe place. I don't know." A sob caught in her throat, and her head ached as she searched for a description of something vague but important.

Again he waited, then asked, "Have you had psychic experiences before?"

When she looked at him blankly, he said, "Have you seen into the future? Or traveled to the past? Even vivid déjà vu episodes?"

"Nothing. Never." She shook her head. "I've never even thought about such things. At least not before moving here. Déjà vu—I've had that with the dulcimer music and for split seconds with Royce. A word he says. A look of concern. But then it passes."

Air bubbles gurgling in the aquarium filled the silence. Molly stared at a brilliant blue fish, mesmerized. Richard moved back to his chair and began to write.

"You've never done that with me before," she said with alarm. "You do think I'm crazy."

He smiled, put the pencil down. "Notes to myself. Some research I want to do. Your experience is fascinating. Over the years I've heard bits and pieces about the family you are encountering. If I can provide concrete facts, it might reassure you that you aren't going insane."

"Oh." Tears trickled down her cheeks.

"Past life phenomenon isn't my area of expertise. I'd like to check with a colleague. Someone more qualified. If that's all right with you?"

"I don't *want* anyone else. Don't pawn me off." *I sound like a child about to stomp my feet and throw a tantrum. But if I can't be honest here, where can I?*

"I'm not pawning you off. We'd all be in this together. And I think you'll like the person I have in mind."

She sank back, set Teddy Bear to one side, and reached for a tissue. After dabbing and blowing, she quieted. "Okay. What next?"

"As soon as I can make some arrangements, I'll call you. You said you're staying at Royce's?"

Molly nodded, picked up her purse, and rose to leave.

"Wait. Let's talk some more. Tell me about your childhood."

She hesitated, not sure where to begin. "Just an ordinary growing up. Typical of a small town in the late fifties. Winters we went sledding and skating, swimming and bike riding in summer. I had lots of friends. Nothing bad *ever* happened."

Richard raised his eyebrows. "Hmm . . . did you attend church?"

"Oh, yeah." Molly shrugged and shook her head. "But I survived."

"Interesting word. Survived?"

"Well, you know. Parochial school and a slaphappy nun or two. Confessions. Not eating meat on Friday when your friends were having hamburgers. That sort of thing."

"And priests? What were they like?"

"One was nice. I remember. But then they transferred him. The next one though. Distant and mean looking. And he drank. I remember smelling booze when he'd come into my classroom. It was like walking past a pool hall with the door open. He didn't last long either. But why are we wasting time on this?"

Richard sat behind his desk, his hands folded on the pad of paper. The clock ticked, fish swam, and air bubbled in the tank. Finally he said, "Right now you are in conflict with two ministers. Two religious authority figures. In this life, your husband. In Sophia's—"

"Oh I see," Molly interrupted. "Well, I quit going to church as soon as I moved away from home and haven't wanted to go near a Catholic one since. There were at least a half-dozen different priests at our church during my childhood. I'll think about that."

"Good. What about your family?"

"I'm a middle child. One older brother and one younger. We didn't have a lot of what other kids had, but Mom and Dad loved us. I felt secure and safe. I fought with my brothers, sure. But just normal family stuff."

"What about your dad? What was he like?"

"Oh. He worked two jobs so he wasn't around much . . . when I was little, he called me Susie. Susie! Why did he call me Susie?"

"A pet name, but . . ." He picked up his pencil, jotted a few words. "So he was affectionate with you? You weren't afraid of him?"

"Oh, I was afraid. Afraid I'd make a mistake. Afraid he'd scowl at me. Sometimes just afraid. Afraid of the dark for years. Why? Why was I so afraid when we were such a happy little family?"

"And you were how old when you married?"

"Only eighteen. But I'd graduated from high school. I was in love . . . Where are you going with this? What are you implying?"

"I'm trying to get an understanding of the people and events that shaped who you are today. You describe your childhood as idyllic, but most childhoods are not. Think about your relationships as you were growing up. With your father, your brothers, those priests, anybody in authority. That's your homework until next time."

"All right . . . I guess."

He walked with her downstairs and to her car. Before she turned the key, he reached through the open window and patted her hand.

When she looked up, he gave her a reassuring nod and said, "Call me. Anytime."

Emotionally exhausted, Molly sat at the wheel and stared at nothing. Starting the old Chevy, she drove slowly down the street. Wishing she had her journal, she let her car drift to the curb in front of a drugstore. Roaming the aisles, she came across herbals and picked up a bottle of kava kava, then selected a spiral notebook. There was something else, some other reason to be in this store, but she couldn't remember, so she paid for her items and left. On the sidewalk, she squinted into the bright sun. Clouds had dissipated, and heat replaced morning's damp coolness. Sam's was just a few stores away, and she thought of Ellen. Oh, to be distracted for a moment by Ellen's banter. Then she'd write about her childhood.

"Speak of the devil! I've been thinking about you," Ellen greeted her. "Take a load off. Java?"

Molly smiled, nodded and settled into a booth. Ellen came with the coffee—two cups. She slid in across from her, leaned forward, and said, "We need to talk."

A roar from the street made them both jump up to look outside. At least thirty bikers, wearing leather jackets and helmets, pulled up to the curb.

"Oops-a-daisy," Ellen sang. "It never rains, but it pours. So much for Sam's day off." Frowning at Molly, she hustled to the back.

Molly watched as the sleepy little café filled with good-humored noise and jostling. Men and women—sweaty, disheveled, and obviously hungry—filled the booths. Ellen scurried around with water and menus. Enthusiastic energy surrounded Molly, and she set her journal aside. Who could think with such commotion? She'd sip her coffee and watch the show.

When she got up to leave, Ellen appeared at her shoulder and whispered, "No rest for the weary. All hell's broke loose. I'll call ya. Royce's, right?" She bustled off, coffee carafe in hand.

*How many people know I've left Jake? I told Richard, and I suppose Royce told Ellen. But why? If Diatrice finds out where I'm staying, then Jake will know. Geez, small town. No wonder I was so eager to get married and leave home.*

Outside, Molly strolled along the empty sidewalk toward the bookstore. A dog ran across the quiet street, and she thought of her first excursion here. With school now in session, no teenagers scuffled but a whiff of rancid air met her as she passed the tavern with its door propped open. The priest from her childhood came to mind. She felt threatened and frightened as if he stood in front of her. Shaking her head, she hurried on and exhaled deeply when she entered the cool dim recesses of the bookstore.

Grinning, she called, "Beth, hi."

Beth, with hoop earrings bobbing, appeared from beneath the counter, dusted off her hands and rolled her eyes. She started to point toward an aisle as if in warning when a customer rounded the corner. Molly's smile faded when Diatrice, dressed in a too-snug white linen pantsuit, met her gaze. Diatrice stood tall, raised her chin, and made sniffing noises as if she'd just smelled something offensive and then strutted forward as only a pious matron could.

"Molly," she sneered before turning to Beth. "I believe I'll check the library for that book. And remember, dear, 1Tim. 6:6, 'There is great gain in godliness with *contentment*.'" With her nose in the air she sidestepped Molly and flounced out the door, leaving a trail of insipid perfume. "You're certainly looking pleased with . . ." she muttered before the door graciously closed, cutting off her uppity tone.

"Whew. I wish I'd been a little later," Molly said.

"Shucks. She's been here fer hours. Makin' comments like that last one and sich. Fishin', seems t'me. I'm right glad t'see her go."

"Was she looking for Royce?"

"No. I reckon she knew he'd left."

"Well, I was just on my way home and thought I'd stop by. See how you're doing."

"Oh, fine. Aside from her the day's been right quiet. So yer stayin' at Royce's?"

"You know? Does Diatrice? Because if she does, Jake and the whole damn county will know."

"Diatrice knows somethin' is goin' on, but not what. It's drivin' her crazy."

"Good."

A customer came in, so Molly waved and left.

After supper, she called Amy and frowned when a machine asked her to leave a message. Destined to be alone with her thoughts, she set out to explore Royce's pond and the grove of trees surrounding it. As the setting sun took its warmth with it, she buttoned up her sweater, jammed her hands in the pockets of her slacks. Evening sounds—the hoot of an owl, a nightingale's trill—relieved her disquiet. If anything could renew her sense of well-being, the natural world would.

Leaves of the yellow birch had begun changing color. Autumn was in the air, and soon mountainsides would relinquish their green cover to undulating orange, brown, yellow, red. As if God had strewn giant gumdrops over the land.

Water splashed, and Molly glanced at the pond in time to meet the masked eyes of a large raccoon before it waddled into the shrubs. Beth had once said something about raccoons. Masks. A sign that someone may be pretending or even lying about who they are. Well, Jake, of course. But what about Royce? She'd been tempted to poke through his desk drawers, but had drawn back, ashamed that she'd even considered violating his privacy. She knew all too well how that felt.

Grateful for the outdoors and solitude, she relished the stillness. She hadn't missed Jake at all. Royce, though, was a different matter. Perhaps because these were his surroundings, she found herself wondering what he was doing and when he'd be home. Where would she go then? Back to Jake, she supposed. No. Not back to Jake; she'd go home, but not *to* him. The very idea made her ill, and she focused on wildflowers blooming along the way. She bent to examine a tall plant resembling a snapdragon, the blossoms looking more like little pink turtle heads. The name escaped her. Black-eyed Susan she recognized and, of course, purple asters. At first she couldn't place why that made her smile. Purple asters or purple assers as Sophia had called them a long time ago. Or just a few weeks ago. Time—its passing, its relationship to now—was becoming more and more muddled. *Stay in this moment,* she reminded herself. The sky had darkened, and she turned toward home. Home? No. Yes, home for the time being anyway.

She'd just pulled a flower book from a shelf when the phone jangled and made her jump.

"You busy?" Ellen asked and snapped her gum. "Can I come by?"

"Sure. When?"

"I'm on my way. Jest a couple minutes."

"Great. See you soon." Molly hung up, surprised at Ellen's serious tone and no clichés. She wondered why Ellen would make a trip over. *Did Royce ask her to check on me? I hope not.*

The teakettle began to whistle as the doorbell rang.

"That was quick," Molly said, holding the door wide. "I'm making tea."

"Just what the doctor ordered. Lemme get rid of this gum."

*Oh good,* Molly thought as she followed Ellen into the kitchen.

They brought their tea to the living room and sat on the couch by the darkened window.

"Some music?" Molly asked. "I finally figured out these knobs and buttons. Why can't they make them all the same?"

"No music. Something's stuck in my craw. I'm hoping you can shine a light on it. So's I can put it to rest."

"I can't imagine me having anything to offer . . . unless . . . is it about me and Jake?"

"Yeah. No. Maybe." They both chuckled at that as Ellen rummaged in her purse and retrieved a pack of gum. "Sorry. I can't talk without this . . . gets the juices flowing, I guess."

She unwrapped not one, but two sticks. Molly sipped her tea and waited as Ellen chomped the wad down to manageable size. *What's next*? she wondered.

"I don't know where to start. Let me just say I'm mighty ticked at Royce running to Cecilia's beck and call. He's such a nice guy but a real pushover for a damsel in distress. No offense. I know you got your troubles. But she knows how to play the game. You mark my words, she'll be coming back with him. And he'll be trailing after her like a kitten following a leaky cow."

Molly couldn't keep a straight face at this image and burst out laughing. "C'mon Ellen. That's pathetic. I can't imagine Royce . . . I'm sorry, but isn't he just going there to help her out of some jam?"

"Yeah, sure. Listen, Sam and I spent lots of Saturday nights with those two. Played card games, brought in New Years. Trust me, she's a flirt and a spitfire. Well, you'll see for yourself."

"It's really none of my business," Molly protested while thinking, *I do not need one more complication. If Cecilia does come back, though, that should keep Royce at a safe distance sexually. Will I lose his companionship too? Please, no.*

"Oh, she'll be your business. She'll be everybody's business. Jest like when she was all gaga-eyed over that preacher she run off with. Well, the shit hit the fan. Pardon my French. The whole church was up in arms. And Diatrice took the brunt of it. Since she hired him in the first place. She blamed Royce for not keeping his wife in line. And I could go on and on."

"Okay. I see what you're saying. That isn't what you came over for though. Is it?" Molly said, wanting to change the subject.

"No. It's not. Guess it's time to cut to the chase here. I can never seem to let sleeping dogs lie. A few days back . . . right before Royce heard Cecilia purr again. Well, there's this guy comes in for lunch and wants to shoot the breeze. I smelled a rat . . ."

"Oh, please." Molly couldn't hide her exasperation. "What are you trying to say?"

Ellen sat up straighter, crossed her legs, and chewed her gum. Finally she said, "Here's the thing. This stranger says he's from Tucson. That he knows you and Jake from there. I asked if he went to your church, and he glared at me. So I says, 'Don't get so hot under the collar. So y'don't like church, I hear ya.' And then . . ."

"More tea?" Molly asked, jumping up and racing into the kitchen to turn on the kettle. Who was Ellen talking about, and where was this roundabout story going? It was clear she wouldn't be rushed. Yet Molly wondered how long she could sit still before taking Ellen by the shoulders and shaking her 'til both gum and facts fell out.

When the kettle whistled, she filled the tea pot, added more tea, and returned to the living room. Ellen, browsing bookshelves, looked at her with a quizzical expression.

"Do you know who I'm talking about?"

Molly shook her head, and Ellen went on to describe a physical appearance so mundane it could have been a hundred different people.

"What did he say that has you so bothered, Ellen?"

"Just that when he got up to leave he said, 'Keep your eyes open and your shades closed.' Which didn't make much sense to me. And then Royce told me what kind of car Jake drives, and I started puttin' pieces together. Are you all right? You look white as a ghost."

# EIGHTEEN

~

*Not knowing when the dawn will come I open every door.*
—Emily Dickinson

Sweat burned her eyes; her mouth felt parched. Yet Molly pursued her quest, one step, one thorny reach at a time. The sun blazed. Humid air dampened her long-sleeved shirt and clung to jeans tucked into hiking boots. September wasn't supposed to be this hot. She had hiked upstream, found a large expanse of ripe blackberries and now filled her bowl while popping almost as many berries into her mouth. Her fingers were stained purple, and, she imagined, her lips were too.

Focusing on each berry and each thorn, she still felt the sting and pull as barbs tore at her shirt and drew blood from her hands. Each nettle a reminder of hurts and wrongs in her marriage. The altercation she'd had with Jake when she'd packed clothes to move out was still fresh in her mind and made her fume. He'd faced her with a cold black-eyed stare when he'd said suicide. Pleading, sulking, threatening. Begging for another chance. She'd finally stormed out. He no longer controlled her emotions, or did he? Menacing words echoed in her head, *I've got a gun now, Molly!* Could she cope with her guilt if his suicide threats were more than manipulation? All her power and energy had gone into creating her dream of a happy marriage, but Richard was right—she had needed Jake to be someone he was incapable of being. Well, she couldn't live like this anymore. Soon Royce would return and then what?

Molly hadn't needed the details of Ellen's observations. Jake's washing his muddy car and the morning he suddenly shaved off his beard were clues she'd managed to brush aside. Would the man from Tucson go away? Doubtful. Had he come specifically looking for Jake? Most likely. No wonder Royce had grown solemn when she'd mentioned Ellen. So they had talked, and he knew or suspected. What next?

Maybe she should just pack and leave. What held her here? Money, for one thing. Twenty years as a minister's wife was hardly a marketable skill. Where could she go, anyway? Amy and North Dakota tempted her, but she wouldn't be that kind of mother—in the way and a bother. Besides, what about Sophia? This whole mess? And what about Royce?

Thankful for the protection of her large straw hat, she gazed hungrily at the sky, searching for a cloud to alleviate the intense sunlight. Heat exhausted her, and she longed for the cool dimness near the spring. The clean, newly freshened pool remained a puzzle. Had she been transported to another time, or was someone kindly bestowing small comforts? Who? When?

When she'd arrived at noon today, she'd been surprised to see that the one-hundred dollars she'd left under the rocker was gone. Dulcimer man must be real and not a ghost or her imagination. Scrawled on a scrap of the envelope—another puzzle—"No rogue finds rest. Kindness be blest."

A crow, or possibly a raven, flew over. So black he appeared metallic midnight blue, he cawed and cawed, squawking at her, jangling her nerves. Blue jays quarreled in the shrubs. Oh, that a dove would coo instead. Oh, if she could hide in happy as she had before moving to Sweet Hollow.

With her container full of blackberries, she leaned against a massive tree, at least fifteen feet around, whose branches spread wide and provided a comforting canopy. Catching her breath, she took a long swig of water and then poured some over her hands, trying to clean her sticky fingers. She splashed a few drops of water on her face and, removing her hat, wiped her brow and nape with a kerchief. When she slumped in the shade of the large leafy tree,

Cat appeared and crept onto her lap. For long moments she petted, and he purred. *A familiar tree,* she thought. *An ancient chestnut?* A few nuts lay on the ground, and she rubbed at one's furry coating. *Odd. Were these chestnuts? Beth would know.*

Molly closed her eyes and sensed the tree's vibrations. From deep beneath the surface, through its roots and then its core, up to the branches energy hummed. A surge of hope sprang in her. She had friends here, people to help her. Richard, Ellen, Beth, and, oh, please, Royce.

She flinched when Cat shot from her lap and growled. He ran up the trail, stopped, hunched down, poised to attack. Had he seen a bird within his reach? Molly stood and followed. Deeper in the forest, the path narrowed; ferns and thistles encroached. Cat darted ahead, paused, meowed, and ran again. He disappeared when she drew near a high footbridge. Her nightmare about falling and catching a baby flashed before her. Molly cringed, watching each step, as she ventured onto the bridge. Careful, expecting a rotting board to give way beneath her at any moment. Halfway across, she stopped abruptly. A gaping hole where a slat should be made her dizzy.

Daylight blurred as if a thin curtain had been pulled across the sky. Goose bumps rose on her arms and she shivered. The hot sun had disappeared. A zephyr increased in strength until gusts whistled through tree branches as leaves faded away and new bud swellings appeared. Music filled the air as if the trees were hung with a myriad of wind chimes. Ghostly dulcimer music. Molly succumbed to familiar sensations of living in another time as someone else.

Sophia stands on planks rickety beneath her feet and gazes over the edge and far down to a stream below. The creek, now a raging river fed by melting snow and rainstorms, is a torrent of power, crashing over boulders and slamming against its banks. A cold early-spring squall cuts through her shawl, wrapped tight around her shoulders, whips strands of rusty-colored curls across her face. Stinging, hot energy pierces her heart as muddy, brown waters pound the bridge's foundation. Driven by the relentless gale, her long skirts of gray calico twist tight around her legs and high-top shoes. Prickly pulses run up her spine. The creek had been frozen over when she left. *Where have I been? Why have I come back to this place?* Tears stream down her cheeks. She yearns to drop, fall forward into the rushing waters. A groan strangles in her throat as she relives the horror . . .

. . .

Sophia had gone looking, calling, listening. And then she'd heard the soft mewing. Biscuit had mated, and when nights were long and snow still blew in furious blasts, she'd given birth in a corner of the shed. Four little kittens squirmed under the white fur of Biscuit's belly. Delighted, Sophia ran and whispered in Granny's ear. Together they brought clean rags, water, and food. They attended to the mama cat as she, in turn, tended her litter. When Papa, furious about the kittens, grabbed three and tossed them in the thicket for scavengers Sophia had wept until her breath gave way, and she sagged to the floor of the shed, her skirts covering Biscuit and the lone kitten Papa hadn't seen. Susie came then and lay with her, dreamed with her as she sobbed. Evening was settling, soft and quiet like new-fallen snow when she crept along with one wee kitten in her arms . . .

Now, hearing violent voices, Sophia runs off the wobbly wooden span and cowers behind a tree.

"Look whatcha done t' yer sister. Yer own kin," a man hollers.

"I ain't done nothin'."

"Why she stare like that, huh? She's crazy as a loon."

"Don' do it," Joe yells, as Preacher Man and her pa, drunk and hateful, throw something from the bridge. A bundle.

"Oh no!" she cries.

"Soph! Soph, wake up," Joe pleads, shaking her. "See, Soph, I'm right here."

. . .

With a slam Molly is thrust back into her own skin. Shaken to alertness, she says, "Oh, Royce. You've come back."

No one was there. Who shook her? Joe? The scene was gone, but she felt another life being played out around her as if a translucent veil had dropped. Swirling burnt-orange strands caressed her cheek and disappeared. Cat yowled. As hard as she focused, nothing would raise the curtain. Anxiety and tension, anger and pain permeated the air, seeped into her, infused her with a deep desire to help Sophia, to help Joe, to stop the mayhem she sensed but could not see. "Why?" she cried aloud. *If I can't help, then why have I been drawn to all this horror?* "What can I do now?" she wailed as she crouched in the shrubbery.

"Ask and listen, Molly" came a soothing male voice. *Dulcimer Man?*

Lifting her head, her eyes darted, searching. A shadow slid behind the veil. Wind and music ceased. Paralyzed, she remained hunched there. A call from a distance reached her consciousness, "Get to shelter, now."

She felt stiff and old as she unfolded, stood erect, and looked about. In this thick forest, darkness would quickly overtake evening dusk. Shelter was far beyond where she'd picked berries and where her pack and flashlight lay. Not accustomed to night in the wild, alone, her heart raced at every noise. Critters scurried about, sending shots of panic through her. The path in front of her ended in a mass of shrubs and berry brambles. When she turned around, two trails opened to her, and she didn't know which would lead her back. "Don't panic," she told herself just as a thrashing in the scrub oak shocked her. Three deer, barely discernable in the gloom, leaped across a clearing. She exhaled. Cat meowed at her feet and then ran on. Molly followed.

By the time she reached the cottage, her lantern beam had dimmed and night had fallen. With no guiding light, she didn't dare attempt the trek to her car. She raced up to the loft and rummaged in a box, dumping out its contents, searching for batteries she was certain she'd brought along. Candles and matches tumbled helter-skelter. Her hands shook as she struck a match and lit a few small candles. The glow and flicker allayed her fears to a degree. Back down the ladder she scurried to retrieve the oil lamp that graced her old walnut desk. Climbing the steps with lamp in hand was awkward and slow. But worth her effort when she lit the wick. A steadier light appeared, and she blew out the candles.

Sitting on the floor, clutching a pillow, she drank from her water bottle and stared at the flame. What had happened to Joe? Where was Sophia that Molly had lost contact? Was that a good thing? No. Something awful was happening. She wished she'd called someone or at least left a note before coming here alone. Her pack lay close, and she pulled out her cell phone. No signal, of course.

*What am I afraid of?* She wrote in her journal. *Bears?* A small hysterical giggle burst from her at the image of a bear climbing to the loft. And what would bring one here? She had no food. But what about cougars? Cat wouldn't have lived this long if cougars roamed these hills, would he? In an effort to calm her fright, she started a gratitude list. Thankful for her pepper spray, the lamp, and oil, she prayed for a loving universe. Remembering the dulcimer, she fetched it, placed it on the pillow in her lap, and plucked the strings as she quavered:

> O, they tell me of a home far beyond the skies,
> O, they tell me of a home far away;
> O, they tell me of a home where no storm clouds rise,
> O, they tell me of an unclouded day . . .

Instead of comforting her, the music and lullaby brought back with a rush the trauma she sensed Sophia endured.

"Ask," the old codger had said. So, while lamplight flickered, she asked what she should do and who had the help she needed. Royce and his loving arms were her last thought before she slipped into a dreamworld.

. . .

Scented candles stood cupped in crumpled foil. A book of matches ready. A man, whose face she couldn't see, filled an air mattress, spread a soft blanket.

The sloped ceiling forced them to move bent over. Without a word, the masked stranger lit wicks while she smoothed pillows and a down-filled comforter to further cushion them. By candlelight they sat and removed their boots and shirts.

A delicate, sweet aroma came to her and she said, "Hmm . . . you chose jasmine. Passion is part of its magic."

He chuckled but said nothing.

"Ah, perhaps the gods are with us," she mused.

When she lay and unfastened her jeans, the unknown swain knelt and tugged them as she wriggled free. He reached, slipped his fingers beneath the elastic of her panties and slid them down her legs. He tickled her toes with his tongue. His hands, as light as satin ribbons, moved from her ankles to her knees and slid across her hips as he leaned and kissed her belly. Warm, strong hands found their way to her inner thighs and traveled slowly down to her feet once more.

Lying close in the nest they had created, her lover brushed wanton curls from her face, cupped her chin, and kissed her until she moaned. As if he were Don Juan, his lips moved over her skin to a pulse point, the hollow of her throat, down to her breast while he caressed her with a silken touch. Molly's fingers fastened in his thick hair and pushed his head until the force of his mouth on her breast made her cry out.

"I . . . I. Please, now," she implored.

"Ssh," he whispered and placed his hand to her lips. She opened her mouth and nipped at a fingertip.

She almost wept as her passion subsided, and she feared the moment gone. But no, with one touch, one kiss, she was aroused again. Again she pleaded.

Again he shifted and blew in her ear.

"Daphne, Daphne, Daphne," whispered the wind as tree branches brushed the roof.

Jasmine fragrance filled the air, and candlelight danced over his body while his face remained in shadow. Intoxicated, she laughed, low and throaty. She straddled him, and with one hand holding his arms over his head in a pretense of dominance, she nudged his face out of the shadows. Still masked, he remained a mystery. She licked his nipples until he squirmed. Having cooled his ardor, she rekindled it by burying her face in his taut, flat abdomen, then fluttering her kisses where they'd have the most power. As light as butterfly wings, becoming more intense until she applied as much pressure as she dared. He groaned, rolled over her, and the two became one.

Two wings of one sleek snow-white swan skimming the waves of a lake so vast no shore was in sight. Faster and faster until airborne. They soared. Higher and higher until the swan dropped away, and one soul touched the stars and swung from the moon. Venus smiled upon them and offered a hummingbird feather to float them gently. Descending until they touched down in a field of daisies. And they slept. Only to awaken and skyrocket through the night, a comet shooting into space.

"Who are you?" Molly moaned.

He said nothing.

Running her hand over his chest, across his arm, her fingers traced the small jagged scar at his elbow, and she cried out, "Oh, Royce."

"What have we done?" she sobbed, waking herself up.

Shock and embarrassment overcame her fears as she recalled the dream. In her journal, barely legible, were the words, "I am not your knight in shining armor."

*I don't dare sleep anymore.* One vivid dream after another, night after night. What was causing this? Valerian root? Stress? *I wonder if I can take something so I don't dream?* Richard might know, and she'd check her herbal books if she ever went back home. She scribbled as much detail as she dared. She'd had erotic dreams in the past, but never with someone she knew. Never so beautifully choreographed. Never leading to such confusion, embarrassment and, she had to admit, disappointment.

Molly stirred, shifted on to one of the pillows. Her bones ached where they met the hard floor. "At least the air mattress could have been real," she grumbled. The lamplight died. Only pale moonlight shone on her surroundings.

Coyotes screamed as if they were at the doorway. Something shrieked. She held her breath and pulled a blanket over her head as noises, too loud for mice, came from the corner. Cat meowed and landed with a thump on her hip. She cried, begged for daylight, and slept again.

. . .

"Dear God, I'm just a little girl," Molly whispered as she dropped a dime—her allowance for one whole week—into the slot and lit a votive candle. She peeked around, saw no one close, and so lit another and another with no coins for the slots. "God, help me. Please."

A strong, heavy hand clutched her shoulder, and she gasped.

"Molly Bell. How many candles do you think one coin will light? God sees what you're doing. He won't answer your prayers," the priest spat. A snake slithered over the wrought iron between the red glass of the votive candles and hissed, "God won't answer your prayers, won't answer your prayers, your prayers."

With her face cast down, she looked up, and tears filled her eyes as she tried to squirm from beneath his tight grip. "Go and sin no more," he snarled, releasing her as someone approached.

Molly darted down a long aisle, hiding her face from old people kneeling in the last pews. With all her strength she pushed open the big door and ran down the stone steps into blackness. Angels and chariots sparkled in the night air. Bright stars—green, white, and red—floated around a golden cross that curled like lace on her mother's apron. In her mind she saw the priest put out the candles she had lit. Sin no more, sin no more, sin no more. The words echoed and she yelled, "Shut up! Shut up! Shut up!"

. . .

Her eyes flew open to darkness. The moon had set. She fumbled for her notebook, and with no light to guide her, she wrote the harsh words that remained with her—won't answer prayers, sin no more.

When she woke again, daylight filtered through the dirty window. A night alone in the forest had left her weary and with aching muscles, but she'd survived. "We did it," she said as Cat fled her grip. A male voice carried up to her. At first indistinguishable. Molly crawled to the window, wiped away cobwebs with her bare hand, and peered out.

# NINETEEN

~

*Like billowing clouds,*
*like the incessant gurgle of the brook,*
*the longing of the soul can never be stilled.*
—Meditations with Hildegard of Bingen

Molly stared as a big burly man ground out a cigarette with his boot. Muscles bulged beneath a tight T-shirt, and she glimpsed a tattoo on his forearm, the image blurred. A brawny black dog ran toward him from the woods. Not being much of a dog lover, she wasn't sure, but it reminded her of a rottweiler or something she'd seen in movies, snarling and pacing in front of a gate. Mean, vicious, huge. The man looked impatiently this way and that. As he glanced upward, she slid to one side, a hand over her mouth. Could this be the owner? Would she be arrested for trespassing? Excuses ran through her mind. *No. If I must, I'll tell the truth and pay the consequences. There's been enough lying in my life.* Without exhaling she peeked out.

"Get a move on, woman. I gotta get the griddle going. You know that," the he-man bellowed as a woman scurried from behind the trees, zipping up her jeans. Molly ignored her own need for a similar visit.

"Just hold your horses, Sam. Let's at least go inside."

As she recognized Ellen standing with hands on hips, chewing gum, Molly released her breath in a long slow exhale. She tapped on the window, waved when they looked up, and then grabbed her boots and climbed down from the loft. Daylight, safety, and someone she knew.

Ellen hugged her, introduced Sam, who was as much a typical short-order cook as Ellen was a waitress.

"Good to meetcha," he said, shaking her hand.

"And this is Fifi." The frightening dog of moments ago now sat, docile at Sam's feet. *He certainly isn't what he seemed to be,* Molly thought as, with fingertips only, she patted the dog's head. *How comforting it would have been if a Fifi had kept watch last night.*

"I gotta get," Sam said. "It's already six and the reg'lars will be clamoring for their coffee and bacon. You comin'?"

"Can you stay a little longer?" Molly asked Ellen. "I'll give you a ride in."

When Ellen nodded, Sam grunted, lit another cigarette, and clumped away. With his bowed legs, Molly couldn't decide if his stride portrayed arrogance or simply self-confidence. His hound bounded after him.

"Bye, hon," Ellen called, then whispered, "A man and his dog. Can't help but love 'em." She turned to Molly. "Were you here all night? Alone? Would of scared the bejesus outta me."

"Don't think I wasn't scared. I was picking blackberries way back in the forest when daylight disappeared so fast I was stuck. Why are you here? Not that I'm not glad."

"Well, when I rang Royce's phone off the hook and you didn't answer, I got antsy. I even called Jake. Who, by the way, is madder than a wet hen." Ellen plopped down on the edge of the stoop with a huff. "Gotta take a load off whenever I can," she muttered. "I paced on Royce's patio til midnight. At the crack of dawn I called Beth. Got her out of bed. She said maybe you were up here. This place gives me the willies, so I coaxed Sam into coming with me."

"It's nice of you to come find me. But why? Is there something I should know?"

Ellen unwrapped another stick of gum and scuffed the dirt with her shoe. She looked around, crossed her arms as if cold, and finally said, "Hey, I brought java. Want some?"

"Boy do I. Did you bring food too?"

"Oops. Forgot. I left the donuts in the car. Well, that'll give Sam somethin' to do while he drives."

"I've got a cooler in the shed. But, damn it, I bet the ice has melted," Molly said as they walked to the storage building.

"Geez, you been in this creepy place?"

"It's not so bad during the day. There's a window in the back wall." When she yanked open the crooked door, Ellen screamed as fluttering, flapping wings whizzed by her face. A bird, trapped and frantic, had shot out at the first chance for freedom. What if she had gone poking around after dark last night? She would have screamed too or had a heart attack. The bird long gone, Ellen and Molly looked at each other and laughed.

When she opened the icebox, Molly shook her head. A solid block of ice sat amidst her fruit, bowls of salad, and bread.

"Thought you said . . ."

"I did. I don't know what's going on." *I should be used to this by now. Has to be the dulcimer man. Who else?*

"So this place *is* haunted. Just like they say," Ellen whispered.

"Who says? No, wait. Before we start on haunted houses, I'm hungry as a bear and want some of that coffee too."

Together they lugged the ice chest up the slope to the porch. With steaming coffee and buttered bread in hand, they settled down to talk.

"About the other night," Molly said. "The thing about Jake. I'm sorry I hurried you out of the house . . . it's just that . . . what you said. I'm embarrassed."

"Listen, hon. Nobody's blamin' you. You maybe got yourself a wolf in sheep's clothing is all. Not your fault."

"Yes, but . . ."

"Somebody's bound to let the cat out of the bag and I figured you'd be better off knowing first. Old Diatrice is gonna be knocked off her high horse too. One more of her preacher picks causing scandal. Mark my words, she'll get her bloomers in a bunch over this."

At mention of Diatrice, Molly cringed. *I bet Diatrice knows I'm seeing Richard. I bet Jake has told her and is sweet-talking her now. Conning his way into people's good graces. Using them.*

"Hey! Hon! You okay?"

Molly blinked, jerked her hand, and splashed hot coffee over her wrist. Her bread lay on the floor, buttered side down, of course. She changed the subject.

"About this place being haunted?"

"Yeah," Ellen said. Use'ta be a nice couple who'd spend a month or so every summer. One year . . . maybe twenty years ago . . . yeah, Sam and me were still all lovey-dovey newlyweds . . . him just back from the navy and all . . ." Ellen sipped her coffee with a dreamy look on her face, her jaws idle for the moment.

Sparrows flitted among leathery leaves of shrub rhododendrons. A spider crawled across the floor. Time slowed, head clamor ceased as Molly, with her eyes, followed the spider until it went over the edge. When she figured Ellen had reminisced enough, she coughed to get her attention, then reached for orange slices on top of the cooler.

"Where was I? . . . Oh yeah. That couple who owned this place. They just packed up one night and never came back. Christmas, the year after they hightailed out of here, we got a card with a note saying there were ghosts from here to hell and back. Even on this porch. Somethin' about a teenage girl in a rocking chair that wasn't there . . . like the one you're sitting in. And an old man. Sam dragged me up here kicking and screaming, for a look-see. I ain't been back since."

"No wonder you brought him and your dog this morning. Thanks again for coming. Did you ever see any ghosts? Has anybody else?"

"I didn't. But I've sure heard lots of talk since. Especially in the spring about that old footbridge. People walk their dogs, and them dogs won't go near that crossing or the clearing next to it. They whine and howl, hackles up."

Were those dogs picking up the scent of evil and trauma that Molly had sensed the day before? How she had wanted to cross over and couldn't. Even in daylight, with a friend, her heart raced and her head felt like it was in a vice.

"Who owns this property now?" she asked, trying to calm herself.

"Beats me. There was talk of them giving the deed to some charity, but I guess there was a glitch with that. Someone could get the whole caboodle for a song."

"The house seems in pretty good shape for sitting empty all these years."

"That couple kept a caretaker for a long time. Pete's still around. Maybe he still tends to things."

"Pete?"

A rustling of leaves made them both jump.

"Hi. I reckoned I'd find you here," Beth said as she came around the corner.

"You too? I'm feeling pretty popular this morning."

"Well. Ellen here rang up afore dawn. Then Jake. Then Royce. All lookin' fer you. I figured I'd best start lookin' too."

Molly felt heat rise from her toes to her forehead. Royce. Her erotic dream flooded her mind, threatened to ooze from her very pores, and she fought the temptation to blurt it out. Instead, she jumped up and walked to the railing, keeping her back to them, hoping her blush would subside before either of them noticed.

Cat came sniffing at the tub of butter and started licking, his little tongue flying over and over it until Beth snatched the butter away. "Reckon that's not good fer you, kitty."

"A black-and-white cat! Yours?" Ellen had pulled her arms and legs into herself as if afraid.

"He's not mine, but he's attached himself to me." *That's an understatement.* "What's the matter? He's harmless."

"There's a cat like that in the haunting story, is all."

Beth leaned down and began petting Cat. "Which haints you tellin' her 'bout?"

"Good grief! How many are there?" Molly looked from one to the other. Then moved back to the rocking chair, and with her elbows on her knees, she placed her palms on the sides of her face as if holding herself together. This was all too much, and she wanted solitude to sort out all this new information.

"I'm talking about the people who got scared out of their wits by a ghost girl crying right here. And the cat. Same coloring as this one, hissing and clawing at anyone coming near that girl," Ellen said.

"Right. That's the latest tale. With dulcimer music. Not much talk 'bout that lately."

"Tell me more about this Pete. You know him?" Molly asked.

"I guess, sort of," Ellen answered, still eyeing Cat. "Pete's a strange one. Comes in once in a while. Spooks me a little cuz I think he reads my mind. Always askin' about new folks in town. I haven't seen him since this summer. Let's see. Right after you came to Sweet Hollow. Yeah. I remember telling him about the new preacher. Next day in you waltz with Royce."

"I think I've seen him . . . this Pete . . . sometimes just felt his presence. I think. Why, I wonder."

"He's a loner. Lives out here somewhere. Maybe he's in cahoots with those ghosts." Ellen shivered and reached for her pack of gum.

"Geez, look at the time. Sure flies when you're having fun, uh?" Ellen stood, brushed herself off, and said, "I gotta get or I'll be up the creek without a paddle. I'm gonna need that lift."

"I best be goin' too," Beth said. "I reckon I can drop you."

The three of them walked to Beth's car. As Molly turned back, both Ellen and Beth said, "Oh, Royce." They shook their heads, and Ellen gestured for Beth to finish.

"He's been . . . You need to . . . uh . . ."

Molly waited.

"Pack up your stuff. He said he was sorry 'bout kickin' you out so soon. They're coming back tonight. 'Bout six o'clock. Him and Cecilia."

"Looks like Cecilia's got them both sipping soda from the same straw again," Ellen muttered.

"And," Beth said. "Jake, uh, gave me a message for you. Said he's got your package from the drugstore, and you'd better come home. Sounded right put out."

"Thanks," she said and waved good-bye. *Package. What package?*

"Hey," Ellen hollered, "call Richard when you get a chance. Bye."

Molly bowed her head. Not even lunchtime and already she felt overwhelmed as if one more complication would break her spirit.

She returned to the rocker, to think. Too much information on too little coffee. Spying Ellen's thermos, she poured the last half cup. Lukewarm and black, the bitter liquid didn't appeal, and she made a face as she swallowed—medicine for her mind. The rocking chair sat in the sun, and she leaned her head back for a few minutes of meditation.

When she roused, her neck was stiff, and her shoulders ached. With no watch she could only guess the time. A crow, startled by her movement, yanked the discarded hunk of bread and lifted as if to fly away with his morsel. Instead, the big, beady-eyed bird simply settled a few feet away and continued his feast. His appetite, obviously, had overcome any fear he might have had of her. Molly sat still and watched, amazed to be so close. Crows and ravens were extremely intelligent birds and were somehow magical, she knew. And something in Roman mythology—yes, according to what she'd read, crows had once been white. Until one of them brought bad news to one of the gods, then they were turned black forever. In the sunshine, this one's many deep-blue feathers gleamed among the black. If only her camera were on her lap, she might quietly steal a picture.

Pictures! She bolted to her feet. Wide-awake. The bird let out an angry cawing and flew away.

Had Jake picked up her pictures from the drugstore? Her mind clicked off the snaps she'd taken, and she winced when the image of Royce, stretched out on a blanket by the lake, came to her. Last night's dream washed over her like warm, sweet cream turning sour. *I'd better get home, now. But my clothes are still at Royce's. And there's Richard. What the hell time is it? I must look a fright.* No mirror, no watch. Not even a hairbrush in her pack.

As she hurried down to her car, panic threatened to swallow her whole and spit her out in pieces. She'd go to Royce's first. Maybe clean up there and then deal with Jake.

At her car, she forced herself to stop. *An angel watches over me. I've been promised.* Self-talk dissipated her anxiety somewhat. With a new resolve, she turned the key. But rather than a sputtering, chugging motor, she heard a grinding noise and then nothing. Not out of gas, she knew that. Now what? She bowed until her forehead rested on the steering wheel.

*Okay. Enough blubbering. What are my choices?* She could walk home cross-country, face Jake and his barrage, depend on him again. Or she could just sit here and fret. *God help me,* she prayed, wiped her nose, took a deep breath in, and remembered to exhale.

Back out of the car, she headed for the spring to wash her face and calm down. She cut through brush and trees rather than follow the long winding trail. Cool, clear water refreshed her and drew heat from her cheeks. She splashed her face and ran her hands through her hair until curls dripped.

The hot sun shone high in the sky. Guessing it couldn't be much past noon, she looked for a shady place to sit. The tree she remembered offering her solace no longer existed there. A boulder stood in its place. She leaned against the unforgiving surface and closed her eyes.

*Damn car.* They should have gotten rid of the clunker back in Tucson. Nothing but trouble, and now here she was stuck in the wilderness. Again she placed her palms on her cheeks, holding herself from falling apart. Opening her eyes, she shrieked as a snake slithered over her boots. A small brown snake. Harmless. Her nerves on edge, she searched her pack and found the kava kava. The capsules being huge and impossible to swallow without water, she got down on her belly and drank from the spring. Too late she remembered warnings about rivers and streams being contaminated and causing giardiasis. But this was a spring, coming up from the earth. Wouldn't it be clean? There was no point in worrying about getting sick now. She'd already drank her fill.

Instead of standing again, she gave in to temptation, folded her arms as a pillow, and laid her head on them. Crawling reptile thoughts snaked through her mind, but she simply did not care anymore. Dirty, unkempt, confused, and unhappy, she was a mess. And so tired, tired, tired. Exhausted from a mostly sleepless night. Oh, to sleep and wake up far away. Again life-restoring sleep eluded her.

With eyes closed, she listened to the rhythmic beat of her heart, the buzz of a fly. Earth's subtle vibrations grounded and centered her. Renewed her spirit. Tears dried on her face, leaving a powdery film that tightened her skin. In the stillness, with only the trickling of the stream, she thought she heard a car engine rumble. Yes. Louder now. Who? Maybe Ellen was coming back for her thermos.

Jumping up, she ran, stumbling and brushing aside thistles and ferns. When she got to her car, a familiar dilapidated pickup was coming to a stop. The old dulcimer man emerged from his vehicle. Without a word he popped the hood of his truck and motioned for her to do the same. Thank God she had backed in against the brier and blackberry brambles. He began connecting jumper cables, and she walked to him, laid a hand on his arm. He was real. Not an apparition, not an angel. Well, not this world's idea of angels anyway.

"Who are you?" she whispered.

He turned toward her, grinned a toothless grin, and said nothing. Spitting tobacco juice, he went on with his task.

"Pete?" she asked. He nodded. Cat made an appearance then, and Pete bent, picked him up, and caressed him. Even from where she stood, Molly could hear purring. She'd purr too. Her shoulders still held the memory of his hands when he'd consoled her that day. She'd thought he was an angel and she was dreaming. A wonderful dream.

Without speaking, he dropped Cat and indicated she should turn her key. When she did, the engine started right up. He disconnected cables and was climbing into his truck when she realized he was leaving.

"Wait, please," she pleaded, hopping out of her car. "Can't you stay and talk with me? How did you know about my car?" Then she got mad. "What the hell is going on, anyway?"

"Yer car is runnin'. Best git to yer chores, missy."

Molly moved away, her fists doubled at her sides, her body aching and her mind going in circles. Feeling childish and helpless, she bit her lip and refused to cry. He must have seen her distress and confusion. With a grunt he climbed out and opened his frail old arms. Gladly she surrendered to the comfort he offered. Her hands unclenched, her body softened. Through bottled-up tears she whimpered, "Who are you? Help me, please. I can't go back to Jake—I won't. I'm afraid."

"We've waited a long time for you, Molly."

"What? What does that mean? Who? Why?"

He stepped back then, holding her shoulders with a gentle touch. She looked into his sad watery blue eyes and he returned her gaze with a knowing, intimate look as if in communication with her spirit.

"Your soul knows, Molly. Your soul always knows." He paused, held her close again and spoke quietly into her hair. "Keep prayin'. You'll be taken care of. Jest remember, nothin' is as it seems, and nothin' happens without reason."

His last words to her were, "Remember yer dulcimer."

For long moments after he'd driven away, she felt the warmth of his embrace and smelled the tobacco and dust of him. A surprisingly pleasant aroma, making her feel safe, as if she had been rescued from a threatening force. Step by slow-motion step, she returned to the driver's side, sat behind the wheel, and inched her old car forward.

# TWENTY

~

*If you but knew who walks beside you*
*on the way that you have chosen, fear would be impossible.*
—A Course in Miracles

"Yoo-hoo. Mrs. Carpenter." A high-pitched nasal voice stopped her before she could make her way to the photo counter. An impulse had brought Molly into the drugstore. She'd check for her pictures, hoping they were still there so she could relax on that front. Now this small wiry gray-haired stranger stood in front of her.

"Remember me? Of course you do. I poured at your welcoming tea. And I came to your home for paintings. Remember? I haven't seen you since, poor dear. I hear you've been so sick. Why, you look just fine." The woman eyed Molly with disapproval, as if she'd committed a faux pas. Belched in her face or something. Taking in her dirty clothes, Molly was sure. Geez, her fingernails were even dirty and still stained from picking blackberries.

"Gertrude, I . . ."

"Priscilla. I'm Priscilla. I know, dear. No need to explain. I understand what it's like to be ill. I've been cursed with, well, mine have all been physical. Why just last week, I waltzed innocently off to my doctor like a good girl, for one of those." She leaned close and whispered, "You know—a colonoscopy."

"I really . . ." Molly held up her hand, backing away.

"Well, wouldn't you know. Four bloody polyps. And now I wait while they determine if I have cancer. Ever since my appendicitis when I was fourteen, there's been one thing after another. I was a dance instructor at the time. Yes, at fourteen. Imagine that. My abdomen blew up like a balloon—peritonitis, you know. Why, I'm lucky to be alive. But you—oh my." Without a pause, she rattled on. "Maybe you have a chemical imbalance like my husband—forty-three years we've been married when he starts putting on weight. Pound after pound. My blood pressure's going up, slim as I am and his is low—100 over 60. That's when I start thinking something more is going on here than just my good cooking. By now he's weighing over three hundred pounds, and I'm telling him to get to the doctor.

"Please, I need to . . ."

"Of course, dear. Let me just tell you so you can think about it. I finally dragged the stubborn old coot—sweet as he is—to my doctor. Sure enough, his thyroid was underactive. Low blood pressure is a sign of that, you know. Now he's on medication for a year already. He's lost sixty pounds and suddenly getting frisky, if you get my drift. Now, I'm not saying you have low thyroid. But maybe menopause, dear." Rather than whisper menopause, as she had colonoscopy, her voice rose a notch. She laid her small, bony hand on Molly's arm. Fingers like cold tentacles with nails polished a gaudy red.

During this whole spiel, Molly had been searching for a clock. At last she spotted one. It read five o'clock. That couldn't be right, could it?

"So nice to have this little chat. I hope I've helped," Priscilla twanged and dashed away.

No one manned the photo counter when she found it, and Molly didn't have time to wait or search for a clerk. So she headed quickly for the door. In her haste, she bumped into a matronly woman about to enter.

"Excuse me," she muttered with her eyes downcast.

"Molly? Molly Carpenter? Is that you? Why, I thought . . ."

"Hello. Please excuse me. I'm in a hurry."

"I'm sure you are. You must be so far behind, after this time . . . away. We've missed you and prayed for your speedy recovery." The woman stood close, and, like a football player, blocked Molly's way, looking at her as if she'd just landed from Mars.

"There's a great sale on tuna here. Solid white tuna."

Why was there such a need for chit-chat today? Or did this go on all the time? How rude could she force herself to be?

"Oh no. Not for Henry and I. Neither of us would ever eat canned tuna. It's for our precious Prince. Our purebred Siamese will eat nothing but . . . It's worth a trip from Sweet Hollow. You have a cat? My, you look frazzled. Perhaps you were released too soon. I'm so sorry. But one gets in this world what one deserves, doesn't one?"

"No. No. I'm not sick. It's just . . . I have an appointment. I'm late!" Molly slipped past her and darted away, leaving Gertrude, or whoever, palavering to thin air.

Where did these people come from, and where did they get the idea she'd been hospitalized? And what kind of hospital? She climbed into her car, realizing she should have left it running like she had at the post office. A letter from Amy lay on the seat beside her, and she longed to read it.

Turning the key, she looked up to see Priscilla running toward her. *Please, start. Yes*. Molly sped off, tires squealing, while in her rearview mirror she saw the little jabber box, tottering on high heels, waving her arm. She had no time for more blather if she didn't want another uncomfortable encounter.

At Royce's, she parked at the curb, ran in, and began gathering her few belongings. No time now for a shower, she scrubbed her hands and face, brushed her hair. As she threw her suitcase in the trunk, a car approached and pulled into the driveway. Should she make a mad escape or face Royce and his—his what? His ex? Or had they remarried?

He stood by his car, handsome as ever in the late afternoon sun. What else could she do but greet them? She wiped her sweaty palms on her jeans. Distant thunder drew her eyes to the west. Yes, dark clouds had gathered and were moving fast across the sky. Slowly she tramped across the lawn. Her heart pounded, the erotic dream came back, and she felt faint.

"Molly, meet Cecilia," he said as a petite bleached blonde sidled over to stand close at his side. Cecilia placed her arm possessively at his waist.

"Hello," Molly said with a forced smile. A cold gust of wind made her shiver as a cloud passed in front of the sun.

Cecilia did not smile, nor answer, but took the offered hand in a tight grip. Molly winced. Next to this perfectly groomed woman dressed in a linen suit and silk blouse, she felt large, awkward, homely, like an overgrown teenager without a date for the prom.

"Molly's been looking after the place while I was gone. Thank you so much." She could tell he was staring at her, and she yearned to make eye contact. But shyness had overtaken her. The dream and the snapshots fresh in her mind chased all small talk to some far corner, and she could conjure nothing to say.

"I'll go now," she mumbled. "Nice to meet you." Without a second glance she rushed to her car. *Start. Please, oh please, start.*

Instead of home she drove directly to Sam's. On the way, she thought she saw Pete's pickup parked on a side street. But then another one in front of her looked like his, so she dismissed the possibility.

Ellen met her at the door.

"A back booth, please."

"You bet, hon. I've got just the spot for you."

The little diner rang with laughter, conversation, and clanking dinnerware. Soon she was spooning hot, rich clam chowder, and reading Amy's newsy letter, hardly able to concentrate but grateful for the diversion. Amy wrote of enjoying North Dakota's crisp autumn weather. They'd already had their first freeze.

Ellen slipped into the booth and faced her, took both her hands and held them tight. "Don't look. You won't believe what the cat just dragged in. No. Don't turn around." She leaned forward and motioned for Molly to do the same. "It's Jake and Diatrice. You can sneak out the back door if you want."

Molly, gathering her things, froze when a hand landed flat on the table. Too late to escape. Jake stood in front of her, Diatrice to one side.

"Shameful. Scandalous." Diatrice curled her lip and waddled away.

"Home. Now," he demanded.

"Sit down, we can talk here just as well." Molly forced herself to sound strong. Deliberately straightening her shoulders, tipping her chin up a degree.

Ellen made a quick retreat and busied herself with customers at nearby tables. With a huff, Jake sat. He looked disheveled, not his usual groomed self. His clothes were clean and pressed and appropriate. Then she realized he was unshaven with at least a three-day stubble. Must be letting his beard grow again. What would his "flock" think on Sunday morning? Why now? Was this part of his injured-spouse act?

"Okay. We've played your little game. Now it's time to come home and get this straightened out. No. We can't talk here. This dump is noisy and crowded and cramped. Come on." He started to get up.

She didn't move. He sat back down and, with tight lips, said, "Do you want a scene? I don't think so, but I'll make one if you don't come with me now."

"I'd think you wouldn't want a scene any more than I do."

"Of course I don't. But I'll gain sympathy. You, on the other hand . . ."

Ellen appeared with pad and pencil. "Can I getcha some java, Reverend Jake?" The sarcasm, no doubt, wasted on Jake.

He shook his head.

"All righty then. How about some pie?" She began rattling off the varieties available.

Jake rose and said, "We're leaving. Give me her bill."

Ellen raised her eyebrows at Molly as if to say, "I'll stand here all night if I have to." But she finally stepped aside as Jake bumped into her.

Molly stood and smiled wanly at Ellen. Moving through the narrow aisle between booths, she suddenly found herself looking directly into Royce's eyes. Averting hers, she saw Cecilia's hand caressing his ring. Without acknowledging them, Jake propelled her forward. At the door, Royce caught up, took her arm.

"Molly, are you all right?"

"Take your hands off my wife. Haven't you had enough of her?" Jake's angry voice rose above the clamor.

"I'm all right. Please go back to Cecilia," Molly said while pleading with her eyes that she was not okay.

Jake paid the cashier, and she watched as Royce and Ellen met in the aisle, whispering.

At the curb Molly fumbled for her keys, and Jake said, "Oh no. We'll take my car." Gripping her elbow, he steered her to the maroon sedan halfway down the block.

"This is ridiculous. We'll just have to come back for the Chevy."

"I don't care. I'm not taking any chances now. You've been pretty elusive lately, and we are going to get this mess settled."

As soon as they pulled away, she heard the clunk of doors locking. Geez. She felt like a prisoner. Had he lost his mind? Would he actually harm her? She didn't think so. He had never been a violent man. But now there seemed to be a desperation about him, as if his house of cards was tumbling, and he couldn't make it stop. Neither of them said anything. Dulcimer Man came to mind, and Molly prayed for help, for guidance. She looked out the windows, searching for his battered, old pickup. Cars, motorcycles but no pickup. The sun had disappeared, and raindrops splattered the windshield. She hugged herself, wishing for a jacket. Wishing to be warm and safe.

At home she was surprised to see a freshly mowed lawn, the smell of cut grass still lingered. Sidewalks had been swept, flower beds weeded. Inside, the house was tidy. His mother's oil paintings she'd strewn were stacked in a corner. No dirty dishes in the sink, no newspapers lying about. Everything had a welcoming appeal until she saw the kitchen table. Her snapshots spread all over, yellow Post-it notes on some.

"That's right. Let's get right to the point here. Add those pictures to this." He held up one of her notebooks. "And I'd say you've got a lot of explaining to do."

"So do you. Ellen has told me—"

He cut her off. "Ellen is a busybody looking to stir up trouble. I've heard plenty about her."

"Give me that journal. And how did you get these pictures, anyway?"

"This is a small community, remember. When you didn't pick them up, they called me. Handed them right over. How much of this hanky-panky am I supposed to put up with?"

"Believe it or not, there hasn't been any hanky-panky." Not entirely true, but she and Royce had exercised restraint. And then her dream came back, and she felt herself blush, lost her ability to concentrate for a minute. She felt guilty, of all things. "I don't think you want a scandal," she finally managed to say.

"You're the one who'd better think about that. How many marriages and friendships do you want to ruin here?"

"What on earth do you mean?"

"Well, for starters, Daphne," he sneered and held up her journal. "There's Royce—your Greek god and Cecilia. Imagine the stir these pictures would cause for them. And then Ellen's remarks about her. He won't think much of that. Your meetings with Richard—well, that's proof of one thing: it's you who has the problem, not me. And he'll side with Diatrice, if it comes to that. Because she's with me on this one. Should I go on?"

His cold brown eyes glazed over, frightening her. Something stiffened within her, and she refused to argue or threaten. What was the point? When he couldn't intimidate her, he tried another tack.

"Just come home, sweetheart. I'll forgive all this nonsense. We'll start over. You can keep using the spare bedroom. And I promise, I'll never read your journal again. Just come home. Come to church. Show them all that we are a family. We'll figure out what to tell them."

"I can't do it anymore, Jake," Molly said, choking on the words.

"What choice do you have? Where can you go? What can you do? You couldn't cope in the real world if you had to."

"I don't care. I don't trust you. I don't like you. And I don't like who I am when I'm with you!"

With that, he placed his hands on the table and rose slowly from his chair, backed over to a kitchen drawer, and pulled out a gun. He came toward her, not pointing it at her. Rather, it rested in the palm of his hand.

"I . . . will not . . . be ruined . . . by you." He placed the revolver on the table at his left side, sat again, and pointed to the other chair. "Sit."

Molly sat.

"Trust me. They'll believe me."

A lump formed in her throat, tears burned her eyes, and, with nothing else to do, she prayed. *God help me.*

They glared at each other until Molly let go of her grip and slowly stacked the pictures, placed them in the envelope with the others and the negatives. She swallowed hard and whispered, "I give up. You win."

The phone rang. They both jumped. Jake held up his hand in a stop motion and went for it. In the split second his back was turned, she grabbed her purse, the pictures already in her hand, and made a dash for the door. Spanning the paved front landing in three strides, her feet barely skimmed the steps. Without a backward glance, Molly flung herself across the front lawn. She ran down the dirt road, tripping on ruts, catching herself, wrenching her back. Rain and tears mixed and everything blurred. Gasping, she paused, looked back. He hadn't followed her. Yet. Frantic, she rushed on until her knees wobbled and her lungs ached.

Up ahead, a truck pulled to the side of the road. The passenger door swung open. Dulcimer Man? No. The truck was familiar, but too new and polished. Closer now, she recognized Royce.

"Hop in." He leaned over her, slammed her door, and they sped away.

"I . . . don't . . . Where did you come from?"

"When you left Sam's, Ellen and I could see fear in your face. We saw you both leave in Jake's car, so we devised a plan. We figured we'd give you a chance to get away from him if you needed to. Ellen phoned your place just now to distract him. Thank God it worked."

Molly sat in stunned silence as they drove back to Sam's for her car.

"I'm going to follow you to that little motel. Make sure Jake isn't trailing you. You'll be safe for the night, anyway."

"First an ATM, please. I don't have much cash."

When she placed her request at the money machine, it spit her card back with the message that her account had been closed. Jake's dirty way of controlling her. But she wouldn't turn back now. She'd just use a credit card at the motel and save what little money she had.

The vacancy sign blinked as they pulled in to the familiar parking lot. Royce parked and went in with her to register. Neither of her credit cards was still valid. Jake had canceled them too. Molly's shoulders sagged. With shaky hands, she opened her purse to see if she had enough money for a night. How in heaven's name had she come to this? Despair washed over her. Homeless, penniless. A waif. Far from the strong, independent woman she wanted to be.

"Never mind, Molly. I'll get this." Royce handed the clerk a card and then took Molly into his arms. She stood still with her arms at her sides and let his strength and warmth seep into her.

"Thank you," she said. To Royce. And to God.

# TWENTY-ONE

~

*The past is a foreign country, they do things differently there.*
—L.P. Hartley

A low, menacing growl came from the big dog as it nudged Molly's arm. She startled from her drowsy half sleep, noticing that the dog sat silent, poised. Fifi, with muscles tense, seemed ready to pounce. Anticipating an imagined hooligan rounding the corner, Molly held her breath while dulcimer music surrounded her, chimed in her head, as if an entity were communicating and strings its only voice. At times the music lulled her, reassured her. At the moment, though, it was a cacophony as disturbing as the crows screaming at each other, and she fought to still the noise. The autumn sun glared hot in the noon sky. She licked her parched lips, exhaled, and closed her eyes.

She hoped it was Richard's arrival that had alarmed Fifi. When she'd called yesterday to make an appointment, he'd told her not to come to his office. Diatrice knew of their sessions.

"Is she making your life miserable?" Molly had asked.

"Don't worry about me. I just don't want to give her more fodder for gossip. Ellen tells me you're camped at the abandoned cabin on the outskirts of Sweet Hollow."

"I've been there for three days, with Fifi on guard. I need to talk to you."

For three days she'd been isolated. Well, not exactly. Beth had come with news that Jake had called looking for her. Ellen dropped in each day to spend a few minutes with her precious Fifi, bringing gossip picked up at the café. The strangers from Tucson were still in town, dropping in at the diner, prying for information. Several people had commented on receiving calls from them and being questioned about problems they may have had with prowlers or anything else.

"Here, hon," she'd say, handing Molly a pot of chili or a wrapper of sandwiches as she related how Cecilia and Royce had been in ordering clam chowder and scowling at each other. "I tell ya, where there's smoke there's fire."

Mostly, though, Molly had occupied her time walking and writing in her journal. Heavy underlining and torn pages marked where she'd unleashed her anger at Jake and herself. Fear made her head ache and her palms sweat. She stopped often to swipe her hands across her jeans, swallow water around a lump in her throat. The fear was not of the unknown future—where she'd go, how she'd survive. No, her fear stemmed from her anger. She'd never known such fury, such rage that made her want to scream obscenities at Jake. "Screw you," she rammed onto the page. And this was not her worst thought. What had she become? Aghast, she'd called Richard. Someone must help her deal with these horrid emotions.

What raised this episode with Jake to the intolerable? Always before she'd excused his behavior or chosen not to see what was directly in front of her. Why now? What had changed to make it no longer possible for her to live in this destructive relationship? Was it Royce? Her attraction to him? His attraction to her? She missed him, but she'd told Beth to let him know she needed time alone. Still she yearned for his whistle now. No. More than that attraction motivated her. This place, the energy here, seemed to insist on her being true to herself, as if a lack of integrity on her part would somehow destroy other lives. As if integrity and eyes wide-open were the keys to solving the mystery of Sophia and her family.

In early evenings, as the sun set, she'd taken to sitting on the porch in the rocking chair. Photos in hand, she'd gaze at each one until the pictures blurred. Searching for answers, remembering the day the pictures were shot; why she thought she had seen a beautiful young woman with long red hair rocking in this chair. In the photo the porch was empty. Sometimes she saw wisps of clouds or shadows. Other times, nothing. Fifi spent those twilight hours on the far edge of the porch as if he wanted nothing to do with Molly or the rocking chair. When dulcimer music grew loud, she thought of the old man—the caretaker—and wondered why he hadn't made an appearance yet.

When it grew too dark to read or write, she'd beckon the dog and, with flashlight in hand, climb to the loft. Fifi would lie down at the foot of the stairs. Flicking off the light produced darkness so deep it took minutes before she could see her hand in front of her face. The first night had been sleepless, restless. Her mind refused to forget the image of Jake holding a gun. She'd made it clear how she abhorred guns, and, as far as she knew, there had never been one in their home. Where had it come from and why? Desperate, Jake's eyes grew cold and hard, frightening her as he held the pistol.

Here in the dark, every creak and varmint noise sent shivers through her. She longed for valerian root or any herbal concoction to sedate her. But she'd sworn off all of them, fearing a growing dependency and not sure if they were addictive. Knowing she must be discerning in the days ahead. Knowing Fifi slept below gave her some comfort, chased away eerie sensations her imagination produced. The next night she lit a small candle safely ensconced in a tin, visualized an angel guarding the door and awoke the next morning to a puddle of wax.

Now as she waited, holding Fifi's collar, her skin prickled, her heart pounded. When the dog relaxed, she did too. Richard stood in front of her, a gentle look in his eyes.

"Molly," he said in an out-of-breath wheeze.

She wanted to rest her head on his shoulder, feel masculine arms hold her close. Her self-imposed solitude had hollowed out a tender spot she yearned to have filled. Instead she released her grip on Fifi's collar and stood with her hands outstretched. He took them both and squeezed, then dropped them.

"Thank you for coming way out here to see me," Molly said, glancing at the black-haired man standing a few feet behind Richard.

"It's no problem." His voice and demeanor shifted from friendly to professional as he stepped back and introduced the tall dark man who stood beside him. "This is Preston, the friend I've mentioned. His family lived in this area in the 1850s. And he's researching for a book of that period. I think he can answer some of your questions."

A warm energy moved through her as the man clasped her hand in both his large strong ones. His eyes were dark and small, with the ageless wisdom of a Native American elder.

They all settled on the stoop with legs dangling over the porch edge. The dog rested in the shade. Dulcimer music, soft and melodic, played on—for Molly, anyway. Do they hear it too? Wouldn't they have said if they did hear music way out here? She didn't dare ask.

"Is this place good for you? I wonder . . ." Richard spoke while his friend remained expressionless and still at his side.

"Well, at least I feel safe with this watchdog. But my dreams or visions of Sophia possess me. Some ghost of an idea that I must change the life she had . . . rescue her somehow. That I won't have peace until I do . . . I know I can't stay forever, though."

"Maybe we can help, but we need to hear your whole story." He glanced at Preston, who nodded.

Molly shook her head, "I don't know where to start."

"Start wherever you're comfortable. Your experiences here, your childhood, your marriage. Anywhere."

"Can we hike to the bridge? That feels important to me. Something happened there."

"All right. Let's go," Richard said when the old Cherokee gestured an almost-imperceptible assent.

She added a couple bottles of water and a sack of trail mix to her already-half-filled day pack. Quickly she tossed in the photos she had been studying. Why take them along? She didn't know, unless just being by the bridge and talking her whole story through would clarify strange shadows and faint outlines she hoped were significant.

What about Fifi? Molly filled his water bowl and fed him, told him to stay and they were off.

Her body remembered the trail, her legs strong and her stride long. Preston kept her pace as dry leaves crackled beneath their feet. Dusty decay-scented air evoked thoughts of inevitable death and rebirth. Soon Molly heard Richard.

"Hey, slow down. I'm not in the shape you two are."

Molly laughed, and they paused until he caught up and stopped panting.

"That smile becomes you," he said as they moved on.

"It feels good too," she said and grew serious, realizing how seldom she smiled these days.

Deeper in the woods, dust gave way to fusty dankness. With a meow, Cat crept from beneath a fern; Molly bent and scooped him into her arms. He had made himself scarce since she'd settled in. Perhaps her other animal friend kept him away.

"Ah, Cat. I've heard about you." Richard stopped, drew in a long breath and wiped his forehead.

"He's been a real companion. I've missed him," Molly said, petting him as they waited, giving Richard as much time as he needed to rest. The Cherokee stood straight and silent like an ancient chestnut tree. She contemplated telling them of her experience with chestnut trees, how they seemed a doorway to the past.

When they arrived at the bridge, Cat hissed and darted off. Winds picked up, dark clouds gathered in angry clumps, and, like the jangle of wind chimes during a storm, music grew frantic and loud in Molly's ears. Gritting her teeth, she let Preston precede her onto the rickety bridge that swayed as if in a tempest.

"I only go a few steps because the wood is rotten. I guess I shouldn't venture here at all, but I feel compelled," she called, looking down at churning, murky waters.

Molly glanced back at Richard and saw color drain from his face. "Come on. Let's get back to solid ground." Without another word they retreated. Preston walked on until he reached midpoint. There he stopped, folded his arms across his chest, and, with head erect, stood like a pillar. After several minutes in this meditative stance, he turned to join them.

Snow flurries swirled, and Molly was lost and alone until the wind switched its course and cleared the air. By the time he came close enough to communicate, snow had accumulated in low drifts that grew before her eyes until she was lost in a blizzard of white.

"Molly, what? You look terrified." Richard stood near her, but his voice barely penetrated the storm.

His arms reached out to her even as he grew more faint and distant. She shivered and grasped for him, but he disappeared, and she stood alone in the snow. Preston plodded toward her covered in snow while behind him the sun had broken through.

"Wait," Preston said to Richard as he took Molly's hand.

They stand in silence as a pretty teenage girl materializes. Her wavy orange-red hair tousles across her face and flows to her waist. She shudders, pulls her shawl tighter. Jewels on a breastpin flash as snowflakes melt against it.

"Do you see her? See . . . see the brooch? I . . . I've seen that somewhere," Molly whispers.

"I see," Preston says softly in her ear.

Molly sinks to her knees and stares as the girl comes closer. Closer. Until Molly can't think beyond pain and fright. Preston holds her hand, and she watches in awe as he seems to age and shrink in stature. The young woman is touching her, covering her as if a cloud is descending over her.

She lays back and screams as a jarring contraction tears through her abdomen. Then another before she's hardly caught her breath. Voices, angry and mean, yell, "Sophia, push. Damn it, push." Someone pulls her legs apart, bends her knees—her body exposed to the cold and to the bearded man with rough hands who holds her against the ground so she can't move. Preacher man.

Warm liquid dribbles across Sophia's lips as Papa yells for her to open her mouth and swallow. She gasps as whiskey burns her tongue, her throat, causing her to cough just as another spasm sears her midsection.

In the distance, in golden light, Susie stands, beckoning her to come. An image of a stooped old man floats behind Susie. His bearded face is contorted, his eyes watery. Sophia cries out. More whiskey pours down until she gags and wrenches her head free.

Preacher man fondles the pin at her breast and Papa says, "Gimme five dollars fer it. And you hightail it with that brat."

Preacher man hands over the money, tucks a bundle under his cloak, and, without another word, climbs on his horse and rides away. Papa sits on a rock, his head bowed, and gulps from the jug until it's empty. Tossing it away with disgust, he disappears into the storm. She sees the faint outline of an elderly man—straight backed, quiet, and still. An angel, she thinks and the world turns black.

Night has closed in when she wakes beneath a quilt covered with snow. The wind has calmed, the sky is clear, and a full moon lights the landscape. She sits up and moans with the rawness of her entire lower torso. Black splotches soil the drifts.

"My baby," she whispers and falls back. Bolting upright she screams, "My baby!" Sobbing now, her hand flutters to her bodice. Her brooch is gone. Frantically she crawls about on her belly, feeling the earth through icy drifts.

The man angel sits beside her, pulls her into his arms, cradles her until her shivers and sobbing abate.

"Sophia?" he murmurs. A thought more than a question.

She nods. "Are you an angel? Did I die?"

"No. Hush." He rocks her gently. "Can you tell me?"

"Papa. Preacher man. My baby? The jewels?" she stammers. "Susie," she calls. "If only," she mumbles and then motionless, with vacant eyes, she stares at him. She is alive but lifeless as if he held only her shell.

. . .

Molly stretched from her fetal position, groaned, muttered, and opened her eyes to see Richard and Preston on either side of her. Sunshine and warmth belied the snow she expected to see. Had she been asleep and dreamed of the storm? The icy wind? She held her breath, turned her head first to look at Richard and then into Preston's eyes. "Sophia?"

"I saw," Preston answered.

Richard looked puzzled. He opened his mouth as if to question. Closed it and remained silent. Preston laid a hand on his shoulder, nodded, said, "We'll talk later."

They helped Molly to her feet, and together all three gathered belongings scattered about. Molly took a gulp of water as she tried to waken from the nightmare she had taken part in. Her mind went to the jeweled pin. It reminded her of something. Had she seen it before? In other visions, dreams or nightmares? Yes. Sophia's grandma had given it to her, and someone had explained its small stones, filigree cross and emerald. Wait. She'd seen all those in real life too. Where?

"Royce," she said aloud.

"Yes," Richard said. "Royce called and wants to meet with me and you. He's had something happen he can't shake."

Richard stuffed the water bottle into her pack and came upon the photos.

"Look. Look at these."

They studied the first picture. Until this moment, all she'd seen on the print was the cabin porch with, at the very most, vaporous blotches in the doorway and where the chair stood now. Suddenly, though, in this light or in this place the clouds took shape, and what emerged astounded her. The beautiful young woman Molly thought she'd seen that day sat in a rocker with hands touching dulcimer strings. Her copper-colored hair fell in waves across her shoulders and down her back. An eerie blank presence about her.

"Yes, this is who I saw that day," Molly said. "Sophia."

As they stared, the blotch in the doorway cleared and an old man with a long beard appeared. *Dulcimer man,* Molly thought. But no. This was not an old man, just bent as if the world's cares rested on his shoulders. He gazed at Sophia with such tenderness it caught Molly's breath.

She looked up to see Richard and Preston scrutinizing her.

# TWENTY-TWO

~

*Without change, something sleeps inside us*
*and seldom awakens. The sleeper must awaken.*
—Frank Herbert

Hot and grimy, they arrived back at the cabin. Fifi wagged his tail in welcome and moseyed to Molly's side. With one hand on the big dog's head, Molly raised the curls from her neck with the other so the air could dry her skin. Her shirt was soiled and her jeans dusty. Exhaustion and confusion muddled her thinking. The baby. The pin. Photos that seemed to come alive as they had stared. Grateful she hadn't been by herself for this ordeal, she glanced at her companions.

Sweat traced down Richard's flushed cheeks. Preston, though, didn't have a smudge or sweat stain on him. He stood for a minute and then, as if tracking an elusive scent, he gravitated to the rocker. On the seat lay her dulcimer. How did it get out here? Who's been here? The reclusive caretaker? Why? Instead of being frightened, the idea somehow comforted her, and she realized music no longer rang in her ears. Silence surrounded them, save for the rustle of wildlife.

Preston hunkered down and picked up the instrument with ceremonious care. He held it in one hand and stroked its contour with the other. When he squinted up at her, Molly answered his questioning glance.

"I bought it for a hundred dollars. I thought I'd learn to play, but . . ."

"They don't make 'em like this anymore," he said. "I know this workmanship. See . . . old Doc's mark."

"What do you know about him?" Both she and Richard leaned forward, alert and waiting.

"Well, he was a medicine man. A healer. Devoted to his family. The story's passed down how he took off after Marta, his only daughter, to keep her from a no-good she'd run away with. He never returned. My people were blamed. No Cherokee woulda hurt him. Respected by most as just an' fair."

Preston looked down at Fifi who had sidled over and laid her head on his bent knee. "Far as I know his body was never found. Everybody missed him except Marta's new husband. With Doc outa the way, he controlled that house. Chased off her mother then worked Marta to death. Been said old Doc haunts the land yet. Some say he won't find rest til Sophia does."

Preston paused so long Molly wondered if he'd gone into a trance. His eyes steadied upon her, as if to say, "Listen, Molly, listen." He spoke again, slowly in reverent tones.

"Molly. They're waiting. All of them."

"Who? What . . . what?"

"You'll know what to do. Don't rush. Don't delay."

He turned to Richard, nodded, and said, "It's time to go. To leave her."

"I'm concerned about her being here alone."

"Not alone" was Preston's reply.

Molly sat cross-legged on the floor and, like an obedient child, listened while the two men talked about her as if she weren't there. Being a child again held great appeal except for . . . she gasped and bowed her head. A picture formed in her mind of herself as a little girl playing, replaced by one of her whimpering, cringing. Like a slide show, this faded too, and then a man's image in black clothes. A crucifix swayed over her face, threatening. Tears burned her eyes. Searing red-and-orange anger swirled around her as if she were trapped in a blazing inferno. Hellfire and damnation. The words, like drumbeats, throbbed in her ears.

The men's voices droned on, pulling her out of the fire. She raised her head, looked from one to the other. Ominous visions disappeared, her heartbeat quieted. She forced her lips up in what she hoped was a smile, but she could feel the strain in her jaws, her forehead.

Preston approached, held her hand in his, spoke, "It's time. You're safe." With long strides, he walked away.

Richard gripped Molly's shoulders and whispered, "Call me anytime. Anytime." His lips felt warm on her puckered brow. She lowered her eyelids, and her frown relaxed.

Molly remained seated and mute, watching them leave, but unable to ask them to stay. When her legs cramped and her feet tingled, she hobbled, like an old woman, to the chair. Picking up the instrument, she sat and laid it on her lap. A yellow jacket buzzed her, stung her right wrist and, with a quick zigzag, disappeared. "Ouch," she cried, then shrugged off the sting as she stared at the beautiful dulcimer. Was this really Doc's? If so, she held a treasure, an antique that must be priceless. Someone had taken good care and refurbished this instrument.

In awe, she caressed the strings, leaned her head back and created a barely audible melody. Slight vibration and gentle rocking eased her cares, soothed her. Breezes had stilled, and clouds floated across the sky, dimming the sun's harsh brilliance. A memory surfaced; the dulcimer man telling her to trust where the music leads. Telling her to ask and watch for the answer. "You are not alone," he'd said. And something about friends who needed her to help them find their way.

She must have dozed then, for when she opened her eyes, the sun was setting and her arm throbbed. A swollen, itching lump where the wasp had attacked. Dragging to her feet, she went in search of her small bundle of first aid supplies. A tube of pure aloe vera gel lay among Band-Aids, scissors, and gauze. There was even a booklet of "what to do in case." She shrugged and applied a liberal glob of gel. The cool contrast to her hot skin gave immediate relief. She'd never been stung before. Should she wait to see how it would progress? The booklet wasn't very helpful, so she smeared on more gel.

Deciding cold water might bring comfort, she called Fifi, and they headed for the stream, now little more than a runnel. Without thinking, Molly pulled off her clothes and lay back in clear, shallow water, remembering her first dip in this brook. A hawk glided high above, reminding her of the two she'd seen that long-ago day. How she'd envied their seemingly effortless flight and congenial pairing. Now only one soared overhead. Had he lost his mate? Or had they even been a pair? Springtime snowmelt had created icy depths and rushing rapids then. So much had transpired since that she, like the stream, didn't even feel the same, as if years instead of just one summer had passed.

She wasn't the same. Sophia and Susie had become part of her. The agony at the bridge, Sophia's loss and anguish, tensed her into a sitting position, and she hugged her bent knees with her left arm while her right hung limp in the cool water, the festering sting barely covered. Sadness, like a thick black cloud, encircled her, seeped in until she felt smothered and hoped to die.

The world of chores and mail and phone calls, even Jake's conniving threats, seemed like an illusion. Something she'd dreamed. Soon she must leave here before she tumbled into the past, down a dark hole too deep to escape. Must contact Amy, her sons too. Do something about her marriage. What next? Inertia held her in the stream. Her face pressed to her knees, she prayed.

The snap of a twig, a whistle alerted her. Royce? But no, this tone not his melodic trill. This whistling sounded fuzzy and unclear.

The autumn creek provided no deep pools to cover her nakedness. She threw on her shirt and struggled her wet legs into dirty jeans. Buttoning her shirt she heard, "Missy?"

As the old man ambled around the brush, Fifi raised her head, eyed him, lay back down, and continued her nap. Molly waited.

"Here. Let's see that arm o' yers," he commanded.

Dutifully Molly approached and held out her swollen red wrist. She didn't ask how he knew about the sting. Was this Doc's ghost? Or was it Pete, the old caretaker? Or were they one and the same? Questions chased each other around in her head as he spat his ugly tobacco wad into his hand. Brown juice oozed as he formed a foul-smelling poultice. He planted this disgusting muck on the bite, fixing it with mud from the creek bed.

He slipped a packet into her shirt pocket and said, "Boil this here and drink it tonight."

"Doc?" she asked.

"Best get on back now. Be dark soon." And he gimped off.

With a weary tread Molly climbed the slope and trudged toward shelter, Fifi at her side. Longing for bed and escape into sleep, still she followed orders, lit the camp stove, and set water to boil. She didn't question, just did what she was told, and when the tea had cooled enough, she swallowed huge gulps, gagging on the bitter concoction.

Night fell quickly with no moon or stars for light. A storm threatened, and the air hung heavy. Heavy like her heart. Like her legs as she clumsily hauled herself to the loft. Not bothering to take off her clothes or light a candle, she fell onto her makeshift bed.

. . .

Trapped in Sophia's body, mindlessly she wakes, sleeps. Joe comes, feeds her, goes. Sitting in the rocker in the sunshine, sparkling jewels of green and white dance in front of her eyes. A cross looms, and she clutches her chest searching for her pin. If she could only find her pin, everything wouldn't be lost. Mama loved that brooch, Granny had cherished it. When she'd held it she could hear her mama sing,

> O, they tell me of a home far beyond the skies,
> O, they tell me of a home far away.
> O, they tell me of a home where no storm clouds rise,
> O, they tell me of an unclouded day.

Now there is nothing but silence. Sweet, lonely, sad silence. Food Joe spoons her clings in her throat, choking and suffocating. She turns her head away. Preacher Man haunts her. Threatening, forcing himself on her, laughing, jeering. Her own screams waken her.

Wincing, she takes up the ever-present brush and runs it through her hair, over and over. It is her only pleasure for it is then Susie whispers, "Stay with me. Nothing can harm you here. But there will come a time. Stay with me. Now is always timeless." Sophia brushes. Her arms tire, her breathing slows. Joe comes running, "Pa done died, Soph. Please look at me. Yer safe now." She falls, falls into darkness. "Good-bye Joe. Find the brooch fer . . ."

. . .

Molly opened her eyes to daylight. Thunder boomed and a man patted her shoulder crooning, "Darlin', darlin'.

"Time?" she mumbled through pasty lips.

"It's after nine. I tried to wake you up, but you were dead to the world," Royce said. "Sound asleep."

"Not sleep. Passed out. Last night I drank some . . ." Her palms pressed to her pounding temples. "Belladonna. Why did he give me belladonna? Oh, Royce, it's so awful here."

"I want you to get away. Run. Anywhere but here," he pleaded. "This tormenting tale of Sophia is sucking us both in. Darlin', your eyes look vacant, far away. Every night I dream of you." He paused for a moment as if seeing the dream again. His hands felt cool and soothing as he touched her cheek. Looking into her eyes, he said, "There is something about the slope of your shoulders as if you are sagging to the ground. You're not merely crying but screaming in terror. I call out to you. Only Cecilia hears me.

"Molly, run. I'll find a place."

She longed to say yes. To abandon her supposed purpose, her personal possessions, and never come back. Instead she shook her head no.

Rain beat on the attic roof. Wind whistled through the chinks in the low walls. Still, she felt overwarm and closed in.

"Let's go downstairs. I can't breathe up here," she said. They climbed down the ladder and stepped over Fifi, curled up and half asleep.

When they'd settled themselves against the little walnut desk, he poured coffee from his thermos, then touched her mud-caked wrist and asked, "What's this?"

"Ouch. Yellow jacket sting. Yesterday. I think it's better." Now it began to itch and throb. She'd wash it later and see. Having him here gently caring for her made her cry, and she blubbered, "Why did you come?"

"I talked to Richard. He said my dream might be important to you. Besides, I've been worried about you. I stayed away as long as I could."

"I've been dreaming too. Let this all be a nightmare and I wake up soon. Tell me, please."

"I dreamt about your little girl, Sophia. Only she wasn't six or seven like you've described, but a young teenager with long reddish hair. I wasn't much older in the dream, maybe eighteen or nineteen. I found her deep in these woods, sitting in a clearing by an old bridge. Her eyes were blank as if she stared through me. I took her shoulders and shook her and said, 'Soph, Soph, it's me.'

"A man yelled and accused me of molesting her, but he didn't use that term. He said I'd been at her again. And I said, 'No. No. I wouldn' hurt my Soph.' He knocked me down, and I hit my arm on a rock." Royce ran his hand over the birthmark that reminded her of a jagged scar. "Told me to get and never come back. That's when I woke up. A nightmare. I haven't been able to forget it, and Cecilia . . ." He shook his head.

Molly slid close and wrapped her good arm around him. He was trembling, and a sob stirred deep in his throat. "Did anyone call you Joe?" she asked.

"Yes. Yes. Joe."

"Sophia's brother. They were blaming Joe for what they did." Molly hesitated, not sure how he would take her idea. *Oh well.* "Reincarnation?"

"No! This was *just* a dream. A *bad* dream."

"And the fall? Joe landing where you have a birthmark?"

Molly bit her lip. No argument would convince him and what did it matter? Minutes passed. Her skin burned even as wind blew cold circles around them, and they held each other closer.

"Royce," she gasped. "I just thought . . . I just remembered. Your ring. The emerald and filigree cross. Where is your ring?" She stared at his bare hand.

Startled, he rubbed his ring finger, frowned at her and asked, "Why?"

She felt feverish, her vision blurred. Then cleared again when the dog bounded out onto the stoop, wiggling with excitement.

"Fifi"—Ellen dropped to her knees, allowing her pet to welcome her with kisses—"ain't you a sight for sore eyes. Come on. Let's find me someplace out of this wind."

Molly and Royce separated but remained seated with backs leaning on the desk and legs straight out in front of them, like puppets at rest. Ellen, with Fifi bouncing up against her, came to them and sank to the floor.

"I brought . . . oh, I see you've got coffee. Well, here." She pulled muffins and a sack of grapes from her pack.

"Listen," she said, "Preston thinks he and Richard were followed on the main highway yesterday. I'm here to warn you. The shit may hit the fan. Though probably not today. Not a fit day for man nor mouse."

Molly almost smiled at yet another cliché, and this one muddled. Was Preston right about being followed? Certainly he would know. But who? Not Jake, she prayed. Maybe Pete?

"And that old rut of a road is gonna be a mess. It's been raining cats and dogs out there. No offense, Fifi." She poured herself coffee and chose a muffin. They sat in silence. Molly, thankful for these two friends, closed her eyes and rested.

Suddenly the dog's head shot up, and he growled. Bared his teeth, hackles up.

"What the hell is this?" came an angry voice from the doorway.

Hellfire lashed at Molly, like the crimson tongue of a wild beast. Like a frightened child seeking protection, she cowered in Royce's arms. "It's Jake!" *Oh no. The gun.*

"Cozy little ménage à trois?" Jake said with a sneer.

Diatrice puffed up alongside him, a smirk of triumph twitching her jowls in orgasmic satisfaction.

# TWENTY-THREE

~

*Dulcimer strings float on gossamer wings*
*While the Balladeer sings to echoes of strings,*
*"Molly, My Own, come home, Molly come home."*
*Dulcimer themes haunting her dreams,*
*Calling her, Molly, Molly come home*

*Molly, come home. Come home.* Molly breathed in the delicate bouquet of the pillow slip next to her cheek, reminiscent of when her mother had hung bedsheets outdoors after the long winter and replaced stale flannel with fresh air and sunshine. Waking with this pleasing fragrance, she heard voices in muted tones and wondered whose bed she lay in. A woman spoke with an anxious timbre as the faint scent of lilacs became stronger. *Spring* blossoms? Warm hands touched hers, lips brushed her cheek. The lilac scent faded. Now a firmer grip and a question, "Molly?"

She opened her eyes, closed them again, shutting out bright light and a fuzzy image leaning close. As a thermometer slipped under her tongue, her mouth puckered from the astringent, caustic taste of alcohol. Cool fingers held her wrist, something grew tight on her upper arm. Murmurs from the far corner ceased as someone said, "Her fever's broken and blood pressure's good."

Familiar faces gathered around her. Beth, Ellen, and Royce. Beth held a spoon to her mouth. One taste of weak beef broth, and she turned away. The room and its furnishings blurred, and she plummeted, stomach dropping. Moaning, she let go and continued a free fall. *Caught in gossamer webs, she floated and a balladeer sang, "Come home."*

When she stirred again, darkness and quiet surrounded her. As she slept, swans had swooped through her belly and landed on the lake in her head. A shadow, cast by a nightlight, approached her bed. "Water. Dream. Swans," she mumbled. Someone must understand the swans in her mind.

"Ssh. Swans are beautiful and mighty. You've had a right good dream. Prob'bly telling you of your inner beauty. I've heard that swan dreams could mean you've got the power to enter another time or place."

"Thank you," Molly whispered.

"Jest now what's best fer you is sleep. Take this." A small hand, smelling of lilac, held a pill to her lips and then a straw. "Sip, sip."

Cool water trickled down her throat. She swallowed and sipped again. A cat cried with a low and forlorn meow. "Cat?"

"I reckon. Don't know how he got here. Jest showed up. We've tried to coax him in, but he jest sets himself on the fence and cries."

"Where am I?"

"My house," Beth said, sitting on the edge of the bed. "We've been right worried about you."

"Why? What?"

"Sleep now. We'll talk tomorrow."

Beth looked like a green-eyed angel with her lips turned up in a compassionate smile, and Molly closed her eyes.

The pleasant, loving atmosphere vanished, and she sat alone, cross-legged on rough boards, in the dark. She shivered, pulled in her outstretched arms, rocked back and forth, hugging herself. Loud voices came through the open window onto the porch, assaulting her ears, and she cringed. Tears traced down her face. With her fist she rubbed her eyes and smeared her runny nose along one arm of her frayed long-sleeved dress.

"She's jest a little girl," her mama said in a weak voice.

"You got that right. *Jest* a damn girl. Of no use. Jest costs money we don't have. No good for nothin'. Never will be good for nothin'." The ugly sound of her papa's words slapped at her through the walls.

Sophia could almost see his scowl. He hated her, and she didn't know why. *I cain't never be nothin'. Maybe if I were a boy or maybe if I could be gooder*, she thought. *If only I weren't never borned. If only I weren't here.*

Biscuit crawled to her lap, purred and patted her chest, comforting her. Even as the fighting continued, a golden light came toward her. A warm smooth hand raised her to her feet.

Sadness lifted. Yelling stopped as they entered, climbed the ladder, and lay together on the straw-filled mattress. She closed her eyes, felt Biscuit at her feet, smelled sweet lavender, and slept.

When Molly woke, sunlight played on the prisms of a crystal hanging in the open window. A brilliant rainbow flickered on the wall, dancing to the rhythm of the breeze. Cat meowed, and a mourning dove cooed. Molly lay still and listened, her senses infused with the idyllic setting. But only for those first waking moments. Fully awake and confused, she tossed one way, then the other.

The pillow, rumpled beneath her face, no longer smelled fresh; and Molly yearned for the crisp, clean air the open window promised. With trepidation she sat up, swung her legs over so her feet touched the floor. Her head throbbed, the room spun, and she lay back on the mussed bed. As she did, Beth rushed to her.

"Hush, chile. Don't move so fast." She bustled around, and soon Molly's head was propped on sweet-scented line-dried pillow slips again. Beth produced a brush and attempted to tame Molly's mop of tangled curls. When her efforts failed, she left the room, returning with a basin of warm, aromatic water.

Refreshed, Molly said, "I'm hungry."

"Good." Beth helped her to and from the bathroom, then went for food.

With a dish of oatmeal in front of her and a friend by her side, Molly tried to sort out how she came to wake up in Beth's bed. As she ate, she listened to Beth answer her unspoken questions.

"'Twas day before yesterday. You collapsed when Jake and Diatrice showed up at the cabin. After the donnybrook, Royce and

Ellen brought you here. We've all been watchin' over you. Called the doctor and followed her advice. Preston brewed a concoction. And you've slept."

Richard tapped on the open door and came in, a relieved smile on his gaunt, tired face. He held her journal.

"Thought you might want this. We'll pack up your other personal items later."

Desperate, frantic, and with all the resolve she could muster, she demanded, "No. No. I must go back now."

Molly clutched the notebook, grateful, as if a long-lost friend had come home safely.

"Ssh . . . you should rest."

"Please listen. I need to talk," she pleaded.

He patted her hand, sat next to her, and nodded.

"I know what happened to Sophia. I know why I know. She's me or I'm her. It's not all a dream. Ask Preston, he saw. I lived her life and now, this lifetime I'm repeating so much of what she . . . I endured before. I can't stop this pattern until I undo her tragedy. I mean, I know I can't make the abuse and pain go away, but there must be something I can do. Everything happens for a reason. I just don't know what."

"I wish you wouldn't stay out there by yourself again. No matter what Preston says. But then again, to have peace in the future, the past *does* have to be dealt with. Perhaps it *is* time for you to do that," Richard said.

"I . . . I" she stammered, stuttered, her glance darting from him to the window and Cat, to the food in front of her. She clenched her fists in frustration.

Richard said nothing more, merely gazed with calm assurance.

Molly tried again to explain. "Everyone in my life right now is here to help me. I have no doubt. And some, especially Royce, will be helped too. And you . . ." She paused, searching for words to describe what she had begun to see.

"I must return to the woods, the cabin, the bridge. I won't be alone. The old man promised me I won't be alone."

"Preston insists you'll be safe, that a spirit protects you. I wish I could believe both of you. But look what's happened. Jake is a very real threat."

"Jake? Where is he?"

Richard and Beth exchanged glances and were silent a moment.

"I'm afraid . . . don't worry. Fifi is standing guard," Richard said. "Now eat up. Get your strength back. The doctor says you're exhausted. And the wasp sting and stress of . . . well, were more than you could handle."

In her mind's eye she saw Jake and Diatrice. The scene flooded back: Diatrice all puffed up smug, looking down her nose at them as if they stank of something rotten. Of Jake's disgusted snarl. And the gun? Had she imagined one? What? She must have passed out.

"I'm sorry, Molly," Richard said, interrupting her musing. "I have appointments to keep. I'll be back this afternoon as soon as I can. There will be more time to talk then. Would you like me to see if Preston can come too? I think he will be more help than me."

Molly nodded and noticed for the first time the weary slump of his shoulders, the circles under his eyes, the sad turn of his mouth. His pouchy cheeks, that once gave him a sweet teddy-bear expression, now sagged and aged his appearance.

"I'm sorry. I've been unthinking. Of course you have other concerns. Come when you can."

After he left, the house grew quiet, but her mind raced. "I need to know," she cried out.

"Hush," Beth said, nearing the bed with yet another pill and water.

"Stop it. Stop. Please tell me what's going on." Molly shook her head, refusing the medication. "I can't sleep forever!"

"Richard's callin' Ellen and Royce. I reckon they'll be here soon's they can. They saw the whole fracas and can answer yer questions better'n me." She held the pill to Molly. "Please, take this jest so's you'll rest til they get here."

"One more. That's all." Molly swallowed, drank more water, slaking her thirst. "But before I'm knocked out again, I want to see Cat."

Beth helped her into a bathrobe, and with an arm around her waist, they walked out together.

The scruffy cat eyed them from atop the fence, leaped down and trotted over to where Molly sat on the lawn. He meowed as if scolding, then head-bumped her leg and rubbed against her arm.

He stepped into her lap, climbed up her chest, and stared into her eyes as if trying to convey a message.

Cat stiffened, alert, and wide-eyed. Nearby, an engine rumbled and clattered. The noise of an old car or truck that sounded like she felt, ready to quit trying.

Cat's body relaxed, blended to the crook of Molly's arm. Beth helped as she stood, and they padded inside, to the bedroom where Cat squirmed free. With Molly settled in bed, he curled in the curve of her bent legs, nuzzled close. They slept.

When she woke, Royce stood looking down at her. He, too, appeared drawn and worn.

"Hi," she said. Cat crawled over her, jumped down, and scurried away as if his job were done, for now anyway. A door creaked, Beth chided, and soon Cat hunched at his perch looking in the window.

"Good afternoon, darlin'. How are you?"

"Better. But I can't think. What happened?"

Before he had a chance to respond, Ellen bounced into the room, chewing gum and carrying a steaming bowl of thick soup.

"Well, look at you. Idling away this fine day. Here, this'll get ya on your feet and feeling fit." Setting her offering on the nightstand, she fussed, propping pillows and placing a tray in front of Molly.

Ellen's fix had arrived. Clam chowder. Molly took a small taste and then wolfed down the delicious, hot, rich soup with morsels of clams and potato chunks. Her stomach ceased to rumble, and she felt satisfied, nourished.

"Thank you," she said. "I'm ready now. Tell me. Please."

Neither spoke and then both at once. They stopped, and Ellen motioned for Royce to continue.

"I'm not sure what you remember."

"We were sitting on the floor when Jake and Diatrice barged in. I thought I saw a gun in his hand."

"Yes," Royce said. "He had a gun and ranted about you and me. Accusing us. Well, he got pretty graphic and disgusting. Diatrice stood there with her mouth hanging open, her eyes wide, looking at him and then us and back at him. I don't think she knew what she'd gotten in to."

"Hey, according to Jake I was even part of the picture," Ellen chimed in with a snort. "And that really threw old Ms. Holier-Than-

Thou into a tizzy. Wiped the smirk right off her face. I think he may have pointed his pistol at her a time or two. In more ways than one, if you get my drift."

"Geez. I'm so sorry. My messes, my stupid mistakes put your lives in danger."

"Don't worry about us. We're okay. He had just started to threaten us when Preston came up from behind and startled them both. Diatrice fainted, and Jake slithered away when Preston knelt to help her."

"Where's Jake now?"

"Gone or hiding out somewhere. No one answers the phone or doorbell. And Cecilia . . ." Royce's voice faded.

"We ain't seen hide nor hair of the two since. Bet she's with him. She does seem to take to preachers. Sorry, Royce." Ellen laid a hand on his arm.

Jake and Cecilia! Shame washed over her, crawled beneath her skin. Jake with another woman. After all these years with her. After telling her he loved her. After just a few nights ago when she'd gone to his bed. He must have had his eye on Cecilia even then. She'd been such a fool to believe his lies, to give him so much of herself. Her throat closed even as the food in her stomach turned to sour bile rising.

"Go, please leave. Now," she said, chasing away her only friends.

"Molly, darlin'."

"I just didn't think. I'm so sorry," Ellen said. "I didn't think you cared."

"I *don't* care!" Molly shouted as she pushed aside the tray, sending bowl and spoon tumbling to the floor. Out of bed, dizzy and unsteady, she stumbled to the window. With her back to them she said, "Just leave me alone, please."

She heard the door close and knew they'd gone. Alone, she released hot burning tears of shame and embarrassment. Scenes of her acquiescing over and over again, scenes of lovemaking, scenes of pouring out her heart to him raced across her mind. Sobs from deep within wrenched her stomach. Afraid she would throw up, she grabbed the wastebasket setting beside the bed, brought it with her to the window. She swallowed, tried to stop the flow of tears, the wracking waves of heartbreaking sobs, the horrid sense of abandonment and betrayal. Tried to focus her attention on Cat as he stared at her. Nothing worked.

When she could cry no more, when her knees wobbled, when she thought she would collapse, she dropped back onto the bed. *God, what should I do? How can I have my heart break like this and still live?* No she didn't want him back. No. If he really was with Cecilia, she could have him. Maybe they deserved each other. So why this torrent of overwhelming emotions? Humiliation, pure and simple. How much could she take? Nothing in her life made sense. Now she really wanted a cigarette. She'd get dressed and go get a pack somewhere. But she didn't even know where she was.

"Beth, Royce, Somebody," she hollered.

Immediately the door opened, and Royce hurried in, followed by Beth. Ellen slinked to the corner, head bowed.

"I want a cigarette. Somebody get me one. I can't stand to be in my skin a minute more."

"Darlin, please." Royce reached to hold her. She cringed and pulled away.

"No no no."

Beth pulled a bottle of pills from her pocket and, with shaky fingers, pried the cap off.

"Hush, chile," she crooned as she poured water and handed it to Molly. "Take this."

Molly shook her head no, but opened her mouth and took the pill. Anything, anything to not think anymore.

The medicine did nothing. She cried. She got angry—at Jake—at herself. Royce stepped back, whispered to Ellen, and they left. Molly cried some more. Finally exhausted, all feeling ceased. Numbly she stared into Beth's worried face. How long she lay in this stupor, she didn't know. Light from the window dimmed. The air grew chilly. Beth tucked a quilt around her and tiptoed from the room.

The doorbell rang. Molly heard a familiar voice.

"Amy!"

"Hi, Mom," Amy said. She sat on the bed, held Molly's overly warm hands in her cool ones and squeezed. When she leaned forward, Molly came up to meet her cheek, placed her hand on Amy's long blonde hair, held her close and inhaled her scent, her energy.

"Oh, Amy. Sweetheart. Honey. But how, what?"

"I took the first plane I could get."

"You didn't have to come . . . your new job?"

"I've brought my laptop and enough projects for at least a couple weeks. As long as I fax work in, my job is secure. I wanted to be here with you."

Molly lay back, never taking her eyes off her beautiful daughter. A gift from a loving universe.

# TWENTY-FOUR

*This moment I shall start a divine life;*
*this moment and not later.*
*This moment is in my hands.*
*My soul will show me the way.*

—Lorenzo

Molly and Amy drifted through late afternoon hours talking. Even though Molly's head ached and she felt weak, she had to ask, "How is your therapy going?"

"Slow. I'm not sure if she's the right therapist. It's hard to know when you've never been before." Amy shook her head.

"What's she like? I guess I mean, do you get a sense of compassion and acceptance of who you are?" Molly asked, thinking of Richard. "That's important for me."

"Oh yes. I feel like I could tell her anything. I've certainly been able to share my feelings about Jake. How he treated me. What it was like growing up under his thumb." Amy hesitated. "You look so tired, Mom. Maybe we should save this for another day."

"No, please," Molly said. "I've got to say this. I'm so sorry I brought him into our home. Exposed you kids to someone so . . . so controlling and mean-spirited. So sick."

"It's okay," Amy said, holding Molly's hand. "I'm going to be just fine. Besides, you were great. And we had a lot of fun too."

"I really want to believe that, but . . . I let you down. I failed you." Molly pulled her hand away and covered her face.

"You're too hard on yourself, Mom. You were always there for me," Amy said, leaning over and giving Molly a hug.

"Thank you," Molly whispered. "How'd you get to be so grown up? And sweet?"

"I had you, that's how. You look like you're going to cry, and if you do, I will. This is way too heavy for either of us right now. And from what Richard has been telling me you've been pretty sick. He's the one who got in touch with me. When he explained what you were going through . . . Well, he didn't have to convince me to come." Amy paused and then changed the subject. "So tell me what's all this about you? Staying at some house in the woods?"

"Yes," Molly said. "And it is interesting. But I'm just too tired to explain today. We'll go out there soon. Anyway, I want to hear about you. Tell me the fun stuff."

Amy related in glowing terms how much she enjoyed North Dakota's rural atmosphere and the friends she'd made.

"Mom, it's a great place to live. Of course I haven't had the pleasure of a winter on the northern plains yet, but I think I'd like to spend the rest of my life there."

*The rest of your life*, Molly thought. *I can't begin to think of tomorrow even, let alone the rest of my life.*

Amy prattled on, hands fluttering, green eyes sparkling. Molly relished her animation and descriptions of her home and the town.

"Sounds familiar. And so pleasant." Molly fell silent, thinking how Sweet Hollow could have been that place for her. If only she'd made wiser choices along the way. Jake had destroyed any chance for happiness here. Sophia too. Maybe when she figured out this past-life mess, maybe then she'd be wiser, more able to rid herself of Jake's negative influences.

If, as she suspected, Royce had been part of that past, could Jake have been too? She'd been shown Preacher Man and Sophia's father more than once. Both of them equally mean and evil, as far as she could tell. I wonder, *Was Jake one of them?* She knew little about reincarnation and now didn't have the stamina to research it. Though she had heard somewhere that souls did incarnate in groups, working out lessons they needed to learn with each other. Perhaps Jake, a preacher in this life, had been one then too. Or had she attracted a "man of the cloth" because of what one had done to Sophia? Oh. Jake more likely had been her father. That would explain why so often she felt like a child with him. An errant child at that. Ugly phrases, like a drumbeat, pounded in her head.

"Wear this outfit," he'd said with disdain. "Where have you been?" and, "Now you've got an attitude," and, "Don't lie to me, Molly," and, "Don't even start with that," and, "Pay attention," and, "You're sick, put your pajamas on now!" and, "I'm tired of arguing with you," always said with contempt. Always she did what she was told. Their relationship hadn't been like that in the beginning. He'd been attentive and complimentary, and she, her feisty self. But when it all turned sour, why, oh why had she stayed? Molly cringed inside, disgusted with herself. She'd lost confidence and any sense of well-being somewhere along the way. Just when she'd had enough of being treated like a stupid little girl, he'd bring flowers or he'd smile with a twinkle in his eyes and kiss her hand, seduce her into believing his love was real. Even their sex life . . .

"Mom?" Amy whispered. Molly heard the bedroom door close. Alone, she mulled over the last twenty years. Twenty years! A huge chunk of her adult life.

Mustering strength, she reached for her journal and began scribbling meandering thoughts, hoping she'd rid herself of angst that, like a thorn in her belly, throbbed and burned.

A knock on the door roused her. She'd dozed with pen in hand, the notebook coil had imprinted its swirl on her forearm.

"Come in."

Amy came with a tray. Dinner for two.

"Let's go to the patio," Molly said. "I want some air *and* out of this bed."

"Okay. I'll take this out and then help you."

"Oh, I think I can manage. What about Beth? Isn't she eating?"

"She's off to a class somewhere. Won't be back til late."

As they ate a simple soup-and-salad supper, the sun set, leaving a pink good-bye in the clouds. Cat settled on Molly's lap.

"I'll have to ask about cats," Molly said, thinking out loud.

"Huh?"

"Well, I dreamt about swans swimming in my mind, and Beth said they represented the power to enter another time. And then there were the raccoons we saw. Something about their masks implying a person may not be who he's disguised as. Both of those sure are real to me. Animal totems, I think she said. Everything in nature, according to Beth, is communicating with us. If we pay attention, that is. Interesting idea."

"Maybe." Amy looked puzzled. "I never thought of that. But, hey, why not? House cats, though, are so domesticated. Even the wild one you've got there."

"Yes, they are. Still, I'll ask."

"By the way, Richard called and has cleared his schedule for tomorrow afternoon so you guys can talk. I told him fine. I hope that's okay."

"Oh yes. Though I hate to take my eyes off you and your smile."

"And Royce has something he wants to discuss with both of you. So they'll be here around one. Don't worry about me. I've got reports to compose—a job to do."

The next morning Molly lazed in the garden petting Cat and listening to Celtic harp music softly playing from Beth's CD. Amy, with reading glasses atop her nose, leaned over her computer at a kitchen table cluttered with paperwork. Beth had gone to the bookstore early, and the house was quiet. To give Amy uninterrupted time and space, Molly had dressed and taken a cup of coffee to the backyard.

The outdoors, always a restful place, soothed her soul. Even this tiny patch of green where a few purple asters and golden chrysanthemums bloomed. Could flowers be communicating too? Mesmerized, she came to attention when she heard a now-familiar whistle she knew to be Royce's way of ringing a doorbell where there was no door.

"Good morning," Molly said. "Oh! You've brought daisies. Where did you find daisies this time of year?"

Royce smiled, set the vase on the picnic table, and took her hand. "You're starting to look like your old self. Charming hat. But, darlin', where's the price tag?"

Molly chuckled at the image she'd presented that first meeting of theirs. What a sight she'd been with the Minnie Pearl hat and biker t-shirt. Her grin waned as she realized how innocent too.

"I'm glad to see you, but surprised. I wasn't expecting you until after lunch. Some coffee?"

"No thanks. Listen, I had a specific reason for coming this morning, and I want to get this off my chest. I've thought and thought about your comment regarding reincarnation. I'm not ready to accept that idea, but I do have something from my childhood that might pertain to your experience with Sophia and . . . and my dreams of you and her and of me being called Joe. I don't know . . . but here's what I have."

"Don't you want to wait for Richard? And Preston will be here too, I think," Molly interrupted.

"No. I want to be alone with you," he said, took her hand and then talked nonstop.

"When I was a child, my grandmother entertained me with tales about my great-grandfather. May have even been my great-*great*-grandfather. How he traveled by horse and buggy from farmhouse to farmhouse, preaching and bestowing his wife's baked bread on those he judged poor and powerless. I imagined some kind of knight rescuing the distressed. Until Grandma's eyes became heavy lidded. Then she'd close them, fold her arms across her chest, and shake her head, muttering incomprehensible noises.

"'Something was mighty wrong with that man,' she'd say with pursed lips. 'The first time he was run out of the territory his wife believed him about a crazy, jealous husband. But when it happened again and again, she couldn't be fooled any longer. What shenanigans was he up to? Rumors were he itched after young girls and took advantage when parents were in the fields or in the woods gathering berries, mushrooms and such. That poor wife of his, when he showed up with a squalling newborn needin' raising. And a fancy brooch to appease her. Some cock and bull about the mama dying in childbirth and the family not wanting another mouth to feed.'

"I listened, not understanding until much later what she meant by 'took advantage.' I'd forgotten all this until I moved here. Especially in your woods. That first day when I surprised you and Beth, I was just as startled. Regaling you with the legend of the family who settled here. About Doc and his herbs. About the young girl. Well, a few nights ago I dreamt about this tight-faced, angry man dressed in black." Royce stood and paced to the flower bed and back. "I just remembered . . . in my dream I saw him pick up something shiny . . . a piece of jewelry . . . stones like those on my family's ring." He frowned as he looked at Molly. "Then, in the dream, the man became my great-grandfather as he jumped on his horse. I saw him riding off, fast. I woke up desperately reaching to bring him back. Make him . . . force him to do right by the family he had mistreated. Doesn't make much sense and yet it does, you know?" Royce licked his parched lips and shook his head.

"Thank you," Molly said. They sat together in silence, Royce with his head bowed and shoulders slumped, Molly deep in thought. When Cat sprang off after a sparrow, Molly straightened and looked at Royce. "The pieces start falling into place, don't they? I don't know what to say, except thank you."

She offered a glass of water, and he quenched his thirst by emptying it. Longing to caress his careworn face, to tilt his head and kiss away the confusion she saw, and to somehow restore the sparkle in his tired eyes, she jammed her fists into her sweater pockets instead. Physical signs of affection could only lead to complications. What she needed was a friend and ally, not a lover. Royce leaned close and reached for her.

They both stood, about to embrace when Ellen bounded around the side of the house. "Hey you two. Gosh Molly, you're looking more and more like your old self . . . Oops. Did I interrupt? I can come back later." She started to retreat but Molly said,

"Pull up a chair. Coffee?"

"No, ma'am. One more cup of java and I'll be nervous as a long-tailed cat in a room full of rocking chairs."

Molly and Royce grimaced, and Ellen shrugged. "Okay, okay. I'll stop."

"We've been discussing the history of my hideaway in the woods. And those mysterious sightings of a long time ago." At the moment Molly couldn't remember how much of the whole story Ellen knew.

"You mean the girl's ghost who haunts the footbridge? I'm all ears."

Molly turned to Royce and asked, "What about your ring? I really want to see it."

"Cecilia hated that ring. Said the design was evil, of all things. So I took it off just to have peace," he said, rubbing his ring finger. "I searched everywhere the last time you asked. I went looking again today. Passed down all those generations, and now the family ring is nowhere to be found. Nowhere."

"Bet the little . . . sorry. Bet Cecilia took the evil jewels and skedaddled."

Molly frowned and muttered, "If your ring was the pin, well, there's a curse on the stones, if you believe in curses. Losing the brooch seemed to crush Sophia almost as much as losing her baby."

"Baby?" Ellen said.

"Yes," Molly said. "Sophia had a baby, and they took it away."

"I'm out in left field here. Who's they? If I may ask."

"It's a long story. I'm sorry, not today," Molly said, glancing at Royce for help. He looked stunned himself. Ellen shrugged and chewed her gum in silence.

"Come on, Ellen. Let's give Molly a rest. Treat me to a bowl of chowder, and I'll tell you what I know."

When they'd hugged her and promised to return soon, they left by the side gate. Molly picked up her clutter and went inside to find Amy at the counter preparing sandwiches. Each with her own concerns, a respectful, almost reverent silence engulfed them. After lunch, Amy went back to work, and Molly sought the comfort of the yard and flowers.

Richard and Preston arrived together. The three of them sat in the shade of a red oak tree in the far corner of Beth's backyard. Cat chose a sunny spot nearby. Even in this comfortable, quiet setting, Molly felt anxious. At least Preston agreed about her moving back to Sophia's haunt. She, of course, could do as she pleased, but she respected Richard and relied on his guidance. After a few remarks about the weather, the leaves changing color, her physical health and his, Richard said, "You wanted to talk about childhood memories."

"Since I saw you last, I've had another vision of Sophia. She heard her father say she was nothing but a useless girl. When I woke up my heart ached, as if that had been my father talking about me. But my daddy loved me." Hot tears ran down her cheeks, and she dug into a pocket for tissue.

"What's behind these tears?"

"Sadness. Hopelessness. Hurt."

"Ask yourself how old you are with these feelings."

"I don't know. Small. Maybe five or six."

"Take some time and ask the little girl within you why she is so sad."

The daisies sitting on the picnic table exemplified simplicity and reminded Molly of the little haven in Sophia's dreams. Cat crawled onto her lap and purred. She thought of Biscuit comforting Sophia. She thought of the hurtful words and then of the golden light that always came when Sophia was most afraid or sad. Right now she wanted that golden light too. Instead, she had these friends waiting for an answer.

"I have no words. Other than I feel Sophia's pain. Somehow I know I can help, and I want to give her whatever she needs."

"It's just not a safe place for you to be alone."

"I won't be alone. Please understand that. Sophia's been abandoned and rejected over and over. I can't abandon her too." Molly turned to Preston for support. He nodded.

The two men stared at each other. They must have come to some unspoken agreement, for Richard heaved a resigned sigh.

"I'm going to trust you two. Your daughter will go with you?"

"Yes. Until she has to get back to North Dakota. And Fifi. I think Ellen will let me keep Fifi as long as I need."

"Let's hope it won't take long. The weather's changing, winter's coming. You could get snowed in up there, and you'll need provisions. Stay here for a couple more days, and I'll see what I can do."

Preston pulled his chair close, took her hand, and placed a small smooth stone in it. "Keep this. Use it as a portal to Sophia. A passageway will remain open."

"Thank you," she said, holding the pebble as if it were a precious gem.

With Amy driving the Chevy station wagon, Molly gave directions down one road and then another. Feeling stronger now and headed into the woods for the day, she'd decided to take Amy on a little tour of their surroundings. First the church. As far as she knew, Jake's mom's paintings were still hung in the fellowship hall, and some of them had been Amy's favorites as a child. It being Tuesday perhaps no one would be around. Before turning off the main road, they stopped and admired autumn leaves now in full flame—crimson, orange, yellow, golden brown. Molly related the analogy of God and his gumdrops as Amy stood by the car snapping photos. From their vantage point, they could see the church nestled innocently among multicolored trees.

"What a wonderful little church. Are the people as pleasant as this picture?"

"Some are, I guess. Richard and Beth, of course." But then there was Diatrice and her retinue of snobbish old biddies. She probably hadn't given them a fair chance, but Jake had done his best to convince them all she was sick and crazy. Aside from the reception tea and one dinner at the Fletch's, there hadn't been many opportunities to find out how nice or not nice they were.

As they wound their way down the hill, Molly said, "I don't have very good memories of this place. I haven't been to services for a long time."

Only one car sat in the parking lot when they pulled in. An old yellow clunker she didn't recognize. "That may be the caretaker. Let's see if the door is unlocked," Molly said.

"Oh my. Look at those." Amy's words echoed in the empty hall. The room was dim, but she'd spotted the wall hangings before Molly's eyes had adjusted to the contrasting light.

"Yes, I thought you'd enjoy seeing some of those paintings again."

"Jake's mom was always kind and pleasant. How'd she raise such a bastard?"

"So that's what I'm called these days. Well, well. Hello to you too," Jake said, coming toward them from an office doorway.

"I thought . . . I thought." Molly shook, overcome by fear and sadness. Speechless and quivering, she stepped back.

"Mom," Amy said, shock written across her face.

Molly reached for Amy with one hand as her other crammed into her jeans pocket. She rubbed the smooth stone tucked there, and an inner resolve, like a power surge, pulsed up her spine. She straightened to full height, her head found its balance high on her neck, and her shoulders slid back and down as she glared at Jake. He hated that stance, she knew.

"Ladies," he sneered even as his eyes shifted from her stare. "I'd like to stay and chat, but I'm finished here."

His strut became a weasel-like skulking as he headed for the door. Molly and Amy watched as he disappeared, heard an engine sputter and cough and then tires squeal. Molly leaned into Amy, like a child seeking safety and comfort.

They hugged and Amy said, "He's a jerk. Let's go."

As they climbed into their own rattletrap, a shiny black Mercedes pulled in. Diatrice huffed her bulk from behind the driver's seat and stood waiting as if to confront them. *Damn it,* Molly thought and slid down in the seat, turning away. Amy hesitated and began rolling down her window but stopped when Molly said, "That's Diatrice. Ignore her. She's nothing but trouble."

Without a word, Amy drove away and turned toward Beth's house, their excursion over.

# TWENTY-FIVE

~

*The soul is capable of knowing all things*
*in her highest power.*

—Meister Eckhart

Three days later, Molly and Amy packed their few belongings and prepared to hie into the woods. They had stocked up on essentials, so the only trip to town would be to fax Amy's completed work. Drawn as if her very soul beckoned, Molly was anxious to get to the primitive dwelling snugged in the forest. She imagined a walk with Amy through the trees and along the stream, sharing the charm and beauty, and longed for uninterrupted intimate conversations to lament and laugh. But more than anything, she wanted Amy to appreciate the ethereal mystery of that captivating place.

"Are you sure you want to go so soon?" Beth asked as the three of them lingered in the driveway. "You could rest easy here as long as you like."

"No. It's time. You must want your peace and quiet by now. And I need . . . I need to be there. And Cat, I'm sure, wants to wander free."

Cat had hissed when forced into the carrier, but now lay quietly, eyeing them as Amy piled the cage among boxes and bags in the car.

"Hey, speaking of cats. Are they a symbol too? Like swans?" Molly asked.

"I reckon. Depends some on their color, I think. I'll check. But I do know cats can mean magic and mystery."

*Raccoons and deception, swans and power to enter another time . . . and cat, as the most prominent, foretelling of mystery and magic.* Dumbfounded, Molly said, "Of course." She hugged Beth and said, "Thank you so much for everything. I think you saved my life."

"Shucks, 'tweren't nothin'. I reckon you'd do the same for me."

As Amy eased the crammed station wagon down the driveway, Beth stooped for the rolled-up newspaper and called, "Take right good care, you two. I'll come visit soon."

Molly, looking back, saw Beth's good-bye wave become frantic. First as if motioning them to return as she pointed to the open newspaper. And then shooing them on their way.

"I wish I'd read the paper before we left," Molly said.

"Want to stop and pick one up?"

"No, let's go. It's mostly gossip and who's been on vacation and where."

Driving through town, she had second thoughts. "Something tells me I should read that newspaper. Would you get one there at the corner drug while I run into the bookstore and tell Royce where we'll be?"

As Molly entered, Royce rose and hurried around the counter, clearly surprised to see her.

"Amy and I are on our way to my enchanted forest." Thinking he might take her into his arms in this public place, she stepped back. "We're set to stay there several days. I just wanted you to know."

Two shoppers came in, laughing. Royce merely nodded, his attention never leaving Molly. "I'm glad you told me. Something's happened. Cecelia . . . but, darlin', it concerns you too.

"Me? How?" *Oh no. Jake and Cecelia?*

A woman entered, looked at the slip of paper in her hand, and walked toward them.

"Mind if I come up after I close shop?" Royce asked quickly. "I'll bring clam chowder . . . yes," he added with a rueful smile, "I'm afraid that's what's called for here."

"Ellen's tension reliever . . . Now I'm really worried," Molly whispered, biting her lip. "But you're busy and Amy's waiting so I'd better go." She turned, gave the customer a half smile, and hurried out the door.

Molly stepped into the street and spied Amy behind the wheel, drumming her fingers on the dash, the car engine running.

"Goodness, you look impatient. I couldn't have been in there that long. You didn't bump into Diatrice or Jake, did you?"

"No, but I've had enough of this town. Let's get out of here. Tell me where to turn," Amy said as she stepped on the gas.

"It's a few miles," Molly mumbled.

"Hey, what's up? You look confused or something."

"Royce is upset about Cecelia. That's his wife. A few days ago she flew the coop, as Ellen would say." Molly paused, not quite sure how to proceed. Should she tell Amy that whole story or just drop it? She didn't want to talk or even think, for that matter. Closing her eyes, she let her mind wander. Relationships were sure hard to figure. Why would Royce even be attracted to the likes of Cecelia? Why had she, herself, gotten involved with Jake? And then put up with so much disrespect and deviousness?

"Well, Mom, isn't Cecelia his problem?"

"*She* is his problem. But Royce has become a close friend. I sure didn't like his wife when I met her. Pretty in a hard sort of way, she seemed cold and calculating. And she's left him before. Ran off with the last minister Diatrice hired. Royce took her back then and will probably keep doing it. For some reason she's got a hold on him."

"What can you do? Anyway, you've got enough to cope with, don't you?"

"Yes, yes I do, but he's coming up later because he says whatever it is with Cecelia will affect me too." She sighed. "What now, is what I'm thinking. If our suspicion is right, that she's with Jake, Royce's problem becomes mine." Molly had been examining her fingernails as she talked. Looking up, she said, "Turn right here."

As they left the highway, Molly cautioned, "Slow down." Amy didn't heed her warning until a bump lifted them from their seats and spun the car sideways.

"Okay. I got ya." Amy laughed.

"Back up into those shrubs. We'll have a clear getaway. Just in case. We walk from here."

"We've got a lot of stuff. Is it far?"

"About ten minutes," Molly said, releasing an antsy Cat from his confines and watching him scurry away. Each unloaded as much as she could carry and headed into the thicket. They walked in silence until the narrow track widened and bothersome shrubbery thinned.

"Ah, fresh air," Amy said, taking in a deep breath. "Crisp and cold. My favorite time of year."

"Mine too." Molly dropped her burden with a weary groan. "Guess it's a blessing I didn't dare go to the house for extra blankets, jackets, and dishes. We have enough stuff right here. I'm sure glad it's not hot. I'm sweating and tired."

"I forgot, you're not quite the mountain-climbing mama you used to be. Not yet anyway. Hey, what were those red bushes back there?"

"Sumac. I knew it would be dazzling by now, and you'd love it."

"Ouch." Amy dabbed at scratches on her arm. "This little trip is dangerous."

"Blackberry brambles. A few weeks ago I was picking ripe, sweet berries, and I had my share of thorns too. The rest of the way is cleared path. Let's go."

When Molly caught sight of the front porch, she stopped again, put down her parcels. *I'm home,* she thought and was both relieved and disappointed to see the rocking chair empty, to hear no dulcimer chime. Fifi bounded toward them, so fast it seemed they would be knocked down and slobbered all over. Instead, the looming black dog slowed, stopped at Molly's side, and barked once as if to say, "Introduce me."

Molly knelt on one knee and scruffed the lively dog's ears. "You've been well cared for, I see. But maybe a little lonely for company, huh? Well, don't you worry, we're here now." Standing again, she said, "This is Ellen's fearless companion, Fifi."

"So this is our watchdog? With a name like that I pictured a friendly little yapper." Amy smiled and patted Fifi's head. "No wonder you aren't scared. Where was this ferocious-looking beast when Jake and what's her name, Gertrude, showed up?"

"I can't remember," Molly said, not even trying. "Funny, you've made the same mistake I did when I met the church ladies for the first time. They all looked like Gertrudes to me."

Once again each hoisted her load and proceeded. The little cabin seemed more homey, more welcoming somehow. Lived in, cozy.

"Look at this," Molly said, grinning. "A door. An actual front door. And a shutter on the window."

"It didn't even have a door? Who's been fixing it up?"

"Heaven only knows. Richard? Royce? The old caretaker? Ghosts? If ghosts do such things." Molly shrugged.

Inside, she surveyed the changes. All windows had makeshift shutters to prevent any bad weather from intruding. A few folding lawn chairs and wooden TV tables leaned against one wall. In the center lay an inflated air mattress stacked high with sheets, a quilt, and pillows. The idea that someone had made such an effort to provide for them gave Molly pause. *Why do I ever worry about not having my needs met? Look at this. It's a haven.* Fifi barked, and Molly rummaged in her backpack for doggie treats she'd brought.

"Cool place, Mom," Amy said. "What a neat old desk. Reminds me of something. It'll be a perfect work space," she added, setting her laptop on the rough surface. "What's this?"

"Ah, my dulcimer." Molly picked it up and stroked the gleaming instrument, its highly polished surface tickling her fingertips. "Beautiful, isn't it? One day an old man with a scraggly beard knocked on my door. Scared me and wouldn't go away. He insisted this was meant for me."

"You can play it?" Amy asked, watching her mother pluck at the strings.

"No, but I'd like to. Even my clumsy strumming produces a vortex of some kind. Transports me back to when this house was relatively new. When a whole family lived here. When smoke rose from the chimney and a sweet, innocent child struggled to grow up whole. The first few times I saw them I felt as if I were watching an old movie. And then . . . then the little girl took over my mind. I *became* her." *Oh dear. Not now.* Abruptly she laid the dulcimer down.

At Amy's incredulous expression, Molly stammered, "I . . . I, it's impossible to explain. Please don't think I've gone mad."

"Oh, Mom. I don't know what to think. You aren't crazy. I know that. But what you're saying is just so far-out. I want to understand but . . ." Amy hugged her and said, "Maybe all that 'other family' is just something you dreamed. You have been pretty sick, you know.

A fever and then all the stress you're going through. For now, let's just get this place settled, and we can relax. Okay?"

Molly started to protest, then gave it up.

After another trip to the car, Molly said, "I'll stay here and start unpacking."

While Amy went back for the last load, Molly made up a bed in the alcove under the loft. If Fifi would sleep at the foot of the ladder, they'd both have protection close by. She toted bags of personal items upstairs. Perhaps they'd have uneventful days and nights—a respite of sorts.

She was sitting in the rocking chair watching two squirrels play chase, the dulcimer idle on her lap, when Fifi sat up, alert. Standing, Molly could see Amy and Richard, both with arms full. They stopped beyond earshot, put down their loads, and talked. Seriously, it seemed.

When they approached, Amy called, "Look who I found and what he's brought."

Richard balanced an upside-down rocking chair on his head while carrying a bouquet of daisies and a grocery bag.

"So you're the one," Molly said, taking the chair. "When did you find time to do all this?"

"I've had plenty of help," he said. "Turns out Royce is pretty handy with hammer and nails. Preston's been here, and Ellen's making curtains or something to cover the bare boards. We've even stacked firewood on the back stoop." He seemed pleased with himself and worn-out at the same time.

"Looks like I'm here for a long stay."

"Let's hope not, but who knows?" he said, taking his parcels inside.

"So our watchdog hasn't been alone too much, I guess."

"Oh no, she's been getting plenty of attention from all of us."

"Does Diatrice know you're doing all this for me?" Molly asked, certain that Diatrice knew every move he made.

"What I'm doing is not my wife's main concern right now." He hesitated with a frown. "Dear Diatrice is in a tizzy about . . . well, at least her flurry is freeing up my time. I've had more sudden cancellations than could reasonably be expected." Richard paused, then added, "It's just not important anymore."

"What do you mean?"

"Well your well-being matters more than my declining practice."

"Oh," Molly said, not knowing what to make of his startling remark. He'd been so supportive yet vague about his personal life. As a counselor should be, of course. Still, he was a friend who now had a lackluster air about him. Gone was his jovial, jig-dancing attitude. Even his comforting teddy-bear expression had been replaced by a drawn and disturbed look. She resisted the urge to place her hand on his cheek and offer to help. First Royce, now Richard, burdened with unexplained concerns. Even Amy, who hummed as she put their temporary home in order, was distracted and edgy.

"Mom, I want you to take it easy for a while, okay?" When Molly nodded, Amy turned to Richard. "How about showing me the lay of the land?"

Preparing to lie down and rest, Molly suddenly remembered the newspaper and began a search for it. She felt a strong sense of urgency. *Why? Where could Amy have stuck it?* Emptying the few remaining sacks and boxes with no luck, she determined the paper must be in the car. Donning a straw hat, she quickstepped out the door and off the porch, smiling at actually having a door to open and close.

A few strides later her pace slowed, and with tired legs, she trudged the path. At the car she saw the newspaper and squeezed the door handle. Locked. *Damn.* And Amy had the key. She leaned on a nearby boulder and wondered why it mattered. Removing her hat, she wiped perspiration from beneath her curls. Let the brilliant sunshine coax what freckles it could, she didn't care. Her vitality had waned, and the trek back seemed a daunting task. *Why didn't I leave a note so they'd know where I went?*

Cramming her hand into her jeans pocket, Molly felt Preston's smooth stone like a promise and relaxed, confident that angels hovered nearby. He'd said to keep it close always and so, trusting in his wisdom, she had. Now, as she sought a level seat on the boulder, she drew the stone from its tucked-in place and let it settle in her open palm, admiring its graceful curves and rises—grateful for comfort this talisman offered.

An eerie silence prevailed. Air stilled—not a rustle in the shrubs, no bird song, not even a trace of music near or far. Words to a favorite hymn drifted through her mind and she strained in hopes of hearing birds sing sweetly in the trees. *Then sings my soul, my Savior God to Thee. How great Thou art, how great Thou art.* A peaceful moment of prayer and meditation. Overhead, a hawk glided in wide circles, serene, free of anxieties and drama. Oh, to be a bird, soaring high. But of course, this free flight was an illusion. Hawks, too, struggled for survival and had their own calamities, their own place in a world often harsh and brutal. Still, could wildlife possibly experience the confusion and heartbreak humans endure?

Ah, the euphoria of nature when slow and calm and quiet—a world at rest, dozing, gathering energy for the next dance of wind or rain or blizzard. Molly's mood often altered with each season's rhythm. And this, autumn, had always been a time of wonder. Gentle, colorful, magnificent. Trees would soon shed their flamboyant raiments and sleep in preparation for spring and rebirth. Varmints would burrow in, snug with their cache of nuts and seeds. Many birds flew south to warmer climes. Those that stayed—yes, they surely must struggle for their lives.

*When through the woods and forest glades I wander . . . hear the brook . . . Then sings my soul . . .*

A faraway booming disrupted her reverie. With not a cloud to be seen, the silence-spoiling rumbles couldn't be thunder. She knew little about hunting season or rifle sounds but doubted gunfire would create such a dramatic disturbance. Somewhere, someone was blasting something. Invasive, unpleasant noise stirred memories of Jake's nasty behavior. How elusive peace was with him. No matter what happened in the future she vowed never to submit to any man again. *But how?* Her head began to pound. An uneasy force buzzed. With an ominous woosh of impending crisis, she stood and started back.

Sumac blazed and brambles attacked, but she emerged unscathed from the thicket to see them in the distance. Molly halted, spellbound, with an overwhelming sense of déjà vu. Invisible power, like high-voltage wires, zipped through the air, zapping her temples with every beat of her pulse. Prickling. Electrifying fine hairs on her arms. It wasn't Amy and Richard, but a manifestation. A little girl carrying a kitten and holding the hand of a boy a head taller . . .

Springtime surrounds them, wild flowers bloom, and the children skip and giggle. Behind them hover faint images of an old man, an aging woman, a golden light. As they near, dulcimer music clamors a chaotic refrain and then ceases.

Suddenly the boy and girl are taller, older. The girl's braids have been transformed into wavy burnt-orange tresses glowing in the autumn sun, like a halo. Sophia, of course. Now with a full-size cat at her feet. A lanky, young man keeps pace beside her. *Joe*? They pause, speak to one another, embrace for a moment. The man and phantom entourage fade, and the young lady in long skirts, trancelike, floats toward Molly, her aura brightening the closer she comes. The cat hisses and darts away. A sudden gust of cold wind implores, "Molly, come home." Sophia draws ever nearer until Molly, consumed with the fear and pain of an abused young woman, drops to the ground. Shifting blurred images dance at the edges of her mind, and she clutches the stone, trying to hang on to a reality that becomes evermore dreamlike.

"*Molly, come home, home, home*" reverberates, bounces off chestnut trees surrounding a secluded glen. Dim winter light casts a gray gloom, and she shivers in the chill air. Icy thoughts prance and collide as she struggles to maintain her elusive identity as Molly Carpenter. Exhausted, she capitulates to Sophia's compelling personality. The high-voltage vibration dissipates. Silence reigns once more.

Hot tears slide down her cheeks as her papa scolds with doubled fists. "You ain't goin' nowhere, no how, Missy. Yer stayin' right cheer to face the mess you done made. Ya hear?"

"Yes, Papa."

"Preacher'll be comin' soon, and me and him'll take keer of that brat you got cookin'." With a snort, he picks up his jug and tromps off.

Molly rouses, bewildered, aware of blackberry brambles, sumac, her pounding headache and the smooth, warm stone clutched in her hand. Forlorn angst descends again like a dense, cold fog; and, with an aching back, she's pacing in the familiar clearing, a fist clenching the thin shawl wrapped tight against the cold. A man coaxes her to sit. He kneels and squeezes her hands.

"Royce? . . . Royce? . . . How can this be?"

"Soph. It's me, Joe. Listen to me. You gotta come quick. I done snuck back to getcha. But I cain't stay."

"I cain't run away now. The baby. Preacher's coming."

"That's why you gotta git. I'll always protect you. I swear," he pleads.

Sophia's hand reaches to the bulge that stretches the worn fabric of her skirt. "Preacher said he'd take me and . . ."

"Don't believe that. Please. They don't care 'bout you."

"But he promised. He wouldn't lie, he's a preacher . . . besides, where'd we go? How'd we get by?"

"I'd find a way. Please let me at least try."

"I cain't, Joe."

Joe spins around at the crackle of branches and the huff of heavy breathing.

Drunk, and with a shotgun on his arm, their papa breaks through the bushes. Staggering, he scowls and shouts, "I done told you I never want to lay eyes on yer no-good face again. Now git, afore I blast ya."

With a final pleading look, Joe bolts, leaving her wretched and wringing her hands. A stone slips from her grasp, falls to the ground; and Sophia stares through her tears, bends, and picks it up. As she caresses the smooth, oddly shaped warm pebble, her panic subsides. Courage, like a velvet drape, cloaks her timidity and confusion. Feeling a blessed relief, she succumbs to this strong phantom personality.

. . .

Molly released the breath she'd been holding. The sun still shone fairly high. Little, if any, time had passed since she'd fallen. She lay with one leg twisted beneath her, the ankle wrenched and swollen. Whimpering and unable to get to her feet, she thought, *Now what?* As if in answer to prayer, a walking stick waved in front of her. The old man, chewing tobacco, held out a hand. With the stick and the boost, Molly lifted herself gingerly. She slipped Preston's precious pebble into her pocket and hobbled toward home . . . *home?*

# TWENTY-SIX

~

*Obstacles aren't always meant to stop you—sometimes they serve as detours, showing you a more rewarding direction to explore.*
—Source Unknown

It didn't appear the days ahead would be uneventful after all. *I will rest and be prepared,* droned a mental mantra, keeping time with the throbbing in Molly's head. Excruciating paces later, she hoisted herself up the steps onto her porch. Unable to climb the ladder, she lay down in the alcove, desperate to sleep but unable to quiet the episode of Sophia and Joe. *Where did Joe go when he ran off? Where are they now?* Sophia had refused his protection, had refused to mistrust the diabolical preacher. So gullible, so naive. Nothing but pain and unhappiness could follow such misguided loyalty. How can I repair this damage and restore a young woman's chance for happiness? For a peaceful life? And why me? Why now? *Quit asking unanswerable questions,* Molly scolded.

She woke to a whisper of voices, the rhythmic creak of rocking chairs.

"I'm awake," she called and limped out to meet them. Dusk had fallen, so she must have slept, though weariness still weighed her down.

Richard stood and motioned for her to sit. He retrieved a stump from the yard and positioned it near her chair. A makeshift stool on which she gently placed her injured foot. Amy held the folded newspaper.

"Oh good, you brought it back. I've been looking for it. Here," she said with an outstretched hand.

"Mom! What happened?"

"I just stumbled and fell. My ankle hurts. I'll be okay," Molly said as another distant explosion distracted her. "Did you hear that?" She shuddered, almost afraid this, too, was a visit from the past.

"That would be coal mining," Richard answered. "I heard it wouldn't be long before they'd move close enough to disturb us and everything in their path."

"It sounds a long way off. But big."

"Well," he said, "You're right. A long way off and big. It's called mountaintop removal. Instead of boring into mountainsides to mine coal, they just blast off about one-third of the mountaintop."

Molly gasped. "Why would anyone do such a thing? And isn't it illegal?"

"It's called greed. And unfortunately this type of mining has been legal for thirty years or more."

"The noise and mess must be awful up close," Molly said. "Isn't anyone protesting? I sure would be."

"Environmentalists have been up in arms for years," Richard said. "Streams are being buried, wildlife either killed or driven from their habitat."

"Mom, please," Amy said. "Don't get all upset. There's nothing any of us can do, especially you right now."

"You know I abhor senseless destruction. What about the animals and the forest?" Molly rested her head in her hands and wished for transport permanently to 1850. Before such outrages occurred.

They sat in silence a moment until a familiar whistle's faint trill reached them.

"That's Royce. He said he'd be by with clam chowder and some upsetting news. What on earth is going on?" As she spoke, Molly looked at Amy, expecting answers but finding instead pain and confusion in her daughter's eyes.

The whistling stopped, and Royce came into view, a pack on his back and carrying his promised supper.

"You don't sound upset, whistling like that," Molly said, trying to convince herself.

"Old habit," he said, handing the soup container to Amy. "I don't want to surprise anyone. Especially a mama bear and her cub. Like I did once. So I whistle."

Molly started to rise, but Amy stood and said, "No, Mom, sit. Keep your foot up."

"What happened to you?" Royce asked as he slipped the backpack off his shoulder.

"The camp stove's on the back stoop. Come help me heat this up, and I'll explain," Amy said.

"Okay. By the way," Royce said over his shoulder, "Ellen'll be here in a few minutes."

Richard settled in the other rocker. Neither spoke. Molly's head was full of mountaintop blasting, full of imagining what awful news Royce might have, and concern for her throbbing ankle. She simply had no words.

"I'm afraid I'm not very good company tonight," she said.

"It's peaceful." He spoke in such a quiet voice, she puzzled at that too.

Fifi merely raised her head when Cat crept up and sidled over to Molly, sniffing at her foot and then springing onto her lap. He gazed into her face with big green eyes.

"He's trying to tell you something, I think."

"Beth says cats represent mystery and magic. A lot of mystery going on right now, wouldn't you say?" Molly's voice sounded petulant to her own ear.

"I know a little about animal totems, thanks to Preston."

Molly touched her pocket where the stone lay. "Thank God for Preston."

"According to him, a cat is a spirit helper and very resourceful."

"I believe that. This cat led me through the woods until I came upon Sophia whimpering and hurt. He seemed to know exactly where he was going. Scolded me to hurry."

"It figures, being black-and-white, which according to my old friend, indicates a need to see issues clearly."

Molly nodded. Even in her confusion, this made sense. "I just don't know what to do next."

"Pay attention. That's all any of us can do."

"To what?"

"You already are alert and aware. Of totems and talismans. Of seasons and this setting. How about your dreams? Are they telling you anything?"

"Here's supper," Amy said as she held the door open with one hand, bowls in the other. Fifi sniffed and came closer as Royce ladled out chowder. The dog's big eyes and slurping tongue seemed to say, "Where's mine?"

"Don't come begging. You've still got food in your bowl," Richard said, patting the dog's head. Fifi sat obediently, and the four of them ate as darkness descended.

After the dishes had been cleared, Amy brought out candles, placing them around their perimeter. When lit, they gave off a tranquil glow, belying the conversation that ensued.

Royce began, "As I told Molly, I've heard from Cecelia and the news is not good. She's been with Jake." He paused. Candles flickered; an owl greeted the night. When he spoke again, his voice was shaky. "It seems they've been seeing each other ever since she came back. When they left here, they were headed for Alaska. They got as far as the Canadian border when she got sick." He shifted where he sat leaning against the rough wall.

"Royce, take it easy a minute. Let me go grab a couple of pillows," Richard said. With flashlight in hand, he went inside.

Another light beamed, Fifi barked and ran toward it as Ellen approached, holding a lantern.

"Hey, cat got your tongue?" Ellen asked when no one spoke. She plopped down, cross legged between the two rockers.

"Sorry," Molly said. "Royce has just started filling us in about Jake and Cecelia."

"Geez those two. What a pair. Or should I say, trio?"

"Not funny, Ellen," Royce snapped. "Maybe you shouldn't have come."

"Ouch. But here I am. I just came to get my dog for her vet appointment tomorrow. I'll hightail it right now if you want."

Richard stepped out, handed the pillows to Royce, nodded at Ellen, and resumed his slow rocking-chair rhythm.

"Stay," Royce said. "I shouldn't have gotten so testy. I know you've never liked Cecelia. But right now I don't need slurs."

They waited. He finally spoke again, this time in a stronger voice as if he'd resolved to blurt out the whole story and get it over with.

"Cecelia is pregnant. When she told Jake, he was livid. Insisted he wasn't the father, and she should 'get rid of the brat.'" His exact words, according to her. She refused. Before I met her, she'd had an abortion and never got over what she'd done. Talking about that was the only time I ever saw her cry. Especially as years went by, and we didn't conceive. Now she's carrying another man's baby."

"Not Jake's," Molly said, thankful for the dimness of candlelight. "He's had a vasectomy. Never wanted kids. Any kids, including mine."

"So . . . this baby is mine . . . mine?" Royce mumbled.

"Not necess . . ." Ellen began and froze.

"When she called me, Cecilia was hysterical. Jake left in the middle of the night. Took all the money they had between them. The car. Even her credit cards. She's stranded. Alone and sick."

Molly's head began to spin, and the meal she'd just eaten threatened to reject her. Who was this man she'd devoted so much of her life to? All the times they'd relocated, all the different churches. Like tiny pieces of a giant jigsaw puzzle fitting together, she remembered how abrupt most of those moves were. How her questions went unanswered or were met with anger and defensiveness. And of course, this last move was to escape *that* scandal in Tucson. He was desperate then, but he had her by his side. A modicum of respectability. Is that why he took to Cecelia? Took her along as he ran away? Why run now? What had he done this time? What? Her face grew hot, her pulse quickened as Ellen's insinuations about a peeping tom crept to the forefront of her mind. Jake? And what of the strangers from Arizona? Did he know about them and feel threatened?

"What now?" Molly asked.

"I sent her money and planned to take Ellen's repeated advice to 'just wash my hands of her.' But now, now if . . . the baby is mine, if I'm the father, I have to take care of her. I'd go right now if I could."

Richard stood, took the few steps to Royce's side, bent and placed a hand on Royce's shoulder. "I think you've made the only decision you could live with. Will you stay here tonight anyway? It looks like you've come prepared. And I have to head home."

Ellen jumped up, attached a leash to Fifi's collar, and said, "Royce, you gotta do what you gotta do. If there's any way I can help, you know you can count on me."

After quiet good nights, she lit her lantern and handed it to Richard. The two cautiously stepped down the uneven rock steps. Fifi took the lead, and they soon disappeared.

"I don't know what to say," Molly murmured.

"Just say you understand."

"Oh, I do. About you and Cecelia. It's Jake's behavior that appalls me. He's being meaner and more self-centered than even I would have thought."

Candles fluttered in a sudden cold wind. Darkness encompassed them as flames died. Coyotes howled. Cat, on Molly's lap, tensed. His claws dug into her thighs through her jeans. With a sharp yelp, she lifted him up, and he scooted from her arms, darting under the rocker.

After long moments, Amy broke the silence. "Let's all try to get some sleep," she said from the shadows. "It's late, and there's been more than enough in this day."

They nodded and made preparations for bed. Molly couldn't climb to the loft on her sore foot so Amy took that bed. Royce rolled out his sleeping bag on the floor, Cat and Molly crawled onto the air mattress in the alcove. With the lantern off, nothing but blackness surrounded them. Molly doubted she'd fall asleep with so much on her mind and she was grateful to not be alone.

As she lay waiting for aspirin to dull her aching foot, she said a little prayer, asking for answers. Praying she'd remember her dreams. With Cat heavy on her hip and the soothing sound of Royce's rhythmic breathing, her eyelids grew leaden, her anxious thoughts hazy, and she drifted.

A giant *A* materialized in the sky. "Ask," a deep, calm voice intoned. "Ask and you shall receive." The *A* exploded into brilliant shards that floated and then danced together forming an *S*. Again the voice, "Seek and you shall find." Another explosion, another dance and a *K* replaced the *S*. Molly said, "Knock and the door will be opened." Her own voice awakened her. *I am asking, I am seeking.*

*Where is the door to knock on? What does this dream mean?* She lay still and petted Cat, who purred and crawled into her arms. The gentle feline curled close to her heart brought blessed sleep. Dreamless and deep.

Daylight and the smell of coffee roused her. Her first thought was, *Knock on the door to inner wisdom*. She knew she would need time alone, uninterrupted, to reach that door. When?

They sat on the porch, drinking coffee, staring at one another. Good morning had been the only words spoken. Molly certainly didn't know what to say. Should she be asking something? All she felt like doing was rocking and gazing at the morning sky where a cloudlike sliver of moon still hung.

"Good coffee," she said.

"Yes."

Amy went in for the coffeepot. After filling their cups and setting the pot on the floor, she coughed and spoke, "Yesterday, in the drugstore, I had a fax waiting for me. There's a shake-up going on at my company. There's rumors of positions being eliminated and possible promotions. It's all up in the air. If I return now, I could get an advancement." She paused, then quickly added, "Which I don't care about. But if I don't go back, I may lose my job. I don't know . . ."

"You go," Molly said.

"I won't abandon you with all this stuff about Jake. And alone out here."

"I'll be fine. Maybe I'm meant to be alone for a while. Besides, there's Ellen, Richard, Beth. And Fifi, will be back, I'm sure." Cat, who had found a sunny ledge, jumped down, stretched, and pranced to Molly's side. "Alone? Hardly," she said with a forced smile and a nod. "You go, I insist. And I am the mother here after all."

Amy paced, stopped at the rail, her back to them, and said nothing. Molly motioned for Royce to back her up.

"I'm flying out as soon as I can make arrangements," Royce said. "Come into town with me now, Amy, and we'll go to the airport together. That way your mom will have her car here."

"You know I can't leave now!"

Molly watched Amy and Royce exchange glances—his eyebrows raised in question. They nodded at each other.

"What? What else is there?" Molly asked.

Amy produced the elusive newspaper and placed it on Molly's lap, front page facing her.

The headlines, big and bold, read

GRAND THEFT AT BAPTIST CHURCH.

> Police are investigating a report of two women having been seen on the premises shortly before the robbery was discovered.

# TWENTY-SEVEN

~

*The door of the soul opens inward.*

—Emmet Fox

The coffee cup slipped from Molly's hand and clattered to the floor. No one reacted to the mess as Amy and Royce watched and waited.

"What?" she gasped. "When? Who?"

Amy knelt beside her, set the cup upright, and dabbed the spill with a napkin. She took Molly's hand, squeezed it, and said, "Mom. Read the rest of the article. The two women mentioned. You and me. They have to be."

Molly read on

> The theft was confirmed late Tuesday morning by Diatrice Fletch, a Sweet Hollow Church board member and president of the Ladies Guild. In an interview, Mrs. Fletch said she'd seen a vaguely familiar gray station wagon in the parking lot when she'd arrived to review the outcome of the yearly fund-raiser. The car sped away before she had an opportunity to speak with its occupants. "I would know the driver if I ever saw her again. She looked right at me," Mrs. Fletch said. "Young, with long blonde hair. Not

> anyone I'd seen before. And there was another woman, but she was wearing a hat, and I couldn't see her face."
>
> According to the police report, several thousand dollars had been placed in the safe the Sunday before. No sign of forced entry could be found. Mrs. Fletch did not note the station wagon's license plate. The investigation continues with . . .

"They can't think *we* stole the money. How could we? But the door *was* unlocked. Why?" Molly mumbled, thinking out loud.

"Mom, remember. Jake was there when we walked in. As pastor, he'd have a key and the combination to the safe." Amy released Molly's hand, stood and, with her arms wrapped tight around herself, walked to the far railing and back again, and again.

"But where was Jake's car? All I saw was that old clunker in the parking lot. Amy, was anyone in that?"

"I don't know. I don't think so, but I thought I heard another car's engine after Jake squealed down the driveway."

In a quiet voice, Royce said, "Richard and I have discussed this. Diatrice has got it in her head that he knows who the two women are and won't tell her. She's even accused him of covering up, or of carelessly leaving the church doors open and the safe unlocked. She's making no sense and is frantic about Jake being gone. When Richard suggested Jake may have absconded with the funds, she was livid."

"Jake! Of course!" Molly's hand flew to her mouth. *Why am I not screaming and shouting, angry and outraged? Instead it is like an eraser has been laid across the blackboard of my heart. Trust, caring, respect, have been erased, replaced by . . . replaced by what? Disgust? Contempt? No. Resignation. I was, no, I* am *married to a stranger.*

Amy leaned against the railing and said, "I'd better go talk to the police. Tell them that, yes, we were there and so was Jake."

"I don't think that would be wise and neither does Richard," Royce said as he, too, stood and paced. "You are a stranger here and your mother is . . ."

"What?" Molly asked, confined to her chair by her still-sore ankle. Unable to physically release any tension, she mentally jumped to the conclusion that he was about to say no one would listen to her either. Why should they? Jake had painted a picture of her as an unstable woman, to say the least. And, of course, in the community's eyes, he was a respected "man of the cloth."

"No one will believe you, Amy," Molly said. "Leave this mess to us. You need to go back to North Dakota. Back to your job. And, I guess, the sooner the better."

Bundled in a sweater and blanket, Molly settled on the porch with her foot propped and cushioned on a pillow. A thermos of chamomile tea and a cup rested on the floor beside her. She poured and sipped. The warm, sweet herbal soothed her grumbling stomach, relaxed her tense shoulders. Alone, she watched as black clouds gathered, and midafternoon stormy gloom descended. Sadness washed over her the moment Amy had turned the corner, out of her view, gone again. It was always this way. Amy left an ache, a hole in her heart. The space reserved just for her daughter and Amy had filled it, warmed her. Now she shivered. Now this door must be closed. It creaked and pained as it folded over, like an out-of-use accordion door, each segment clinging to its neighbor. To ease this ache, to feel it subside, she'd turned to her journal. She would express her emotions there and let them go.

Amy had argued, "Mom, I won't leave you alone." When that approach failed, she'd pleaded, "Come with me, then. At least for a few weeks. We've hardly had a chance to talk."

Molly had been tempted but knew, somehow, she was meant to be here and to face whatever challenges came. If she ran now, something would be forever missing in her life. And Sophia—poor Sophia would never rest. Amy finally acquiesced when both Molly and Royce assured her they'd keep in close contact.

Anticipating nothing, Molly sipped her tea and stared at trees dripping droplets. The gray day softened and quieted her mind and heart. Seemingly alone, she knew she was safe, with unseen spirits waiting to guide her. A gentle calm, like a deep blue lake, pooled within, surrounded and waited. She rested in that nourishment. Cares slipped away to dusty corners, and her heart closed over the space left gaping by her daughter's leaving. A yearning niggled to clutch this moment, to put brakes on it, make it last forever. She let the thought slide away and breathed. Certain of the living process, she pictured her blood traveling through her arteries. Focusing on her breath, she realized how often she had to remind herself to exhale. And yet there was a sense of being fully alive, of breathing for the first time in her life. The atmosphere in this cabin and surrounding forests seemed to take the lid off society's claustrophobic box of rules and propriety. Open to fresh air, she refused to be imprisoned again. From the very first when she'd tossed her clothes to the wind and sunbathed nude she'd startled herself with uncharacteristic behavior. When after she'd crammed herself into a sweltering suit for high tea and then moments later had donned baggy shirt and shorts and bebopped to a "Miss Molly" melody. When she'd fallen for Royce and lied, implying she was a merry widow. She'd certainly come out of the box and wasn't even sure who she was anymore. Now, she'd take time to get to know this new personality emerging.

Thunder clapped, rain fell, and still she sat—journal open on her lap, pen in hand—blank page before her. As if in a trance, she stared at the white paper until it blurred and a sketch took form. A filigree design overlaid by a Celtic cross. The overall shape was oval, edged by small circles that seemed to sparkle. She blinked, shook her head, and rubbed her eyes. The pen in her hand moved across the page, beneath the design.

> Baubles for naught. Love 'tisn't bought.
> No rogue finds rest. Kindness be blest.
> On to the last. The spell is cast.

Mesmerized, Molly stared as a vapor swirled into a ghostly apparition that settled beside her, and with the energy of a tormented spirit, prodded her to recover the brooch.

"But I don't know where it is," Molly whispered.

"Yes, yes you do." Her hand wrote on the page. "Your soul knows. Your soul always knows."

*The brooch is now Royce's ring, this I know,* Molly thought. The sketch in her journal took the shape of the ring and then blurred. *No rogue finds rest* leaped out at her and she scribbled "Jake!" Aloud she mumbled, "Jake has the ring. He's stolen it. The curse is on him." But she didn't know where he'd gotten to by now.

"Ask, ask, ask," the shadow, or the flutter of falling leaves, begged.

"Where is the ring?" she wrote.

An unfamiliar city street materialized. Molly searched for signs, a city name, anything that would place her there. But no, she was seeing this image for the first time. A weary-looking woman, dressed in a tight mini skirt and scanty V-neck tank top, lingered on the corner. Scraps of paper and debris twisted in the wind. A row of small seedy stores lined the narrow, dingy route. Casey's Bar and Grill, Resale Mart, Cash Advance, Used Books, and Adult Pleasures. Molly felt dirty just mentally walking down this sidewalk. Jake appeared in a doorway. Above his head a neon light with bulbs missing flashed, "E . . . . on Pawnshop." Counting money, he stepped off the curb, and a car horn blared, tires screeched. The scene faded. A sick old woman and a crying child took its place.

She jerked to alertness when Cat jumped into her lap and knocked the pen from her hand. Just as quickly, he leaped down and off the porch. He turned and meowed at her, urging her to follow him.

"Biscuit, I cain't today," Molly said, her voice sounding strange to her own ears. "Mama is daid."

Her fingers went to her throat, seeking an amulet there. Nothing. Cat meowed and paced. Picking up the pen, Molly scribbled. I said "cain't" and "daid." I called him Biscuit. Have I *become* Sophia? She looked at her hands. No, they were not a young woman's hands, nor was she dressed in long skirts and a shawl. Jeans and a sweater clothed her.

She felt the child's giggle before she heard it. Soothing words waltzed in her head. The thunderstorm moved on, its power spent. As her senses sharpened, she felt an impetus surround her, transport her. In sunshine, with journal open, she smelled sweet lilacs before she saw them. Fairies danced and angels sang. Cats purred—all of them—lions, tigers, cougar. A sleek black panther belched, and flowers bloomed in the gas of it. Ripe red strawberries hovered, as if lobbed by gods. Juice trickled, she smacked her lips and licked sticky fingers. She napped on a lush lawn and the grass cried, "Ouch." Hugging trees, she teased them, and they sassed her right back. Pirouetting through a field of daisies, she laughed and laughed until her laughter woke her, and she saw Richard sitting in the other chair, smiling at her.

"Sounds like a lovely dream. I envy you," he said.

"Oh yes." Even as she nodded, the fairyland dream disappeared. A wisp beyond her grasp, but the promise of future joy lingered. "It's gone. All I know is that I've had this dream before, and I always wake up laughing."

# TWENTY-EIGHT

~

*Your sacred space is where*
*you find yourself again and again.*
—Joseph Campbell

"I've brought food and news." Richard opened the cooler next to him, offering lemonade and a man-sized sandwich. "Hungry?"

"Starving. Well, not exactly starving," she said and laughed. "But I haven't eaten since breakfast." She sat and unwrapped the supper. "This looks delicious. Homemade?"

It was his turn to laugh. "Not quite. Ordered by Royce, created by Ellen."

Ah yes, hearty whole wheat, with roast chicken, jack cheese, and familiar southwestern flavor of green chili. They ate in compatible silence until Molly remembered. "News? You said you had news?"

With a long swig, he finished his drink, crumpled the food wrappings and frowned.

"Not more bad news, I hope," Molly added

"Not exactly. I just don't know where to start."

"Wait. I need to ask, has Royce left yet? I know something about where his ring has gotten to."

"All right, I'll start there. He and Amy are on the road right now. He's taking her to Knoxville, where she'll catch a plane. Then he's driving north to rescue Cecelia."

Disappointed at first, she remembered they all had cell phones and weren't out of touch. She'd have to go into town to make a call, though, and she dreaded that. If Diatrice should see her car, she'd surely connect it, and her, with the church incident. Besides, her gas gauge was showing empty and so was her wallet. Too bad she'd left the $100 under the rocker that day. That money would have come in handy. Certainly more so than the dulcimer it had purchased, which now lay silent on the desk. Molly reminded herself of all the times she'd worried and then been provided for. *I will not let my lack of money be an issue*, she told herself.

Richard didn't know her financial situation, and she really didn't want him to.

"Maybe when you get home you could call Royce for me," she said.

"I was hoping to spend the night here. Royce left his bed roll, I've been told."

"Gosh, that would be great. I hadn't even thought about a dark night in the woods alone."

"Have you considered going back to your place? Now that you know Jake isn't apt to show up."

"Hmm . . . That hadn't entered my mind." Molly paused. Dulcimer strings whisper, as if saying, "Please don't go."

"No," she said. "I'll be staying here."

*I'll walk over to the house tomorrow,* she thought. *I could retrieve some old journals, a book or two, and more clothes. There might even be some money in a pocket or purse. Any amount would help. And I could get cell reception from there. Silly. I'll just use the landline.*

"Along with sandwiches, Ellen sent news. She won't be bringing Fifi up for awhile. Poor dog seems to have had a bad reaction from his shot. Which has her pretty upset but still concerned about you. She's gotten a couple calls. That man from Arizona. He'd tried calling your house. Says he knows where Jake is but would only talk to you. Oh, he left a phone number." Richard pulled a scrap of paper from his shirt pocket and handed it to Molly.

"I'm beginning to think more went on in Tucson than I knew about. Why is this guy in such pursuit of Jake? And, I wonder, what his plans are."

"That I don't know and neither does Ellen. But we can't contact him tonight. Maybe tomorrow you can get some answers."

Molly shook her head, smoothed the crumpled note, and tucked it into her back pocket. Confused and tired, she wanted nothing more than to run away. To not have to clean up Jake's messes. To not feel responsible for Sophia or anyone else. She had to clear her head, and she knew only one way to do it. Molly winced in anticipation of pain when she stood and challenged her bruised ankle. The wince turned to relief as the ankle held her weight without complaint.

"Let's take a walk, okay?" she suggested. "I need to move and stretch. Believe me I feel a lot older than fifty right now."

"Sure," he said and stood.

"Let's go to the stream. I've always liked it there."

Side by side they strolled. The air was fresh from the rain. Mosquitoes and no-see-ums gathered in hordes but flew off in the slight breeze that carried Celtic rhythms of harp and dulcimer to her. When Molly stumbled on a loose stone, Richard was quick to catch her, and she leaned against him, felt the comfort of strong arms. They continued to walk with his hand on the small of her back. A reassuring presence. A sense of being cared for.

At the stream, they sat on a boulder and stared at the shallow ripples as if they told a fascinating story. Molly retrieved the smooth pebble from her pocket, held it tight.

"Do you hear music?" she asked in a soft tone she half hoped would go unnoticed.

"No," he said. "But I don't doubt you do. Preston has convinced me that two worlds or two time periods are layered here for you."

"I wish Preston were here. Will he come back, do you suppose?"

"I'll talk to him tomorrow. I know he's very interested and concerned. But he also thinks you need to be alone some. He's the only one who believes Royce and Amy leaving was a good thing for you."

"When eerie things happen I feel safer with him close by. At least I have his stone." Molly opened her palm, revealing her treasure.

"Thank you for your company." She reached, squeezed his warm hand, stood, and moved closer to the water, what little there was.

Molly pondered the significance of this creek, now, here, not much more than a trickle. A gentle, quiet place to think her thoughts through. But in springtime, far upstream this waterway had been, and would be again, a torrent of rushing snowmelt and danger. Goose bumps rose, and she pulled her sweater tight. Remembering frightful scenes she'd been a party to and those she'd witnessed from a distance made her shiver. Music grew louder, and she wondered if the dulcimer man would appear. Memories came—of the bee sting that had made her so sick, the old man's poultice of tobacco juice and mud he'd packed on. Herbs he'd given her to make a tea. Amy arriving at Beth's. An ache returned, she shrugged it off. Jake. The church money.

Fear and anxiety began in her groin, swelling as if a witch's cauldron bubbled. The intensity shifted and, as if by magic potion, turned to excitement then fizzled, leaving her cool and with a clear sense she was exactly where her spirit was meant to be. She closed her eyes; a smile tempted her lips. "Yes," the whippoorwill sang.

Often she was unclear as to what her role was, why her, in this misty drama that played out here. With her eyes still closed, she swayed as if on a moving train as the picture unfolded and folded again—wavy lines of insight that puffed into thin air, then reappeared. She said, "Ah." A sensual, almost sexual, current pulsed through her. She yearned, but for what she did not know. A rhythm echoed, and her feet itched to dance. A polka full of laughter and gaiety. Or hips undulating to an erotic rumba beat. Instead, she turned to see that Richard had come to her side.

"The light's fading. It'll be dark soon," he said. "We'd better head back."

"Yes," she said and joined him on the path. They walked slowly, without speaking, together but separate. Inside the cabin, he lit the oil lamp and surprised her with a bottle of wine and two small goblets.

"I don't even know if you imbibe," he said, offering her a glass.

"Not often. Not much. Thanks." She accepted the drink, again aware of the warmth of his touch.

"Won't Diatrice . . . ?"

He held up his hand, stopping her. "I don't want to get into that right now. Let's just say she's not expecting me home tonight. You need to know, though, the police are looking for two women. It's only a matter of time before Diatrice remembers your car. She's determined."

He spoke with a tinge of disgust, she thought. "Why don't you just tell her?"

A chuckle escaped before he could suppress it. "As long as 'the car' has her stumped, she's relatively harmless. But my wife . . . well." He shook his head. "This is the third minister she has insisted on hiring who has been a disappointment, to say the least. I doubt if any of us would have seen through Jake, but the decision was hers. So she's desperate to save face. Still, I've never seen her this defensive and mean-spirited, and we've been married a long time.

"Molly, she's accused me of having an affair with you."

"Why on earth . . . ?"

"Her imagination. Her need to fix blame, I suppose. And of course, Jake told her you had been seeing me for counseling. Which I won't talk about when she asks. But . . . and I hope you don't misunderstand this, I've changed since you've come here. And she's seen that."

"What do you mean, changed?"

"I guess I've been rocking the boat at home, and Diatrice, well, isn't pleased. It's just that you have so much courage and integrity, I've had to look at my own. I'm taking a stand for what I consider right."

"I don't feel courageous at all. There just seems to be no other choice for me."

She rose and moved to the desk, ran her fingers over the dulcimer strings, and then walked outside. Richard stood beside her as an owl hooted, low and calm, evoking an ancient melancholy. The day sighed to a close, they returned to shelter and whispered good night.

Molly climbed cautiously up to the loft. Moments later the downstairs quieted, lamplight died, and darkness enfolded her. Wide-eyed she lay, unable to stop the episode-by-episode replay of the last few months, turning and tossing with each change of scene. When she'd exhausted those events, her mind went back to Tucson and the last days there. Worn-out, she forced herself to lay still and soon heard familiar scurrying noises. With a thump, Cat landed upon her belly. Soft and warm, the kitty purred as if to say, "Sleep, sleep and dream." She closed her eyes and imagined Cat did too. Both to sleep and dream.

# TWENTY-NINE

~

*If the sight of the blue skies fills you with joy . . .*
*if the simple things of nature have a message that you*
*understand, rejoice, for your soul is alive.*

—Eleonora Duse

When Molly woke, rumpled and groggy, the sun shone across her face, and she knew it must be late. She was alone, Cat having departed, no doubt, for a calmer bed. A faint aroma of coffee spurred her to rise. She dragged on yesterday's jeans and raked her fingers through her unruly mop, patted the curls down as best she could. Mindful of her ankle, she eased herself over the edge and onto the ladder.

"Richard," she called. In the stillness, her voice sounded hollow and loud. The bed in the alcove had been tidied, and a thermos sat on the desk, the corner of a note under a mug.

> I hope this brew is still hot when you finally start your day. You were sleeping like a baby, snoring softly, and I didn't have the heart to rouse you to say good-bye. I'll be back later today or tomorrow, depending on what Preston advises. Remember, call me if you need me. Take care.

> PS. There is an envelope from Royce in the drawer. It was in my jacket pocket so I forgot to give it to you last night.

After pouring coffee, she opened the drawer, finding not only Royce's envelope but five twenty-dollar bills in a neat pile behind it. Did Richard know she needed money? But wouldn't he have said something in his note? She spied a slip of paper with her handwriting: "For the dulcimer," it read. *The* one hundred dollars. Was this intended for her use? Could that have been the reason for the payment all along? Her dulcimer man must have foreseen her future need. Once again, a loving universe provided. Coincidence? No. If Richard hadn't forgotten about Royce's envelope and then hadn't merely left it with his message, when would she have found this much-needed cash? Molly smiled from inside out and sang, "Thank you!" She heard no chorus sing, "You're welcome." But she knew her gratitude hadn't gone unnoticed.

Settled in the rocking chair, she gulped strong coffee, glad to have it but wishing for some cream to allay its sharp taste. Opening the bulky envelope from Royce, a ring of keys fell out. The accompanying letter, written in fine penmanship, read

> Dear Molly,
>
> Darlin', I wasn't thinking clearly when I left you. I will be gone for several days and hope you know you are welcome to stay at my house if the woods get too uncomfortable or spooky. Anything you find at my place that you can make use of, help yourself. And you may want to use my truck for any business you have in town.
>
> I admire your courage and tenacity, darlin', and will always treasure the time we've had together. I wish we could relive the day you, beautiful in your white dress, mirrored Daphne and made me feel like Apollo. You and the sweet softness of ambrosia will be forever linked in my mind and heart. I loved you then, I love you now.

> I leave here today not knowing what to expect, but I hope you understand I must try again with Cecelia and the baby I never thought I'd have.
>
> I remain always, your friend.

Tears burned her eyes, ran down her cheeks. She sniffled and read the note once more. And then again. She saw herself wearing white, standing barefoot with wavelets lapping at her toes and watching a magnificent swan skim across the blue silken lake. She could only imagine what a sight she'd been when she emerged from that lake, water dripping from her curls and from the dress clinging to her body. It had been a magical day. But only that—a magical moment in time. He was married and so was she. Her emotions defied description. Heartache, pleasure in the remembering, a deep yearning unfulfilled. Across the screen of her mind, like an erotic movie, played the dream she'd had of the two of them. The scent of jasmine and flicker of candlelight, the sexual intensity. Filled with both relief and regret that it was just a dream, she moaned. After reading his words again, she kissed the page and folded it neatly, pondering why two men in her life saw her as courageous and told her so at this time. "It is what it is." She spoke aloud as if there were someone present to hear. Perhaps there was. Clutching the keys, she stood and went in search of breakfast.

With sturdy boots laced tight, an empty backpack and a bottle of water, Molly closed the new front door and walked away from what she now hesitantly thought of as home. As far as she knew, she had this day to herself, and there was no hurry. She found the hole where the fence had rotted through, and after slipping between two rails, she looked back. There on the porch, in her rocking chair, sat Sophia, her wavy red hair shining in the sunlight. Molly blinked, shook her head, and looked again. Shadowy, ashen figures stood behind Sophia. Ghosts. They were all ghosts, of course, but Sophia appeared in vivid color. Not only her hair with its golden highlights, but her royal blue and brown calico dress and white pinafore. So real, Molly waved and called, "I'll be back." They seemed to wave in return and then fade, as if they'd made an appearance to remind her she wasn't alone.

Without considering the strange promise, she proceeded, soon engulfed in nature, where she felt most at home. It had been what seemed a lifetime since she'd taken this cross-country route, and the rolling hills were now vibrant, as if she'd entered one of Jake's mother's gaudy oil paintings. "This is Godly gaudy," she said, pleasured by the sound of her clever phrase. She stooped often to examine wildflowers in bloom. Brilliant purple coneflowers. Sweetly scented blue wood asters. Assers, Sophia had called them a long, long time ago. Queen Anne's Lace, its creamy white flowers almost spent. With a gentle squeeze, she slipped its delicate fernlike foliage through her fingers, held her hand to her nose, and inhaled the fragrance of carrots. And, here, like an angel in a crowd, blossomed the periwinkle blue bottle gentian. Tiny sparrows landed on tall-stemmed goldenrod and ironweed. What a splendid garden. Planted for her enjoyment by wind and rain, birds, and bees. She guessed at the birds that sang with such sweetness. Warblers? Eastern meadowlark? Oh, to have Beth by her side to name them. Or, at least, have her reference books with her. She'd bring them on the walk back, stop again, and identify.

With long strides she strolled, pleased with the strength of her ankle, the stretch and strain of her muscles. The air felt cool and fresh, even as the sun warmed her. Though her destination held unknown impact, this journey through fields of flowers on a clear autumn day connected her with spirit. Every scent, both sweet and fusty, every butterfly and bird in flight spoke of a reality far removed from egos and lies and deceit. Wilderness, sometimes cruel and harsh, was nevertheless honest and straightforward. A realm she trusted, accepted as is, and experienced as a tingling of her skin, a rush of blood through her veins. Doubts and fears, anger and jealousy slipped off her shoulders with every step she took until, for a fleeting moment, she felt weightless, bodiless, at one with everything.

On she trod, growing tired and wondering at the distance she'd covered with still no sign of her old backyard. Her body reminded her she'd just been ill, and she sat amid flowers and buzzing busy bees. She drank long gulps from her water bottle and chewed on a stale granola bar she found in her pack. As she lingered, her worried mind awoke and began a litany of what ifs. *Suppose Jake has come back? Suppose the lease on their house had been canceled? Suppose strangers were there?* Now Molly grew anxious as if her world would crash while she dawdled in a flowerbed, picking cockleburs off bootlaces.

A faint, distant melody sailed to her, as if on a sunbeam, gently reminding her she had no need to rush and nothing to fear. After all, she had awakened this morning believing herself stuck with no place to go and no money to get there; now she had keys to a house and truck, and one hundred dollars in her pocket. She grinned and hugged her knees, feeling much like a little girl just given another few minutes on the playground swing. Releasing all traces of tension, she threw her head back and gazed at a sky so clear she thought she could see right through to heaven itself. *What is heaven, really? This. This is heaven. This moment, now, cockleburs and all. But what about those who haunt the cabin? Where and when is their heaven?* A pointless pondering, she knew, and shook the thoughts away. Geese honked and flew overhead, their open V formation a symbol of new beginnings.

With a seemingly slow-motioned pace, she completed her journey. Through the back gate, her eyes took in a few straggling daisies that refused to die, tall weeds, and spent flowers. And Cat atop the fence. *Cat atop the fence?* Hesitating, not knowing if this property still belonged to her or if she were intruding, she knocked softly and then louder. When no one answered, she jiggled the backdoor knob. Locked. Under a flowerpot in the side yard, she found the key and cautiously let herself in.

Before her eyes became accustomed to the dim light, odors assaulted her, warned her of what she'd find. Sour, stale, rotting smells lay, one on top of the other to the ceiling and back down again. Molly threw open both kitchen windows. She flipped a light switch and saw incredible disarray as if someone had ransacked the place. Clothing lay on the table, draped over a chair and puddled in a corner. Jake must have packed in here, as if in a panic, deciding what to take. What had been going on in his mind? Was it fear that drove him or guilt or greed?

Dirty dishes, with dried-on food, were piled on the drain board. Not like Jake at all. Always neat to a fault. She almost felt sorry for him and the state he must have been in. Wrinkling her nose, she took the smelly garbage pail outside to the trash. Disgusted, all Molly could think to do was start cleaning. Cleaning up another of Jake's messes.

Filling the sink with scalding, soapy water, she left the dishes to soak. She gathered his discarded clothing, searching all pockets for loose change or a wad of bills. Finding none, she dumped them in a clothes basket. Her next stop was the bathroom where she experienced an unexpected delight in seeing a flush toilet. Then she made the connection. Running water and a shower. Immediately she stripped, stepped in, and luxuriated as the full force beat upon her, as hot as she could bear. She shampooed and scrubbed and let her head roll to the side, back and around while water cascaded over her until it cooled. Even then she was reluctant to turn it off. How did they manage a hundred years ago? Of course no one had been spoiled and pampered this way.

The phone was ringing when she stepped out. Before she could wind a towel around, the ringing stopped. She waited for her own voice to say hello. A click and then silence. The machine tape must be full.

Quickly she donned clean jeans and shirt. It seemed all she wore these days. Not that she missed the confines of suits and panty hose and high-heeled shoes. No, she'd gladly wear jeans and boots for the rest of her life. Feminine trappings just conjured up images of pretense and facade. Maybe if everyone walked this world naked there'd be less chance of uppitiness. *Diatrice naked,* she thought and shuddered, banishing that image.

The refreshing shower, hot water from the tap, a telephone all tempted her to stay here and just visit the cabin. True, she'd said she'd be back, but she hadn't said when. And it was, after all, a promise made to ghosts. But there she could breathe. Here she felt suffocated. Here an evil energy seemed to lurk. Spirits resided there, of course, but she knew them to be benevolent. No, her peace of mind and integrity demanded she return to the primitive little log house as soon as possible. She'd better get on with the tasks she'd come for.

Jake's dresser drawers were at various stages of open, and her jewelry box lay upside down, its contents scattered in rumpled sheets of an unmade bed. Molly owned only a few trinkets worth any money, and she poked about for those. Her mother's pearl ring, some gold chains and charms. Gone. *He would get next to nothing for them.* But this petty theft certainly showed his desperation. She spied the tiny key in a fold of the pillow slip. *Yes,* she thought, *her journal boxes.* Flat on her belly she squirmed as far under the bed as she could. Her outstretched hand made contact. Grunting, she stretched again, but could not get a grip. Locked, untampered with, out of sight, she'd leave them for another day. Suddenly everything seemed like a monumental chore. Why had she come here today? Oh, yes, phone calls.

Since the telephone and electricity hadn't been shut off, she wondered about the mail. On the front stoop she looked askance at the many yellowing newspapers strewn at her feet. That answered her question, and, stepping over them, she wasn't surprised to find the mailbox stuffed. Flyers, catalogues, and bills. Back in the house she dropped the bundle on the couch and began sorting through. The utility bills were two months past due. Those alone would wipe out her thin wad of twenty-dollar bills. At least the rent was being paid by the church. But for how long? Should she call the landlord? No, she'd ask Richard. She could have sworn she'd seen Jake at his desk writing checks not that long ago. Back to that room, she found it cluttered with papers and folders scattered.

The answer machine's blinking red light caught her eye, 20, it flashed, and she was sidetracked again. She grabbed paper and pencil, punched the play button, and prepared to jot information. Three hang ups, Diatrice obsequiously requesting a call back, the police, a reporter, another snooty tone, this time commanding one of them to return her call. More hang ups, the police again. A man identifying himself only as being from Arizona, addressing her by name, he left a number where he could be reached. He rattled it so fast, Molly had to rewind and listen to the entire tape before she got the digits right. Only then did she remember Ellen's slip of paper in her pocket. Finally, what she longed to hear, Amy's voice saying she'd arrived home safely and asking, "Mom, please call when you get this."

After leaving voice mail for both Amy and Royce, she hesitated. Next on her list was the man from Arizona. A stranger with an unknown agenda. *Okay, God, this is yours,* Molly thought and picked up the phone again. The doorbell jangled, and she jumped. Who? Was she ready for this? She could just hide back here until whoever went away.

Hiding was not the answer. *Let's see that courage everyone tells me I have.* With shoulders back and down, a silent prayer in her heart, she marched down the hall to the door. Two men in suits stood facing her.

"Mrs. Carpenter?"

"Yes," she said. Closing the door behind her, she bent and picked up the scattered papers. "I've been away. This delivery should have been stopped." Molly heard herself babble and clamped her lips together.

# THIRTY

~

*When I hear music, I fear no danger.*
*I am invulnerable. I see no foe.*
*I am related to the earliest times, and to the latest.*
—Henry David Thoreau

Belligerent. She'd been belligerent, refusing to allow the detectives or whoever, to come in, to look around. She'd answered their questions with short, snippy replies. Why? She had no reason to feel guilty, feel threatened and absolutely no reason to cover up for Jake. They'd stood on the stoop for at least an hour, the men asking questions, she with her hands on her hips, staring eye to eye with the tall one and down her nose at the short stocky one. When they had finally turned to leave, they thanked her for her cooperation, and assured her they'd be back with necessary papers. Whatever that meant.

In her journal, Molly recorded as much of the conversation as she could remember. Her feelings, though, defied description. Anger came out on the page. Frustration and confusion mingled there too, but beneath them all lay an unclean sensation as if she had been sullied. Violated. Of course. Not only had Jake been having sex with a teenage girl but then with her too. Disgusted, she wished she could throw up. Cleanse herself somehow. Another hot shower tempted her, but there was no time. Writing helped and finally the deepest cause of her angst revealed itself. If the accusations were true, it meant he had lied to her about *everything*. Even the vasectomy he'd claimed he'd had. A cold sweat beaded on her forehead at the possibility she could have gotten pregnant. How would he have squirmed out of that? When no more words came, she lay the pen down and reread what she'd written. Something else niggled at her thoughts, poked, and then ran away. There was no use trying to force revelation. It would come when it came.

Now she stared at a sink full of dishes, a heap of laundry, and a mess. Shaky with hunger, she pulled bowls out of the refrigerator. Everything was old, dried up, or worse yet, moldy. She dumped it all, piled still more dishes in the sink, and opened the freezer. A hamburger patty on a plate and in the microwave would have to do. What she really wanted was a big bowl of chocolate ice cream and a cigarette. What she needed was a salad and either a long conversation with a friend or a good cry.

Silence hung over her like a death sentence while she ate and then did dishes. When the phone rang, she jumped. Shocked, she stared at it for two rings and then pounced.

"Amy. Oh, Amy," she said before her throat closed.

"Mom. What? You sounded really good on your message."

"I . . . I . . . two men were here and . . ." She bit her lip, trying not to cry.

Molly did as her daughter instructed. She sat down, focused on her breathing and managed to relax. And then she talked. About her emptied jewelry box and her mother's missing pearls. About the disgusting disarray she'd found in her home. About two men who'd identified themselves by showing some sort of badges. Police or detectives or agents. She couldn't remember and felt out of her realm.

When she paused, Amy said, "I should have stayed. I wish I hadn't listened to you guys. Hey, why don't you come here? Just pack a bag and get Richard to take you to the airport."

"I can't leave now, Amy. I've got to see this thing through about Sophia. And I don't have any money. No job. Not much experience anybody would want to hire either."

"I'd hire someone like you in a minute, Mom. You're dependable, intelligent, and so capable. I've been made supervisor here, and believe me, qualities like yours are going to be hard to find."

"Congratulations. See, we were right to send you back! Thank you for your faith in me, but I'm afraid it isn't too well-founded. If I really were all the things you and Richard and Royce are telling me I am, I wouldn't be in this muddle. Wouldn't have made such stupid choices." Molly heard tears in her voice again, felt her throat begin to close again, felt herself sinking into self-pity. She hated that.

"Mother," Amy said softly. "No one is saying you're perfect. But you aren't responsible for Jake. Your only fault might be that you're too trusting. If that is a fault. Think about coming here soon, please. Meanwhile, remember you aren't guilty of anything and neither am I."

"No, no. Those men were looking for Jake. Not about church money but something in Tucson. And they acted as if I knew all about it and was covering up for him. It isn't possible he would do what they suspect him of."

"Mom. Jake would do whatever it took for him to come out looking good. I wouldn't put *anything* past him."

"Murder?" Molly whispered.

"No! No way."

"Well, not murder, exactly. They . . . these two men. Detectives, I guess. They said he paid someone twenty thousand dollars to do it for him. Hired someone to kill a girl from our church there."

"Oh, my god! What? Why?"

"Something about statutory rape and, and a baby. I don't understand this at all. I, I, I . . ."

"Mom. Slow down, take another deep breath."

"It's just that I feel so betrayed. I can't believe this. If I do, then . . . then I can't believe anything. All those years together. All lies."

"Maybe they've mixed this up," Amy said. "Maybe they were looking for someone else. First of all is the money. You've always kept such close track of money. Wouldn't you have known if twenty thousand dollars just disappeared?"

"That's just it, Amy. I haven't been paying bills or paying much attention either. Now past due notices are piling up. But there was an inheritance of twenty thousand that I asked Jake about this summer. And he said . . ." Molly hesitated. Did she want Amy to know she knew and didn't do anything about it? *I will not keep secrets anymore,* she resolved.

"Mom! What?" Amy said in a controlled shout. Molly could just see her pacing and running her fingers through her hair, pushing it off her face.

Automatically, Molly's shoulders went back and down, strengthening her determination. "Here goes. Jake told me he'd used that money to bribe a judge to drop a case against him. Yes, I knew he was in trouble with the law. That he was suspected of indecent exposure . . ."

Amy interrupted, "Well, that doesn't surprise me. Even the girl. But murder, hiring a hit man. Mom. Get what you need and get out. You aren't safe. And not at that isolated place either."

"Jake's on the run. He won't come back. Why would he? But you're right, I feel powerless. Royce left his keys. I may drive over there tomorrow."

"I wish you'd go now. Richard called and said he'd been with you last night but wouldn't be coming up tonight. I don't like the idea of you being alone, and I told him so. I didn't like it then, and now I really don't."

"Richard left me a note saying he would take Preston's advice about tonight. I guess he thinks I need solitude."

Molly reassured her as best she could and sadly ended their conversation with a promise to call again in the morning. Her pack heavy with books and clothes, she was about to leave when the phone rang again. This time Royce's comforting drawl. She thanked him for his keys and offer. When he told her about the money in a strongbox in his closet, she remembered her one hundred dollars, and they laughed at the coincidence. Then his tone became serious.

"Your message said something about my ring?"

"Yes. Yes. I had a dream or a vision. We've got to get that ring back. I know it was Sophia's brooch, and it's a key to ending this saga. But, as Ellen would say, it'll be like looking for a needle in a haystack."

"Darlin'," Royce said, sounding tired and out of patience. "What was your dream? Where is my ring?"

"I saw a pawnshop in a slum of a big city. I saw Jake walk out counting money. You did say the ring was worth a lot, didn't you?"

"It's an antique, and some of the stones are valuable, yes. What big city, Molly?"

"I saw a sign starting with *E* and then several bulbs burned out and then an *N*, I think. Where are you headed?"

"Detroit. Cecelia is in Detroit. I'll check a map for towns starting with *E* around there. Now, besides all that . . . I miss you."

Molly felt her face flush, her heart quicken. "Royce, thank you. I don't know what to say."

"Just tell me you're okay."

With that, Molly explained about Amy, the men, and Jake. Words tumbled out on top of each other until, breathless, she paused.

"Darlin', have you talked to Richard about all this?"

"No. I just found out. But I will tomorrow."

"Where are you spending tonight?" Royce asked, his voice husky.

"I have to go back to the cabin. My car is there and so is Sophia. I'm frightened, though."

"Molly, darlin'," Royce said with such tenderness she felt as though he were holding her, and she wanted only that. "Be careful, please. Stay at my place all you want. I mean that."

"Thanks, I will," she said, trying to sound strong and capable. After they'd said good-bye, she whispered, "I love you too."

Molly hoisted her pack once more. Once more she set it down and answered the phone. Beth's voice greeted her.

"Yer right hard to get hold of. I've been thinking 'bout you all day. Ever' time I called, yer line was busy. How are you?"

Without including the sordid accusations about Jake's behavior, Molly described her day and said she'd better head back before it got dark, though she was leery of spending the night alone out there.

"Shucks. Come here. Yer no trouble."

"Thank you. But no. It's important that I be there. Preston believes I'm under some sort of protection, and I'm trusting him."

"All right then. Jest so you know, Diatrice has been coming in here asking about you, about Jake. In a real tizzy, worse than ever. She's wondering where Royce has got to. If you and him are off together. You best get now. I wish I weren't so busy, I'd come keep you company. Maybe Ellen could? And I'll see you as soon as I can."

When Molly hung up, she shrugged and lifted the receiver, dialed Sam's café to talk to Ellen.

A stranger answered and informed her Ellen was at the vet. They'd know tonight whether Fifi would recover or need to be put to sleep. Did she want to talk to Sam? Molly looked at the clock. Six thirty already. The café's busiest time.

"No," she said. "Tell her I called, and I'm thinking about her."

Poor Fifi. Poor Ellen. She had no idea an allergic reaction to a vaccination could be that serious. *I must go in tomorrow and see her. See them both if Fifi is still alive.*

The phone was ringing as she closed the back door. She was anxious to get away from its incessant jangling, from doorstep inquisitions, from negative energy that infested every room. As it was, getting back before dark meant hurrying, and she was already weary. There would be no time to enjoy wildflowers and birdcalls, not that she was in any mood for that now. No, this trek would be only about destination, not the journey.

Soon after she set out, first stars appeared faintly high above. She picked up her pace even as her pack grew heavy on her back. Why had she taken so many books? For comfort and companionship, she knew. Having books at her fingertips made her feel less isolated, less vulnerable somehow. But lordy, they weighed a ton now as she strode purposely toward her wooded refuge. She set the pack down, arched her aching back, rolled her neck.

Night slowly settled, like a blanket floating to earth. An owl hooted, and she took a deep breath and pushed on. She'd grabbed a flashlight on her way out. Now she turned it on only to produce a light so dim it was useless. Could she find her way? Would she miss the mark and walk right past her goal? The fence. By the time she'd get to it, it really would be dark. How would she find the way through? A passage from the Bible came to mind. Paul telling someone to not worry about anything, but pray about everything and to not forget to thank God for the answers. So she prayed. Prayed for a guiding light to direct her path. As she crested the second hill, she thought she saw a light flicker in a window, but she wasn't close enough to be sure.

Yes, there was a candle burning, welcoming her. Who? Richard must have come after all. Molly sighed in relief. But after she bent to crawl through the hole in the fence, her beacon disappeared. Truly frightened now, she didn't know which way to turn. Who would do that? Darkness descended, aside from the stars directly overhead. Where was the moon? She'd lost track of its cycle, of its rising and setting. Her flow with nature had stalled in this turmoil. This lack of awareness appalled her.

The owl called again with an eerie tone as if to say, "Watch for shadows that aren't there." Of course there are no shadows in the dark, only strange noises. Snapping branches, leaves rustling, and worse—silence. Molly picked up her pack and ran toward the cabin. And safety?

The door was open. Hadn't she closed it when she left? Yes, she had. She knew she had. Afraid to go in and afraid to stay out, Molly trembled and tried to calm her racing heart, tried to catch her breath. The word *courage* bounced in her head. Where was her courage now? Something bumped against her leg and she screamed. Cat screamed back and was gone. Holding her breath, she went in and fumbled to the desk, remembering a flashlight in the drawer. Yes. Clicking it on only made the nightmare more frightening. Now shadows did dance. She forced herself to light candles, her hands shaking so that wick and match did their own opposing cha-cha. When the lantern glowed and candles flickered throughout the tiny space, she calmed some. She prayed, reached into her jeans pocket, and retrieved the talisman Preston had promised would help keep her grounded in now. *He promised I'd be protected and not alone.* Dulcimer music glancing off walls, looping through still air, evoked, for Molly, the hymn "How Great Thou Art." This reassured her, reminded her no harm would come.

Cat crept in and bumped her leg again. This time she saw him. This time she bent and petted and cooed and thanked him for his presence.

Gulping down valerian root capsules, Molly thought of something she'd read a long time ago. As she clutched the stone in one hand and petted Cat with the other, she recited the phrase, "there is nothing in darkness that doesn't shine in daylight." Repeating that affirmation, she blew out each candle and carried the lantern to the alcove. She'd sleep downstairs tonight. The idea of resting her head upon the same pillow Richard had used the night before comforted her.

In bed, she turned out the lantern sending her into total darkness. With the words "then sings my soul my Savior God to thee, how great Thou art," she surrendered her worry, pain and confusion.

She slept.

# THIRTY-ONE

~

*It's not half so important to know*
*as it is to feel.*

—Rachel Carson

Molly roused with beads of cold sweat on her forehead, hot tears sliding down her cheeks. The night was deep and dark. By flashlight beam she recovered her journal and, with trembling hands, scribbled the nightmare's details. The strange house she'd entered uninvited. The hole in the garden she'd dug and clawed at until she'd fallen in and dirt clods rained on her. Covering her head and cowering she'd awakened. There was more, but the details faded. Cat crawled to her face, kissed her nose, and nestled his head at her neck. She snapped off the light and surrendered once more.

Her father looms above her, his features changing like a slow-motion horror film until he is Papa. Angry. Drunk. Sophia, her hair flowing over heavy breasts to a swollen waist, wails as if she were being attacked and tumbles into the hole. Now Molly reaches down from a cloud and whispers, "Take my hand." Instead, she is drawn into Sophia's burdened body. The priest approaches, but Sophia cries out, "Preacher Man, no!" in a voice much younger than her years. Searing pain rips through her.

Molly's screaming wakened her. Cat howled in an eerie guttural way, hissed but stayed close. Shivering, gasping, she panned the room with the flashlight beam. Nothing. She pressed hard on her abdomen. It was flat, and no pain resulted. Fingers tracing over her face confirmed she was fifty, not fifteen. Clumsily she lit the lantern, its soft glow hushed her trepidation to a low roar. How much night was left? She didn't know. How much pain could she endure? She didn't know. Trusting Preston's promise of her safety seemed foolhardy now. And yet nothing had actually happened to her. But would she soon lose her mind, become a stark raving lunatic locked in an eternal scream? She dutifully recorded what had occurred, leaving written evidence in case she awakened unable to communicate.

With the lantern casting a warm light, and Cat heavy on her chest, Molly closed her eyes and prayed a child's prayer, "Please God, help me wake up in the morning." Something rested hard beneath her buttocks. It was the magic stone, and she clutched it tight in her fist.

Menacing men appear. Her father, the priest, Preacher Man, and Papa. Their faces slide together, their bodies merge, and the group is coalesced into one man. One sick, angry, frightened man. A mask of calm strength creeps over his face, and he smiles. Jake.

"I love you, Molly," he croons. "Come with me, please. I will make you happy. I will never leave you."

Something heavy falls from her as Molly rises. To take his outstretched hand, she unclenches her fist, and an object drops to the floor. It is important, and she bends, searches but is pulled, almost yanked away. They walk, hand in hand, out the back door, down wooden steps and through a garden of daises to a chain-link fence and through a gate. Along the path they stroll, smiling at each other. Farther and farther into deep forest they journey.

Jake's smile shifts to a sneer, and his soothing words are replaced by condescending ridicule. Pushing her to the ground, he looms over her, and his face becomes four. Four bodies—four diabolic men—taunt her. "Good for one thing," they jeer. Pain throbs through her as the priest, the preacher man, her papa, and Jake tear at her night clothes, grasp her breasts, force her legs apart. A big hard hand clamps her mouth shut, forcing her strangled cry back down her throat. A golden light appears. Susie.

Molly sinks deep into an emerald green pool. Like a velveteen cloak, soothing water envelops her as if in a cozy cocoon. A massive swan swims to her, and she climbs on his back. They fly high and land on a sapphire lake where Prince Charming, with open arms, awaits.

"Is it morning yet?" she asks.

Not Prince Charming but Preston whispers, "Almost. A little more. You can."

"That's it. That's all I remember," Molly said as Preston refilled her cup with sweet, warm liquid. "It was a horrid night. A horrid night alone."

"Yes." He nodded. "But you weren't alone."

Molly clutched her mug with both hands, hoping the heat would quiet her trembling. The drink was hot and honeyed with the hint of familiar herbs she couldn't place. They sat on the porch in early-morning light, Molly in the rocker with a blanket tucked tight around her and Preston on the floor, cross-legged. She looked down at him and asked, "Can you explain any of this? Does it make sense? What about the hole I dug?"

He said nothing for so long she itched to jump up and pace, but she was too weary. Instead she leaned her head back, closed her eyes, and rocked. Dulcimer music lulled her, and she longed to fall. Yes fall and fall into peace. Into the velvet lake. Into oblivion.

"What were you digging for?" Preston asked.

"I don't know."

At his insistent but calm gaze, she shook her head. "I don't know!"

"What were you wearing?"

"Oh my gosh! I was naked. No, wait. Jeans, I was wearing jeans. Why did I think I was naked?"

"Symbolic."

"I was naked when I came to the house. I remember now. A man on a white horse galloped out of the garage and vanished. What does that mean? There were people everywhere. No one paid any attention to me. I went to the backyard for a shovel. Two men were in the shed, they did not move as if I weren't there. I felt like a ghost. A ghost with no clothes on. I ran. Up the back steps, through the big kitchen full of people. They talked and laughed and didn't even see me. Why didn't anyone see me?"

"Were you dead?"

"Maybe. But I didn't feel dead . . . I, I, I think I was *between* dead and alive. What does that mean? I felt naked and invisible. I wanted someone to see the real me. But I wasn't sure who me was. Molly or Sophia or nobody."

"The house?"

"I knew the house. I knew right where the stairs were. Where I'd find clothes to wear. I thought if I had clothes on, someone would see me and help me."

"Help you what?"

Molly shivered with cold. Her hands loosened on the mug, and she gestured for more tea. While she waited, she watched shadows on the frosty yard shift and disappear as dark clouds closed in obliterating any sunshine or blue sky. The clouds hung so low, morning appeared more like dusk. She almost smiled as Cat shot out after a sparrow. Preston came back with the pot, poured a steaming cupful. She recognized the fragrant scent but couldn't name it.

"This concoction may quiet your conscious mind, freeing your subconscious to speak your truth. Only drink if that's okay. Drink slowly. Relax. What did you want help with?"

Molly drank and retraced her steps through the dream, asking herself what she was looking for. "Parsnips. I needed to find the parsnips, and no one heard me. In a panic I dug and dug, but the roots wouldn't loosen. I felt desperate as if doomed to dig forever and never unearth the roots." Molly stopped. Her hand went to her mouth. Something teased around the edges of her mind. What?

Without a word, Preston brought her mug to her mouth. She gulped the hot liquid, swallowing and opening eyes she didn't even realize she'd closed.

"Belladonna," she whispered, shocked. "There's belladonna in this, why? Why are you poisoning me?" She pushed his arm away, squirmed from his touch.

"Hush, Molly. Trust me. This won't hurt you. My people have used this potion for eons. There is no belladonna. Just healing herbs." He sat back on his haunches and made no attempt to touch her. A safe chasm between them.

"But why?" She felt tears well up even as her surroundings grew hazy, her head light, and her eyelids heavy.

"Why belladonna? It isn't in use. Anymore. Unless to poison someone. And belladonna is bitter."

Molly mumbled, leaned her head back, and fell asleep. When she woke, snow was falling in huge flakes. The scrubby yard and tree branches cloaked in white. Her stomach rumbled, and her nose was cold. She smelled coffee and something meaty. She groaned, lifted her head, tried to stand, and fell back.

"Good. You're back," Preston said. "The tea did induce messages from your subconscious. I have them on tape."

He didn't smile, but his eyes were kind when he stooped close and handed her a mug of coffee.

"Drink this. We'll walk, and then sit by the fire. After you eat and get warm, we'll listen."

"Then it'll be too late to leave. I have to get out of here. I can't endure another night here alone." Molly managed to keep her voice below a shout. "Please, I'm not ready to know," she whimpered.

"You can. You aren't alone. I'm here. I was here last night."

"All night?"

"Yes."

"But why didn't I know that? Why didn't you let me know?" Molly heard the accusation in her voice, and she grew angrier as she thought of him there while she faced terror alone. She jumped up, strode to the steps, ready to run. Realizing she was stocking footed, she stopped short and whirled around.

Preston caught her in his arms, held her, and said, "You needed to learn to trust your soul. You have the answers. I think I know, but that is all. Tonight I stay as you seek."

The very length of his speech quieted her. She'd never heard him put so many words together at onetime. He released her then, and she acquiesced.

With coats and boots on, they stepped off the porch and onto a white carpet of new snow. A smidgen of space separated them, and neither said anything as they walked. First to the creek, now shallow and beginning to ice over. Then up the slope to the back of the house and to the privy. Not a pleasant place to be under any circumstance, but in this cold winter afternoon, Molly had to force herself to bare her bottom.

Hurrying now, they made their way back, stood for a moment, and watched the snow fall. It showed no sign of letting up. It would keep her trapped here tonight, but my was it beautiful. Through the door to warmth and comfort and an enticing aroma that aroused a sense of Sophia's grandmother, stirring a hearty meal. A Dutch oven of beef stew simmered on the cook stove. Stomping out of her boots and hanging her jacket on a hook, she expected to hear, "Sophia, 'bout time you come in outa that cold." Hunger fetched her back to the present as Preston placed the cast-iron pot on the table. She sat as he served her a bowlful of steaming vegetables and chunks of meat swimming in gravy.

Outside wind howled, promising an October blizzard.

# THIRTY-TWO

~

*The distinction between past, present, and future*
*is only a stubbornly persistent illusion.*
—Einstein

On the tapes, Molly's voice sounded dreamy and far away, at the same time very much her own. Long periods of quiet, like softly falling snow, floated between the words.

"All the strange fears I've experienced . . . Sophia's," she said when the last tape clicked off. "The old man and his dulcimer. The music almost constant. Now on tape too."

Preston said nothing. He needn't. She'd spoken aloud mainly to hear herself. To dispel out-of-body sensations her own taped voice evoked. Words strung together, held in place, sliding into stillness. Messages elicited cloudy déjà vu wonders, as if today were then and tomorrow too.

"The flashbacks. I've known I was Sophia. I just didn't understand they weren't flashbacks. It is all happening now. Isn't it?" Her mind, like a wide satin ribbon, wrapped around the idea. But before she could tie the bow, it, this monumental life-changing concept, vaporized and slipped away. She reached out with her hands, grasping at seemingly empty air. Finding no answer there, she turned to Preston. "What?" she asked. "Please just tell me what I'm trying to know."

Preston remained mute. The only sounds were howling winds and sparks spitting in the stove. The kettle whistled, and he slid it from the heat.

"Tea?" he asked.

She shook her head no. "Yesterday and tomorrow are the same? But how can that be?"

"It can't be spoon-fed, Molly. Think. Everything is lined up to aid you."

"What? What do you want me to do?" She shook her head again. "All right. I understand spoon-fed. You aren't going to tell me. I need to know for myself."

"Yes. Allow it. Let your logical mind rest."

The fire burned low. Preston rekindled and positioned a heavy log. Wind and fire blended their voices with low, sweet dulcimer music. Molly drifted. They sat silently until they both spoke at once. She laughed and waited. Finally, Preston said, "This is your opportunity. This comes because you have courage to stay."

"I know. I believe that. But it doesn't make it any easier."

Molly relaxed her hands that had been tight fists in her lap. She straightened in the flimsy lawn chair, stretching her shoulders back, rolling her head on her neck. Major events in her life reran through her mind. Risking hell and damnation by running from an oppressive religion had taken some courage, she guessed. But look where that had led. To the Baptist church and into Jake's web. Hadn't that been a major mistake? Or had it? Was it courage that had made her stay? Or cowardice? How could she discern? Still, staying had brought her here. *Let your logical mind rest, Molly.*

"Jake's gone," she said.

"As it should be. His problems are now his alone. Wounds will heal. Write."

They rose and retreated, Molly to the loft steps and Preston to the alcove.

"Morning I'll be gone," Preston said.

Molly's eyes shot open in the dark. Noise hadn't awakened her. Silence had. Silence rested on her chest, like giant gnarled hands pinning her down. She had no idea what time it was. No idea what lay ahead. It must be early morning, for Preston was no longer there. Not his body anyway. How she knew this, she did not know. A shiver ran through her, a shiver of expectation that her life was about to change in ways beyond her knowing.

Surrendering in a child's prayer, she whispered, "Take my both hands, God." With that, her fingers uncurled, her toes too. The hands of silence lifted slightly, she breathed deep and slow, relaxing her eyelids, allowing them to close. Closing out the meaningless darkness increased the volume of the silence. No wind blew. No fire crackled. No joists creaked and settled. Cat, like a lump, lay at her feet, heavy, dead to the world.

Days passed in silence, blurring one into the next. Molly no longer paid attention to time or date. Instead, she wrote page after page in her journal, spilling out every thought, every question, every feeling she experienced. When her fingers cramped and her back ached, she laced up her boots, grabbed her camera, and tramped through the woods. Small pockets of snow lay in shaded areas, but otherwise the ground was bare. The path spongy and damp, the sun warm as if its fire had been rekindled for a last hurrah.

One day she took comfort in leaning on the twisted trunk of an old chestnut tree, there to be shaded beneath its wide branches. It was summertime there, and dulcimer music rang through the forest. Sensing a presence, she looked around and, on her knees, came face-to-face with a shy little girl hiding behind the tree. Molly held out her hand, nodded and smiled.

"My name is Molly. What's yours?"

"Sophia," she said in a voice small and hesitant.

"I thought so. Will you come sit with me?"

Sophia took her hand, and they sat side by side on the soft earth, holding hands, saying nothing. A soothing warmth spread through Molly, and she leaned her head back, closed her eyes, and thanked God. She yearned to hold Sophia forever, to ask questions, and reassure her but kept still and quiet so as not to scare her away. And yet Sophia didn't seem frightened, just shy.

"Mama's wantin' me," she said.

In awe, Molly watched her disappear. She continued to sit until the earth beneath her became cold and hard. Rising, dusting off, she made note of exactly where she was, planning to come back every day. This breakthrough left her strangely calm and enthusiastic.

Most times she stayed in the present, in late autumn with the oak trees bare of leaves. She accepted whatever came her way. Comfortable, at ease and more relaxed with each passing sunset.

She ate when hungry and drank for thirst, mindless of any yearning or craving. Food and drink sustained her with no need for pleasure in it. When coffee ran out, she drank tea. When the day came that there was no food, Ellen appeared with a homemade concoction and canned goods. She didn't stay long and uttered no clichés. Fifi had died. Molly opened her arms, and Ellen folded into them. They wept and then Ellen left.

Each evening, as soon as the sun set and the air grew cold, Molly would start a fire and huddle there until the room warmed. While water heated for her sponge bath, she'd sit and write by candlelight or listen once again to the tapes Preston had made of her subconscious whispering words of wisdom and truth. Portions were profound and thought provoking. She paused the tape often and wrote what she'd heard. Time and her sense of it caused her to ponder. Time had always been linear. A straight line from one moment to the next, day after day, year after year. Now her own voice told her this concept was merely an illusion. Society as she knew it lived an illusion. So what then was real? *Let your logical mind rest, Molly.*

Secure and at peace, she slept long nights of dreamless sleep. The few dreams she did recall were of deep vivid blue and green rolling hills, layered with thin patches of swirling fog. She'd waken with a taste of heaven on her tongue.

An early morning walk produced another encounter with chestnut trees and summertime. Even though Sophia wore the same tattered dress, she seemed older, slightly taller, a bit gangly. She held a black-and-white kitty, and she quickly curled into the crook of Molly's arm.

"I'm glad to see you," Molly said. "Are you playing here?"

"Nuh uh. I been lookin' fer you. Papa's mad. Biscuit been bad. I'm scared."

"Ssh," Molly crooned. "When you're with me there's nothing to be scared of. I'm here to help you."

"I knowed that. Kin you stay?"

"I don't know. I don't know how yet. Keep Biscuit away from your papa, okay? Someday Biscuit will have babies, and you need to carry them far away and tend to them." Seeing Sophia's confusion, Molly added, "But that's a long time from now. Want me to sing you a lullaby?"

Sophia nodded her head and snuggled closer.

Molly closed her eyes and sang,

> O, they tell me of a home far beyond the skies,
> O, they tell me of a home far away;

"Are you an angel?" Sophia asked.

Molly chuckled and shook her head. "No, but right now I feel like one. I wish we could stay like this for a long time. But won't your mama be looking for you?"

"Mama's sick and Papa's mad."

"Can I have a hug?"

They hugged until Molly's arms were empty and Sophia nowhere in sight.

Indian summer stretched on with brilliant blue skies. Warm enough in daytime, she needed only a light jacket. Nights, though, became increasingly colder. The pile of cordwood dwindled until the night she burned the last stick. She shrugged and put on another layer of clothing. Next morning Richard arrived with a bundle of wood, a pound of coffee, and news. When the man from Tucson and the two detectives could not locate her, they had contacted him. They'd seen Jake leave the church on the day of the robbery. The police were still investigating, but with this new information, their main focus was no longer on two women in a grey station wagon. Jake had disappeared somewhere in Canada. Yes, he was his own problem now.

"What about a pastor for your church? Have you found someone, and will they need the house?"

"I no longer attend, so I don't know. The last I heard a visiting minister was holding Sunday services until things quiet down. As far as your house goes, I believe there's no rush about vacating. I'll check though."

"Thanks. I don't know what I'd do without you."

"Amy's called several times," Richard said. "She's sent letters to your P O box. I promised I'd report back to her on how you are. How are you?"

Molly fumbled in the desk drawer for her keys. "Next time you come, would you bring up any mail?" She handed him the box key and her house key. "I want to hear from Amy and talk with her. But I can't right now. Please tell her I'm fine. Actually I feel better than I have in a long time."

"You look rested and calm."

"Maybe it's because Jake has left the country," she said with a playful lift of her eyebrows. And maybe that *was* the reason. Not him leaving the country so much as her having distanced herself from his energy. For twenty years she'd lived with the intensity of his dishonesty and conniving. Now it was gone, he was gone, and her spirit relaxed in the stillness. At once detached from and connected to everyone and everything, slow motion waltzed through her days and caressed her dreams.

"You'll find this hard to believe, but I'm having visits with Sophia. Friendly little chats and getting comfortable with each other. That's a big part of why I'm so content. I really know I'm exactly where I'm supposed to be. Funny, I haven't been the least worried about the cops or being a suspect. I'm just taking each day, each event as it comes."

"Mellow, that's what you are. Good. I'll tell Preston. Though I'm sure he knows without me telling him."

"He's right about all this." She tapped her pocket, touching the ever-present stone. "Will you walk with me now? You might have a chance to see firsthand what I'm talking about."

"I wish I could, but I promised Preston I would only stay a few minutes. Anything else I can tell Amy? Maybe you'd like to write something, and I'll mail it for you?"

"Good idea."

Molly picked up her notebook and pen, dashed a note and handed it to Richard who was standing and ready to leave. "I wish you could stay longer. I enjoy your company," she said softly. Standing, she went into his arms for a gentle embrace.

"I'll be back day after tomorrow," he whispered.

They smiled at each other, and when he took leave, Molly realized he'd not put any pressure on her to hurry or to vacate this place.

Deciding to stretch her legs anyway, she called after him, "Wait, I'll walk out to the road with you." She ran to catch up, almost skipping like a child.

As they walked, Molly noted a slightly quicker pace, and she glanced at him to see him looking at her with an expression she couldn't quite decipher, as if he questioned who she was. He'd lost some weight but no longer had the woebegone sag to his face. She let it be, and they continued in silence, only speaking a word of good-bye at his car.

Molly watched him drive away and then turned toward the stream. It was not anywhere near her "encounter place," but where she felt led to go. The sky clouded over, blocking the sun, cooling her, and she wished she'd grabbed a jacket. Nevertheless she continued on, with an urgency, as if she were late for an appointment. At the creek she sat, waiting, wondering why. With the first drops of rain she rose and started for shelter. A whistle stopped her. Royce? No, Richard had told her he was still in the Detroit area. Turning toward the sound, she saw the old handyman, or dulcimer man, or whoever he was, gimping toward her.

# THIRTY-THREE

~

*If we all did the things we are capable of doing,*
*we would astound ourselves.*
—Thomas Edison

Molly held out her palm in greeting. "Hello," she said.

The old man took her hand in both his gnarled ones. "Howdy, missy. Be raining hard soon. Best get back yonder."

Together they made their way, at first with a pace so labored Molly could hardly maintain it, each step excruciating in its slowness. After a few minutes, though, she noted a quickening. Glancing over, she was shocked to see a handsome younger man. Scraggly gray wisps had been replaced with a short full, dark beard. Molly gritted her teeth and ground them. Her stomach ached as if she'd been punched. *Let your logical mind rest, Molly. Let your logical mind rest*. This a common mantra now when her consciousness couldn't grasp some bizarre new level of life. Hurrying along, she felt her tension ease, as it always did when she walked fast, with purpose. They sighted the cottage just as the sky opened and a deluge dumped on them. Laughing, she ran. Laughing, so did he. Up the three boulders that served as steps, they stopped beneath the porch overhang. She felt a pressure on her shoulder, a slight squeeze, and an indication to sit.

They sat in two rocking chairs and faced the rain. Trees bent and swayed in sudden gusts of wind. She shivered and he rose, entered the house, and came back with a towel and an unfamiliar cape. Molly tousled her hair and dried her face and arms. Figuring out just how this unusual wrap he offered was to be worn, she donned it. A flowing garment in soft shades of green, it appeared to be hand knit or knotted in some way. Hidden beneath the overlay were fabric sleeves that came to her wrists. Even though the homespun material scratched her neck, she pulled the drawstring snug. A perfect fit and warm, she ignored its coarse texture.

"Looks right nice on you," he said.

"Thank you," she said and they both sat once more. "I call you Dulcimer Man sometimes. And Handyman. Ellen thinks you might be the caretaker. Are you? Or are you Sophia's grandpa?"

"Yep," he said. "There kin be no rest without you. We all been awaitin' fer you."

"I know that now. I'm in awe of this whole experience." Molly interlocked her fingers, rested them in her lap, and rocked as rain poured and thunder rumbled. "This is good energy. Did you conjure it?"

He smiled, and a row of even teeth showed. No yellow tobacco stains, no chaw bulged in his cheek. Even with his beard, he was tidy, almost clean-cut. Molly knew she had again stepped back in time. As soon as this thought formed, she shook it off. No. More likely she had stepped sideways in time, a dizzying idea.

"I don't conjure any more than you'un. 'Tis what 'tis. Iffin' I could conjure, you'd a been not so long in coming. We've jest been a-waitin' fer you."

"You and Sophia?"

"Yep. Couldn't leave her. And she ain't goin' til she makes things right."

"What about Sophia's mama? Is she here too?"

"Ah. Marta. My sweet Marta. No. I sent her packin'."

"You can do that? When you're . . . uh, uh, dead?"

"Not rightly," he said, but explained no further. "Matters is yer here now."

"Yes. Here I am. Ready, willing, and, I think, able," Molly said in a futile attempt to make light of the ever-unfolding drama encompassing her. "I just don't know what I'm to do. How I can help?"

"Not by warning. She won't git that." At Molly's raised eyebrows he added, "I heard you tellin' her 'bout the kittens. It don't work that way."

"Then what?"

"First, you got to make Joe understand and do his part, fer hisself."

"Joe?"

"Joe was always a good lad. Watched over Sophia. Took care of his mama. Thought I didn't need to worry. I come close to leavin' when he growed big. But he were no match for her papa and that preacher," he spit the last words as if he'd just smelled something rotten. He spit again. "Joe was chased off. Had no choice but to run. He goes by Royce now. Tryin' to rescue Sophia. Over and over. He don't know that. Been here fer years. But he won't listen, won't see. Won't hep hisself. He's blind. I seen how he is with you. You, missy, got to make him hep."

"But how? I . . . I think he's to find the brooch that was your mother's. He's looking for it now."

"Good."

"What else?"

"All she needs is fer you two to listen . . . That George," again he spit. "He kilt Marta sure as if he shot her dead. That young'un needed her mama. Chile, come out here. C'mon. Don't be shy now," he called as he got up and walked to the rail.

The door opened, and a young lady appeared with a blank, faraway demeanor. She gazed about as if she were alone and lost.

She sat as if commanded to do so. By her appearance and flaming red hair, Molly knew her to be Sophia. But not the happy little girl, nor the tender teenager giving birth by the bridge. No, this person was older, fine lines creased her face. Rough red hands lay lax on folds of her faded calico skirt.

"Hi, Sophia," Molly said. When there was no response, she tried again. "Do you remember me? I sang you a song when you were a little girl. You thought I was an angel."

Stillness. Even the thunder and rain seemed far away. Aside from the rocking chair's rhythmic creaking, all was still. Sophia turned to her with a vacant stare.

Molly looked to the young man at the rail for some signal or cue. Instead, her glance was met by the watery eyes of the old codger. The peace she'd enjoyed and taken for granted shattered. Her head pounded as if a thousand demons were trapped and struggling for freedom. With jaw clenched and hands to her ears, she jumped up.

"No no no!" she screamed and ran down the steps into the woods. She needed to move, to get into nature where time and aging could be counted on.

When she could run no longer, when every breath rasped from her lungs, she sank in dry, dusty pine needles, and dirt that should have been soft and wet. She had run far, but the time phenomena had kept pace. Was it today, or was the rain from another yesterday? Somehow she'd managed to cope with living in two different worlds, but this . . . this she could not hold. Even nature contradicted her understanding. The old man had moved through years in seconds. Sophia came when called, sat, but saw neither of them. Where was that child's mind? *I cannot do this. I can't. Please.*

Her breathing slowed. Searching for a tissue to wipe away her tears and runny nose, she jammed her hand into her jeans. Nothing. Poking around in the shawl she found a small patch pocket. As if in answer to prayer, her fingers touched a smooth, cool pebble. She yanked it out, clutched it, and swayed back and forth. Preston's talisman that he promised would hold her together reminded her she would not shatter. The demons quieted. Her jaw relaxed. Then it hit her. The stone hadn't been in *her* pocket! How did it get in this old wrap? Thinking it must be a different one, she patted her jeans. She had never gone anywhere without that precious gem. Through burning eyes and with shaky hands, she examined the stone she gripped. It had all the wavy lines and curves of the one Preston had given her. In a stupor, she crawled to a large tree, sat, and leaned against it. When the shock wore off, she capitulated to whatever was to be. Resting there, her back and head against rough bark, she felt a slight vibration and heard a low hum. Instinctively she knew the tree was sending her a message. She closed her eyes, caressed the stone, and listened. Energy surrounding her softened.

Thoughts seemed to come from nowhere. *Your job here is almost done. Helping Sophia helps you. Someone else needs you. You'll be moving far away soon, but not alone.*

When she opened her eyes, rotting chestnuts littered the ground, baby birds cried for their breakfast, and somewhere a woman cried too. It was springtime here, now. A time of awakening, renewal, and new growth. Relaxed and in the moment, she was suddenly overcome with an urgent need to contact Royce and Amy. Her thoughts became questions. Why Royce? Because of his role in this healing of long-ago wounds. Why Amy? Just because. Is that where she'd be moving? North Dakota? Close to her lovely daughter? But how could she move anywhere? There had to be a way, but she had only $100 and a beat-up station wagon. And who or what would go with her? Wishing a notebook were at hand, she began to make a mental list: to house for belongings, get rid of everything but necessities. Maybe she could sell some stuff. Fill up with gas, make phone calls. Soon the list became too long and only served to distract and annoy her. With an imaginary eraser, she eliminated each item until her mind was blank.

No longer fretting, she sat and waited. The woman's weeping ceased and was replaced by dulcimer notes. With an innate sense of someone's presence, she waited. Only moments later, a beautiful young woman, with head bowed, walked toward her. Sophia, of course. Molly rose slowly and held out her arms, almost instantly filled with warmth. *Listen to her*, she told herself.

They sank to the ground, and Sophia began to talk in a quiet voice, almost a whisper. Molly strained to hear. She leaned toward the words and focused all her attention on this hurting young woman. This ghost of herself.

"It's all my fault. I should've been better. I should've been a boy. Joe's gone. It's my fault. They done hurt me bad." She sobbed and lowered her head, as if waiting to be scolded. "My mama's pin. I got to make it right. I got to fix things. Where's Joe?"

Molly didn't know what to say. Finally, still not sure, she ventured, "Joe's searching for that pretty pin right now. I hope he finds it. But no matter what, remember this, none of this is your fault. Joe knows that. And so do I. You only did what you had to do." *And so did I. The choices I made hurt my little girl. But I only did what I thought best. I must forgive myself for the mistakes I've made.*

Molly smiled and reached to lift Sophia's chin but found her hand filled with air. Not even warm air. The energy was gone, she was alone, and daylight dwindled. The ground she sat on was damp and cold. Another time shift? Yes, and she'd better hie back to shelter before dark.

She rose and, without even brushing off the dirt and pine needles, hurried along the path. Running, stumbling, catching her breath, she paid little attention to rustling leaves, eerie hoots of an owl. Darkness descended and brought a bite to the air. How far had she come? When would the cabin loom?

# THIRTY-FOUR

~

*Forgive them for they know not what they do.*

Exhausted, but determined, Molly made her way to her car. She'd endured a restless night even after recording every event of the day and making a list of what she needed to accomplish. A list that became so long she resigned, believing it would take a week rather than a day to work her way through. Sometime during her nocturnal thrashing, Cat had jumped down and disappeared.

In dawn's dim light she'd dressed in clean clothes and groomed herself as best she could. She'd not taken time to fix breakfast or coffee. But she had left food and water for Cat, though he had managed just fine before her arrival. As she walked, with a backpack flung across her shoulder, her concern turned to the old Chevy waiting where she'd parked it long ago. Or was it long ago? Yes. Too much had happened to not have been. Would the clunker even start? Maybe the tires were flat. Maybe it had disintegrated. Hardly, but who knew any more?

She stomped through frost-blackened brambles and saw that at least the two visible tires were fully inflated. A silly worry anyway. The windshield was filthy, as gray as the car itself. *Guess it didn't rain here,* she thought as she slipped the key into the ignition and turned it, holding her breath when the engine coughed and hacked. "Start. C'mon start!" Cold sweat beaded on her forehead. Then the motor purr—lovelier than dulcimer chimes. With motor idling, she rummaged through backseat clutter and found a bottle of water and an old towel. Windows smeary but clean enough to see through, she slowly moved along the rutted lane. The gas gauge was below empty, and she held her breath once more, as if that would somehow make the dregs go farther. All she asked was to get off this deserted road.

Once the tank was filled and windows sparkling, Molly's shoulders released their tension. Her hands rested loosely on the steering wheel, and she proceeded to the house to gather anything of importance. The place was as she'd left it. If anyone had been in, they'd done no damage. Journals were the first task, and she slid on her belly under the bed, dragging out one heavy box. Sitting cross-legged amid dust motes, she pulled a notebook at random and let it fall open. Poetry met her eye, and she read the rough draft of "My Best Friend"—a tribute to Jake. Tears welled up at her description of soft eyes, gentle hands, tender moments. With so much love, forgiveness, and devotion, why could they not have been happy? Damn it, because he never was who he pretended to be. When would she get that through her head? Right now, she resolved. Right now. He's gone. It's over and time to move on. Back under the bed she hauled another box out, this time not giving its contents a second look. When all three cartons were safely stashed in the car, she went to the closet. In a suitcase she packed only good, practical clothing. Leaving it on the bed she proceeded through each room, taking a mental inventory. Jake's mom's paintings leaned against one wall, and she selected her favorite, a small bowl of lavender African violets. Some sentimental items would need to be put in storage, she supposed. Nothing had much monetary value, but she'd have a moving sale anyway. Get what money she could and give the rest away. How could she feel this confidence when she had no idea where she was going or when or even how?

In the kitchen, she unplugged the empty refrigerator and propped open the door. Her hands trembled, and she felt faint. Low blood sugar had begun to take its toll, so she rummaged through cupboards but found nothing nutritious to appease her hunger. Way to the back, behind stale crackers and cereal, an unopened brandy flask looked forlorn and seemed to say, "Take me with you." And so she did, setting it next to her purse. Why? It no longer mattered why.

A sad smile crossed her face when she entered Jake's office and gazed at his books neatly lining the shelves. In alphabetic order by author. Newly married, she'd found this quirk of tidiness charming. But when he imposed his standards on her books, her clothes in her closet and even spices on the kitchen rack, his quirk became an obsession and drove her to revolt with uncharacteristic messiness. A part of her yearned to return to the innocence of that minor disturbance. Sorrow, like a dark veil, enveloped her and temptation to crumble almost overwhelmed her. Where had she gone wrong? What could she have done differently? Nothing. Nothing. Nothing. Molly frowned, scolding herself. The time for tears had expired.

Jake's Bible caught her eye. He hadn't even taken his Bible, for Pete's sake. What does that say about all his rhetoric? Like a sharp, piercing scissors, anger shredded the newly donned cloak of sadness. Muscles in her face tightened as she squared her shoulders and tilted her head slightly.

*In quietness and trust shall be your strength,* a woman's voice whispered. Molly turned sharply to see who had spoken, who had intruded. The room was empty but for her. She must have voiced those words from a passage she'd memorized when it mattered. Unable to remember the complete verse, she opened the Bible to Isaiah. A sheet of fine scented stationary lay on the page. Several lines of a feathery scrawl blurred in front of her. *My dear Reverend Carpenter*. Blather followed about his wonderful sermon and how Sweet Hollow was so blessed to have him and *your dear wife, bless her.* There was no date on the letter, and Molly assumed it must have been written soon after they arrived. Until, toward the bottom these words, *our whole church family prays daily for you as you struggle in dealing with your poor dear wife's mental condition and her seduction of my Richard.*

Molly's head ached, her eyes burned, and she could not remain in the oppressive energy that hung over everything. Jake's energy. After opening several windows, she headed out, Jake's Bible in one hand and the bottle of brandy in the other. If anyone saw her they'd cluck and dismiss it as just one more mentally disturbed behavior.

Another day. She'd come back another day. In the car again she made note to stop at Richard's. Her mailbox was empty, so he must have already been by. And she wanted his reaction to this letter his wife had written. Sam's café and Ellen were far down on her list, but she headed that way. A cup of good coffee and a bit of food, a friendly face were what she needed.

"A sight for sore eyes," Ellen hollered when Molly entered the quiet diner. A real smile crossed her face as Ellen rushed toward her. "Look at you. Just look at you. Come, sit, I'll get java."

They took a back booth near the kitchen, far from the few customers having early lunches. Neither spoke for a time, but simply sat in companionable silence looking at each other as Molly gulped the hot, strong brew. She could feel her headache ease but her hands still shook.

"I need food, please," she said. Her friend jumped up to fetch her a meal. "No clam chowder," Molly added, letting Ellen know and affirming to herself that she would be all right. Ellen turned, grinned, and gave her a thumbs-up.

"So while I feed my face, tell me what's new around here."

"Well, a couple days ago that old codger finally reappeared. Hadn't seen hide nor hair of him since you moved here. I asked if he knew you. 'Yep,' he said. Then he added he'd be movin' on soon and told me I should do something about that blasting. Like what, I asked. Didn't answer, just gave me a nod, ate some soup and hightailed it outta here. I'm guessing he's going to kick the bucket, is what he meant by movin' on. You think?"

"Hmm. Something like that. Are you going to follow his advice? Do what it takes to stop that horrid mountaintop removal?"

"I don't know what I can do. But he seemed to think I can help somehow."

"Believe him. He knows and you'll find out. On another subject, have you heard anything about the church and Diatrice?"

"Oh yes!" Ellen said and then stopped as if she wasn't sure how to begin.

"Come on. What?" Molly asked, biting into chicken salad loaded with green chilies.

"Well, that woman is a piece of work, let me tell you. She doesn't grace our establishment, of course." Ellen paused and unwrapped a stick of Juicy Fruit. "Ya know, money talks and she's loaded. I hear she's got the whole church council at her beck and call. All hell's broke loose. They've impeached Richard."

"What do you mean, impeached?"

"They ousted him from the board. That's what I mean. Claiming he was in on the robbery. How foolish can people get?"

Molly pushed her half-eaten salad away, her appetite lost. Ellen scurried off and came back with a thick slice of apple pie scooped high with vanilla ice cream.

"I'm sorry, I'm too upset. I can't eat anymore."

"Course you can, put some meat on those bones. Here I'll help," Ellen said picking up a fork and digging in.

"I just saw Richard a couple days ago. He didn't say anything about this. I wonder . . ."

Ellen swallowed. "Delicious pie, if I do say so myself. Now this, this is eating high off the hog." She wrinkled her nose at the odd connection she'd just made. "Have a bite. Go on now or I'm putting clam chowder in front of you."

Molly did as commanded and was surprised at how good it tasted. Fresh and tart with just enough quality cinnamon. She took another bite as Ellen went on.

"Gotta wonder when that broad is going to wake up and smell the coffee. The police have all but pinned the crime on Jake, but she still says you did it and Richard helped. Yeah, right. She even thinks Beth was involved. Can you imagine?"

"Oh, dear. Poor Beth. I was going from here to Richard's office, but I'd better stop at the bookstore first. She is still working there, isn't she?"

"Yeah. Comes in here for supper some days. She's leaving soon as Royce gets back. Getting out of this one-horse town. Can't say as I blame her. People talking about her and Richard, her and Royce, even her and you, for God's sake."

Molly cringed. Everyone who had been kind to her here was being besmirched by that woman.

"I'm leaving too, Ellen. I'm not sure when, but I think soon." She set her fork down, sipped the coffee grown cold in the cup. "I don't have much money, and I don't know where I'm going, but it's almost time."

"Well, that's a fine kettle of fish. You've been the bright spot in my life and Royce's too. Now with Fifi gone." She stopped then and bustled away, soon returning with a fresh pot of coffee. Molly noticed Ellen's hand shake as she poured and splashed a bit in the saucer.

"I'm sorry," Molly said. "It seems to me I've been more of a bother. And I'm so sorry about Fifi."

"Funny thing. Most of the time it feels like she's right near me. Sometimes I see a shadow just her size and expect a lick on the face. And you haven't been any bother. Look, you're cleaning up that haunt. Now the cabin can be put to good use again. It's a nice place."

"Yes, it is. Maybe I'll come back and visit. Meanwhile, I'm still here and have lots to do today so I'd better get going. Let me pay for my lunch and give you a hug. I'll be seeing you again soon."

"Chow is on the house. But I'll take that hug."

Molly walked the few blocks to the bookstore, remembering the first time she'd gone there and been startled to see the man she'd just met behind the counter. What a day that had been. She having just escaped from the church ladies. Her Minnie Pearl hat came to mind, and she chuckled, tempted to skip down the street.

Bookstores had always been a favorite place for her. Being surrounded by books and the smell of them filled her with quiet warmth. Libraries once had that effect, when she was little, but no more. Too noisy now, too many computers and people yakking about movies to rent. As she stepped into Royce's store, she inhaled deeply and sighed, letting her eyes accustom to the light, letting her mind mellow, her body relax.

"Beth," she called. "Anybody here?"

"Molly," Beth answered, appearing from behind a stack. "You've come to town. Gosh, it's right good to see you. I've been meaning to visit and check on you. But this has kept me so busy. And the scandal an' all."

In her cream-colored sweater and brown wool slacks, and with a big smile, Beth looked as youthful and charming as ever. But when she drew closer, Molly noted premature deep creases around her eyes and across her forehead. Fatigue and stress lines, no doubt.

"I hope you're taking care of yourself. This place will survive if it's not open every day, you know. Ellen's filled me in on some of the gossip. It must be hard. And yet here you are with a big smile."

"I'm totally tuckered. Reckon I can hold on a few more days of this, 'til Royce gets back."

Molly forgot her concern for Beth and asked, "You've talked to him? Has he had any luck? Finding the ring, I mean?

"He called jest yesterday. Didn't say anything about a ring. Jest said he's coming home, alone."

"Cecelia?"

"I asked, but all he'd say was he'd tell me when he got here."

"Oh," Molly said, disappointed. "Say, I hear you're planning on moving away. Where are you going?"

"I don't rightly know. Jest gotta leave.

"I'm leaving soon too. And the thought of packing up and, well, it's daunting. But you . . . you've lived here nearly all your life. This has to be difficult."

Beth's face puckered, and Molly thought she would start crying. Instead, she shrugged.

"Shucks, there's a heap new fer me to learn, new folks, new places and sich. Jest that you'd think people would think more highly and kindly than believe what one woman says."

"I'm so glad I met you. You've been such a good friend. Thank you," Molly said and gave her a hug. "I feel like this is all my fault. The nasty rumors. You having to move."

"Pay no mind. I reckon it's fer the best. A person can git too comfortable where they are, so the universe gotta' give a shove sometimes. Could be by this time nex' year I'll be thankin' you."

They consoled each other, reminisced for awhile about good times. The Bible study fiasco, their hikes, wildflowers, Cat, and haunts. Molly finally pulled herself away, saying she had errands to run but for Beth to be sure and not leave without saying good-bye.

All the way to Richard's office, she thought about Beth. Really this was one more mess Jake had made. Anger snuck in the back door and almost succeeded in ripping away Beth's sweet energy that had enfolded her. No. Beth was right. Jake and Diatrice and their behavior were catalysts, moving both of us in the direction we were meant to go. They know not what they've done. Much like Judas with Jesus. The comparison dissipated angry residue as she arrived at her destination.

Loud voices penetrated the heavy wooden door, and she paused before knocking. She'd have left unnoticed, but anticipating Amy's letters spurred her on.

The door flung open, and there stood Richard, scowling. Behind him, a stranger in a dark suit and Diatrice with a sneer.

"No. Go. Quick get out of here," Richard said.

Too late. She'd been seen.

Diatrice, puffed up, hissed, "You. You little hussy. Where's the money? What have you done to Jake? Officer, arrest this woman. I demand that you arrest her now."

# THIRTY-FIVE

~

*You gain strength, courage, and confidence by every experience in which you really stop to look fear in the face. You must do the thing which you think you cannot do.*
—Eleanor Roosevelt

Stunned by this "church" woman spewing venom, Molly stumbled back as if she'd been hit with hot pepper spray. Richard quickly caught her or she would have surely fallen. As he righted her, his expression softened to one of compassion.

"I wish I could have saved you from this. But here you are, and I suppose there is a reason."

"Yes, I suppose," Molly said, straightening her shirt. "What now?"

"I'll tell you what now." Diatrice, her stout body pulsating, elbowed past Richard, and looked like she might spit in Molly's face. "Why don't you get in here, and we'll put an end to your disgusting behavior. We have an officer of the law standing right here." She leaned forward almost nose to nose with Molly. "And, if I have my way, which I mean to, you *will* leave here in handcuffs."

"Diatrice, back off. Keep still for a minute." Richard took Molly's arm and ushered her inside. With quiet deliberateness, he closed the door.

"Let's all calm down now and see what we have here," the police officer said. "Why don't you all just sit down, and we'll get the facts."

Diatrice, still huffing, glaring, and trying to maintain a self-righteous pose, did as she was told. For once. Hairs straggled loose from her bun, lipstick smeared outside its definition, and a button on her silk blouse had popped open. She looked like a fat old trollop, Molly decided and then chastised herself. Still, the sight amused her since the woman obviously believed she displayed great dignity.

Richard leaned over and whispered, "Diatrice, your shirtwaist is unbuttoned. You look disheveled."

Diatrice looked down, and with a great to-do, rose and strutted to the restroom.

"Excuse me, you are?" the officer asked, turning toward Molly.

Molly heard her voice quiver as she identified herself. When he asked to see her driver's license and then copied all the information, her nervousness intensified. What other questions did he have and how should she answer? Just being accused of a crime made her feel guilty. Nonsense, she told herself. I've done nothing wrong. But innocent people do get sent to prison. And guilty ones go free. Jake for instance. *Let your logical mind rest, Molly, and trust.*

A tidier Diatrice returned, and no one spoke for a moment or two.

"Mr. Fletch, let's start with you. Your wife states you've conspired with this woman to steal church funds.

Diatrice sputtered, and the officer held up his hand, silencing her.

"My wife thinks because I will no longer follow her orders, I must have found another woman. And she's focused on Mrs. Carpenter. Which is ridiculous." Realizing how that could be interpreted, he shrugged at Molly.

A friendly gesture Diatrice chose to take offense to. "Don't get cute with . . ." Again the officer held up his hand, and she stopped as if by magic. Surprising how much control such a young man had. Molly doubted anyone had ever hushed her before in her life.

"By the way, Ms. Carpenter, I'm Officer Martin. Tom Martin. Now, before we waste any more of everyone's time, let's get to the bottom of this. Mr. Fletch, you've said you were with patients the afternoon of the robbery. And," he said, looking at Diatrice, "the crime is all I'm concerned with at present. So I'll ask you the same question, Ms. Carpenter. Where were you, and who were you with that day?"

Knowing she was not a convincing liar in any circumstance, truth was her only option, even if it meant being arrested. Molly explained about showing Amy paintings at the church. That Jake had been there when they arrived and left before they did. Yes, it was her car Diatrice had seen driving away. But she didn't know what happened to the money. "I suspect my husband took the money. He had . . ."

Pointing at Richard, Diatrice demanded, "Ask him who those patients were. Ask him if he hasn't been keeping her hidden somewhere. Ask him. Even if he was with patients on that particular day doesn't mean he wasn't behind all this in the first place," Diatrice said, ignoring Martin's raised hand.

"Good Lord, why would I do anything like that?" Richard, angrier than Molly would have imagined he ever got, refused to be silenced.

"Because you're so pedestrian. So, so common. That's why. And people like you do this sort of thing."

Richard shook his head and, with his elbows on the chair arms, clasped his hands in front of him. A posture that said, "Go ahead, have the last word."

Diatrice continued her rant until Officer Martin stood and raised his voice louder than hers, finally cutting her off.

"We won't go into that today. I think my work's done here. And no one is going to jail. At the moment, anyway. Be available for questioning. That's all I ask." He placed his hat on his head, smiled at them, and said, "I sincerely hope I won't be called back here. Good luck and have a good day."

"How dare he," Diatrice spouted. "He doesn't know who he's dealing with. I'll see to him."

"For Pete's sake, be quiet. For once in your life, you are not calling the shots. Accept that and behave with some modicum of Christian charity," Richard said.

"You can't talk to me that way. Just who do you think you are?" She pushed herself off the sofa, snatched up her purse, and slammed out.

Molly and Richard stared after her. "I'm sorry you had to see that. But I've just had it with that woman. I could use a drink," he said. "Want to go get one and we can talk?"

"Well, if you have a couple of glasses, there's a bottle of brandy in my car. I'm shaking, and I'd rather stay here. Besides I like your office, the . . ." Molly suddenly realized the fish tanks weren't gurgling. They were empty. "Where are your fish?"

"You get the brandy, and I'll find something to drink it out of. Then maybe I can explain."

"I had lunch with Ellen, so I know some gossip," Molly said, sipping her drink and coughing as the liquor burned her throat. She didn't care much for alcohol, had usually passed on it except for a celebration toast or an occasional mixed drink at a party. This was different. Strong but also satisfying, it warmed its way to her stomach where she lost track of it. "Ellen told me Diatrice ousted you from the church board. How could she do that?'

"I left her. Moved out. I expected reprisal. And the fish? I've given them away and closed my practice. What little was left after she got through."

"I'm so sorry. This whole mess is because of Jake and me. Beth's leaving town, your marriage and practice ruined. It seems like I've been apologizing all day. If only we hadn't come . . ." her voice trailed off. She emptied her glass and welcomed the heat.

"It is a mess, I agree. And some of it is Jake's fault. But not yours. I should have left her a long time ago, but I always had my work. And she couldn't be bothered with 'my little hobby.' Now, though, she's desperate to save face in this community. So she hangs on to her belief in Jake by making us guilty." He poured more brandy and, before he rested his head back, asked, "What about you? I was surprised to see you'd come into town."

"Well, I've got a list a mile long, so here I am." She raised her glass and let a biting swallow slide down her throat. With each sip, the drink became less intrusive and more welcome. She felt her face flush and her muscles relax.

Liquor loosened their tongues, and they talked then about when they'd met and he'd danced the Irish jig. How comfortable she'd been with him from the very start. She reminisced about her first visit to this office and her confusion about her relationship with Jake, about Sophia, the music, traveling back in time.

"It all seems to have come together for me. Or fallen apart, maybe. I clearly see the similarity between Jake and Sophia's preacher man. She trusted that he would take care of her, and then he betrayed her. I'm reliving her experience, and I did it in my first marriage too. Because of the men I've been attracted to I came to the conclusion I must have been molested and had blocked it all out. Or was trying to please my father . . . it seemed the only things that made sense." Molly paused, caught her breath, and waited for Richard's comment. He said nothing, just nodded. "Well, yes, I had been molested. And yes, I was, at some level, needing my father's approval. But not in this lifetime. And if Sophia's dilemma isn't resolved, I'll be hard pressed not to make the same mistakes over and over. Exactly what I did with Jake. Trusting the wrong people, while those who love me and want the best for me get shunted aside. Now that he and I are through, I have a chance to . . . I don't know. I have a premonition Sophia's torment is almost over. And when it ends, I'll have a clean slate and not be led by unfinished business from a century ago. That's what I hope anyway." She watched as Richard poured a splash more brandy. What could it hurt?

"I was aware of your expression as I told the Trail of Tears saga. Then you came to me and spoke with such honesty about your encounters in the woods. I saw you as someone special. Someone who would shake up this complacent community. At that time it wasn't my place to say this, but now I can. You've been good for all of us, Molly."

Tongue-tied by his praise, she leaned forward for her drink, sipped, and cupped it in her hand. That reminded her of his teddy bear.

"Did you give away your stuffed animals too?" she asked.

He reached behind his chair and held up a tattered teddy. "This? It needs a new home." Taking the few steps toward her, he held out the bear. "It's yours."

Their hands brushed, their eyes met, and she smiled her thanks. Molly had a brief vision of the old man nodding and wearing a toothless grin. What?

"It's getting late," Richard said, breaking the spell. "I'm hungry, how about you?"

"Yes. I think I am. But I'm feeling a little woozy. I'd better not drive anywhere right now."

"I'll drive. It seems I've built up a bit more tolerance for alcohol than you." He rolled his eyes.

"You indulge often?" she asked, surprised.

"Well, no. But obviously more than you do. Sam's okay?"

"Is today Friday? In this realm?"

"Yes it is. Why?"

"Catfish night at Sam's. Or doesn't he have that so late in the year?"

"Let's go find out."

Molly pictured them sitting in the café. The town busybodies were already flapping. Maybe they should invite Beth, really have them buzzing. No, she didn't need whispers and gawking. A solution came to her along with another nod from the old man.

"Listen," she said, "Royce offered me his place. He's not due home for a day or two. Why don't we get takeout and eat over there?"

"Great idea. I'll call and order."

At Sam's, he retrieved a bundle from the backseat and said, "Here's your mail. A little something to do while I get us some fish."

A little something? Though it appeared he had separated flyers and general throwaways from the personal. The first envelope, from the Sugar Creek Antique Shoppe, she dismissed as probable junk and slid it to the bottom. Amy's handwriting on a small packet delighted her as if she were a child with an unopened birthday present. She slipped her finger under the flap and then put it down, reaching instead for her cell phone. Disappointed when Amy's machine picked up, she left a brief message ending by saying she was holding her letter and about to read it.

She'd only peered into the manila envelope when Richard was back with dinner.

"That was quick."

"Ellen's busy and distracted. No time to chat. As she put it, 'the natives are restless.' Some sort of meeting going on. Said you'd know what it's about?"

"Hmm. All I can think of is the mountaintop mining issue we talked about. But that was just this morning. Hmm."

On their way to Royce's, she considered Amy's letter, but she wanted to savor it and reading on winding roads would make her carsick so instead she took in the scenery. They traveled narrow lanes lined by simple bungalows already lit against twilight gloom. Kids played outdoors making the most of these shorter days. Good weather had held long past what could be expected. A sense of urgency pressed on Molly. Being trapped in the wilderness by winter snows held no appeal. But she would stay until her work was finished and trusted she'd know when that happened.

"Brr," they both said when they entered Royce's home. Richard went in search of the thermostat while Molly prepared plates and set them to warm in the oven. She flipped on lamps and the stereo. Lights and Celtic harp melodies filled the room, banishing the November chill.

"Hey," she called. "Look here. We'll have a fire."

Royce had left one laid in his small fireplace. One match strike completed the room's ambiance. When the coffee was ready, they fixed a tray and then sat cross-legged near the hearth, enjoying good food, a warm blaze, and each other's company. When they'd done the dishes and stored leftovers, they returned to the living room. Richard sprawled on a pillow while Molly curled up on the couch with a second cup of coffee.

"You should know, Beth isn't the only one leaving here. As soon as I can wrap things up, I'm going," he said.

"Me too. But I don't know where."

"Me either."

They looked at each other and laughed, then he turned serious.

"Molly, thank you," he said with a catch in his voice. "This is the nicest evening I've spent in years. I don't want it to end."

"I know. Me too."

Molly averted her eyes, not knowing how to respond to emotions his expression so clearly exposed. She felt too vulnerable now. But if not now, when?

A key rattled in the lock, and the door opened. Royce was home.

# THIRTY-SIX

~

*Around the corner there may wait*
*A new road or a secret gate.*
—J R R Tolkien

"Oh, gosh," Molly said, jumping up. "I didn't think you'd be home so soon. This isn't, uh . . ."

"Darlin'," he interrupted. "I've been driving all day and expected a cold, empty house. This, this feels like home. Better. A warm welcoming fire and two good friends to greet me.

"Are you hungry? We have leftover fish and slaw from Sam's."

"It just keeps getting better. Sounds good." Royce turned toward the kitchen, but Molly beat him to the doorway.

"I'll get it. You just relax. Take your shoes off or something." She hummed while fussing with the food.

"There's a bottle of wine and glasses on the shelf over the fridge," he called.

Molly poured three small goblets. *Why not*, she thought, tasting before serving. A light rosé with a hint of sparkle on her tongue. Nice. Nice too, that this afternoon's brandy had worn off. When the fish and his plate were warm, she added coleslaw and a roll and brought the tray to Royce, who did have his jacket and shoes off.

While he ate, Richard related some of their afternoon and why they'd come here instead of to a restaurant. Royce, hearing of Diatrice's diatribe, groaned. Molly sat by the fire in contented silence, considering these two men she hadn't even known a year ago. Last year at this time had been turmoil and conflict. Not so much between her and Jake. They were on the same side then. She shook her head in amazement, sipped wine, and watched flames leap and sparks fly. The men's voices droned as background music, replacing Celtic harp and dulcimer. Mellow and sleepy, she was glad her attendance wasn't necessary. Soon enough her questions of Royce would need to be asked. Soon enough.

"Wake up, Molly," Richard whispered, patting her arm.

"Hmm. Not asleep. Relaxed."

"Very. Listen, I'm leaving now, so if you want a ride back to your car tonight?"

"You're welcome to stay here, darlin'. I'll crash on the couch. Don't worry, it won't be the first time."

"I'll take you up on that, but I'll take the couch."

Molly walked Richard to his car. "I need to talk to Royce. Soon. Call you tomorrow?"

"Yes, do." He held her as if he'd never let go.

She stepped back, watched as he drove away, and then hurried into the warm little house.

Seated again on the floor by the fire, Molly asked, "Cecelia and the baby?"

Royce retrieved the wine, filled their glasses, and, with a bowed head, answered, "Cecelia isn't coming back, ever. She insists the baby isn't mine. That it's Jake's. He sent her a note mentioning a small town in Canada. Promising he'd send for her when he got there. When he got another preaching job. Absurd, but there was no convincing her otherwise."

"I'm sorry." Another apology—what a day. "I've learned some things while you were gone. It could be Jake's baby. It looks like his having had a vasectomy was just another lie."

"Hmm . . . I guess that makes more sense. It's awful what she's headed for, and I can't stop her."

"Cecelia? Uh, did she tell you the town Jake was going to?"

"Yes. Here, I wrote it down."

Molly's hand shook as she took the paper from him. She knew what she must do. She'd call that Tucson private detective. Surely they'd find him, bring him back, and make him pay. He deserved to pay for all the laws he'd broken. To suffer the consequences for all the heartache and pain he'd caused. She'd help the authorities in any way she could. Royce would, no doubt, object so she kept her own counsel.

Sadness, like a gray cloud, surrounded Royce. Sadness emanated from his eyes when he muttered, "You know I don't love her. All I wanted to do is protect her, and she wouldn't let me."

"Royce," she said and then paused. Should she wait until morning? When he was rested and clearheaded? When they both were? Intuition told her to speak now, while he was tired. He'd be more open. In her mind's eye, the old man nodded.

"There is someone. Someone you tried to protect a long time ago. Someone who wouldn't let you. You can help her now."

He made no reply. She sipped her wine and waited.

"I don't know what you mean. Who? Who needs me?" he finally asked.

"Sophia." Molly waited again.

"Even if that's true, I'm no good to her either. I tried, but I don't have the ring."

He sounded so despondent she longed to take him in her arms. Instead, she hugged her knees to her chest and waited, the wine forgotten, the fire dying.

"I found the pawnshop you told me about. I talked with the owner, and he remembered Jake and my ring. Not because Jake pawned it, but because the owner made him an offer. Jake answered that no way was he letting go of it. The ring was his good luck charm, and he meant to keep it. What he did pawn were these." Royce rifled through his duffel bag and handed Molly a small velvet pouch.

Her pearl ring and choker lay in her hands. Among the few mementos she had of her mother. "Oh, Royce. Thank you. These are priceless."

"I'm glad, darlin'. Glad I could do something for someone."

"About Sophia. Not having that jewelry isn't what's keeping Sophia trapped here. It's guilt. She needs to talk with you. And the ring? Well, Jake may be sorry he's hanging on to it. There's the curse.

'No rogue finds rest.' Remember?" As an afterthought, she added, "Something tells me you'll get your ring back eventually."

Royce smiled at that, turned serious, and asked, "But about your Sophia. How can I listen to a ghost? I know you do, but that's a gift I don't have."

Molly pondered. Gift? Was her communication with Sophia, with the dulcimer man, a gift? Or had she been ripe, ready for this step? Preston would know. An idea took shape, and she said, "Preston. Ask him how to listen."

Finally at her humble home in the woods again, Molly, dressed in a long denim skirt and wool sweater, petted Cat and waited. "What's going to happen to you, when this is over? Poor kitty. Are you going to be all alone?" Then it dawned on her. "Are you one of them?" Cat eyed her and must have sensed her tension, for he stopped purring and his ears perked up. "I'm sorry, kitty. I'm just nervous and confused. Sweet kitty." With effort, she cooed. Cat jumped down and off the porch, obviously not fooled.

Trying to relax, she picked up the mail bundle again. Reread her daughter's plea to come live near her. "I want my mommy," Amy had written, drawing a happy face beside it. Still, Molly had a sense of real need being expressed. She'd even enclosed a job description for an open position with her company and clippings from the local newspaper. Perusing them brought back happy childhood memories, and she was tempted. Could she deal with harsh winters, though? Of course. Trudging in knee-deep snow and below-zero temperatures would be nothing compared to the path she had walked this year.

It wouldn't be long before she'd need to leave here. She'd worked hard this past week, crossing jobs off her list and adding new ones. Her bags were packed and in storage with the few household items she'd take with her. The yard sale had been worth her time and effort. Richard and Beth had brought their own odds and ends, making the day almost fun instead of tedium. Crowds came; she hadn't known so many people lived in the area. Amazing how much they were willing to pay for junk and possible treasures. Jake's mom's oil paintings sold immediately, at a good price. The day had brought in close to a thousand dollars, but money remained an issue. Even the antique-store stuffed shirt had nosed around. He'd tried to engage her in conversation but she had no antiques to speak of and so had brushed him off.

Now she paced, back and forth on the porch. Where were they? Royce said they'd all meet her here at ten.

Wait a minute. Hadn't there been a letter from that store? Sitting again, she churned through the junk mail she still toted with her, looking for the Sugar Creek Antique Shoppe envelope she'd dismissed as a mass mailing.

> Dear Ms. Carpenter,
>
> Regarding your agent's appraisal request of several months past, we apologize for the delay in responding. We have carefully researched this item and are pleased to offer the following information:
>
> Not only the age but also the one-of-kind, detailed workmanship and excellent condition of your dulcimer leads us to place its value at $20,000.
>
> Should you now, or any time in the future, wish to sell this instrument, we are prepared to purchase it at that price. If, of course, upon examination, we find it in the same pristine condition it came to us originally.
> We look forward to hearing from you . . .

Sell her dulcimer? No, she couldn't, she wouldn't part with it. How could she? And yet why had he—and it must have been the old man—why had he taken it for appraisal? And then asked only one hundred dollars from her? Which he then gave back. What? Clutching the letter, she stood up sending flyers, unpaid bills, and Amy's packet tumbling to the floor.

The dulcimer lay on the desk where she'd left it last week, and she ran her fingertips over its polished dark wood. Plucked the strings. How could she entrust this fine instrument to that uppity antique dealer? Didn't it belong here? But she'd be moving away and couldn't just leave it here. Could she, if it was really worth $20,000? Probably more if that was their offer.

"Darlin'."

Molly jumped. "Oh. You startled me."

While Royce and Preston bent to pick up the scattered mail, she slipped the letter into the desk drawer. She would not chance being advised to take the offer. How could she possibly sell what had become like a friend? A companion. A portent.

"Where's Richard?"

"He's found someone to sublet his office, and they want in as soon as possible, so he's packing. Said to tell you he needs to ask you something, really wants to talk with you. And he'd be out later," Royce said.

"Better this way," Preston added. "You ready to go?"

"Uh. Yeah." She picked up her day pack, and they began their trek.

On the path, Royce said, "I still don't know about this. I've never talked with a ghost before."

"Remember the work we did all week. How you felt, what you saw during meditations. When we get there, I'll lead you through the meditation again."

Royce nodded. With a stronger voice, he asked, "Where are we going?"

"To the clearing at the footbridge. I may be wrong, but I think that's where we'll find Sophia waiting," Molly said.

Gray clouds hung low, and a cold wind blew. She could see her breath and expected snow before night. Indian summer had held far longer than anyone predicted. Now winter had arrived. No doubt. As if the weather had grown impatient with these mortals and their plans. Grown impatient with their need to wrap things up all tidy before proceeding. *I hope I haven't delayed too long,* Molly thought. Her answer came quickly. *It's never too late.*

"And then what?"

"What? Oh, we listen. We let her tell her story if that's what she wants."

"What if I can't hear her? I never have."

"That's why I'm along," Preston said.

Molly reached into her skirt pocket and handed Royce her stone. "Hold on to this." At his puzzled look, she explained its meaning and how it had worked for her.

They walked in silence until, almost there, Royce broke the spell. "I hear the music. I hear music. Do you? That's a good sign, isn't it?"

"Yes," they both answered.

At the clearing, Molly pulled a heavy towel from her tote, spread it for them. She and Royce sat and watched Preston walk onto the bridge. He stood at midpoint with arms at his side, trancelike, for several minutes. Then he turned, came to them, and sat cross-legged. With hands open, palms up, he led them. "Breathe in, one, two, three, four. Exhale slowly to the count of four. Again, inhale . . . exhale."

With each breath, Molly relaxed further until she felt limp and warm.

"Your mind rests. Your heart is open. Be present now," Preston intoned.

Molly pushed up her sweater sleeves, inhaled deeply, and thought she smelled lilacs. She reached for Royce's hand, saw a shift in his demeanor.

"Look," he whispered.

Sophia, like an angel in long flowing skirts stood in the center of the clearing.

"Joe," she sobbed and crumpled to her knees.

Royce looked to Preston who nodded. With faltering steps, Royce approached her.

"Soph, please don't cry. It's okay. It's okay."

"Joe. I'm so sorry I let you down. I'm sorry I couldn't run with you. I was afraid. It weren't yer fault what they did. My baby, Mama's brooch gone, cuz of me. You cain't fix things fer nobody. You need to understand."

Sophia rose to her feet, gliding away from Royce—Joe. He followed, and together they walked to the bridge, where he knelt on one knee and looked up at her. She seemed to be patting him on the head, as if consoling him.

Molly turned to Preston. "It's good, isn't it?"

"Yes," he said. "Finally he broke open. All it ever takes is willingness."

Dulcimer music grew louder, and she heard, "Missy."

The old man, leaning on his walking stick with Cat at his feet, stood so close she reached to touch him. Her hand filled with empty, and a knot formed in her throat.

"'Bout the dulcimer, missy. It's fer you to choose. Bless you fer what you done." And he, along with Cat, were gone, leaving Molly with a vacant place deep within.

"You've done good," Preston said.

"I feel so sad, as if I'm losing a grandpa I never knew. As if my protector has left me. And Cat. It's the end of something important."

"A beginning too."

Royce returned looking astonished. His coloring had shifted from gray gloom to pink lights, and Molly realized she was seeing his aura. That he'd been cleansed of ancient guilt and grief. That his whole life would take on a new, healthy glow. But not with her. Their romance was never meant to be.

"Molly," he said, taking her hand. "I've loved you from the moment I met you. I'm so sorry that I confused that love. I'll always love you. Like a brother." He held her then, and they wept.

Preston laid a hand on her shoulder, and she knew it was time. With humility and awesome respect, she moved away from the present, away from winter's chill. Toward Sophia and the bridge.

Molly and Sophia stand, perhaps three feet apart, in dappled sunshine of this early spring afternoon. Leaves, having emerged and unfolded from their budding nests, still retain delicate shades of green seen only in nature's rebirth. Far below the rickety footbridge, the river awakens. Winter's icy blanket recedes, and snowmelt froths on its downhill tumble, dancing to the dulcimer's tune. Turbulent waters eerily beckon Molly. Over the cascading euphony, she and Sophia confide and soothe each other.

"Sophia, I just talked to Joe. He understands now that you had to do what you did. He loves you. He loves me. And he respects our courage." Molly hesitates, searching for words to assure this beautiful young lady that all has been forgiven, and Joe is releasing them both. "He's going to be just fine from now on." Tears stream down her face, even as hope fills her heart.

In barely audible words, Sophia whispers, "Thank you."

With outstretched hands, Molly tentatively moves closer. "Come," Molly says.

For a moment it seems Sophia will fold into waiting arms. A golden light hovers and then envelops her. She steps back, over the side of the bridge. Molly cries out, but seconds before hitting the roiling river below, Sophia disappears. Dulcimer music fades until the only sound is the icy water's joyful song accepting nature's invitation toward an unknown destination. With winter's biting winds yet to endure, Molly stands alone—surrounded by and filled with the promise of spring.

The end—or the beginning.